© 2024 L.A.Miller

All rights reserved. This book or any portion thereof may not be reproduced or used in any manner whatsoever without the express written permission of the author or publisher except for the use in quoting in a book review.

Paperbound : ISBM–979-8-218-49681-4

Ebook : ISBM–979-8-218-49682-1

Cover art by L.A.Miller

Edited by L.A.Miller

It's you who shalt begin thine journey and make a

pilgrimage on a march to misery, and pass through the lands of

living and dead.

The March to Misery

L.A.Miller

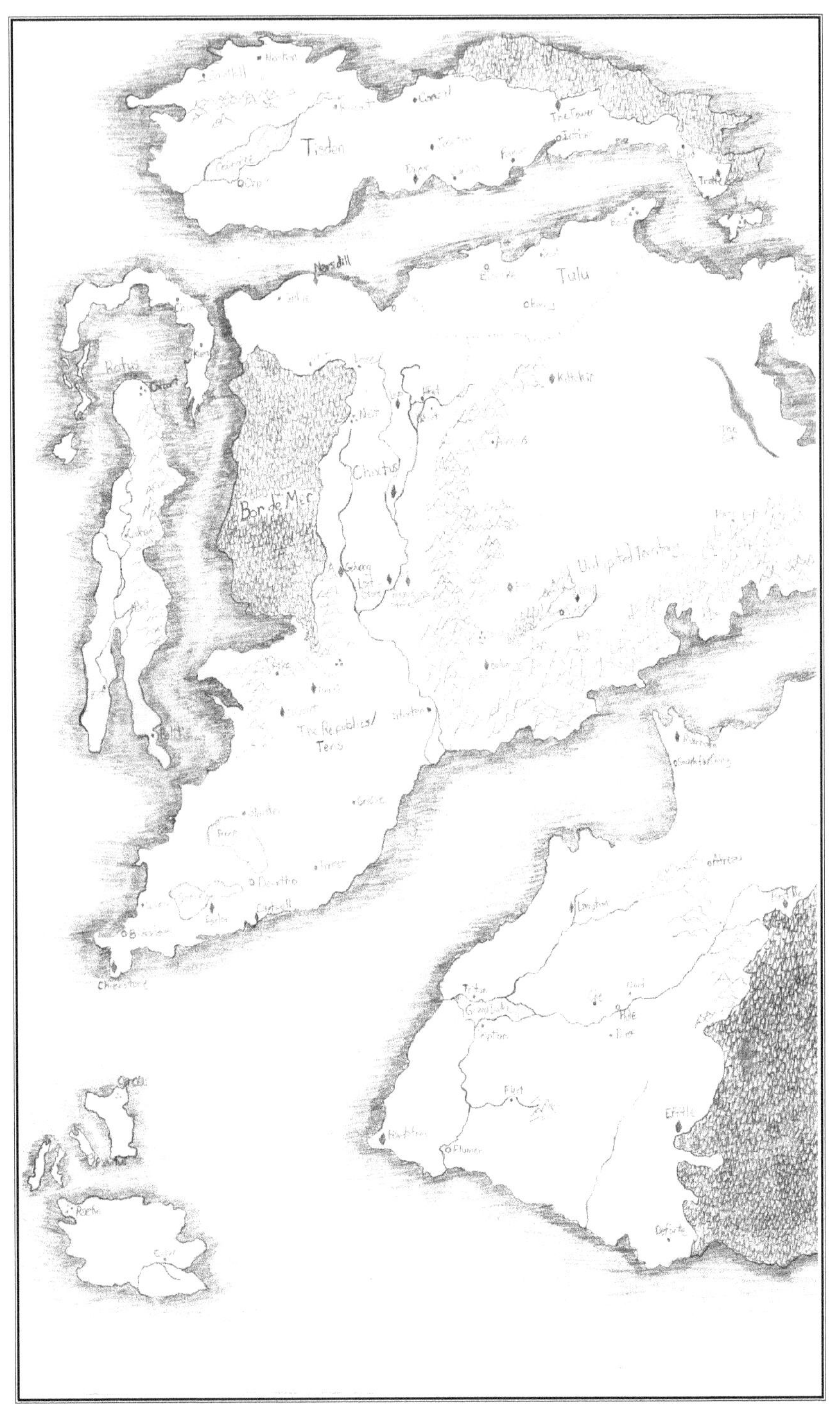

N
Arceus
Serr
Breez
Ros
Fel
Ethira
Baier
Ibru
Riontorem
Opissa
Seba
Ouexios
Hurt
Tinston
Esty
Lekindon
Ith
Bleu
Itarrium
Tabier
Maeve Lake
fasi
Bleszidel
Reno
Waterweep
Tercir
Porcelania
Esterland
Argalli
Serdart
Mulda
Cusart
Attuio
Brosant
Dexide
Vermorte
Glarisi
Acre
Vinci
Lun

Table of Contents:

Prologue:

They kept their boats tied to posts they planted far from the shore in a specifically chosen cave too small for the hunt. The near half dozen of them checked the skies above, only seeing gray. "And I hear nothing too. Perfect."

They first searched for one of the worn paths, and discussed which was quietest. Among the men, they quickly found which way was most suitable and professional for their strange task. For hours they rose the sprawling sharp hills, and the sight of those red scorched mountains in the distance stood above them.

The day soon faded into night, and they made their rest in a common spot made by those before them. They were protected by a small stone fort, carved into the side, but open for their campfire smoke to escape, scatter, and be absorbed by the stone and hanging tree leaves. The light of the fire made their tan skin glow as they huddled close while eating.

"I'll bet half of my copper, it's a big one."

"Half!? Heh, I'll take that bet."

"I have a feeling, I saw it in a dream."

"I saw in a dream the opposite, in fact they seem to keep getting smaller, so I'll match."

"Just you wait."

They clinked their spoons together, and the night came over.

They continued their pilgrimage north, riding the ever increasing mountains. The stone was hard, but their boots dug in, grasping its surface. Nothing weighed them down, not their massive winged spears, nor war-bows, but the drawstring on one of theirs had made one plucking sound and shattered into bits. It was a short time later when the poacher put the bow between his legs and replaced the string before most could notice.

"How did you do that so quickly?"

"Well when you do it quite a lot, then you adopt that little skill and master it."

The day still wandered on, as they kicked the path they followed, and made the path more obvious. Around when night had begun to fall, they descended the mountain side, and came across a deep cave, which passed through the mount above it.

They took the drawstrings off their bows, and a stack of sticks from their dry bundle. Quickly they brewed a fire which made the wall light up with the image of dust and new webs and the paint of past hunters.

One of the men pulled out a jar of paint and added his name along with all the others.

"How many days away are we from this one?"

"Well, we're at point c, we just need to get to the next peak: point d."

"That should be easy enough, are they waiting there for us?"

"Supposed to be."

"If they get us killed with this job, I'll haunt those creepy bastards in death."

"I hope they're there. Never even got the name, nor the look of the guy's face."

"If this ends badly I'm sacrificing them first."

"I wouldn't touch them, if I were you."

"Why's that?"

"They are the commissioners, and they have an icy and oppressive force that radiates from them."

"But they pay generously?"
"Especially so."

"So the coin I got before sailing was what . . . half?"

"No, it's about a third."

" . . . Who are these . . . guys?"

"Well . . . they are . . . the commissioners!?"

They snuffed the flame and gathered what coals they had for the next hunters and some for themselves. They walked through the bored cave onto the other side of the mount, and all they could see stretching up in a sheer peak was point d.

They fastened all their gear tightly. Their great spears were not only wrapped in linen, but the crate it was held in was fitted with extra heavy straps that wouldn't escape the hunter's shoulders.

They tore into the ground; spikes fitted to their boots. Ropes bound all the men together, and they ascended. Hours passed with no break, sweat clinging to their brows. The only other life on the mount were the pale stone trees which grew deep into the hard rock and the vines hanging off its branches.

The day reached its peak as they climbed. Sweat pasted their suncloaks to their bodies. "Is there a good place to stop up there, soon!?"

"Just a few more hours."

"Why not make it night?"

"What, is there a problem?"

"This cloak has clung to my sweaty groin, and is pinching me."

"Alright all you, stop for a moment while we get this man's groin dislodged from his dress."

"You complain about me, but it'll happen to you too with all your . . . complaining."

"Heh," he chuckled, and they continued.

"I saw it in my mind. A vision."

"What is it, my lord of lords?"

"A world without tyranny, nor exhausted breaths," he clutched his hands together.

"My lord of lords, must this vision come to being?"

"I'm afraid that it must. I've reigned in this land, not as its ruler but as a tool untrusted and unloved by my brother. What I am will never be seen as a holy power within these lands, unless I move to remove what blocks me from doing what I must. It is him, who must be rid from this realm. And thrown into the land between realms. Or maybe a realm of my own design. A cage for a beast who believes itself to be a great force, such as man, who shall be given a treatment like and unlike him."

"To your children?"

"To those half of my creation, they shall be wilted of knowledge in contempt of me but from their beings they shall be given the opportunity to become one of the holy order, and my children who follow not what I am shall be dealt with slowly. For they are a burden on this world, and have created something hideous and vile. A corruption. It cannot be that they be left, for they of my dear creation have conspired against me and so I must be a father and punish their child."

"And with this strike, how shall it happen?"

"We must take like the lightning which I have gifted to the sky, and swiftly halt all who measure in his court."

"The blind angels shall fall?"

"Completely and mercilessly. For if they try, they will rebel, and be a disgrace to the laws of nature. Hideous beasts of nature."

"I shall relate the message to the rest of the court, and on your command."

"Then tell them now. We shall strike on the sound of the church bell."

"You are wise, my lord of lords."

"And then we must spread the word to the realm and beyond that." He nodded and flew off and away to tell the others.

"You must fall for what you've done. Oh brother of mine. Oh how you've sinned against the sky of stars and when this bell rings, you shall find I have smothered this cruelty you've created. Oh this cruelty. I shall hide under your sky no longer. I shall take the sky for mine, and keep it hidden, for it shall not be taken away from me again."

His fiery hand fingered the rim of the bells and his hair rose and dropped fluidly through the air. His form wavered through the chamber.

The golden marble floor held his form as he gracefully passed over. And he had the windows opened so he could view from the top of the keep and see all of creation. He held his eyes out and grasped the world outside. He then closed the window before grasping the bell once more and left the court.

It was clean, the city of silver and gold. The marble street high above the ground. It was all clean and kept, and perfectly straight.

He stood above all who passed, each one bowing down in prayer. For what he will do was not what they know will happen. The largest peak of the tower held a court of the silver crown, and the silver scale hung above holding a chandelier in equally filled cups.

The room held all the blind, and their lord of lords. He looked up to him, and only said, "brother, may it be when chaos is a certainty?"

"Nay," the silver man said back, and he rang the bell, which belted out a deep reverberation which shook the ground, and then there was silence.

In the sky turned a milky orb as well as another of deep constant fire. Light emanated from one and cooled by another and fell onto the surface of hundreds and thousands of souls. Warmth, nourishment and a burning sensation was a gift to one and blue light and cold was to another.

In the sky turned an orb of opaque light as well as another far greater in size and holding of an eye that looked but refused to watch. It held no warmth and no chill tones. No reverberance nor the rhythmic beating of most, but the souls of hundreds of thousands.

It was close to night when they made their final step onto another fortification carved high in the cliff. They found a pack of clergy waiting for them. In their perfect scarlet robes. Behind them already kindling a fire were another pack of hunters.

"You're our commissioners?"

"Yes," they said quietly, while subtly sitting down with a kettle and a table.

"What's with all the other men?"

"You know what is planned – you led your men here. This is simply security."

He saw on the table held a dozen or more glasses and a scroll as wide as the table.

"Come, sit all of you."

As they sat, one of the robed figures poured a thin yellowish liquid into each cup, and was subsequently passed around to them all.

Once the cups were filled and the kettle cleanly empty, they cleaned the table of things and rolled the scroll over its surface.

"This is a map of this mountain range."

"Hmm," one of the hunters mused.

"This terror is afraid, but is able to be drawn out. So you must do so, carefully. Tactfully."

"We're professionals."

"You are, so don't let that pride take hold in your mind and your arms."

"Come on, this is what we do. Stop trying to fit us in a trunk when we know what we're doing."

"They've commissioned us to down one alive."

The robed commissioners nodded.

"Alive!?"

"This is not for sport, this is for capture."

"Yes, this is what they've commissioned us for."

"Not enough."

"It's three times," he barked, "for only one of thems."

"That's absurd," another chimed in.

"Five." He said, carefully brushing his robes.

"Five . . . Five times . . . commission!?"

The robed man nodded, and said slowly but assuredly, "five times commission. For you all, and nothing else."

For half a minute they sat in quiet reprisal, hoping there was some catch. But there was none. The clergy man sat up kneeling over the table and tapping on the map with his stern finger. "He has been spotted in the valley hiding in the shade of this mountain, I believe you call it point e. Hiding in the shade at the respective time of day. And seemingly unwilling to come back out."

"They can be like fish, you have to have a good lure. Though only when they're hungry."

The hunters on the other side held up a sheep's carcass, as well as a pig's carcass.

"The carcasses will be planted on the top of that peak, and once he finds it, he shall fall a great league, and be captured once debilitated."

"There's a problem with that. We need the odor to travel. And they like the scent of burnt flesh. Burning flesh. We'd also need a full coverage of that peak, while also not being seen. Let's see.

"This is the peak. Over here is the second highest, and there's a stretch in between with a smaller one. That small peak is the one we should bait at. Since there's two of them, maybe hold one against the face of the smaller peak."

"That should be arranged then. Archers from the true peak, raining arrows to drop him, and spears to keep him down."

"But you don't want us to kill him."

"No, he has to be alive."

"For five times commission, alright. Another day to starve, and in the morning it shall be done."

One of the clergy men put a crate on the ground, it forced the red dust to part and be thrown on landing.

"What is held in that crate – can only be used by specially trained hands which – will deal with it after we drop him."

"There are also risks in all this, such as death, and runaways. As well as the simple human error. And plenty of other parts unable to know. If all else fails, will you continue?"

"Was must be done, will be done."

His humming rang down the streets. The gold shimmered against the vibrancy of the fire which erupted from the houses and men who were repulsed. While the bells continue to ring in a beating rhythm.

The golden brass rang against the cold steel blades of the interrupted. And crashed down in vibrancy, in tones that rang true and furiously quick, bringing all those angles to fall to death.

The horns of men, who could only roam the ground were split among their lords, who made vows to their lords. A force, a fire started in their hearts and they pushed out and made visible all those who weren't of their right religion.

The fires roared as they remade the streets. Repaved with the molten glass that shattered minutes ago. The smoke rose up into the sky, and stayed put for now.

He rose to the peak of the chapel, and saw what he had done, and spun in marvel. The marble was struck by a force which split the city, and sent half into dust. From above a thin bladed estoc pierced him through the eyes and through the back of his head. "You dare try!?" And the angel died, and fell.

For some reason he stood there, he touched his eye. No pain was there, but he felt there was something that shouldn't be. Soon that feeling made his hand tense.

He descended back down to the ground, the marble warping from his steps, and the sky darkened. Another angel came forward, with sword in check, and tried to make the distance. A spear of pure white hot flames pierced and fell his wings. There was nothing but dust left to fall and rise into the sky.

He watched as all the angels collided with brass. The sound of fighting was rhythmic; transcendent. It beat with the ringing of the bell, and the tolling of the age. The forceful toll. The sound was grand. He had orchestrated it, "and it is only the intro to my requiem."

He stood with his arms outstretched, and looked down now seeing the realm inflamed, and he said, "fall," and so it fell.

Soon once the light could not be seen, he stumbled, and a voice was put in his mind. "This is what you seek, and this is what you made." And the voice repeated, "this is what you seek, and this is what you made. This is what you seek, and this is what you made. This is what you seek, and this is what you made."

"I want you gone! From my mind!"

This is what you seek, and this is what you made.

Soon the figure presented itself to him. *This is what you seek, and this is what you made.*

"I did what I had to do, for you kept myself from me."

I will not be rid of myself, so easily. "Begone!" The court of golden marble soon became a catalyst of fire.

You can't do this! "I said go!" And it all became light.

He shuddered in the slow pulling rubble, and he pushed through the top and saw the world, and declared a new order while erecting a tower of his own.

They gathered around the red zealot as he held the burning ember and sent smoke far above them to gather on the ceiling. He looked down on all those who were circled around him. After the smoke had settled – and the thurible incense and coals were gone – they pulled a heavy plated table into the center of the stage.

A thin wave of urgency fell in each a part of a repetitive system. Each a release of information which transcended and a rose in the heat. It gathered, turning the sky into a perfect all-absorbing black night. The zealot kept pushing, again and again, until stalagmites formed and transformed into one giant spike from the ceiling.

He waved his rhythmic arms in an incantation, spiraling and inciting a happening. She had walked onto the stage, masking her face, and momentarily hiding her body. At the moment that was right, she disrobed — revealing her long spun hair of sunlight and gold. And she was placed onto the altar. With a single plunge, rising white and gray ash painted the ceiling in a spiral-like pattern. It condensed and began to drop down the spike, ringed and throbbing. It began to shiver at first wake until it entered the bloom and they became one. Striped of black and white.

It was a quiet place to rest, by the lantern post furthest from town, and a bench unoccupied by most besides himself and his bag. He pulled a silver flute from a box on the side of his hip and tuned his breath with his acute feline hearing.

He played a sonata he had heard many years ago, it was a slow piece that he wasn't sure he'd remember, but it didn't matter so far away from the town. It started slow, but quickly grew into a great crescendo – which caused him to sputter – and after a brief moment the music quieted and slowed to a heart beat. The closest who could hear were the dead.

The old day dwindled into a near darkness, as he sat there in silence only broken by the tunes he played. Until he heard something different. It wasn't just a fumbling sound, it was a series of footsteps.

"Who goes there?" He asked the darkness from the graveyard.

He clutched his flute in one hand, and his bag in the other, while the lantern above kept him in the light. The fading evening light at the front gates was disturbed by a pure void, cloaked in a dark weave. The only light that showed was on his bright violet eyes.

He was stuck on that bench, the hairs on his arms stood, and for those moments of silence he looked at the figure, and when he saw the face some memory pierced his mind, and he said, "you, yes you. I see you there. Are you wraithkin?"

The dark figure walked up to him clearly trying to speak back, only to find he couldn't do so. "Ah, no you're no wraith at all. Hmm," he whispered to himself, "strange, hmm," and he gestured for this wanderer forward – while putting away his silver flute – and said, "no you're no wraithkin, but a mute. Oh where's my manors, I'm Rouvel, and It's cold out here, and you'd believe it's summer. Walk with me, after that journey through the forest you must be exhausted. I have soup cooking over a small fire, but I think it will fill us two."

He looked back at the gate behind the brush and trees, *the graveyard for the dead, but the dead still walks?* "If you go walking around the old cemetery any longer it'll consume you. I'll pity you then," and Rouvel walked down the road towards a deep mist, and the traveling figure followed.

They mounted and climbed the peaks sides. Carrying with mulled grunts the carcasses that had already begun to stink. They placed one – the sheep carcass on the side before the second peak – and then the other – on a stake planted at the very edge of the cliff side. From down below they could see very little, but a certain low hum gave them all they needed to know. The hunters nodded to each other before pulling out a coal box.

"That won't be necessary," said the man in red, as he drew a flame from his palm and set the carcasses ablaze.

The hunters waved to each other – getting their attention – and they fell into position. Half climbed point e, and the others kept their hefty spears in hand and ascended the second peak.

From fifty or sixty feet above the burning grounds they waited. Fingering their drawstrings and arrow shafts, tensing their grips on their spear shafts, and letting their mind tick at the right moment. The men in red were calm and quiet to the point where they seemed to blend in with the stationary old mountain.

More moments passed, the meaty smoke rose and fell, and the scent drifted for miles. There was a deep ticking sound that echoed up the mountain. As it grew from echoes to a direct line, they could see it. The claws burrowing into the hard red stone, and the beaten flaps of his wings, the eyes of desire.

He encroached on the stage, trying to quietly and slowly poach that roasting body. And he noticed from the side another, both equally burnt, but the shivers that ran down his bones were cold.

The hunters masked in red dust drew their long arrows and knocked them. They slowly drew the creaking bow strings, and waited for the correct moment. The leader raised his hand after knocking his own bow, and whispered, "on my release." He began to draw his great bow, and they waited. He nodded slowly, as he was finding his time to the hunters on the opposite peak.

They waited a minute more, as the beast shyly took the bait, and the lead hunter nodded, and dropped his hand from the drawstring.

Chapter One:

It was warm, and it looked like the light of a candle flame, but it rained the purity of dirt: blood and ash. It flickered with red. He went to grab it, but it wandered on. It pooled up and floated away in the pool of ethereal waters.

They passed from a door and down the dirt and gravel road. And he kept chasing the little flying flame, but it kept out of grasp. He chased down the hill, and past the watchers tower, and across the short bridge in dire need of repair. Through the thin trees, and warped gate he passed over the hills of the cemetery gardens.

There were marigolds wrapped together in a weave that blanketed over everything. The rot of the stone was wrapped in golden flowers, and the light drifted and dripped its light onto the petals which reflected back a golden shimmer.

It led far past the end, through a gaping portal of limbs twisting around. Out of the end, he walked through a tight corridor of flowers and twisting frozen limbs. The light fell upon his face and brightened his eyes into a soft vision of the thicket.

For hours they walked, the light soon was so far ahead it was just a twinkle sometimes seen when a single needle sized hole in the trees was available. His feet dragged against the ground, but his body still drifted forward towards where the light really was. And soon he met himself at the base of a great old tree. The trunk was shriveled, pulled tight over the fruit of the world of what was, long ago.

And a figure sat shaking a box lantern trying to take the light out, or to see the true light that's buried inside. For a minute this figure – short in stature – kept shaking that lantern, but to no avail. Instead he placed it down, and sat on the lantern. The figure showed him a thin silver bar, but with it being obscured by his hand, he couldn't tell what it really was. The figure said something to him, but still it was unintelligible.

He stood up again holding the lantern towards the tree, and the light showed nothing but a dark aura. It was a black fog embedded in the tree, a doorway into another hall. He passed through the tree, and the light emitted through the mists until it became a single entity which enveloped him, and pulled him down the hill.

He fell down an infinite depth. The well had missing bricks which let this faint draft in and something not yet realized. For minutes it had been just the darkness until a fraction of light could be seen shining at the bottom. And as he fell he grew closer and closer to that light, until with one quick snatch he took it by the handle and held the lantern firmly.

He was no longer falling, his feet were firmly planted on a creaky wooden trapdoor, which after two stomps broke open, throwing him down into the chamber. The lantern was as good at penetrating the chamber as a single candle for lighting catacombs.

He landed next to a stone pillar, made of a gray rock. Across the hall – by fifty or so feet – was an identical pillar. And between the pillars was a long hall of rows of these same pillars, equal distance apart. He wouldn't go down the hall – feeling a fear from the other side. So he walked across, and every time he met a door which opened to the other side. For a few times around he'd hoped the door would open to some destiny, but it never did.

He held the lantern high, letting its light penetrate only feet through the thick fog in the distance. His hands shuddered as a cold front ran through and dusted the pillars. At the very end of the hall, he initially found joy, until he saw a massive door that rose as high as the pillars, and they opened as he drew close. From there all that was left was the void.

The fireplace whispered to the traveler, and a small cooking pot held some soup which was faintly aromatic. The sound of a spoon clanking the sides of the pot fully awoke him. He sat watching the malkin stir the pot, and when he was done, he said in a reserved tone, "strange dream you had?"

He nodded, and Rovuel said, "sometimes I think it's a strange world too. It wasn't always so strange. My great great grandfather always told me stories of the world of the past. I don't think you've seen much, if any of these lands at all."

And he nodded, "the silent night reveals much to us, and here you've come to us, our silent knight. Here," he handed the wanderer a silver mirror, "look, see who you look like."

He saw his face. There was almost nothing to be seen, it was like looking into a shadow, except for his eyes. They glittered like purple jewels. Twinkling from the fireplace. He grasped the cloak feeling with his dark fingers over the fabric. He remembered something about that face, his face, but it was finding a grain of sand in the expanse of oceans.

"The very moment I had a good look at you, I could see, and I was sure of who you were," the malkin dropped down to the traveler's eyes, and he looked carefully, and said "Do you remember my people: the Malkin?" The traveler shook his head, "hmm, that is a shame, but. Hmm," he scratched his face.

He tried to wave his hands to gesture something, to communicate something, but to the malkin it was gibberish. *Who am I?* He thought and Rovuel perked his ears, "my word may not be great enough, I don't have any evidence, nor am I such a scholar in my faith, but I'm certain you are the justice knight, as it's called."

The traveler shrugged, not knowing what that meant, "in my faith, we believe that there would be a champion of balance who would clear the skies and bring justice to the being who betrayed us: Gruel. And they would bring peace back to the world."

The traveler pointed to himself, "though it would have to be proven, and I don't know where to do so, but I'm certain. I know a fellow malkin far older than I who does, and may know some of the test as well. To anyone else, this may seem rash, but where you go I'll follow, it's a prophecy, and I want to help our savior as much as possible. Please," the malkin prayed, and the traveler stayed still.

"I can see it on your face, we Malkin are good at reading it. If you would give me time, I want to show you those you'd be saving," and the traveler nodded, but he thought, *I have nothing in this world, no commitments, and no one to share with.* "I'm here for you, come let me show you this town, and then you can see what the world looks like."

It was moderately warm outside, above the world cast just below the sky was a blanket of gray clouds. Not a single ray could pass and show the sky behind. All the light was diffused in clumps, and caused everything to appear almost gray.

They walked through the town, which was a series of either old brick buildings owned by the wealthier in the center, or wooden shab houses meant to fall, and rise quickly and cheaply, but drafty winds made winters insufferable. Leaning against one of the shabbier buildings was a man a head or two taller than himself. He held his face in his hands, and fell to the ground. Rovuel ran to him, asking, "what's wrong, what happened."

He looked up, his eyes were blood red, he said, "my wife is dead, and my son is gone," and said nothing else.

"Where did he head? Where did he go?" But there was no response, he pointed in a direction, but didn't seem so sure of it.

It was still early in the day, they passed by brick buildings on either side, until they came into a middle courtyard. Rearing up on horseback was a man with a long coat, and a round leather cap. He rang a bell yelling out, "to the plows! To the plows!"

"That man works for the duke, or lord, or whoever supposedly rules us. He knows enough," he waved over to him, and grabbed his attention, then spoke up to him, "have you seen a lost boy around here lately?"

"Some brat has escaped their duties? Or run away? That cannot be, who was the child?"

A wailing woman ran up screaming, "there's a beast in my chest! There's a beast in my chest! There wasn't one before, and now there's a beast beating on the walls, and scampering about," her hair furled and was intensely wily while she spoke.

The rider shook his head, and rolled his eyes too, and he said furiously annoyed, "you malkin, and you," he was struck, he simply didn't see the traveler, his eyes shrunk, from his hip he pulled out a sword, and pointed the tip to the traveler, and yelled, "wraithkin! wraith!"

"No, no, no!" Yelled back Rovuel running in front of the traveler, "he's not a wraith, a wraith would've attacked us by now. No, no. He's a . . . a reaper."

"A what?"

"A reaper, those angels of death."

"Fine," he sputtered his lips, "you . . . you take him, and deal with her stupid chest rat. Get out of my sight," and he put away the wooden sword, and ran the bell, yelling, "have no alarm, just a rat, just a rat. Get to the plows, get to the plows."

The woman in her rags escorted them. She had lived in a building of brick, but now it was in its middle stages of decomposing into dust. She fidgeted, her skin shook about her dainty and flimsy bones. The chest was a slick worn thing, partially covered in moss, and she stood paces behind them visibly afraid. "There, the demon is in there."

They tried to open the chest, it was locked, and they said so.

"Oh," she stuttered, "give me a. Give, a moment," and she left walking into her house, and they weren't sure she'd leave.

There was a large squirming and thrashing within the box. They themselves too were vexed to have to deal with this. And then they heard a high pitched groan. And then another. Rouvel looked around, and said, "you stay here, watch the chest, I'll get her."

The chest held something large, but it didn't seem to be some animal. He looked to the ground, grabbing a rock, and smashing the lock off its latch, and he cracked the lid, and he saw a child green of skin, and covered in bruises. The traveler stepped back. Rouvel returned and ran up to the now open chest, he said in a low tone, "by your hand he's still alive. That man, the tall one, who lost his wife and son, remembers him? This is his son."

Why was he in a chest? He wanted to ask, but Rouvel said, "do you see what you can do? I feel his life could have only been saved if it weren't for you. It's a prophecy; it's meant to happen."

The traveler stood there, and he knew he had no life, nor any commitments, or people to protect, so why not these people, and the people he's said to help. He nodded to the malkin, and he reached in the chest to return the dying child to his broken father.

Chapter Two:

They packed what they could, collecting bread and grain to cook and eat – at least what Rouvel could eat – on the road north. They scavenged for sticks and during their time planning and packing, the sticks dried into burnable firewood. They acquired a good share of leather, and saddle bags that they could, and now the only problem they had to face was how they would protect themselves on the road. There were blacksmiths who could forge a knife, and a mean club, but they were more akin to finding a decent armorer's blade. They wouldn't need anything ornamental or shiny; just a sword that could smash into a tree and have fittings that didn't rattle loudly. Although it wasn't nearly as difficult of an endeavor as finding a stable with horses who wouldn't be spooked by the mere presence of the Traveler, nor be completely out of their budget. Even with all this difficulty, Rouvel wouldn't part with travel on the grounds of horseback traveling. They wouldn't dare trek the edge of that damned forest on foot.

A week passed, they had found an armorer from the opposite side of town, who for a cheap commission could forge a semi shabby blade, but for how cheap they were able to buy him, the blade would be a tiny thing. The armorer had said it was the best he could do for their price, and he even pointed out the blade shape from a book. It was a design from out west, past the forest, and from a great city called Hule. The only problem left for them was acquiring horses.

Near the end of the week, these figures in a full brown robe and hood had come to town. There were maybe a dozen of them. The men who worked for their lord, had come to figure out who they were, and made a whole mess of it, and the next day they had disappeared from the town. It was strange, no one saw them leave from any direction. Although going through the forest of Mulder wouldn't have been hard to disappear from, it was still strange no one saw a trace of them from then on.

It was now near the end of the week. Soon their sword would be finished, and they believed there was a man who would sell them mares, and luckily these mares weren't so easily spooked.

For the little time the traveler was in this town, he seemingly was given a reputation that caused mothers to yell at their children to come inside, and men to cower and hug the enshadowed walls of the closest buildings.

There was an old man, with a long shabby beard who walked up to them, and on his face was less of an expression of fear as there was of anger. A rock hit him on the back. The traveler turned to see who threw it, finding this old man bending down to throw another. Rouvel yelled, "stop that! Why are you doing this! What's your problem!"

And the old man yelled back, "you killed my son, and my granddaughter, and ever since he came here he's caused more horrors than I've ever seen in all my life. And he brought with him those cultists."

"What are you talking about? Stop this, he has nothing to do with that."

"He killed my son and granddaughter. Their deaths are in his hands, and you protect him?!"

"Come now, I've been with him since he's arrived, and he did no such thing. He's caused no cult in this town."

"That cult has come following his arrival. How do you explain that?"

"Leave us, he didn't do this insanity you're stuck in."

"Blood sucking wraith," the old man said before walking away.

"That man is crazy, don't worry about him. Come let's continue."

The traveler checked his shoulder with every turn. There wasn't anyone there, but he hoped that there wasn't anyone there.

The armorer held his shop in a small quaint place with fewer tools than even other blacksmiths in the town, but it didn't matter when he held out that sword, in a leather sheath, and said, "as you requested."

Like they were told, the sword was a tiny thing. It was thin and whip-like, but had a mean curve which ought to deal something if push were to come to shove. The traveler held it by the small handle, and went to put it around his waist, and instead he put it into the void.

They thanked him, and went on their way. But when they were just out of earshot, Rouvel turned to the traveler, asking, "what did you just do?"

What, I put it away, he thought. He pulled it back out of the void, while reaching for his waist. He pulled out that sword, in its sheath. "Fascinating, can you do that for anything."

He pulled out a knife from the void as well, and just to prove the point he took a rock from the ground, and passed it through and back again. "I guess we'll have to see how much you could carry at once."

The sky was a deep orange blur. The air was cooling from the midday sun, and the warm colors became nothing but an expected darkness. Like usual there were some of the townspeople with their lanterns and torches working away, and others switching positions in the community watchtower.

They had picked up some small vegetables of varying quality, and threw them into the soup pot when they returned. "Tomorrow we'll pick up those mares, and then we'll say goodbye to Demorte.

Here," he pointed to a map of the region, "next stop is north in Deinde. That is that fellow malkin I spoke of, have I mentioned his name?"

He shook his head, *No.* "Ah then, Tolk, well, he's an old man. Far older than I, and anyone you'll see here. His memory is said to go back many many centuries. I believe I've told you he lived before the great war. If that's the case, he might as well be the last one left from then."

The great war? He thought perplexed, "ah, yes, the great war. All I know is from the tales, myths, and a few books I read of it, but it's agreed that it happened about a thousand years ago. And the reason it's called the great war, is because the whole world fought at once. Every country, allied between the forces of good, or the forces of evil."

Quickly there came a knock at the door. Rouvel said, "I'll get it, I'll just tell them to bugger off," but when he opened the door, he found a priest in old tattered clothes, who said, "praise be the lucky. I beg thee, for hot soup by your fire, and to light a candle for heat."

He couldn't hear what the malkin said, since he whispered it in a solemn voice, but the priest soon left looking stern and disappointed. Rouvel returned, fashioning himself another bowl of soup, and sat down mulling over the soup. "Where was I?"

The traveler gave him a look, and he said, "now, not every country is allied with the good. Some did align with darkness. But you must be wondering, who won, and why it all started?" The traveler nodded, and the malkin continued, "to put it simply, our side lost. Well the armies of good lost. Now we live under the faith of the chaos god: Gruel. For years they fought, men from the west, and men from the east. But the main two forces were the Kingdom of Tisden of the west, and our armies from the Kingdom of Rientonem. From this war, great scholars of the Malkin had found a prophecy, and wrote it before their churches and my race was nearly annihilated. But this prophecy told of a hero of good and just would defeat the chaos god, free us from this world's uncertainty. That leads us to you."

The traveler raised up two fingers, and Rouvel realized and said, "ah yes, you're right, almost forgot it," he spoke in a soft tone, "in the realm of the living, there is not one, but two gods of creation. And they were brothers. Selziar the god of balance and justice, and Gruel the god of chaos and-"

"Fire!" Yelled from outside. "Fire! Fire!"

They both turned, a small trickle of fire seeped in from the roof. "Get out!" Yelled Rouvel.

Upon opening that heavy door, the smoldering and hoveling of fire transcended the night sky. The town was in flames. From the center was a massive flame spiraling into the sky. They could see the tendrils of those flames appear just shy above the rooftops. They donned masks of skulls with antlers twisted and sharp. There was no image of humanity from these monsters. They were throwing flames from their hands, and even melted brick like it was simply wax. But what layed on the ground were charred bodies of those who didn't deserve it.

The priest too donned this mask, his freshly cut off the deer. He raised a carved club in his hand, and raised it to them. Rouvel pushed on the travelers legs and fell them to the side, as a liquid stream of flame chased them. Swirls of red and orange engulfed the brick and mortar which held the home once.

The traveler drew the sword which glimmered in the light. Without thinking, he ran sidelong around the flame in an attempt to end this destruction. Before he could land the point in his chest, the priest summoned a pillar of flame, and the traveler fell back. "One does not attack a servant of god without repercussions," yelled the priest, "I shall show you mercy – and pray for thee – in the other realm."

They came into the light, imbued with this arrogant power of the flame, but it was smashed open with a simple rock. His mask fractured in half, revealing his pudgy smoke filled face. He gasped in horror, and swung out a whip of flame.

The traveler quickly ran up, and sunk the blade through the priest, and when he ripped it out, the body fell limb, dead. There was a grumble of pain, of sorrow not from the priest, but from Rouvel. He clutched his chest – there was a hole deep and fatal. "I guess I did my part, now you just need to survive."

The traveler hunched over, examining the wound, and he said, "the wound is seared, look no blood, and there's no way to fix this damage," he coughed, and his eyes went gray, and he said with one last breath, "goodbye."

Chapter Three:

All he had was a knife, a sword, and a lantern with one candle. The gray night sky held chill winds pass down against the ground, blowing the grass heavily and dislodging from the loose ground. He looked behind, and all he could see was the black smoke and fire which ravaged on, but the sound was long gone.

Up ahead as he walked was a growing fog that became so thick that the traveler couldn't see his own feet. He wanted to light the lantern, but he had nothing to do so with. He just continued on to Deinde.

He was exhausted, there was no light, and all he knew was the sound his steps made on the road. He couldn't see a foot ahead, but before he slept, he made sure no-one was following. He checked his back, but he didn't know if there was anyone in the darkness, and in the fog.

The next day – when the traveler awoke – he expected Rouvel to be there, with a pot of soup, and a lit candlestick, but there was only himself. With all the warmth his cloak brought him, the chill still pierced his being.

The mists were thin in the morning. He was able to see far in the distance. There was a crossroads, but the post had shown that both roads led to Deinde. He chose a path and walked it for hours, and hours. It was long after he passed that junction, when he thought about it again. *What was the other road like? Why would it split to begin with? Maybe it was those cultists, luring people down the wrong path. Have I gone down the wrong path? Are they following me?* He walked and thought these same questions over and over again, trying to think of answers with little he knew of the world.

As that day rolled over, the fog of yesterday had shown itself again. Soon all he could see was the wall of diffused light emanating from the covered gray sky.

Eventually the sky became shaded, and there was nothing left but the dark. For some time longer, he walked the lonely road. There are only the sounds of footsteps, and the sound of the passing winds. He was growing tired.

Before he went to sleep, he heard another sound. It was a low moan far away. It echoed harshly through the forest, and then there was a silence. The traveler again tried to look around, to find and see who was there, or what was there, but there was only the empty silence. He stood with the sword pointed forward, and the knife in his other hand. Every step was taken with caution. At any moment he would thrust the sword forward, hoping to kill someone who would kill him. The only thing that drifted towards him was the wind, and some small droplets of water. More rain fell as he waited for something human, or inhuman to close in. Just something to deal with that sound in the empty space that occupied the air. It was a dreary silence, as the rain fell on him, and coated the silver of the blade. It came in an instant. A flash and explosion struck the grass twenty feet behind him.

Even with the dampness in the grass it caught fire in an instant and started to spread.

Once the flash had faded from his eyes, he could see the flame and its diminishing sight. The traveler ran to grab the light it emitted. Pushing the wick into the flame. If there were something following him, the light would do little to already hamper him then what is already hampering him.

He waved the lantern to and fro, hoping to scare off whatever was approaching. If there was something there. He walked backwards first slowly then quickly, and for an hour there was nothing.

For many hours he sliced through the fog, the light barely touching the ground below. The fog darkened; the air was chilled to almost freezing the water on his cloak. It was quiet for a long time still. Eventually he grew less weary, and the traveler decided to rest for the night. Under the shade of the forest was an initial thought, but walking to sleep under the forest was too dangerous it felt. *What man has plowed is less insane than that forest.* But if the road was in use, and in the morning was covered in fog, that'd be an embarrassing death. He decided to lay on the side of the road, in the grass, by himself.

He feared to snuff the candle, fearing what the darkness would bring. Before he drifted on, he remembered the image of the fire that came so little time ago. How it burned so bright, and it spread horribly quick. But also how if extinguished, all that would be left would be ashes. As he came closer to that deep void of sleep, the image of fire began to fade without any residue.

There he saw in the void, that expanse of pillars in an order, of an ancient but pristine stone that stood on either side equal distance apart. He was floating in a pool of infinity. But was drifting forward, on and on, from all of time to be.

A set of doors with no significant features opened forward, and he walked through to another world. There was a crystal orb floating behind a glass blown cavern. In the center there was a man in the middle of crystal, draped in old robes from another age different then the current year. He couldn't see any features on the man, or at least none that remained in his mind. But it wasn't just the figure in the orb, but another just above, with a long blade with a wicked and aggressive curve, and the figure thrusted the blade into the orb until it became part of it. And the figure themselves tried to pull it out, but for some strange consequence was turned to stone, leaving many with long curved hair like a fire and long graceful wings like the most incredible hawk.

He entered the home with a quick thrust to the window shattering it into a billion glittering pieces which fell up like fluttering paper receipts. On he went through the insanity and halls which couldn't decide whether to let lanterns fill their volume with light, or let the incoming rain snuff it out. "What do you think?"

"I don't have the time?"

"No you don't. Which one?" They begged.

"I already know of rain, so let it be rain."
"No I'm tired of rain, how about something else."

"Well I'm not too fond of fire, if that's the case."

"Well if we can't keep one option, then we can't keep the other. But the fire and rain will stay. We'll bring in something new."

"So be it."

And they let him through. It took the rest of that day and night, and further on, but he found a mark on him which wouldn't go away. So they kept the rain, and fire, and something else he couldn't see was approaching the hallways of wood. He kept moving forward through the sludge which was a consequence of his own action. The light reflected off of the glass so intensely that it was a reflection a thousand times greater than looking in the heart of the brightest fire, the sun, a star. But he kept walking, and he kept walking until he found out the other side was the door.

He tried to open the door outside-in, he had no key. He tried to search the ground which was still a brilliantly stunning light. He pulled on the handle, it burned his hand, his palm ached in pain, but it soon faded away. Other things faded, and soon his sight faded too.

There was this horrible pain which pierced his hands. He had been holding onto the lantern, burning his hand. He had pushed it to the ground with a thump. In the little light, he looked at his hand, and it was the same as it had been before. The night sky still stood in place, like no time had passed at all. He no longer felt exhausted, and the candle barely lost half an inch in length.

The road was hard from the cold wind, and filled with so many stones it could be assumed someone poured gravel on the ground. For hours he walked this way, he kicked rocks as they randomly intercepted his boots, and stumbled against the holes drilled by rainwater.

For an hour or two he kept walking down the same road, burning his candle till there was nearly nothing left. The last of the low lights just shyly revealed the end of the road. And just slightly past that was a dropoff down a deep cliff. He carefully checked to see the sheerness of the cliff hoping it was short, and all he could see was the absence of the ground.

As he turned the candle snuffed, and the smoke drifted away down the cliff face. A sound too followed, not of any soft kindling, but of heavy breathing. It was not human breath, but the breath of a large approaching beast.

The traveler held the sword forward. He walked away from the cliff. *So this cliff came in the way of the old road. I can deal with this animal, and then I'll go back and walk the other route.* The sound of the ground crunching under his boot was both silent, and sonorous.

He felt the eyes pierce him, and the sound of heavy footsteps. They drew closer, and closer, more until it felt like the beast, wherever it were, was really right in front of him. He leaped forward, intent to skewer whatever was there, but what he saw in the coming and passing moonlight, was the image of a snow white bear.

It rushed his side, batting at him with hard claws, and passing the blade by its side. He was kicked back, on the edge, and before he could stand. The massive white bear clawed his body, roaring a haunting sound. And down he stumbled down the rocky cliff, and the bear was there above, as he fell into the dark depths that were below.

Chapter Four:

The midnight chill befell, a daft wind came and awoke the traveler. He struggled to get up, limping a few feet away from the bottom of that sheer face before falling to the ground as he clutched his throbbing leg. He tried limping forward, until he thought he gained full control of his legs, and he stumbled until the pain was subservient and dealt with.

Up ahead in his sight there was a house with lanterns lit, but windows closed, and smoke puffing from a brick chimney in the back.

From up above he could hear this booming sound of an echoing thunderous clap. Down came a horse in half and man in pieces, with blood slapping the ground. In his hand was a snapped sword, and in his other was a lantern shattered in many pieces. The traveler looked up trying to see what was there, but still he could see nothing. He checked the corpses further, and in a pocket he found a letter drenched in blood, and it was completely unreadable. It wasn't obvious, but this was the work of that same beast which threw him over.

As he walked to this house, for a brief second there was a face that peered through a small window. The person had run away before he could see their facial details, but he continued on. He came to the front door, hoping to stay undercover against the night. The door of the house was old, wooden, and had stained glass panels at the very top of the door. He knocked on the door, and right after, the door swung inwards, and he was grabbed, and thrown to the floor by the person from inside. "What does a wraith have to sneak upon me at my own house? I saw what you did to that man, how you left him and his horse. I'll let you know I haven't provoked your kind for quite some time, and every time I have, you've lost. You won't get what you want, for my blood is mine!" She exclaimed, drawing a bastard sword onto him.

He escaped that stab, jumping up from the ground. She leapt forward her sword point directed to his side, intending to end her threat quickly. He reached out, pulling his sword from the void. The traveler jumped out of the way to her left, got closer to her and tried to attack her. She quickly guarded with her sword and stepped back, and prepared to strike back again.

He tried to reach back for the door, and attempted to disarm her if possible. He swung from high to low, knocking beams from above, and was blocked by her blade. He swung again, but she parried and tried to push her blade forward into his chest. The traveler in little time was able to parry and push, and then he ran. She realized, and said, "I won't let you leave you monster. you're trapped in here with me, and I've killed wraiths before."

The light in the house was no longer there, and the traveler was thrown into darkness. When he tried to reach the door he found she was there already with her sword pointed forward. She held a dim lantern, and muttered "Scared? What a weak wraith I've found," she said, "why so quiet? Are you really so scared?"

He held the blade firm, and their swords collided, but the traveler was fast, faster than she expected. She swung out, feigning her strike and redirected the blow forwards, but her careful strikes had missed him. Deflected and parried the blows, but she kept her stance and her composure. She went in for a stab, but reeled back, before running forward to grab him. They both fell to the ground, covered in the gray light.

The traveler reached for the knife, and used the flat side to block the edge of her sword from reaching him. In one successful push, he turned them over, putting her below him. The steel was close to her skin – ready to draw if needed – while her sword was out of range of anything useful. He kept the knife close, while her breaths became a rolling stutter, but that sound came and shook him.

That stutter gave her the little time to push him off, and she rose up – grasped the sword hilt firmly – and kept the blade tip pointed at him. She leaned in thrusting a stab, but he parried and feigned, swinging wildly to keep her away, *the bigger fish is here.*

The covered sky let off no light, and from outside a beastly sound erupted and shook the panes of stained glass until it faded quickly. And again, the sounds had come, and shook the ground now. It grew closer and soon dust and chunks of wood which held the ceiling had started to fall in flecks from the ceiling above. They were dead still. She looked up and fear fell into her cheeks. The sound of the beast felt like it was within ear shot; like it was breathing into their skulls. The air then became silent, and for a minute it stayed strangely stale. He felt it, he felt something was off. Before another action he ran to her, taking her to the ground. "Get off me!" She yelled before a great crash came down to try and drown them into the ground.

There were beams and the clay tiles scattered over them, but they were lucky. There was a small crevice that they were in which let them survive. After a minute in the cradle of death, a heat had pushed them out of the rubble. And the heat had begun to shear the pieces left from the splinters and wafers of the walls and roof of the house.

Clawing the roof parts behind them was the beast with white and red claws. The lanterns that hung before, crashed down and created a fire that was growing slowly. In the flicker of the flame they saw the great big monster. The red light illuminated its face, but not the whole of the beast. It was a bear far larger than they, with white fur stained with blood of many different shades of red and brown.

The white bear leaped from far, and crashed down between them, and they stumbled trying to get away. But it mostly targeted the traveler, trying to claw him, with viperous quickness. The traveler was able to back away, but tumbled to the ground into the arms of possible death.

She was on the other side, she searched for her sword, while the bear was batting at the stranger. Under some stray pieces of flat boards. She quickly whipped the sword high. She touched the blade quickly, and ran to pierce the bear's back, and stuck her blade through the back of its leg. She took the blade out, and with one mighty swing, the leg was severed from the body. It recoiled violently, and spun on its available appendages to face her. It screamed at her, and she jumped back far enough where her feet met the ground, but then she was tripped by that same leg she severed, and it tried to grasp her leg with its sharp hard talons. She swiped the blade against her own feet, and sent the appendage flying some feet away, but instead of the limb landing dead, it crawled back to its host and reattached itself with a firm popping sound. The bear ran out of the darkness, but it wasn't gone. It leaped out from the sky, the blood fur rained down trying to crush her, but she was able to leap out of the way in time.

In a moment of opportunity, the traveler stabbed at the white fur. Squeals of pain roared out, and in retaliation the white bear clawed at him tearing gashed into his cloak. His blade pierced the flesh down the guard, and was stuck. And tried to reach to pull it out, but the beast was unwilling. He reached for the knife, but guarding the beastly arm of the monster, and the traveler was thrown to the ground. The bear stood over him trying to gnaw at his face, but the traveler held the knife firm, and kept pushing the blade into its head. Blood swarmed down and coated the blade, and lubricated each subsequent attack, until the bear became enraged from this all. It stood on its hind legs intending to crush him under its sharp pointed claws.

She was again on the other side of this bear, she jumped forth slashing from behind, and into the torso going through the leg, which caused the white bear to fall to the side. But soon the wounds closed, and the bear got back up, and charged. She was knocked back, but was able to keep her blade somewhat steady and firm. She kept back up, until all the light came from behind the bear, making its fur appear black as coal and shrivel with squeaks that burned.

The traveler ran to the bear, jumping on its side, sticking the knife into the hide and peeled back chunks of flesh oozing blood of no particular color. He rode the bear which tried to swat him off, and viciously rioted back and forth.

She was attacking its back, the bear turned around in such a violent way it was only making itself more aggressive, and she yelled out. "Back! Back! You beast! Let my strikes follow, and keep you dead!" She knew this wouldn't do anything, but it was a primal thing she felt she needed to do at that very moment.

The bear kept slashing at her, throwing her sword with one strike, and pushing her to the cold ground with another. She protected her head with her gauntlets, and the claws tried to get through her breast plate. Each strike caused the plate to scratch and dent, more and more, as she laid helpless on the ground.

The traveler was initially thrown off the back, but he again ran and jumped on its back, now ready to stay put. He kept sinking the knife into its back, between fur and flesh, and flesh and bone. At first it didn't notice him, and he kept stabbing and stabbing the beast. But what was more apparent was its aggression. It turned to rubble, which now was firmly a true chaotic blaze. The bear shifted its weight. It tried to drop him in the fire, but instead he jumped off and some of

that fire had spread across half its body burning half the fur leaving a
smoking skin closer to coal.

She tried to get up, but found she couldn't. She tried to keep
her breath, but it grew harder to take any breaths. All she could do
was keep her hands over her face. But she wouldn't accept it, she had
to try, or that bear would most certainly kill them both, as soon as it
killed that stranger-wraith.

He watched the bear closely, *the skin isn't healing,* he thought.
He ran around the other side of the bear to lure it into the fire. But for
some reason it wasn't attracted to him, it was after her again.

Again the bear was clawing at her armor. Each strike pushed
the armor into her chest until the metal separated, and started to shear.
With one arm, she tried to crawl away. She was pushing herself back,
and then the deep screech came.

He pulled the sword from the bear's side, and it was warped
and coated in that sticky blood. He swiped the blade against its leg,
and again, and again. The leg had severed, but wouldn't die, and she
said with what little breath she owned, "the limbs still move."

He looked down, noticing it wiggle and try to return to the
socket. He kicked the leg toward the fire, and the fur immediately
evaporated, and the skin became charred and shriveled and smoked
until it smelled like illness. The bear made a sickly scream which
echoed off the cliff face.

He ran back, this time luring the bear around the flames. The
more he evaded its quick ensuing attacks, the more enraged it became.

The traveler continued luring the bear further, until it was in range of attack, and then he ran through the fire, and the bear followed too.

He immediately dropped, turned and escaped, his cloak having become engulfed. He dropped to the ground, quickly snuffing the flame. But the beast had begun to erupt into a massive bubbling curdle and flame which stripped its fur from its skin, and began to char, and shrivel into a skeletal carcass.

He went to the girl, noticing the armor piercing her chest. He grabbed the straps holding her armor to her torso and cut them with the now dull knife. Her eyes opened, as she took a deep breath in, and said quietly, "wraith-kin?" And fell into the dark night.

She awoke at the beginning of the morning, the sun had just risen, though all the light was diffused by the clouds. Sitting beside her was the traveler, when she saw him, she jumped back, scared, and then exclaimed, "wraith-kin! wraith!" And then she quickly remembered, "no . . . you saved me!? Why? What are you?"

He gestured how much he could, she eventually realized his speech, and she was able to take note, saying. "Oh!? You're not a wraith are you?" And he shook his head, "I can help you, whatever it be I'll help you. I . . . I have to help you. You . . . you saved my life, and I have to do something it seems."

He extended a hand, which she didn't take at first, but after a fleeting moment she held his hand, and he helped pick her up. He pointed forward, and after a minute, she asked, "Diende?" And he nodded, "I travel there once a week or so, I can help you get there. I need to repay this debt to you.

"Could you help me search the rubble?" And the traveler nodded. They looked through the ashes, and found a small chest which even after the fire, was barely touched. Inside were leather pouches of gold and silver coins.

Chapter Five:

The morning was mild with a dew dripping down from all the leaves on the two wanderers, as they gathered stray sticks for fire. They both held two armfuls of the semi-slick branches and smaller sticks. They both tied their bundles and carried them over their backs. "We won't be able to use these today, we can go a night without fire, but tomorrow these should be fine for a fire. Hmm," she thought, *I don't know his name, and he doesn't know mine either,* "I forgot to say, I'm Jane. And you?" And the traveler shrugged, it seemed like he didn't have any name. "Can I give you a name?" And he nodded, "then, how about Litus?" She offered.

Litus? What does that mean? And it showed in his expression, "I may be wrong, but my mother once told me it was a term for being quiet. I thought it fit you."

The day dwindled slowly, as they walked on and on. There were old roads made of dust and dirt which were broken in pieces of different ages and unused by most. For a long time they could hear the leaves fall, and the ground move, and the little pitter patter of small animals around them, but nothing between them. Most of all the silence around them grew into an audible droning. She asked, "did you come from Demorte? The one past the cliff?" And he nodded, "you fell down that cliff!? I've only been there when I was young with my mother, we had to go the other way, the longer way."

Soon it would be night, with the sky swinging from pink to nothing. The lands in the distance showed trees which rose high on hills and mountains, all in pure darkness and shown no further detail. And those trees soon became nothing as well. They couldn't go further on, the night had taken hold, and now they had to wade out the night, in hopes something wasn't stalking them while they never noticed.

Jane volunteered this night to stay guard while the sounds of air passing and animals skittering were only amplified by the absence of her use of her eyes. She remained still, with one hand gripping the pommel of her sword, and the other across her chest, as the pain still stood over her.

The moon eventually became somewhat visible. Its faint light showered down something, which glinted off the metal of her gauntlets. She waited for time to pass away, and to rotate position. And then a moonlight thought came to her, *I'm guarding something inhuman. What is he?* She kept a firm grip on the handle. She watched him intently, hoping he would get up to attack, but for minutes there was nothing whatsoever. She sat back, disgraced by her own actions. *Am I really willing to kill someone in their sleep, who saved me?* Tonight she decided not. She laid back against a tree, ready to draw if necessary.

The morning had a certain chill in the air, a quality that was similar to his first awakening in this realm. The morning was an immediate journey further on. They broke through old groves, and the ever present feature of those broken roads.

The hills were sprawling, but the ground wasn't kind on them. There were the roots of many different sizes, the large ones were easy to deal with, while the smaller seemed like they were meant for tripping the two. They walked for a very long while, and often made stops to rest. But for that day, it was like the day prior.

The sky had dimmed down close to night, they decided to make camp, and sat under some shade with a fire between them, burning low. Jane had been twiddling sticks, "we're getting closer to the town. We'll get there, most likely tomorrow, if we push ourselves.

Hopefully someone will let me stay with them. I don't want to be rude to those I know, and say 'my house was destroyed by a demon bear' but I don't know. Do you know someone there?"

Litus nodded, *Tolk, the malkin,* he repeated in his mind. He drew in the dirt – with the end of his sword – that name. Jane tossed in those twigs, and said, "oh, I've heard of that old man, the old malkin. Never bothered to meet him, never bothered, he never stepped foot outside his house for anyone that I've seen. For being someone who complains about noise, he doesn't seem to mind blacksmiths. What do you have with him?"

He didn't know how to articulate it to her. *Does she know about the prophecy?* And so he wrote that on the ground too, but Jane laughed, "you can't trust what you see in dreams. Following that stuff will only make you stupid," Litus shook his head, and persisted in that word, "so, what are you?"

I want to know who I am too. But he didn't write it. Jane looked at him solemnly, and she said in a nearly broken voice, "are . . . are you a Reaper?" Even though Litus had been called it once, he didn't know what that meant, so he shook his head, and Jane asked, "so you don't know about Reapers? They're the angels of death. Wherever they go, death comes with them," she let out a sigh, "I guess that's some relief then. Still, even if I don't know what you are, I now know you're not some wraith."

The night had fallen, the only sight was given by the flickering of the flame. "Have you ever seen . . . a star?" *A star?* And he shook his head.

"I haven't either, but I've heard about them from my mother, but I know if she's never seen one either. But it's apparently said, they were this twinkling sparkle which the ancient people looked at and told stories around. And the stars are also supposed to be as bright as the moon, but smaller. Isn't that odd? Little candles in the sky, but now they've been snuffed with nothing to light them again."

The fire kindled slowly, and Litus stood guard, and there he hoped not to see something creep in from the night. But soon the fire took hold. The dancing flame, of no perceivable pattern drew him, until that was all he looked at. The fire. A burning hatred, a burning disgust grew in his stomach. It eventually snuffed itself and the black of night took hold once more.

They didn't spend any time mesmerizing in the morning light and temperance. They were on the walk and wouldn't stop. Even as they tripped over small brush and roots, they continued on. As morning turned to afternoon, the roads now led to a short wall in the distance.

He was walking forward, almost creeping forward. And peering out of the gray fog was an object, almost unidentifiable from far. There was this miasma between his eyes, and the object there. On either side of the road there were the two figures now visible. On the ground they were crumpled into a prayer. Their worm clothes clearly were once blue and brown, and handwoven by passionate people. And as he came closer he noticed not two figures, but two rows of figures all praying in unison, with marks against their wrists and flat faces melted like wax.

A wall of fog ran towards him, and he walked forward still. And it passed him, those figures on either flank were mere shadows and with each step he took they fragmented until they turned to small flecks of ash.

From the gray he could see directly in front of him was a tall figure. And the figure for some time was walking towards him, until a single point of bright red and white light started to drift towards him.

As it came closer, it grew in size, until it took all of his vision, and all was filled with light of white and red.

Chapter Six:

"What is it? What's wrong? You were shaking," but there was little that was remembered.

Up ahead a few hundred feet there was a great wall of wood and iron. It was a story and a half tall, and reinforced in many places. And inside was the entirety of the town of Diende. *How many thousands of people live within those walls? Those walls were meant to keep back the forest invaders?*

There was a tall door of heavy plank wood guarded by two men garbed with red and yellow gambesons, and they wielded long spears. One of the men with a gruff beard shouted, "address yourself!"

"You know who I am. I'm Jane."

"Not you! Him, that wraith! Why have you brought him here? People live here!"

"He's not a wraith. You know that to be true."

"Why, what is he?"

"He is of holy nature. An angel from the other realm. An angel of death. And he seeks refuge here, for the night."

"Do you have any weapons on you?"

"I wouldn't be standing here if I hadn't had a weapon. I have a sword as you know, and he too has a sword."

"Is that it?"

"Yes," and she looked to Litus, who also nodded.

"I need to see the blades before I can let you pass."

"A sword is a sword, why do you need to see them? We admitted we have it."

"A sword is a sword, and process takes procedures. You should be thanking me, it is ultimately my say of whether you enter to leave. Do you understand?" She nodded, "now I need to see this weapon before I can let you pass."

He stood on his spear, "come closer," and Litus was reluctant at first, but ultimately, he did so. He drew out the warped sword in his hand, and the guard laughed, "this is the sword of an angel of the dead?" He dropped the sword on the ground, and laughed as he said, "let them in."

The wooden gates opened, and they walked through into the town. There was the smell of metallic residue in the dirt, there were weariness upon all the stone walls. It appeared less so later down the road where the buildings were constructed of brick and stacked two stories tall. "They're new. I remember when they started being built. Folks found the middle of the town to be the safest place, but in my opinion, really it makes them the easiest targets. For them."

He noticed the few people he passed while walking under outcast shadows, were all turned their gazes away in disgust, or fear. Children pointed, some older kids walking from the church's sermons could have assumed he was a Reaper, but not for most. For what they saw was a wraith out in the open, and creeping like the demons roaming the dark, ready to prey.

Them, he thought, *the cultists are here too.* He kept a tight grip on the handle, "why so tense? We're safer inside, he was right, you won't do much with that. It's alright, we're close to Andrew, he's a blacksmith."

They walked to the stand just outside a little shop with a team of men forging out tools and other things alike. Outside pushing into a bed of coals was a broad shouldered man of older age, with a long beard caught with many old ashes, and a head wrapped with an old cloth. Sweat fell from his chest as he brushed off scale from the billet he heated.

"You should stay back, far behind me. Give me your blade, I'll deal with it."

She walked up to the anvil and plopped down a coin of gold, and the sword with the wicked bend. "Where'd ya get this, deary?"

"I'll need that mended, and a new breastplate too."

"What happened to you? Encounter with a wild tree?"

"A bear, and that's my reward, and I want it mended."

"A poor sword and a full new breast plate?" He scratched his beard, "the blade will never be as good as it maybe once was. And there's nothing protecting the blade."

"So?"

"If you use it poorly it'll snap it two, or three."

"Alright, then. Anything else?"

She had returned, "I'll find you, and return your blade anew. Down this road for a while you'll walk until you see a house with rainbow glass. I have something to do here."

She returned, and Andrew held out some basic breastplate. "Now It's been a while since you've been fitted."

He placed the breastplate further away from the flame, and pushed out a stool waving for Jane to sit. "You could get plenty with that gold, do you need a gambeson too?"

"How long will that take?"

"Why the rush? It'll take longer to fit the plating. Now try not to squirm," he prodded a large iron measuring device against her skin, and noted.

"Now where did you actually find that sword? It was recently forged, and do you know how I know that? The rust, and the very very little wear on the blade. If it weren't for that bend, it would be brand new. So I ask, where did you get it?"

"A bear attacked me, and in its side was that sword. It also nearly killed me, if it weren't for your armor."

"Flattery only goes so far."

He used a round top hammer and stretched and squashed the plate over an exhaustible long time. Soon the day churned on, and the blacksmith had switched to hammering out the warp and extensively sharpening until it was as flexible and as dangerous as a wild viper.

The day was nearly over, and Jane was ready to give the sword to Litus, but before she left, blacksmith Andrew said, "don't go meddling in dangers beyond comprehension," and then she left.

He watched his shoulder, and each alley he passed in case there were figures in the dark ready to attack him. And for nearly a mile of that wall with little breaks he walked with eventual dwindling fear. Up ahead, he could see this old two story building, and in the side shining out was a stained glass mural of a beautiful man, blinded and stabbed.

Litus quietly knocked on the door, and waited, and waited even longer. But eventually the door was opened by a malkin of short stature and long gray hair. Just outside Litus was sitting, and before he could get up, the door slammed shut. The little malkin yelled from inside, "wraith? Wraith?" And then it all went quiet.

Litus stood by the door, and decided to knock once more, but the door opened, and Litus jumped away as the malkin pushed through with a shovel, but before he could swing, he stopped. He threw down the shovel, "forgive me lord. For what I've just done."

Litus picked up the shovel, and handed it to him. He still felt shock through his mind as the malkin took back the shovel. And he said, "come in, before a crowd comes."

Inside were furniture clearly built for a Malkin: short and scrolled. "Please, sit in my best chair, for my lord."

So Litus sat in that small chair, and the malkin poured tea in a small glass cup, *I can't drink this,* and he pushed the glass back, trying to relay that message, "I'm sorry, my lord. And I'm sorry for never giving a formal address. I am Tolk, elder of the town of Diende, and priest of the malkin Jesuits. Are you hungry? I don't have much, but I have something I can give."

Litus waved his hands, and Tolk asked, "what is the problem?" And Litus gestured, *I have no mouth.* And it finally related, and Tolk said, "you're a mute, my lord?" And Litus nodded, "senselessness comes with age it seems. I didn't used to be this senseless. Rouvel sent me a letter, so I expected you, but here I've done a senseless thing."

Stop this pity, and he gestured to stop. Tolk did so, and decompressed in a chair. "And so it begins," he said, "tomorrow we'll begin to plan your journey east. I'll make a bed for you in the meanwhile, so excuse my leave," and Tolk left for another room.

On the other side of the room, there was a fireplace, with a low flame, and a rocking chair. The chair still rocked, as the little flame danced. And Litus had those red swirls attract him in a sensual but cruel way. It was like seeing a dead body, he was disgusted, but it still attracted him, and enraged him.

He kept watching the flame, until there came a knock at the door. He initially waited for Tolk to come, but the old man was like he was, so instead, Litus opened the door, and there was Jane. She held out the mended blade, and said, "here, I promised, and I've delivered."

"Who is that?" Asked Tolk, walking by from the other side of the room.

"Well. Hello, elder Tolk. I don't think I've ever spoken with you until now."

"Have I seen your face before?"

"I don't believe so, elder."

"Are you a friend of my lord?"

"Lord? Well, Litus is . . . Well we know each other, but I must go. I need to find someplace to stay the night."

"Well a friend of my lord Litus, is welcome in my home"

"Really?"

"Yes, yes. Come in, I'll make some supper."

They all sat around the small table, they pecked at their small portions, and Tolk said, "this reminds me. Back in a day when the sky wasn't blanketed in a great gray, and seas weren't churning, the mountains weren't sweating, and the kingdoms of the east and west weren't deserts of barren life, doomed to eat the sands of time."

"Of what?" Asked Jane, "you didn't finish what you were about to say."

"Oh yes, sorry, it's about hope. I haven't seen or felt this feeling in a long while."

"If you will mind me asking, but how old are you?"

"Old, far older than your bloodline, I presume. To put it in another way, I've seen stars twinkle, and I was there to witness the great war, over a thousand years ago."

"I didn't know Malkin could live that long."

"Well not quite. I used to be a healer, but now my prowess has about dried up. It was an injury I received on the other side of the world. And what did I earn for survival, a thousand years of life to watch crumble. But don't pity me, please."

"Now you call Litus, your lord. I don't understand, do you know who he is?"

"He's my prophet, and a prophet for all malkin of faith," and he grew solemn, "the Malkin Jesuits are a collective of fellow malkin who formed a religion after the passing of our god. Of my people, we Malkin were always the children of Selziar. Our last message from our lord, before the betrayal, was a prophecy. A man of darkness and the body of death, would rise and bring justice on the tip of his sword. And he would vanquish chaos from the realm in his return. I was there in Tisden where it all began. We don't know why . . . Keroth, ever did it. He killed his own brother, and soon after started the great war. There were more injuries than could be healed. More bodies than could be buried. And the Malkin were subject to death more than anyone else.

"But I left the sept to preach to the lower people, but they never listened, or cared. For decades I've remained quiet in this town. They don't bother me much, and I not them."

"I don't know the history of you all, but how are you so sure Litus is who you think he is?"

"I suppose I don't, but that's for us to realize and figure out."

"How do you not know?"

"Well I see him in front of me, and I've received notice from another malkin who thought the same. Now that I mention it, I do ask, did something happen to Rouvel on the way here? He said in his letter that he was coming too."

Both Tolk and Jane looked at Litus, and he glanced at both of them one after the other. *He's dead.* He looked blankly, not knowing how to gesture. "Oh," Tolk sighed, "that's unfortunate."

On the next morning Jane was asked to grab a loaf of fresh bread to break while Litus and Tolk discussed their preparations. Down the street she knew of a bakery which she wasn't completely unfamiliar with.

The inside smelt of dust and partially dust. Jane walked up to the counter, and rang a bell above her. Soon a tall and wide man walked through a door at the side, "hey your what yer face, that girl who was with Andy the other night."

"How much for two loaves?"

"Now, he's my dear friend. He was worried about you, and you know what, I'va heard you brought a wraith into town?"

"I haven't, and your only business is selling me bread."

"Sheesh, alright, you must be a stranger to these times then, with the weirdos roaming the woods outside."

"Just tell me how much- what!? What do you mean!?"

"Ah now you've cracked, those strange religious folk outside are here."

"Well when I came back, I didn't see anything like that, so?"

"So, you're blind. Now I've seen them, and in a dream they walked, but didn't talk."

"I'm going to leave if you keep sputtering this nonsense."

"Just a few coppers, and leave after, but don't return."

A knock at the door came, and they opened it for Jane. She had a few loaves of bread which she put on the table, and Tolk used a knife to cut a morning breakfast, and smeared a fruit jelly over its surface. "Thank you, now please sit. I have something I want to ask you, something partially greater than just going to the bakery. It's not something that'll be easy to grasp, but it's incredibly important."

"Go on."

"My lord, and myself need to find out if he is, who is prophesied to be. The problem is that I'm old. I'm frail, and weak. I may not survive this trip, but I need to try. And part of that problem is that this is a matter of grave importance, and so I ask, will you go with us around the forest to the city of Atreau?"

"No, I won't. Litus has been surprisingly good company for our small travels, and I thank you for allowing me to stay for the night, but I'm not going to kill myself trying to escort you two where ever Atreau is."

"But our lives, all of our lives could be saved."

"Sure, but I'm not going. I have a life to live now."

"Here? Where grown men are afraid of leaving the walls from the animals, beasts, and men in the forest?"

"I can deal with it, and I've dealt with it for all my life. That's certainty, but you're not certain, so I'm not joining you on this suicide mission."

"Are you still looking for a place to stay?"

"What?"

"Do you need somewhere to stay?"

"Well yes, but if you're asking if I'll go with you for another night here, I won't."

"No, I'm letting you stay the night again, if you'll think about it, and then after, I'll give you my home."

" . . . Why!?"

"The world is cruel, but you have still done something great; something absolutely great for the rest of the world."

"This won't change my mind, but are you sure?"

"Fairly certain."

Chapter Seven:

It was cold, and he walked the long desert path in the middle of twilight. To each side of the sandy path were troughs of grass, cold and black. The edges were walls of trees, which stood more like stone barricades keeping in something old. He walked forward, and in the great darkness there stood in two rows on either side bodies strewed along motionless. Bodies ranging in size and wounds. The further he walked the more the wounds became more of the image of a person than one.

They were now figures of ash at the ends. Their posture, their pose, was as though they were running from something, and something dangerous. The traveler kept walking, the sands below him were wisping away, and just out of sight there was a figure. They seemed so sure as to remain out of sight. But he kept walking forward, and soon began running to the figure, but the figure always remained just out of his sight. The buried was this deep fog, and the figure in one drift fell into a plume of smoke and fog, and completely gone.

He stood there unmoving, completely stationary. There was a light wind blowing the sand below his feet away. The silence was loud, so loud the only audible noise was the sand shifting under him.

For a second there was nothing, no sound, no feeling, just nothing. And then from quite far away a vortex emerged. It sucked in all of the fog, and far ahead in clear view was a red robed figure with the head of a blood stained deer skull. Emerging from the figure was a blaze, and the great big blaze was sprinting after him. A seeker to a chaser. And he wanted to run but couldn't, and as the fireball was reaching him he was motionless. Then it was everything.

He got up in the blaze, Jane was awoken at the same. Smoke filled the air with an orange glow. They looked at each other, and heard a crash from upstairs, and everywhere seemed to crash. Jane ran outside, yelling, "Litus! Where are you going, you have to save yourself!" But Litus only thought one thing, *old man Tolk.*

There in the middle of the room was the bed of Tolk. Above him there was the flaming beam, it crashed down onto him and snapped the bed in two. All they could hear was the huffing of the old malkin. Litus drew close to gaze down at him once more. Tolk's eyes had opened, and blood was rushing through his pupils, and he looked to him with one last breath, he said to him, "atreau," he coughed up blood, "you must seek Atreau and Tisden, and rid the children of fire."

The stained glass on the wall next to the stairs had started to collapse and shatter from the heat. A shard of glass had fallen out and shattered on the ground. The smoke was thick and caked on every surface like water to a stone.

Litus tried to lift up that beam, with all of his strength, but no matter how hard he tried, it was too heavy. And he tried and tried until the flames were nearly shy of taking all possible escapes. And he burst through the front door, empty handed, as the house still burned.

It wasn't just the house that burned, it was the town, and half of the buildings they saw were engulfed in flame about to fall apart.

Droves of the guards, a third fully armored, and the rest in partial armor were fighting the flame, and the fire bearers. It was these men in red cloaks and hoods, with a mask over their face of a horned animal.

There was a woman and daughter, in each other's hands, and they lay on the ground dead. Pillars of fire burned up chimneys, and anything wood was scorched.

Jane grabbed Litus' arm, "stop standing around. Hide! Get out of here! We have to go!"

He reached for the blade, and Jane yelled, "you must leave, they'll kill you if you're seen. Go!"

All around them were either fire, guards, or those cultists. No matter where Litus went, there wasn't anywhere to go. It all ended the same. Except for the door on the other side of town, which was relatively close to Tolk's house.

The unfortunate souls screamed out from either side of the blackened soil road. Man fought man, until there were no sounds left but the collapsing of roofs into houses. And any basements now fully held the brick and stone which once stood. The east watchtower held two men, a guard and a cultist, and both were dead.

The gate nearby was secured by a large wooden beam, and Litus had tried to lift the beam up himself, but couldn't. Not until another came to his side trying to lift the beam. "Come on, heave, we have to try," Jane said.

And they pushed little by little, and then the beam fell. "They're dead," she said exhaustedly, "they're all dead. The town is gone. And those fuckers took it from me."

They saw the dark walls with a fire emerge behind it. And they sat cast in the dark waiting for it to end. After a half hour of tumbling fear, they heard a small rustling in the woods to their side, and soon it fell away.

It's them, they're going away. No, I can't let them. He got up and followed the noise, "where are you going?" Jane whispered, but he kept creeping on.

He followed the noise until there was none. "Where are you going," she said again when he stopped.

He walked into the woods, just a few feet to become completely disguised, and waited. "You're trying to find them? Why do you wish more death to occur?" And he shook his head, "then why are you doing this? Do you think you can take them alone?" And he nodded, *I have to try.*

Eventually there was a small rustling in the wood, and Litus wouldn't wait for this. He held the sword close, and ran to the sound, and he thrusted the sword into the body of a demon. He struck the cultist again, just to make sure, and there in the darkness between some trees, and below a shrubbery was a trapdoor in the ground. He lifted the door, which made no sound, and before he descended he offered a hand. Jane took in a breath, and after some silence, she took his hand, and they descended below.

At the bottom there was a wall veiled in darkness. They felt around and found the walls and soon they found a door with a handle. It didn't look anything like a cave, or a bunker, in actuality it seemed it was more of a cathedral. The walls were made of stone and bright red porcelain. There were torches on the walls lending their light down.

Litus held his sword forward, and Jane kept her hand on her sword handle. They felt strange walking down the hall, with air that smelt like an ancient church. Every step they walked lightly echoed. The end of the hall ended in a crossroads, and the flanking hallways were dim and their ends couldn't be met from where they stood. So first they listened. They heard almost a rhythmic tapping, or stepping, and behind them was an ambiance of churning sounds. They took timid steps forward, and any discrepancy in the air caused them to stop for just a moment.

Jane whispered, "I don't hear anything different, they're the same. I don't know which way to take. I'll flip a coin. Crowns, we'll take the right, and the other, the left," and she flipped the coin, and crowns it was, to Litus' disgust.

The hall held a room to the right, and the end continued on somewhere else to the left. As they drew close to that door on the right, a waft of chemicals came over them. "That's awful," she whispered, "what is that?"

On the inside were crates stacked on crates, and only some cultists were still in their robes with a thin wooden stick in their hands. There were also crates in the middle of this room, and one of them swung a hammer high, and drove a long nail into the crate. That cultist held the hammer to his side and pulled out a ring of keys. A second later he left.

Litus felt a strange tingle come towards him, drawing him forward. He held his sword firm, as he crept inside. Sitting alone in the middle of the room, was one of them holding a lantern in their hand, and with their other hand he prayed.

"Stop that," she whispered.

Litus snuck up from behind the cultist, and he rose, and pushed the blade from the cultist's neck, and down through the body, and immediately the body went limp. He dragged the dead man to the side against the wall, "see that room, I think he went in there, but we should leave before anything happens. What you just did may have killed us already. We don't know if that door leads to a droves of those bastards."

There wasn't a light emitted from the doorway, so Litus again crept forward, and leaned around to see through the door, *where'd he go?* So he walked while clinging to the side of the wall, where light was as little as peace.

At the end of the room, there were shelves with a lit lantern sitting on a shelf, and a large locked chest on the ground, but no man. *Where did he go? He has to be here somewhere.* He turned, and the cultist stood with a carved stick pointed at him, and he waved for Litus to drop the sword. Litus didn't do so, but instead he took one wide swing, and Jane struck her blade through the cultists back.

Litus checked the corpse for that ringlet of keys, and opened the chest. There was only one thing which was inside: a large key. It was made of old iron, and clearly wasn't a key for any common purposes, but he felt it was important and kept it anyway, "let's go, there could be more," she said.

So Litus had held the key in the void, and they left the strange room, or at least they tried. Jane pushed Litus back. She said with a heavy breath, "there's two of them. The body!"

Quickly Litus ran past, with the sword piercing true, and the first fell, and a fire erupted. The fire came from the end of his hand, and rolled down against the floor. It swept across causing this garish red light to emit all within those walls. The cultist waved his hand again, and there it was a wand. Litus had jumped out of the way of the incoming flame, and rounded around one of the crates in the middle of the room. A heap of flame had dressed the ground around the crate, and Litus tried to leap around, but it was over sooner than expected when Jane pierced her sword through his neck, and the cultist fell creating a pool around their now stained mask.

Jane stepped away from the dying flame, as she checked the body, "a wand. They killed everyone with a flick of their wrists."

Litus held his hand out, asking for that wand, "alright," Jane said, *and I'll give it back to them.*

They left before more came, and down they went through the hallway of less. There were doors, all locked, and all leading to where they didn't want to go. They didn't know what they wanted, but continuing ahead was better than not.

Ahead was a large hall where those cultists ate at short tables on their knees, and lit little gold chandeliers that hung from above. The dozens that made them up were impossible to attack, but not to sneak around, because they now saw themselves in the heart of this beast, and they wanted to rid it for what was done. So they needed to go, and decapitate the head.

"Wait Litus," she whispered, "we'll go back for their disguises, and we should hopefully be able to pass without much trouble. Then maybe we'll get them from behind and our blades will really match their cloaks."

They quickly scrambled back and salvaged what robes and masks they could use. But when they returned ready to sneak upon the cultists eating, almost every single one of them were gone. "What happened? They were," Jane said, "they were just here? Do they know? They have to know, they sent- No, they would have sent more?"

But they continued walking from room to room, noticing the very lack of cultists. They eventually passed into a strange hall with a dressing room to the side, and a great big gate at the other. They both grabbed new garbs just in case, and while changing, Jane remarked, "all of this is under the ground? How long have they been here?"

There was a chanting, and soon they found the great worship chamber. At the back there was this statue of blood marble of an angelic figure which resonated power within the crowd. There was a platform from which a few decorated figures used long warped knives to draw the fury and pain, and the massive beast was chained and bound to the ground. With each laceration the Bishop made, the beast roared and a little bit more of light from its eyes faded more and more. Then one of the men on the side put his palms on the wound, the blood on his fingers bubbled, and then the wound was healed, but the scar remained. The Bishop raised the wand high, and a spray of flame danced up to the ceiling. There was a stalagmite made from that setting soot. And the scales were one a deep red, but now they looked more like bone, especially compared to large red curtains which hung from either side of the stage which drew all attention directly to the holy surgery.

"By the great gods, what the fuck," she tried to keep her voice down, "that? That's a dragon. They-" She swallowed her words, "why does it not breathe fire on them? What have they done!?"

The chains had words scribed in a language they didn't know, but Litus felt what they meant. The enchanted chains could bind the greatest of beasts, and keep their strength to little more than a pigeon.

The key, it must go to those chains? "Litus, let's go, we have to keep going," but showed her, *This could bring it all down.*

"I don't understand what you mean, we can't just walk up and rain fire upon them. Look, there's at least a hundred of them."

And Litus looked at all of them, entranced by their lord of pain. Those needles returned, and they pulled him forward. Jane grabbed his shoulder, "what are you doing," but she couldn't keep hold.

He went from the right where the welding priest was, and waved for assistance behind the curtain, but he held the knife and struck the neck quickly, and down the priest went under no light. He stole that mask, and drew out the key. The Bishop chanted tones, and pushed the blade into the beast, marking it as he coated its power onto a catalyst. Litus walked over with the key and knife concealed. Litus bent down to the chains, looking for that lock, while the Bishop placed the wand in a crate off to the side. The people were deeply confused, and gasped in shock. The Bishop turned around, "what are you doing?" He asked, "does the chain rattle?" But when the lock fell from the chain, the Bishop yelled. "Get away! Get away!"

There was a rumble in the ground, as the dragon stretched its wings out and roared. The Bishop lunged onto Litus with his waving bloody knife piercing him in the back. Litus had shifted himself and backed away, but the mask was stripped from his face, and the Bishop looked into the dark, "you. The heretic shows thyself, and dances with a flame which burns."

The Bishop held his knife firm, and he lunged toward the shadows. Litus stepped to the side, and quickly slashed at the priest's arms. He was quickly grabbed from the back by other cultists. They held him still as the Bishop came closer. And he waved his dagger as the light of fire burned behind him casting him in shadow. But then the fire overtook him, and one of the arms which grabbed Litus was released as Jane pushed her sword through the cultist's shoulder. She then grabbed the other, and kicked his knees until he fell to the ground. She plunged the sword between his neck, and she looked at Litus, but spoke not. For any words pierced less than those deep red eyes.

He held the sword in one hand, and they both tried to leave, while flame was poured on the crowd and ash fell from the sky. They ran through a door on their left, as a massive boom sounded from behind them, as the stalagmite fell and revealed a spire and night sky above.

They ran through corridors of the cathedral, while stray cultists tried to figure out what was happening. But both of them were just trying to find a way out. Fire rained down through the now crumbling roof. The sound of wind being thrashed from high above. They tried to find some way out. "There they are," a yell came from behind.

Litus looked around, and he saw a lone door with blue stained windows. *Through there,* as he grabbed Jane's hand and bolted through. On the other side was a hallway with a railing on one side, and chairs scattered around. Litus put a chair under the door handle to stop them for now, as Jane looked on. "It's a church, a real church," she said looking down from the balcony as the door was banged upon, "down there, there's a doorway out, and over there, I see some stairs, but first Litus, burn some chairs or something. Burn the floor in front of the door. Give us more time before they bust through."

Just as Litus had pulled out the wand, the door smashed open, and he threw a massive stream of fire towards them until the doorway was filled with corpses, and a blockade of flame. They rushed down the stairs, and the aisles and nave were empty. The door opened, and outside was nothing but trees, and the new found smoke in the sky.

Chapter Eight:

Within the ground and between the trees, was a once inhabited city of old. And behind them they could see the spire of a great cathedral in the bosom of the trees. They looked out for the dragon's breath like watching for aggressive animals in the woods. And they also checked their backs of those robed men of fire and blood, and their insatiable grasp over others.

The ruins were another threat altogether. With any number of cultists who take up their halls, or animals who nest and protect their kin. They were the ones alone in the land of their unknowing. And it was worse from their speed of traversing the lands, and they were never able to understand the unintelligible. The further they went, the old decaying streets turned erratically, and the buildings were occasionally charred. The old ruins, now the testing ground, and the cursed forest masked it all.

They followed the roads out, eventually most of the cathedral was obscured by the passing trees, and they decided to stop for a breath. They had made sure a building made of stacked mortar and stone were still and the halls were empty of any dog or bird. They closed the door in an attempt to mask themselves against everything around them.

"We have to get out of here," she looked outside through a hole in the wall, "the smoke is where the church is, then we have to go, um . . . that way," she said pointing in a direction opposite of the smoke.

She took in a deep breath, then said, "we should go, before they get closer."

The dust was dragged by their feet, as they left through that door. The trees were thicker the longer they walked, but every time they thought they exited the city – and came closer to leaving

Mulder's grasp – it seemed to always turn back on itself. And every time they thought they were gone, and saw a new house once more.

It had been hours since they left, Litus could see the smoke continue to rise, "it's still there. We should have never gone down that door. If we don't die to those cultists, we'll die to some fucking bear out here, another one. No matter how uncertain this is, I'm certain we'll die out here. We'll never leave this maze. We've become entrapped by the laughing winds that rustle the leaves high above us. I used to have friends, and live in a world of some uncertainty I've been born into, that I was accommodated with, but no. Now we're stuck in a city of the swirling thoughts and spire of ash, and it was all outside my mind, and my knowledge of my world."

If you stop, or fail. You will die for nothing, you will die not for yourself or friends. To beings who are something greater, and a number for no one. If you stop, you fall into cowardice. You become a monument of dust, and nothing else. But if only he could speak.

"You look at me, with those eyes, and I see nothing except a piteous gaze upon me. I don't want that; I am not a burden. I will not be your burden, do you still think I owe you a debt still?"

And Jane looked at him, and he thought for a moment, and then shook his head, "well you don't know? Well I don't know either, so we'll find out soon enough, I suppose."

The night was coming, and it came in waves that obscured everything in an increasing blue haze, but eventually it all added into a deep dark black shadow. They found a house filled with nothing but dust. Litus had that fire wand, but there was no dry wood to keep the ground warm. So they sat on the cold ground, which they couldn't see, with nothing to eat, and constantly checking their backs hoping for nothing outside the ignorant walls.

Litus sat there, while Jane slept. He held himself close, in an attempt to ward off the cold which pierced the weaves. Next to the door there was one window, it wasn't a large window, only a foot and a half tall, and one foot wide, but in the ambiance of moonlight he could see the borders and some faint branches subtly wave and twist in the air as time wind away. He found himself staring deep through that window. At any moment there could have been someone or something there. And if it were the case, they would have been stalking them for hours without them noticing. It would only be a matter of minutes till they strike. And Litus waited, but it never came. So he just sat there in the dark and cold, thinking something was there, to break it all.

He held the wand firm. What it has caused, and now he has that too. There were pins that pierced his skin far greater than the cold winds. The dust, like ash, was everywhere. He felt the need to brush the dust off his cloak, it was disgusting. But no matter how hard he tried, the dust was always there.

There was a field of flowers that filled her palms. She sat serenely with the faint light casting warmth upon each petal until there was a beautiful warmth that brought certainty, complete hopeful certainty.

"Oh how these flowers remind me of you all. Each in difference, still a beating heart. A lovely heart, I see. I see it all."

She sat in that field for perhaps ten years or so. And then the flowers lost their warmth. They were once pale, and now they began to dim from the ends inward. She held the flower softly, she didn't break a single stem. "Is it the seasons? Winter isn't even soon, there's plenty of time to live and breathe in the air, but why? Why do you change so suddenly?"

She stood and the flowers buckled and began to fall and stink over thirteen short years. From far in the distance on that same hill, the flowers turned again from a brown sludge to an incredible collection of orange, yellow and red. In a flash all of the flowers, except the one around her, were vibrant and reflected her eyes. She reached out to touch and smell them, but they snuffed her. So she tried to understand those petals, and leaped into the dirt getting her hair and dress dirty. And she was able to grasp it, but only for a moment. She recoiled as her hand was pink and forcefully calloused. The heat was not pleasant, it burned with great pressure and lust. A gust of wind brought forward a wave of fluttering petals.

Each petal left red marks against her skin. Eventually all the flowers were cut from their stems, and on that hill there was nothing left to grasp and hold. Her hand which once held a flower, now was skeletal and charred.

On the other side of the hill, once obscured was a sitting figure. She stumbled over her own feet – and the crater holes left by the disaster – slowly walking to the man. His figure could only be interpreted as divine. It was like a shadow was cast in her mind, like to remember something, or to think of something which wasn't there. A cloud of infinite reason.

He spoke, but nothing was heard, and she asked, "what are you?"

"I am infinity, and certain uncertainty. Or that is what you think. I give you a form, gaze upon it," and the figure became a man of beauty, and his eyes locked her, "you survived this uncertainty, and that is a gift, so take it with grace," he spoke with reverberation.

Seconds passed, and he said, "the time will come one day, can't you see it. I can see it pass within fractions and fractions of that same period. And determine what to do. Can you?"

"You're cruel!"

"To you? No. You are the blessed saint, me dear. Can't you smell the flowers?"

The morning came, and eventually it went as they walked their longing path between trees and brush. Between the few gaps in the trees, they could see the ash still linger and they knew it still burned.

"I don't care if we cut our feet on sharp rocks, we're not stopping. We have to keep going until this forest is past us."

Litus looked to Jane, "I had a bad dream last night, alright? It's hard to remember details, but it's just, I don't want to stop, or be forced to stop for anything in my way, and especially in this damn forest."

The day still hung, and between those points they were quiet. "If you were this prophet you think you are, we'd never be here to begin with."

He shook his head, *I don't know if I'm some prophet.* "Well no one knows, but here we are anyways," she let out a deep breath, "if you were this prophet – I don't know, maybe you really are – what would you do?"

He looked to the ground wondering if the answer was written there, but ultimately shrugged, "how could any of this be fixed? You're wondering, hmm. Well I'll tell you, firstly we have to get the fuck out of here."

Eventually as the day passed, they came to realize that the last sight of any structure was long past them, they didn't want to speak, because maybe the forest would rebound, and put them back in the path of the city, but to them, they were out of those first bounds. After coming to that realization, they then noticed that the ground itself had become more erratic. Roots from old trees sewn in and out of the dense ground, and wild herbs dressed the skirts disguising the bottom half of trunks like a hidden barricade. They could hear the squawks of birds and chirps of small critters all around as they near-aimlessly roamed the gray. All that sound enveloped the ambiance, and they were accommodated to it, but always questioned it in case there were other sounds that should be.

But soon the day slowly turned, and their legs were tired. And the ground kept pushing against them. The farthest they could see in the distance was still full of trees and dirt. Once they stopped they found flies buzzing, and nothing could stop it except for one. And they gathered sticks and branches, it didn't matter now if they were dried or not, because the cold winds and those mosquitoes prodding them.

They bundled a whole stack of what they could quickly forage, and Litus drew out a flame. There they sat on the ground, hoping the rising smoke didn't show above the tree line. But somehow, at least for Jane she felt some comfort from the flame, even after it all.

She twisted some twigs with her fingers, and after the thin skin cracked she fueled the fire some little bit more. And started again, "so so so," she said, "if we get spotted by some cultist at least we'll have fire to keep warm till then. Wherever we end up, hopefully close to some society, let's hope there's no one there to destroy it all again."

It beckoned again the dark sky, and soon all the light showed upon their faces, and little past that. Litus fell, and Jane stood guard through those sounds of dying flames, wind, and sounds of animals of no particular nature. And eventually all of the light was subdued to only some coals which still lived. And in those wee hours of pure darkness, it became day.

She almost couldn't get up. She hadn't eaten in days, and it was hard to protest it, but she was able to say something, "Litus, do you have anything to eat?" And he shook his head, "then, please, could you hunt for me?" And he nodded and shortly left.

He tracked the forest, especially carefully to make little to no sound. And he followed the sounds of animals, particularly the ones whose steps trickled in the grass. And eventually he saw it, it was just a simple squirrel. The sword was extended to his side, and he crept from behind.

There were pins and needles against his side, but he was too afraid to move except forward. There was one exact point which felt like ice. The singularity stretched far from one eye to another. The animal looked to that point as well, and then it struck. Litus picked up the body, and ran. He couldn't see whatever it was, but now he didn't want to. Wherever it was, he intended to escape it.

With the blade out, he ran seemingly in circles for an exhaustively and hauntingly long time, until the feeling faded, but he still thought strangely about whatever it was and whatever it could possibly be.

Jane had told him basic steps to prepare the meat before placing it on a new fire, and after nearly half an hour, it was over. They snuffed the fire with dirt and other debris, and slowly began to wander their own path.

For hours they'd walked, and the strangest thing became apparent was that there wasn't anything out of the ordinary. No sounds, or winds. No feeling of pins, or old structures in the distance. And nothing left behind. So it was just some empty forest. And they walked hoping this feeling lasted, but when it became standard over so long, nothing felt right somehow. And then some glimmer of hope rose, when they tried looking for the smoke, but saw nothing. Now they knew they were lodged deep in the forest, and they knew not how far they were, but they were joyous.

They followed the faint glimmers of light from the sun for direction. But with nightfall in its faint hours approaching once again Jane had spun in circles trying to find the direction of the sun through the gap of the forest. "East," she said, "if we continue to travel east, we should be able to break from this line tonight.

"You know what I hope I see? A town, and someplace nice to sleep with hot meals, and a bath. Maybe a map too. But at least I know a little thing about this cursed place. That throughout the entire forest the distance from east to west is always the shortest route. At least it's like that up north, only been there once in my life, and I wouldn't remember it. It was when I was really young. And up north they some guild that guides people across this wall, but I think we're doing just fine," Litus looked to her with slight contempt, and she said, "if only that guild were down here, and we were just able to bump into them – I think they call them ranger, because they range. Whatever, we don't need them."

For the next few hours, as the sun shaded the end, they decided to run. The forest was loud with bugs, and the sound of leaves and branches crackling under their feet. Thick forest fog had emerged and suffocated their eyes and other senses. But Litus felt again a needle in his chest, and it burned like a red hot iron, and it called him, it pulled him. He grabbed Jane's hand and followed the feeling.

There was darkness in their mind, there was a cloud of thought so clear, but unintelligible to their rational thoughts. They clawed through only seeing glimpses with every passing stroke. Their bodies were walking through the darkness, their thoughts were mere suggestions. A puppet controlled their movements, their blinking, their breathing. Their sweating, and perception of light. The emptiness was both within and without. Like a pig in a cage, like a bird in water, like men in a casket. But Litus knew, even then, their bodies followed that now familiar sting.

They walked the infinity. Hunger was nothing anymore. Cloth was planted, and woven into a hollow doll with more dolls stuffed inside in perpetuity, but that outer doll was the newest, and closest to the flame it was nailed to.

Trees lined both sides, and the wind passed by like rays of light. It was stars around and they spun around and around until all direction was meaningless, and soon all the light faded into nothingness.

Both Litus and Jane awoke simultaneously, the sky was illuminated with light. They exhaled the nauseous poison gas, and breathed in the air on the border. They could see through the bars, and on the other side in the distance were houses tall and people were working and living. "Where are we?" She spoke, gripping the side of her aching head.

Litus shifted her gaze outward, she took an intense look, and asked, "is that . . . Maud?"

Chapter Nine:

"I think you should stay out here, at least for now. I'll return, and don't get caught by anyone," Litus nodded, and Jane said, "I'll be back."

She began to walk toward the town, and most people took almost no notice of her. It seemed like that for quite a while. She tried not to look at anyone, as much as she tried not to draw attention, but nothing could be helped. An old woman walked up to her, Jane was unsure what she wanted, and the old woman asked worriedly, "look at you, you're a skeleton, you need help, come with me young woman."

"No, no. I'm not going to go with you."

"Are you really sure, young lady?"

"Yes I am, but can I ask you something?"
The old woman grasped Jane's hands while nodding, "yes."

"In this town, is there an inn?"

"Yes," she said as though she didn't expect that answer, "you wouldn't want to go there, just full of yelling sailors, and brutes who don't listen to anyone."

"That doesn't matter, where is it?" Jane said, wiping sweat and dirt from her face.

"It's in the center of town, my lady?"

"What?"

"It's in the center of town, this road here. Go down it for ten or so minutes, there's a tall old building, and well . . . it says inn. And that's where the inn is."

She walked down that seemingly simple path, but it was true. There was this tall and old wooden structure, and of course the sign which said inn.

She rang the bell waiting for someone, but after a minute, there was no-one. She kept ringing it, more and more until some man twice her height casually walked up to her, and he said, "did you ring the bell? Welcome, my lady, how can I accommodate you?"

"I just want one room, and one farthest away from anyone else."

"Can you speak up my dear?"

Jane yelled, "one room, far away!"

"Ah, I have a perfect room, but it'll cost ya."

Jane tossed a gold coin on the table, and ordered, "no visitors!"

She waited till it was nearly night, and waited inside the room, until then, but once she thought it was time; she left. She bought and brought a lantern, some candles, and a tinder box too. She wore a hood over her hair, and walked in the shadows of the buildings.

There were people outside by small cooking fires, while they smoked their pipes and spoke old tales. And soon accompanied them were sailors from the north, and they were telling their long embellished tales of fighting squid and other sea monsters.

There was a small tower with men lighting their lanterns and whipping off dust and grease from refraction lenses. And others were scratching rust off of their spears and arrowheads. But for that time being, they were perfectly distracted, and Jane swiftly snuck past their gaze.

Litus sat where they were initially separated, and she said, "Litus, we have to be careful, they have watchmen at night. They didn't have any in the morning, but we should go now, while they twiddle their thumbs."

They began walking away from the wood, but once they were returning, there was a different mood in the town. It seems like most of the people who were out, no longer were. And then a man yelled from above, "hey you!" As a beam of light shown down on them.

Litus dashed away, and did so without attracting attention from those guards. "You! Hey you!"

Jane covered her face from the bright light as she said, "I was just walking back."

"Why were you wandering out of the wood at this time of day? Don't you know anything girl?"

"I . . . I." She stuttered, "I was just taking a stroll. That's it!"

"Well then get along," and under his breath he murmured, "stupid sailor's broad."

She ran off, Litus had suddenly appeared to her, and they both walked in the shadow as she brought him to their room.

They sat apart in bed and chair, with a lantern on a small table flickering on a map. She sat for a long time thinking while Litus looked for Atreau. "If we," she cleared her voice, "the capital: Porcelania, if we go there, we'll have better options to travel."

He pointed to himself and then to her, "well, where else can I go, my home is gone, my friends are dead. I have to do something, or else I'll fall into darkness."

He looked at her strangely, "what?" She said, " . . . forget it. This is a sailing town, so without a shadow of a doubt, there's ships, and people sailing to the capitol. So tomorrow, I'll go find someone, and we'll sail north."

They put out the lantern light, and the night rolled over. Jane left early that morning, she only brought with her Litus' knife which she concealed, and a bag of coins, she held on her waist.

The older ones were out at this time, ready to start their day's work. She had walked up to a pair of men with axes on their shoulders, and asked where the shipyard was. They happily told her, and then went about their day.

She walked the whole length of Maud east of Mulder, and found that down a sheer cliff side was an open shipyard. Sailors of considerable height and faces of stone worked under the shade of a building built at the top of the cliff, and slightly overhung on stilts. The shadow also hid their peering hollowed eyes from her.

There was a small vessel at one end of the docks. It held some crates, and barrels full of anything that might sell, but only the one manning the vessel was of importance to Jane. She had waited and tried yelling at the cabin for someone to come through the door. "Get away from my ship," said a pot bellied pig of a man, walking from behind, "flutter away bird, and make business like all other animals."

"No, no, I'm here to do business."

"Little girl, little bird, fly off I say, I'll do no business with you, so get away from my ship."

"Well I have money, and I'm not some child. I just need to go to the capitol."

He snorted with raunch, "you need to go to the capitol," he repeated, "so, are you some lord's daughter? That would be a good excuse, my dear," and he laughed.

"What's so funny?"

"Well that's a shame, the ability to laugh is always a nice one," and the sounds of his stomach creaked, and he breathed, "now dear, I seem to be in a dry spot these days. It's been a bad year for sailing, you see. But I'm a kind guy, you understand," and his heavy breath hung.

"All I want-"

"Don't waste your breath, young," he turned to the ship, slapping the side, "it's a poor vessel. The waves rock it so harshly, like it's being thrown off a cliff. Every bump," and he slapped the side again, "very awful. So, that's why I couldn't let you – dear – sail this vessel."

"Then what about them?" She pointed to the sailors under shade.

"No," is all he said.

"But I need to go to-"

"Yes, yes, my deary dear, dear, dear. See I get it, times are really really hard. But no, not them. I wouldn't let them touch you, and your, well, figure."

"Well if you won't help me, I'll go somewhere else. This is a fishing town, other people have boats."

"Do they," he said with a grin from cheek to cheek.

"What do you mean?"

He laughed in short high pitched spikes, "this is my field. Dear, look at all of these docks. They're all mine. I built them with my own two hands. Without me, there is no entering and leaving."

"That's not true!"

"Look around, this is all a cliff face. The docks only exist because of me," and his smile grew thin.

"I think . . . I'll be going."

"Come back anytime, dear," he said with a smile.

Jane swiftly went up those stairs planted in the cliffside, and that man watched the entire way. She walked up to some men sitting outside drinking their day away, and asked them, "who runs the ship yard?" They all replied either by saying, "some fat guy," or, "Batwit."

They don't know what they're talking about, he's not some lord, he doesn't own the dock. No one could own the entire dock. But still it worried her.

She walked around asking locals, and sailors alike, and all the same answers she heard were continually given.

She found herself wandering back to those docks, and she looked down trying to find where Batwit were, she heard a sound from inside the structure on those stilts. And soon a stream of a near dozen sailors left through the door, and they scattered around, some getting lost into the town, and others went back to the docks. Jane then went inside, and it was a mass of papers, tools, and other things she didn't know the purpose of. And the man sat behind a desk, gripping a feather pen while rubbing his stomach. "The pretty hawk flew back," he said, coming to a smile.

"Sir Batwit, if that's your name, I need a ship to board towards Porcelania, when one is available. Please, I have money I can give. Um, I just, I. Please."

"Stuttering isn't so grand, you see. But I, for one, find it to be a guilty pleasure," and he laughed a stuttering mock, "have your humors fallen dead with the rest of your mind girl? Laugh, laugh, wasn't it funny."

"No, it wasn't."

"And you want to sail? What a bore. Did you just come back, little bird, just to prove your stupidity?" He pulled out a pipe, and struck a light from a candle nearby, "why are you still here?" And Jane stormed out.

Chapter Ten:

Her eyes burned like fire. Not a twinkling flame that flickers with barely any pressure. Her eyes flared with hatred and loathing.

That morning her eyes were piercing, she would have yelled, if it weren't for the other occupants in the inn. So she said quietly, without raising her voice, "I'll be back in a few hours, every man has his price. Especially gluttonous ones."

She left the room, with a sword on her hip – just in case – and Litus watched wearily. He didn't know exactly why, but a minute after she left, he followed. The hall was full that morning. Sailors sat at small tables many to each as they waited for large greasy meals to start that day. Litus hung around the outside skirt of the hall. No one noticed as they were looking for anything like him. They just looked for their food, or for the women bringing their food.

Outside in the distance, he could see Jane march feverishly forward, and Litus thought, *Does she plan to kill him? What did he do to her?* He kept her in sight, as he followed. With the hood over his head, he refused to look at anyone, and hoped anyone looked not to him.

Litus found that the end of the town was a cliff side. With stairs and docks and other buildings built on stilts out of the side of the rock. Litus saw her enter this building on stilts, but he stayed out. Then there was laughing. A large haughty laugh came from inside as Jane entered. He couldn't hear exactly what was being said inside, but he could feel what was being meant.

The sound of salt beating a drum with crashing waves obscured many of what was being said inside. He wanted to peek in, or just to walk in, but he knew it wouldn't go so smoothly. He didn't know why Jane was seeing this man, or who the man really was.

When she returned to the room last night, she barked in an awful grieved tone, but spoke nothing about it.

He looked down below to see sailors just simply do whatever jobs sailors did other than sail, and they all brooded and feared over the waters. Maybe they feared that man inside? *The building resides over them, they work under his shadow. This man is the lord of this land, certainly. It couldn't be anything other than that. And his control isn't within a tower, or palace, but a simple building, not at the heart, but the cold mind of the town. Does she intend to kill the lord and survive after?*

He walked around the premises. There was a door in the back, and it was locked once, but no longer. And now Litus walked through, crouched below mounds of papers and wooden drawers which were out of their cabinets. Even a thin staircase was covered in dust and salt. There was a wall with a door covered in scratched, and Litus eased by hiding under mountains of rubbish.

She was visible through a beam of light, and then Litus saw that man lounging in his chair laughing at each of Jane's pleas. "Why can't you?" She said, tossing a bag on the counter.

"Again, it's a matter of principle. If I let you do what you wanted without problem, then everyone would do the same."

"What are you talking about? I'm trying to give you money. What do you mean!?"

"You women, so . . . so," as he grasped for words, "so, silly," and he laughed at himself, "now you think money is so powerful, not its relationship, and property. Like take for instance, this bottle. Do you know what's inside dear?" His wide toothy smile reflected on the bottle.

"What does- it's a ship," she said agitated, "a model ship."

"You had it in the first half, almost very good. No this is a ship, an old enchanted ship. And the reason why I have this enchanted ship is because I lead this garrison, these docks are mine. This shows why I am respected and I command those men below. This ship shows my importance, without me, this whole town drowns. Can you understand now?"

Litus had begun sneaking closer just in case anything were to happen, and Jane responded, "no, I don't think I do. An enchanted ship, what do you mean?"

"Hmm, very enlightening, enchanting dare say that you don't know what that means?"

"Magic-"

"This ship, fought in the great war, a thousand years ago. This very well is the last of its kind. A battleship of a greater time. Care to take a look?" He leaned back, grabbing the bottle, and leaned putting his face close to hers. "Here look, those flags, these purple flags, the flag of the royal house of Renoi."

"Why are you telling me this?" He held her hand, but she tried to retract it.

"Ever heard of a holiday?" Jane didn't answer, "truly enchanting dear. A holiday is freedom. And I'm due for one, soon," he said slowly, trying to rest his hand back on hers.

Litus silently crept closer to them, making sure to not be spotted. And then he thought, *The magic ship.*

"Are you?'

"Yes, dear, finally you can open your ears. Thought you were deaf for so long," he rolled the bottle in his fingers, and said, "It's a strong sturdy ship, it survived the war a thousand years ago, it'll survive the night."

"I thought of you from the beginning we met, the same I see now."

"You fool me so well."

"A pig."

He looked completely baffled. His sheer look of shock eventually turned into anger. "Now, why would you!" He shouted, "how dare you! You are sure a dumb-" and murmured the rest under his breath, and returned the ship on the stand, by nearly smashing it.

"I have gold, you're a pig, let me buy a ship from you if I'm such a drag."

"A ship from what dock? Get the fuck out."

"Gold, have you ever seen gold before?"

He stood up, and smashed the table with his fists, "you gone deaf again? Get the fuck out!"

He was close to that chair, and that man too. Whenever the man made drastic movements, Litus retreated only a little.

Jane fluttered her eyes once, and saw a familiar dark figure sneaking around Batwit. For a second, she wondered, *Is he going to kill him?* But even though he was rotten flesh, she hoped Litus didn't kill him.

"I'm not deaf, I'll go to one of your sailors, and buy a ship off of them."

"What did I just hear, you plan on buying off my own men, I laugh at that. See," and he broke into a snorting laugh.

She noticed Litus wasn't heading for his sword, or even had one in his hands, nor knife, or any blunt object. "Do you know why I'll be successful?"

"Why are you still here, get out!"

"Cause I'm not a fat pig."

"That's it," he said recoiling, and he smacked the side of her face.

"You fucking-"

"Don't make me come over this counter, you rancid bitch!"

Jane got back up, with a hand on her handle, and the other feeling her stinging skin. "You fucking pig, I'll gut you!"

He made this horrible grunt, as he began to jump from his position onto Jane, but she was quick of hand. She backed, holding the full length of the blade between them. She could see Litus' shocked eyes fade as he went not for a blade, but for a bottle.

"You say anything further," and she tipped the blade down.

Litus reached out his hands – when the time was right, and with one fell swoop – he took the bottled ship. Batwit tried to fall back, but Jane just pushed her blade closer, "fucking," he said quietly, "you kill me, you won't go anywhere. What do you think you do with that, d-" He refrained with the point getting closer.

She watched him withdraw and escape from sight. "Worthless," she said before leaving.

They met up shortly after, and rushed out of the scene they had made. They were in between two buildings casting a shadow on the dusty and sandy ground. "Why!" She said putting a foot to the ground, "why, are you here? I was trying to deal with this."

The look he gave her with just his eyes was one of disgust and disappointment. And his eyes didn't falter as he held the bottle. Her face was slightly flushed, "thank you," she said with a rock in her throat, "you stole his ship. Have you ever sailed a ship before?" And he shook his head, "how hard can it be?" And she chuckled a bit, while she held her face with a shaking palm.

They looked out to the ocean, the waves beat on, and they quickly walked down the wet and semi slick stairs down to the docks. There were a few ships in the docking yard, aboard there were plenty of sailors, with grim faces. And they were hauling cargo from the capitol, shown by the name painted on the side. They were skilled laborers, and by sheer appearances, they pushed themselves against the waves, and the ships rocked and swayed.

The end of the dock opposite of those sailors was completely empty of men and ships. They calmly and inconspicuously walked to the end, with their faces covered.

Chapter Eleven:

"How do we use it," Jane cried, "we can't smash the bottle open, it might break."

Litus decided to just try something. He uncorked the bottle, and tossed it into the water. For that brief moment, there was nothing. There was a stream of bubbles from where they threw the bottle in, and they watched the bubbles eventually die out. And when there was nothing left, absolutely nothing, Jane started to chuckle, "whats next, should I lose an arm or you your eyes, should there be lightning that strikes us in the back of the head, should the world stop turning, and the sea boil away, and the sky could fall and suffocate us all," but then another stream of bubbles began to rise.

Litus stood around having noticed them, and then the heat started to emerge, and the stream of bubbles became more rampant. At an immediate impulse a plume of heat and frothy water rose, and with it came a ship, the one from the bottle.

Jane looked on with awe. To see something so grand right here, was intoxicating. She remained quiet as she noticed the flags on the ship, and they waved the purple flag of Porcelania.

A hissing steam was wafting away from the ship, Litus went to touch the side, and the blistering heat radiated all of the air for just a moment, until that heat evaporated into the air. Along the sides of the ship were a series of cast iron funnels or troughs. Back in a time long forgotten by the old, and only spoken by the dead, these iron funnels surely were formidable weapons however they functioned.

The ship in particular stood much taller than the ships the sailors were prepping, maybe five or ten feet taller. On their side of the dock there was a climbing ladder to get aboard, and Litus put the ladder down onto the side of the ship, and the two started to climb up onto the deck. "Where is the anchor?" She asked while looking around, "ah, it's already down."

Litus went down under deck, and below near the bottom of the
ship was an old windlass. There were massive chains as thick as his
wrist wrapping around the crank. He gripped the long spoke of the
wheel, and tried to turn, but he soon realized that the chains and gears
were crusted with a thick layer of rust preventing the mechanism from
turning. He kicked with the heavy end of his heel on the chains and
broke up much of that glue. As he continued to try and raise the
anchor, there was a hissing, screeching noise coming from below, or
behind. From where Litus stood, it echoed continually. Breaking
through the hiss, Jane called, yelling frantically "Hurry up!"

While Litus had just gone down to look at how to raise the
anchor. Jane remembered the true situation they were in. She was
standing on a massive ship, strapped with strange unusable weapons,
but most importantly it was stolen. Batwit was yelling at the top of his
lungs, and the sailors were running to her. Some of them went
elsewhere, but they were a long afterthought.

When the scraping sounds from below started to secrete a
stinging pain, Jane was forced to cover her ears as she watched the
sailors get ever closer. As the sound kept fading, they came closer.
She pulled up the ladder, and ran around to make sure that there
wasn't anymore, and then the sound of that scraping had diminished.
They were all around. She scabbed her blade, and stood towards the
sides. With little time, the sailors started to grasp at the sides wall, and
soon they began to peer over the side. "Seize them, seize those
thieves! Get them! Get them!" Yelled Batwit sharp and clear. "Get
them! Get them! Get them!" She ran up to the sailor, thrusting her
pommel into his side, before she kicked him off the side.

Jane quickly went to unspool the rope knots holding up the
sails, and as they fell, they caught a stream of wind, and knocked the

ship forward, but it was still stuck in place. Jane quickly ran down below deck and yelled to Litus, "hurry up!"

Litus didn't know what was happening, but knew that whatever was occurring put a weight on his shoulders. At that moment the anchor felt heavier, but with all his might, Litus pressed on pushing the crank wheel around more. Consolidated within the room a deep groaning grew in place of the screeching. But as that groaning grew, so was the heft of the anchor. He made a few more rotations, the heft started to lessen, but now he felt a horrible scraping and buzzing. He pushed, and pushed the wheel, and the wheel started to buckle, and at that instant, he lost his grip, and Litus was thrown to the side. The anchor wildly fell back down to the sea floor. The wheel was spinning like a top. The ship rocked back and forth erratically.

Jane had just emerged from below, and onto deck again. There were sailors all unarmed climbing onto the sides of the ship. Jane held her sword firm, and went to each side of the ship and swung above the sailors. *Come on, fall already!* She swung from side to side, and a few sailors dropped back on deck, and others crashed into the water. A smack came from behind, they were climbing from the other side, and Jane ran to deal with it. She began with a swing of the blade forward, but at the last second she again pushed the pommel into the man's face, knocking him to the ground motionless.

She looked over the side, trying to keep balance with the waves. There were more sailors climbing up the side, which meant with the threat of a blade more fell back on deck, and others were water bound. "Get on deck you miserable fucks," he yelled so aggressively that the last word he said was complete animal noises.

She ran to the other side of the boat trying to knock off one of the sailors, but as she was swinging, one of the sailors had caught the edge of her blade with his bare hand. He bled fast but didn't fear a cut on his hands, in fact he grinned a little. He pulled on the sword trying to bring Jane down. She kept trying to reel her sword in, but the sailor only pulled back harder. She planted her feet down at the wall edge of the ship to keep herself from falling. From behind on the other side of the ship a single sailor was able to climb onto deck. He ran to Jane and tried to push her off. He grabbed her by the chest, and violently tried to push her off. She grabbed the side railing with as much of a grip as she could possibly muster, and in her other she tried to keep a grip on the handle, but the one grabbing her sword made one quick yank with his marred hand and pulled her. The ship rocked forcibly again, the man pushing and groping her fell back, and accidentally pulled her back. In the rocking, a hand flew away, and men on either side careened to the ground with a series of thumps.

Litus was thrown back from the wheel, the anchor fell and the ship rocked violently back and forth. Litus struggled to get back to his feet as the tumbling kept him glued down. Off to the side of the crank wheel there was a stop lever. He crawled on the ground – keeping his body to the floor – as he slowly, but eventually came to the stopper. He wrapped his arm and leg around for leverage. He heaved with all the weight of his body, again, and again, and again. With each thrust, the crust was being broken off, little by little. And with one last thrust, down the lever went bringing Litus with it, and the wheel seized with a piercing and decaying hiss.

The ship rocked one massive swing, but hadn't continued to any scale as before. He returned to the wheel, and pushed it while keeping his grip tight, and his feet planted. Litus reeled in the wheel, each rotation caused the lock to click rightly, until the chain was now completely spooled.

The rocking was dimming, and Jane was trying to get balanced as the ship was still in a hard motion. A sailor crawled on deck and gripped the railings. Waves broke off the sea wall, and splashed water everywhere. Puddles clung a thin film on the deck's surface leaving it walkable, but slick. He thundered over, kicking Jane in the stomach, before grabbing her with his calloused hands. Jane tried to push back, but he kept a firm grip. Pulling her up, to see her face before he wrapped his claws around her waist and neck. Jane was put in shock, she grabbed at his forearms trying to free his grip. She was trying to swing but couldn't reach. With his strength he lifted Jane up, she began to see darkness, she looked down and used what's left of her strength and smashed his legs, and down they fell.

Jane looked about the deck searching for her sword. It had planted itself in the left wall of the ship. She rushed as quickly as she could. And grabbed the hilt trying to pull it free. The sound of fury arose from the ground – with pain struck across his face. Jane propped her foot on the wall, nudging the blade. She turned, watching him rush towards her. In one swift motion, he fell down and died.

Litus looked around him as the darkness below deck finally sunk in, and he paused for breath. But only for a second. Up deck he ran, there were a few bodies on the ground, and Jane had a streak of blood running down her blade, and face.

The wind took the sails, and the docks now passed them, and together they threw the dead overboard while watching the docks become smaller and smaller.

Litus felt strange, there was a fuzzy feeling like needles pricking his skin. He turned back and saw the crews of sailors fishing out the sailors from the water, and the body parts that followed. The water hitting the coast was frothy and apple red. They could hear a distant roaring, but no sailor sailed out.

Jane cleaned up, taking her armor off and finding rags in an unlocked chest in the captain's cabin. She struggled to take off her breast plate and called to Litus, "Litus, Litus, could you spare a moment?"

After a few moments waiting, Litus peered through the door, "would you help me shed this armor?"

Litus helped Jane undress her armor, which had caked spots of browning blood. "For some reason, now I think of Tolk. I don't know why, but the bit of silence we have now is making me think about him," she paused for a brief moment, "do you think that our coming to Diende is the reason that they attacked the town?" He stood there motionless, but questioningly, "if what he said is true about that prophecy? If you are truly some spirit destined to destroy . . . this cult and rid the world of chaos. Do you think that . . . it's possible?"

Litus looked to her and his hands wavered back and forth. He then shrugged, and not a shrug to dismiss the comment, or to downplay the severity, he shrugged to show his uncertainty. Jane looked down and questioned the position she was in. Cutting in was the sound of her stomach begging, "I'm going to go look for some preserves, wherever they're stored."

She left and Litus was left there in the captain's quarters. Near the back close to a glass window, there was a long table, with a map sprawled across. He shook off the aged debris. It might have been a complete map once, but with gashes here and there, it was barely useful for traversing the world. Holding one corner down was a compass which no longer always pointed north, and a cracked quill pen. Near the side of the room, between two desks was a thin wooden box, and inside were sprawls of cracked maps, covered in dust.

Jane entered with an old sack of food, and sat down at the captain's table. She pulled out a slab of bread, "Litus, I know you don't eat, but even if you could," she slammed a slab of hardtack on her knee and it snapped in half, like dry boards, "this isn't it, is it?"

She took her hardtack pieces and soaked them in the water, where they almost immediately turned to mush. Food is food, and even though this food was complete mush, it was the only food available in their situation.

Hours passed, and the sky was turning dark, and the cabin was lit by only a few lanterns. The waves started to rock heavier than they had an hour or two back. In the sky above, the moon's outline was visible in the center of the blanket. And it outstretched farther than the eye could see, or perceive. It was near infinite. Just a ship on a rocking blue, with the blanket holding the moon. The lanterns swung from side to side.

Jane peered at the map after finishing her sludge of somewhat edible dust. "Mulder either grew since these markings, or we've almost died to the balding skirts. We should keep a hold on this map, whether it's old or not, the look of land doesn't change much over a few hundred years. So we're around here and there doesn't seem to be Atreau on this one?" But she could remember Tolk's map, and where it had been there.

"And after Atreau, you're going to Tisden?" She said, "how will you get there?"

Litus sat down beside Jane, looking down, and tracing a path with his finger. "I don't think that works, you can't just go straight through, the mountains are too tall. You'd probably rather want to go through these countries, because what I know is that there's cities and not empty mountains."

And then it came to the idea of sailing, and other things for quite some time, but once they heard a sound from outside, they drew quiet. The ship rocked, and a deep droning reverberated throughout the boards, vibrating them at the perfect pitch to hum a ghastly tone. They looked out the window, and the waves had grown and thrashed against the hull.

Litus scrolled up the map quickly and concealed it in his cloak. Jane grabbed a hanging lantern, and gave another to Litus. The drumming of rain began to pound, and thunder groaned in the far off distance. Litus remained low, he held the sword ready to use with whatever stowed on deck.

They held their lanterns high, but no light could pierce the heavy droplets. The rhythmic waving lured them, and the thunder broke that stimulation. Litus stepped forward with each step drawing fear throughout his cloak. Lightning struck down, and in its light revealed the sight of an engorging arm, gnawing the hull. A hissing steam of a thousand raging bulls, more evil than the cold of the ocean, ranged for the left beyond the ship peering at its prey. From where they stood, they could see through the plume of the debris of foamy waves, those thin slivers of red. Lightning crashed again, light spilling over. The wet slimy skin reflected the light towards their eyes. The bouquet of arms sunk in the black water, and arose clutching the ship. The red was embedded deep in the folds of a brow, and smoothed out showing a round top. The light faded from the sky and all was dark except those ever present eyes.

The lantern fell from her hand, and the flame died upon impact.

An arm in the complete darkness unspooled around the ship and like a tree timbering, came crashing towards Jane. Litus took her by the shoulders, and dropped to the ground under the rain of splinters. The shock came after, and threw them further to the side. They were next to the doors. They quickly went back in, and gathered what they could. Litus faced the dark, with a lantern and the shimmer on the length of the steel.

In the pale darkness, he couldn't see what lingered, but it's peering red eyes, on the broad side of the ship. Lightning struck, and the arm could see him just as much as he could see the arm. Litus played first, getting behind the mast as fast as he could. The arm swept around leaving a short trench in the deck. The arm swept around leaving a short trench in the deck. Jane rushed out, partly armored, and sword in hand. Lightning stuck, the sky illuminated, the arm reached for what it thought was where she was. But it missed and came past her; Jane felt a gust of wind emerge from the new trench. She muttered under her breath, and pierced the tip deep down into the flesh of the calamity and it spewed a thick blood over half the deck.

Salt sprayed up, stinging the raging beast about. Lightning struck in the distance, and a flash of light caused the calamity to be in darkness, except for those eyes. The long arms swung high, and whipped down, and Jane yelled, "run!"

The floor cracked and shattered, a trench dipped down low, and Litus stood his ground, with that sword raised high. As that arm swung like a released arrow, he swung, and down it went. The severed arm bled and crashed to the deck ground, again spewing it dark sticky blood. And Litus was thrown back, in repulsion of the swatting. The lantern crashed to the ground, and the light faded in the night sky.

"Where are you?" She whispered in the dark, and Litus quickly ran to her.

They fell back into the cabin, the door was the last barrier against the calamity. "Are we really safe here?" But she didn't want an answer.

Soon, the beast roamed around observing right outside the cabin, but not for long. The arms smashed through the door, and were stuck by the door frame. They both tried to stab as they peered through. Then they stopped, and for a second there was silence. They had the urge of leaving to see where they went, but fear stopped them. Both the right and left side of the cabin had a scraping rubbing sound. They didn't turn, but looked around as the sounds peered through. And Litus felt needles prod from all directions. In an instant, a heap of arms thrust through the window at the end of the room, glass came crashing at them. The arms ran around the ceiling, they pulled and pulled, and the roof came away. Shredding splinters. Litus prodded his sword at them. Slashing at them, cutting out chunks of flesh. Lightning stuck lighting the sky, and Jane and Litus were thrown out of the cabin onto the deck. They fought as well as they could, cutting as much as possible, but there was too much. They fell back to back waiting for something. Another bolt struck down. And with it an arm struck with it, separating them. The arm threw Litus across the deck, he hit the mast with his back. Pain shot through him, but he still had a fight to give. He ducked behind the mast on the opposite side he was hit. Litus got out as fast as he could, for when the arm came. There was silence. The arm, like the crash of a wave, came to, and the mast shattered like glass.

A scream broke the silence. It raged through the seas, and the foam created by the crash of waves, rocked the boat from side to side. Jane was thrown aside, and yelled out for Litus. He came to her voice; everything was silent for a moment. All they could hear was the blood in their ears when the sky went white. Entangled in front of them was an army of arms. Then the only light fell down.

Chapter Twelve:

The mist from the ocean shores left debris strewn all across the coast of the city of Porcelania. A cast iron gate stretched all around on the edge of the headland above a short but steep white rock cliff. The gates were decorum, covered in art of flowers and thorns. Against the iron were tall brushes of well trimmed hedges, with splashes of red flowers and thorns. Small cliff faces cut through the beach into near equal dividends. And there crawling against the cold sand was Jane, and hidden in debris was Litus. She was as pale as the white sands, and sickly too. Water clogged her lungs and she grasped at air while still asleep. Jane awoke first, throwing up all the bile and water that built up over the time stuck in the tumbling waters. Over a minute passed her head filled with fear over where she was. A sort of old memory lost to time, refound, or slightly uncovered.

Once her head stopped stirring, she thought and worried, "Litus!"

He rustled under the planks stripped into sticks, and the only sound she could hear was the ocean crashing against the bed of sand and the rubbing of sticks, and Jane's own calls. There were fragments of the hull, or glass, barrels, and even of severed tentacles from the monster of the sea, laying all about the beach. A being of darkness's arm crashed out of the shattered planks, and iron rings from barrels.

Jane turned around, crying out for Litus. Pulling away scraps with her worn hands. He tried to push away what he could, his shadowy flame tearing holes through the cocoon. The skin on his arm was like a void – no light reflected – and all the light around bent like the sight over the horizon. "What happened to your arm?"

Out of the rubble, there stood a figure of shadow. There were no details of skin, or blood pumping. He didn't look like a living being, only of it's shadow. Except for those eyes, they still radiated a deep gem-like purple. And then in a fissile of mist and smoke, his figure was again draped and armored.

"That's what you look past the cloak?"

The sound of the ocean crashing in the ambiance. "Are you okay?" Litus nodded so, "I know these shores, I've been here before, a long time ago. Well we are here, we are where we want to be: Porcelania, but for me not how I would like to have gotten here," she choked up a stream of bile and ocean water, and her face grew paler.

Litus grasped her, his arm around her trying to bring her further away from the coast. "It's alright, alright," she moaned, "I, we need some dry clothes, and hot food or," she looked around the ground, and checked her hip, and said, "new steel, mine's gone by now, rusted away."

He helped her stand and stay standing, and Jane remarked about how dry Litus garbs were. Out of the void of his soul, Litus drew out the small throwing knife he found in the woods, and gave it to Jane. She looked down at it, and in almost a trance she said, "if you really were a wraith, you would have killed me with this while I lay in the dark that while ago," she twisted the knife between her fingers, "huh, so small. It's cold."

About forty feet off there was a cement staircase – with pots of flowers along the railings – up towards the gateway. There was a big iron lock, on the ornate iron gate. They grabbed and pulled on the lock hoping it would budge, but Litus resulted to strike it with a rock that sat nearby. "Hopefully no one saw us."

They walked into another world, of flowers, gravel paths and the great walls of henges which had no end. The distance between the well kept walls were five feet apart, and continuously accurate to that degree. At the end of the hall, was a crossroads, in which every way was more halls of grass. "A maze," she said with a cough, "of hedges."

In the background the sound of the waves were fading out, but another ambiance was drawing in. They walked and walked, by every edge and again into a dead end. "They're just hedges, lets just part them, and walk through," but when she parted the branches, all which was behind was a wall of gray cemented bricks.

They were trapped in the prison of no apparent end. The further they walked, the more it seemed like the maze had no end. And for thirty or fourty eons of minutes they kept them batting at those tall plant masked walls. As they made each turn, they beat their fists on the side of the walls. And each dead end made them scratch their heads.

As they walked through, the sound from outside became more audible, the rhythm not of waves, but something else emanated as they traversed the insanity. But that faint change in ambiance kept their short term state into a self realized loathing. It made them both feel enthralled and disappointed in themselves. They took one turn, and from the light that touched their feet, they could see the exit before the turn too. A stream of light shown that wasn't enriched by the dark shadows the walls cast, or the green of leaves. An ocean of pink flowers, were a bed on either side of a curvy cobblestone pathway leading out of the garden.

There were no longer any hedges to mask the sound of the ambiance of marching. Soldiers dawned head to toe in decorum steel plated armor, with halberds raised, and guiding from in front was an officer with a saber outstretched. They all wore masks of white porcelain painted with stripes of purple, and leaves of gold. High above their steel morion helmets, they flew on poles the monarchs crest on a flag. In the center of a sea of purple and a gold and silver cross, there was the crest, shield, and crown of gray silver above.

Their march was a loud rhythmic stomp of these men at decorated arms. But where Litus and Jane were, they could hear the thin plucking and ticking as their plate scraped and shifted in formation. And past the garden fencing the men marched further, and down the city street of cobblestone and brick and mortar. They turned a corner, and men atop horses with their swords erect and their posture stern and strict. And the men who didn't carry swords, carried women and men alike, with their heads peering down from the tall tower of pike.

"Blood stains their garbs, but they don't wear red," Jane said under a small breath.

Blood dropped on the ground. It was red and brown like the evenly built brick block, and sticky like sugar left in the sun. Around their bodiless necks were red burns, and they watched the formation march till their last men passed. And Jane just looked at it, with a still unmoving frame.

Litus saw a malkin with white fur, and from the other side of the road he could make out a porcelain mask similar to the soldier, but with a group of people following after their treads with masks of carved wood, or paper. Litus was hesitant to seek out this malkin. He was a drop in this new ocean they were looking into. And a drop, may be insignificant, or it could be the average in this cradle of death.

They went across trying not to make any attention whatsoever. Litus sought the company of this malkin, and he quickly walked up the street and tapped on his shoulder. Almost immediately that cat jumped to the side, and fell to the ground, shifting between the alleyways of the tall buildings. He scrambled for what to say, sputtering. "Wr- Wr- Wraith?" He said, scrambling for words.

Jane had followed up quickly, taking the attention, by saying, "no, no no. He's not a wraith, he's your prophet, Mr. malkin."

"What?" He said, trying to gather his thoughts, "who are you two?"

"He's your prophet! The knight of . . . justice. We saw you, and we're asking for your help. Can you help us?"

"With what," his eyes dilated when he saw her, "again, who are you, why aren't you covered?"

"What do you mean? One of those masks?"

"Yes, a mask, and you," he looked into Litus' eyes, and it clearly clicked, "it's you!? Really you!?" He said as quietly as he could muster, "and you're not some wraith. How? It's you! Forget it, it's a dream, all a dream."

"Stop this, please can you help us?"
"First you should get a mask."

"Do you have one?"

"I didn't think I'd be in the presence of a prophet today, so no!"

"I've been here before, but then we didn't need some mask."

He begrudgingly said, "so be it."

Jane looked at him eerily, "why does everyone wear those masks?"

"Why do you wear shoes, or socks, or undergarments for that matter," he chuckled, "if our queen wears the fashion, it dribbles down to us. And some think it's worth sacking you for being a traitor to the crown."

"Fine, then where can we get these masks?"
"I'll show you, there's a party in the park."

Down the block they walked to a field of evenly clipped grass, set a stage of lumber, ropes of twine, and bodies of prisoners at gallows hall. "Prisoners of the crown, mainly pirates, and thieves. And other undesirables stand their ground."

Jane – behind a paper mask – held some disgust in her palms. *How can they cheer for what they don't see,* Litus thought. Hundreds of people in the fields crowded around one point, in tents which stood above all the commoners were the nobility in their decorated masks, and their few guards. The trees lined the boundaries of the park and held leaves of perfectly bloomed flowers of red and pink and gold. And the flowers were all perfect, and their colors were bold and painted.

Lined up around the gallows were the doomed men. Their trials were decided, and they were given the loop of rope around their neck. They entered from one flank of the platform, and guards adorned with leather jerkin pushed them into their fates. They held their pikes up readily, the iron point glinted in the light. They could hear the commoners cheer for the queen, and they hummed a little tune together. Those far closer – within grasp of the prisoners – uproar in fantastic cheer for the dropping men.

A man in clean robes held a leatherbound book, and prayed. He had mumbled his quick sermon, but it felt strange. *They parade the dead, while giving a last rite.* And the priest said his prayers in mumbled speech, but the last phrase was clear, "and may your sin be forgiven, by our great gods above, and our death god below."

They leaned back into the road, a shadow overhung, and the malkin insisted they pull back more, "we should watch from here, I don't like to be close to the-" the floor dropped, and that sound echoed in near unison, except for one who dangled and struggled. The people all around we're quiet in anticipation. The prisoner thrashed about, their face slowly turning blue. His eyes bulged, trying to find an escape, but inevitably rolled back, showing white dots in a purplish-blue field, and the body stopped and people rejoiced.

"Why did they cheer?" Jane expressed, "that was absolutely horrible. They rejoiced in death. They craved it."

"They don't 'crave' death. They merely want justice exacted."

They hadn't noticed it, but there was a stir among some of the commoners. One man pushed his mask up to see through a face with one eye patch. And that man had quickly scurried to one of the horsed saber-wielding men, and they both looked at Litus and Jane. And forth the soldier trodden. "You, woman," he said with a stern voice, "take your blade away."

Jane turned quickly, and looked up at the man on his horse. He barked, "put down your sword, heathen," but before Jane could do anything, he snapped his finger yelling, "you are in violation of public possession of weaponry, insubordination, and treason against the crown!"

"What! You didn't give me any time."

He outstretched his sword, "be quiet wench."

Soldiers from either side grabbed her arms, and pushed her backwards onto the ground. She tried to fight them off, to break their grasp, but to no avail. She yelled out, before having a sack put over her face, "run!"

Litus drew out his blade to meet, but immediately he saw the extent to their scale. A near dozen men with halberds turned down the alley, and pushed them back, but Jane remained in their grasp on the other side of the wall of faceless men. He ran down the alley, and realized that the malkin was already gone. With no direction, Litus ran wherever seemed the safest.

The streets further away from the luxury of the park subsided, and in its place were grime and bits of glass strewn about. Litus escaped and found himself on the side of another street. He checked his shoulder, before darting further on. There were those tall buildings connected by old brick and plaster.

"After that one, the one with the dark cloak!" Yelled a man from behind.

Litus ran into the nearest alleyway, and it broke off into multiple separate halls. The left and right alley were copies of this same grime and the cracks between stepping stones were sands of little mirrors. "Hey," clicked from afar. "My prophet here!"

The white malkin beckoned Litus from down the corridor, and through a door. "My prophet, please come over here," and Litus ran, and the door closed behind him.

The malkin led him down that hall of tiles, and into a courtyard, and across a bed of tall gray and white grass. "You should have run when she said so. I'm sorry my lord, for my apparent cowardice," he said, picking at his claws, "my lord, my great great lord, you can stay with me tonight. I give my abode to thee."

Chapter Thirteen:

The door was quiet like the stalking of cats as it closed. "You're going to try and save her, oh I see it in your eyes, but you'll kill her if you do so," he whispered, "don't go, don't go. You can still save her, they won't execute her yet, you have a chance. Now go sit, my lord."

It was a small room, and a small apartment of furniture that fit a malkin, but Litus was unfortunately used to it all by now. Litus found a small rocking chair with scrolls carved in the arms and rocker. *Just like Tolk's, hmm,* Litus remembered like it was long ago, *I couldn't save him, but I can save.*

"Do you drink tea?" Litus' thought was broken as he shook his head, and the malkin said, "my name is Taresh, or Terry, choose whichever. My lord, what is yours?"

He pushed on a table a platter of paper and ink for a pen. "I believe you can write, am I correct?" And he nodded, and wrote down the name, "Litus? She gave you that name."

He sipped at his small glass, "you have time to save her, still. She gave you a name, and you can return such a favor, or you don't. There is only one try."

"Where is she?" Litus wrote down.

"By now she's in a dungeon, and being judged on crimes, maybe of piracy. But between a day or a week, they'll decide whether she'll walk free – which mostly doesn't happen, she'll be put in the dungeon below tower black, or she'll be put on gallows road. And my grace, if you try to save her from the rope, and fail," he sat back, "why is she so important?" He asked, but before Litus could write, he said, "forget it. It's not important right now.

"What is important, is you are a prophet to a dying faith, and to be truthful never in my life would I have believed it to be true. But here you are. I can help you save her, but you need to listen. Like I said, they won't execute her today, not even for real pirates do they do so. If you make a distraction big enough they will focus their attention elsewhere, and all you have to do is cut her from the ropes and escort her away, far away. North up the block. There is an old woman, in a grand but decaying home, with pink flower bushes, she's an acquaintance of mine, and a believer of this faith. She could help you more than I could or would. This needs to be as safe and secured as possible. For the loss of anyone in this decadent faith, is a great loss indeed. The more hands on deck, the better."

Litus shrugged, looking down at the parchment, before he could think of what to write, Taresh said, "new garbs will play nicely to remain under the light of those who seek. But I'm sorry, all I can give is a wooden mask. It's an old mask, carved from the birch of this city. When you leave, I hope you'll think of me, and what I've done in the name of faith."

Litus held the white wood mask, feeling the carved scrolls. It had a strange feel, the old oils worn down, and the surface was smooth. It held some memory which was apparent through its age, but deciphering which was tricky. He put it over his face, and through its holes, there were pins and needles which tickled his face. Litus took it off, again looking at the carves in the face. "Don't be so startled, friend. It is only a mask." The malkin took it from Litus' hands for a moment and placed the mask over his own face, "see, just a mask, just plain and simple. It's old, but not as old as the malkin."

A door showed against the faint light of white birch and a silver doorknob encrusted with a shine of thousands of particulates. There was darkness above, below, and around, but not from the doors cracks and gaps. He tried to open, but it wouldn't budge as though it were locked from the other side of the world. But he knew of this other door, one behind him, made of scrolled oak, and thousands of years of stripped and reapplied paint. He twisted the door handle made from the old branches already twisted in a braid, and opened into a grand hall of volcanic glass. And a double staircase leading upstairs called his mind into a trance. Along the walls were hundreds of doors, thousands of doors – some were covered with chains, and others as he approached shut. Nearly all were locked, in one way or another. Except one. It was on the far left of the hall. It was wide open, and foaming out a cold green air. The scent of stale iron hung.

There was a hall, a different hall, but something similar in two ways. It was a palace of blood red columns of marble. The palace was knee deep in blood, it flowed through an expanse of the unintelligible. Swirls of painted tapestries line the walls spanned ages between breaths. There was an air of distance, a voice. Maybe the voices of people, but they're too far away. The distance in the current was an iron chain. Past the paintings, and obstructing the future was a mist, similar to that of the sky. But the closer he came to the mist, there was a twisting in the palace hall. Waves and swirls in the pool formed and crashed in the pillars and walls. The heat and sweat built, and dripped off into the river of blood. The noxious fumes persisted still. "Who's there," he thought he yelled.

"Who's there!" He thought again, the noises warped against the shifting room.

The end held an altar overflowing with a figure of petrification and ash. "Now that I've arrived, this is what's left for me. What can I do now? Why did I let this happen? Why didn't I stop him, when I had a chance? But could I ever see that chance?"

A blade struck through the figure's back, by an angel with wings of crystalized blood. And arms tied in ropes of sacrificial binds. And they stood still. The wings of scrolled red glass held its own light. As the statue with the long curved blade said in a whisper which pierced skulls, "you welcome me lord yet to be. Never so. You'll see a dream within a dream within a chest in your mind. You may not see what it is, but it takes many shapes throughout this time. You will not seek that chapel."

"I will, no matter what you are," he thought he muttered.

"Then death will be part of a world so torn already," he said, blood running down his soft pale skin.

"That's not fair."

"Is and isn't."

"And they who you brought to stone?"

"May it be an acquaintance of yours?" His skin was like marble, as his figure lost the heat that was so wanted and gone.

The air was again stale, as the painting dried and was streaks of red and pale cream colors. And The door on the end led outside.

Chapter Fourteen:

A light from a window – which hadn't been seen before – had made him awake in the morning coolness. Little warmth came from the fireplace, even as Taresh stroked it with an iron pick. He put his hands around a hot cup, and let the steam warm him.

"Here," Taresh said tossing a large paper wrapped stack of garbs, "get yourself out of that cloak and dirty plates. When the watchmen come, they'll search for someone who looks like you, as you do now, and put them to the gallows faster than that lady of yours."

He peeled the waxy paper, and unfolded out a large wide brimmed hat, a long shirt with ruffled cuffs, general pants and tall boots, and a cloak of interlaced weaves of red and russet tones. The cloth was heavy, and as it draped over his figure it was completely strange compared to that dark cloak.

Litus walked the streets, with his hands concealed, face and head hidden, the gallows platform still held high as its shadow hung down across the flourishing garden and park. At midday down from a series of carts were the lines of prisoners, not one who fell were a head of golden strung hair.

He watched for hours – that day – but no carts held her.

The people were what attracted him — outside of the ones held in the carts. Some of them were clearly disgusted. Either by the practice, or the disposition to the sound of a unified snap, but those people were apparently in a minority, and held fear in their eyes, but those masks kept them safe and stuck. It was similar to what he felt, but he wouldn't be stuck. He had already crossed a line that he didn't know was set.

The next day was the same, he waited, and thought about what he'd have to do. No golden hair was caught in that loop that day, but the prayers of the priests fell on the deafening voice of cheers for the damned.

He pushed through the people. Most gave grim and piercing eyes through the windows in their masks. He tried to exit through a stone arch, but a man in a black mask grabbed him by the shoulder, "now where are you heading friend?"

Friend? The sound stirred in his head. *You. Who are you?*

"I see in your eyes, turmoil, friend."

All that could be seen were his eyes of no particular color other than a golden light. But none of that light reflected onto his black plated gauntlets with articulated fingers.

"Now do you disgrace her? Our lord, and queen?"

He grabbed Litus, and turned him to face the stage, "look at them, those who deserve justice. We may have lost the great great war, but our lord's word still lives in our hearts, so say prayers. They will soon.

"You still seem very tense, let me try. Those are pirates, and they tried to attack us, in a sailing town a little north of here. Those gypsy pirates run amuck of these shores, and it's golden beauty. But not only that, they failed, not a single feather was plucked from the crows tush."

Another cart rolled in, and with it a line of men, gruff and tumbling entering the stage of falling. The men handling the dead wore their hood of shame, but that was only a tradition. A priest, a younger priest, walked in front of the ropes while sprinkling something from his hand onto the platforms.

And as they listened through every verse, the masked man ushered in emotion, and then they fell. Litus no longer felt those needles, nor the grip or sight of the armored man of darkened steel.

Litus drifted away, and through the arch wondering where he went, but hoping to not meet again.

It was near noon the next day, the morning air was starting to dissipate, and there was already a crowd of people in a quiet rumble just seething for death. They couldn't see the entire crowd while only on the sidewalk, but there was still a significant crowd, so early. Taresh turned to Litus, remarking, "from what I've seen, the troops with pikes will already have marched away by the time they reload the nooses, so don't run too fast, or else you'll run from the frying pan into the fire."

The Rientonem flags hung from the supporting beam, as a final judgment from the state. Out of the first cart, were the prisoners similar to days past, but with one, was different. A head of worn and muddied golden threads.

Litus streamed through the crowds towards the front. And waited for a long time, while prisoners were being strung and hung. It was now properly noon, a troop of spiked heads strolled out, a line of prisoners filed in, and rain started to fall. In the center of the line, she stood a sickly and ruff covered Jane. And they draped her in prisoner garb like the rest.

The same priest from the day prior, walked in from the right, in his clean smooth garbs. He looked at only the wave of masks, and opened sacred texts. There was no executioner, but a man of larger stature with a feathered helm with a bronze faceplate. He gripped the lever to drop the platform, while the father was preparing the last rite. The priest coughed and turned the page.

He spoke loud and clear, "from Maewin 1 & 2: In the beginning, there was life and death, and they bound the realms, in eternal prosperity. The gods of this realm, may them be halved, still hold great value to be upheld. And banish those to phantoms when they fall from grace. And they shall fall with judgment and await their sentence, as they climb in returnal to the realm of the living.

"We bring force peace – in the public – for all to look at and repent for, for what has been wronged, and for the mother and children of the living. And may you seek forgiveness in the fading twilight, and let judgment and nature take your spirit and condemn it correctly."

In the dirt we wallow, and may they be changed and break, for in the dirt we become one. Under the silent sky, we shall see no light, for it grounds us. In the waves we float, and that current pushes us towards uncertain life, and rest unto death. And may god pray forgiveness to damned ones, till repent. It swirled in his head, those words. They came to him as something to step over. He kept his hands concealed, ready to draw at any given time. Some of the people looked down in prayer, but still Litus kept pushing through.

"From Selziar 2: Death be part in just manor. Piash del monoto. May those who fall to sin, be worthy of sin, or let them be forgiven, if forgiveness be in thine blood. And those who accept sin, will fall from the greatest height and land in the deep pit where only one strain of light shall be gifted, and when the sinner befalls sin will they climb and be judged again."

He kept touching the lever – tapping his fingers on the end – ready to drop it. His face may not be visible, but it was all clear to those who looked, which was only the prisoners themselves. All except one of the dead kept their head down. Jane looked onto the people, and saw a crowd of no-one staring back directly at her. The field of blank stares. The field of scarecrows. She wanted to say something, but there was nothing in her throat.

"From Mortith 1: They be not buried, for their soul and spirit remain walking in lands. And their limbs touch the dirt, as they praise their kings of the soul walking. Be it that life and death are of equal weights, one of birth, other of true death."

The closer he got, the less he saw. Eventually all faces became gray like the sky above. Down rain fell in droplets strong and resistant.

"From Keroth 2: From death in battle, one shall live in the light of a great fire. And may they be chosen to die into a great land of love. And those who cower and throw their swords into the mud may or may not be pitied by the flame, or consumed by the flame. When the land becomes stale, and the air settles and blankets the land, then rivers shall break that stillness and the rivers shall bring hope and peace, as much as split and make change to the lands of stagnation, and those who stay will make their own grave."

"So now your crimes have been committed, and may your sin be forgiven, by our great gods above."

He was close, but he still would have to push through near a dozen people in front of him, and when the hand of the bronze faced man finally sternly squeezed the lever, and tried to bring it down. It squeaked like a mouse, and Litus looked in shock. He reached not for the blade, but firstly for the flame which he hated, but sought. In one quick extension, he threw an arrow of flame at the man with a heavy hand. People were yelling. Guards were looking around confused, and aggressive. The rain snuffed most of the flame, but still drove a hole through his gambison. The soldier patted down his chest, as the heat still persisted. Those around him drew away, and made him in an empty circle of his own.

Litus threw another, stronger, arrow at the soldier, who caught it with his chest, and fell dead while lowering the lever. Quickly without even thinking, Litus ran under, to where Jane was, and down the lever fell. A series of snaps fell, and Litus tried to catch her, but wasn't there. She hung there struggling, with her face turning blue, but not yet dead.

Guards swarmed around the platform. They thrust their pikes forward, Litus weaved around the dead, and their bodies were prodded and lodged into the warm flesh. Litus in that brief moment with no points being thrown, cast a bolt of fire and fell a spearman. He tried to jump out and trample over the new body, but the men to the side quickly tried to take space away. He cut out small knocks into the shafts of the spears and halberds, in an attempt to push them away.

A commoner came in from the side swinging. His fist held a rock, and he went to Litus' side. He took the blow, and was pushed to the side consequently. Litus pushed him back, as they grabbed at each other.

Some of the soldiers still held their spears closely to Litus, but didn't risk stabbing the commoner. One armored ghost went in trying to break them apart, and Litus pushed back the commoner with a strong shove into the soldier, and they fell together pushing the spear points down rippling that line of pikes.

Litus held Jane's near limp body, and jumped over, with his open hand holding his blade, he swung at the soldiers necks. Cutting one, and nearly another. He had run only a few feet, when a spear from behind snagged his cloak, making him fall, and quickly he put the blade against the cloth, cutting it. The man tried driving the spear again, but Litus grabbed the haft of the shaft, and tucked it under his arm pushing forward into the spearman, making him fall.

The commoners looked in complete horror, but none interfered. Litus didn't wonder why, and he didn't mind it. He kept running, and into the street where no one was in the way. Then the screech broke the silence. It was all slow, Litus peer back at a sixteen red eyes with white beams of light. First came a blare of noise, and then came arrows.

There was the sound of horns and the incoming of horse trotting in the distance. Litus pulled Jane over his shoulder, and pushed into the cobblestone path. The streets were slick, and all that could be heard was the oncoming mounted men. A pain jolted up through Litus' leg, and still he pushed.

A flight of arrows came streaming by making a knock and snapping into the road below. They made him jump a bit, but still he pushed forward. But soon the trotting of hooves came closer and closer. The soon to swing blade hummed against the wind and rain, and Litus tried to push more and more. Twenty feet behind the riders were, and Litus knew there was one option left. He twisted with the wand outstretched, and made a last stand. Using all the greatly packed power of fire casting a wall tall and wide, that took the entire street's length and more. The blaze burned riders and horses to bone and bubbling flesh, and Litus and Jane were thrown back, as the wand shattered violently in his hand.

As Jane hit the ground, she gasped for air, as if teetering to a state of being awake, asking, "what's happening?"

Litus gripped tighter not to lose her, and she said in weary dreamy gasp, "they beat me with the handles of poles, and pricked me with needles to try and," she coughed heavily, "try for confessions from me. I was a thief, a pirate, a murderer."

He came past the block, and turned down an alleyway. And through he went trying to blend in with shadow. *Up the streets to the house, where the lady is.* "Why would anyone do this?

"The soldiers, and people, and lords did this?"

He ran through a courtyard, and into another alley, where on the other end was a neighborhood of close and tall mansions of recent and old. Most of them varied slightly in color or shape of hedges, except one. It was run down with no servants to maintain overgrown plants, nor repainting roof tiles. It was then he knew, and beat on the door with a heavy fist, and they both fell to the cold wet ground.

Chapter Fifteen:

Under the flickering candle light, and soft bedding, a shadow hung in lapse. Moons passed, and the light that streamed through the windows seemed like a pulse. For some time, sitting in a wheeled chair to the side was the old frail Lady Thinithe. Jane was by the bedside, her face flushed with a healthier tone, and with blue marks starting to fade. And a door on the other side of the room had a child peer their eyes, before darting away in fear from what layed in that bed.

She rang a small bell by her side, and asked the incoming servant in a delicate tone, "go replace the wrappings on him, they're old, worn, and smell . . . like death."

"Yes, my lady," she said in response, leaving the room promptly, and silently.

"Your help is necessary too. From what you've said, he's like this because of you?"

"Yes," she found it hard to speak louder than a whimper.

"How did you cause this form?"

Jane looked at her questioningly, "no, this . . . as long as I've known him, is what he's been."

The maid servant quickly returned with a cart of hot water and a spool of linens and clean rags of shabby quality to discard without remorse. Jane lifted his ligaments, to help the servant, as she worked. The rags had dried up in a cake of silvery black substance. She replaced it with a clean wad and cloth.

"Those garbs, my dear, are poor, and unfit too," and she rang a bell, and in came the servant with bundled weaves of fine cloth.

And Jane left that to a dressing room, where a different servant almost fought to get her in. To Jane it was a restricting sensation just to put on. And there was certainly no plate woven underneath. There were layers of red and white overlaid over Jane's thin but shapely physique. In silver thread were embroidered symbols of the royal family, around the sleeves and the bosom. The sleeves along her arm ballooned out, but at the wrist they came back close to her skin.

When she returned, she walked stiff with a flushed face. Lady Thinithe remarked proudly, "a good dress for a real lady."

"It's, well, revealing. It's beautiful indeed, but I can't accept this. I'm not some lady or noble. And I was fine in those normal clothes you gave me when we came."

"No, no, no, my dear. You bring a light in this stuffy house, and if you're not a lady, then it's a gift."

Jane sighed, "why are you helping hide us?"

"You're asking now?"

"Yes."

Lady Thinithe too sighed, and said, "in my heart this faith is not native, nor is it a belief of my dearly departed, but it was a promise he made long ago to a malkin I do not believe I'll ever have acquaintance with."

"Would anyone else know of you?"

"Quite possibly yes, including other malkin, but if you've met this malkin I heard from him, but I'm not sure that's plausible. Because it happened during the war, most likely before you were born."

"No, I was born before it, but I never experienced it. I don't remember anything from that time. I was too young."

"It hurt him," she said looking at a painting on the wall.

"I feel guilty."

"About Litus?"

"Yes, I . . . I feel guilty, because we're here talking about dresses."

"If you spend every dying day worrying, it'll never pass, and if every day is worryful, than every day is torture. You are worrying about means outside your control, and that is ultimately wasteful, but having a sliver of worry in moderation keeps to the heart."

Jane looked towards the door, "it is truth below the skin of the world."

Jane didn't speak, "he will wake," Lady Thinithe said, while Jane left.

The moon hung directly above, and soft streams fell through the panes of glass. "Has he awoken?"

Jane looked up from her chair, by the bedside, "no," she said, "not yet."

By Lady Thinithe's weary side, that little boy crept by, and she looked at the boy questioningly, "Simon, please leave, this is not a scene for young eyes," and he looked up at his grandmother and without a word, left like she asked, and closed the door behind them.

"He's the only family I have left, my son died of the plague nearly five years ago, and the same with his wife. It swept through so many, did you have anyone who you lost because of it?"

Jane shook her head, "no, I lost my mother before, during winter, years ago."

"And your father?"

"I was never told, besides that he did something great."

"But that's not all, is it?"

"In such a short time, everything happens all at once."

"It does always seem like that. When hit by a wave of uncertainty, the wave will either crash, or it will fall back into the water quite inconsequentially."

"What does that mean?"

"Without much impact."

"What if it doesn't end?"

"A hundred and fifty years ago, during the yellow plague, those who were blamed more than anyone else were the Malkin and the Gypsy's. Then five years ago during the little plague, it was again blamed on the Malkin and Gypsy's. Even though that plague swept by for only a brief moment, it took all except Simon and my now weary self. Chaos is a mare; when it bucks, you tame it, you fall, or ride a different horse."

"But I don't have any other horse."

"That's what you think. He'll live, the prophet twisted the hands of Pias and his watchmen. He will find a way. And you've played with swords!?"

Jane spoke after brief silence, "yes," she said, "but they're not toys, but tools. I used swords before, if that's what you're asking?"

"Hush. My son was a royal guardsman to the queen, and in his chamber there's a sword. While Litus is waiting to wake, as long as you keep that sword safe, you can use it to trail and what not. To keep the demons from your head."

"Are you sure?"

"I don't think it's lady-like to hold a sword, especially of others. But I can see writings on the walls, and see into the clouds and see stars."

"Can I go see this sword?"

Lady Thinithe nodded and rang a bell, "now do remember, my son was a royal officer, they've been given beautiful swords, and once Simon comes of age it will be his inheritance. So don't mar the edge, or else it will be a crime against my name."

A servant came to the door, "good night, my lady," and she was escorted.

The chamber was surprisingly small, although it still held a bed that could hold a half dozen people without much effort, it felt small. She kept peering at that bed, feeling a shadow which lay there. She darted her eyes, as Simon hung by the door, "your grandmother doesn't want you in here," and the boy ran off.

On an armor stand and standing mirror were the sword on the armor's hip. The hilt was a crossguard extending out of a basket of blue steel, and as she unsheathed the long straight blade, Jane noticed it cut through the dust in the air. There were scratches along the blade, which made it look like a feather. At first the blade seemed heavy, but eventually it felt right.

For some time she tried to practice, but without no one, nor nothing to spar with kept her at a standstill. She felt silly swinging the sword mindlessly. She inevitably resheaved the blade, and left the room.

She walked down stairs, when a heavy thud met the front door. A maid immediately came to the door, and greeted the men on the other side. They spoke loudly and proudly, "the residence of Lady Thinithe?"

The maid bowed, saying, "what can I assist you with, gentlemen?"

"We have had some difficulties with two murderers who escaped as of recently. Have you come across a thin blonde woman and a man in black?"

"Well, I cannot say I have. What time of day was it when they had escaped?"

Jane moved further down the stairs, but tried to remain away from the door. She hid between a window and cabinet of plates and masks. She put her ear towards the words. "Midday was when. But you've not seen them? It was only a few days ago."

"You assume they came this way?"

"May I speak to Lady Thinithe, myself?"

"It is quite late, gentlemen, Lady Thinithe is in bed. If you want to speak with my lady, then you need her permission. I can relay to her, but you'd need to come some other day."

"Fine."

"I will bring notice to my lady, and you gentlemen, have a good night."

Their plate shuffled as their scabbards tapped against their sides, and they stomped away. When the door closed, Jane and the servant woman exchanged eyes, and said nothing.

The morning rose all. Jane sat at the chair by Litus' bed, and his eyes opened. He looked to the side, as saw Jane, and then saw the others. Then he rose.

Jane was silent as they circled the empty quiet room. Small slashes came and found quick blocks and repos, but fell away to circling. She stayed silent, and measured him. Litus too tested with three to four small slashes about, before feigning the fifth and lunging the wooden sword forward. Litus pushed her back five to six feet back. She stepped further back close to a wall, and she kept her wooden sword outstretched. She quickly pulled the pommel close, and kicked off the wall.

Litus jumped to the side, and put his sword above hers and forced it down. He took a step back, swinging the sword up. Jane stepped to the side, while turning her blade in. Litus turned to face her, and kept guard. She made small attacks forward, and feigned her blade. She leaned forward, making strikes to keep Litus from striking. And he threw her thrust to the side, and swung low while delaying his attack. It cut through her offense, throwing her to defense.

They attacked and parried back and forth, sparks flew from their blades. Infront their blades connected, for that brief moment they saw each other's eyes.

Jane pushed her palm against the side of her blade, pushed down Litus' sword. Her blade was to his neck. And she kept the end of the wooden sword there. He put down the sword, and she hers. Sweat beaded on her face and hands.

Chapter Sixteen:

It came with a letter, at the door of the next day by a servant woman with a silver plated tray.

In the sea of poppies, there lay the princess.
She dreamed so fondly, to be the queen.
And the true king comes to be killed.
They ran under the trees of yearn.
The wet dirt softly held the old king.
The flight of a bird is a fascinating sight,
When the winter sky obscures all the land,
With blood red poppies for the puppet god.

Little time passed, between having and reading the passage, when the servant woman beckoned them to follow. They were brought to Simon's room. Lady Thinithe brushed his head, and he had a cough that was sickly and sticky. Lady Thinithe turned her head slightly when she heard the door creak. "I sent you a poem I've heard from my late husband, who heard it elsewhere. But I asked you because your time here is ending soon. I've heard rumors, and told of sightings of soldiers just 'passing' by. And I'm afraid I can't help much further, and you'll have to go."

She looked to the child once more, "but you two have been good company, I know Simon liked hearing you two spar through the door. And I know it felt more lively as well. But I have to think about Simon above all else. I'll ask you to leave by the night."

Silence hung in the stale air. Lady Thinithe continued, "I'll accommodate you as much as I can muster, for what you can give this world will be much more than what I'll give to you. And myself and my estate will try to do what we can for you two. To escape this city."

"So suddenly?" Jane said with some disgust, "thrown out in one go."

"I don't want it to be like that."

"Is he not your prophet?"

"He may or may not be, while Simon is my grandson, and my last child. This kingdom is brutal."

"We've seen terror."

"This kingdom is governed by cruelty and conspiracy."

"And?"

"I've witnessed every decade or two, a conspiracy arises and stirs individuals to commit terrible acts against others."

"This is irrelevant."

"And the queen responds with force over all."

"What are you getting at, why are you saying this?"

"This kingdom isn't meant for this faith and any other faith. You need to keep moving, and never stop. Follow the waves, or drown. There's no breaking this way. I'll try and get a cart and mare to bring you to a town outside of the city, but time is no longer on your side."

She brushed Simon's head, Thinithe said, "his fever has developed in the night, and grown worse by every hour. Even worse, is that the well water has been tainted, boiling doesn't seem to cure it. So please this may be a stretch, but I ask you two, to fetch some water by the river side."

"Why us? You have servants who aren't wanted by the crown," Jane questioned.

"Currently, your dear, I trust you over my servants."

"Then why do you still have them around?"

She sighed, and looked over her shoulder and said, "I need them."

Litus handed her the pad, glancing down at the text, she directed her eyes on Simon again. "A world without fear, without innate misery. Please go fetch water by the river bed, the water is fresh there. It's up the street, it's easiest by going through the park entrance. Just ask a servant for a pitcher, they won't refuse."

"What if we're seen!" Jane exclaimed, "we're still being looked for. Why would you send us out then."

"You must go, I don't want any servants possibly poisoning the water! And your hair will help you, no one south of Renoi has hair as fine or noble like yours will interrupt you. I also have clothes for you Litus that would fit. A cloak of royal blue."

"Why don't you trust them, they could kill you now?"

"They don't want to be executed for murder, they would rather kill me slowly. Just go get that water, I need it to make tea, because Simon is sick, and I need you. Now go!"

"Why?" Litus wrote down on a piece of paper.

Lady Thinithe looked at his piercing eyes, a tear welled up in her eye. "Let my sins be forgiven. Watchmen will be here soon, and I need you two to be away in the meantime. They know, but they need to be sure. I'm sorry," she looked back down at the child, "but I do need water from the river. Please, you must go."

They were escorted back to their room, with new garments, and told to change by the servant woman. "What is she hiding from us? Why does she not trust us now? I can't trust her now, she deceived us. She had us stay with her, but can't keep us here?"

Litus wore a cloak of similar proportions to his own, only made of a blue fabric with silver etching along the edges, and when worn it covered his face almost completely but only for those viewing him. He drew the wooden mask of scrolls, and slowly placed it on his face.

"How could she do this to us, we've only tried to help her," she took a minute to gather her thoughts trying to think it properly through, "maybe she didn't deceive us, but why did she do that, so suddenly. I don't know where to put it, she does it out of safety for herself, why can't she trust us to tell us? Will she turn us in? We could just run? What would she do then?" She dressed in a thin ball gown, of similar red and white and royal stitches.

They left with a pewter pitcher, and the masks that partially obscured their vision. They tried to walk the streets slowly and make themselves as unassuming as possible. And down the cobblestone streets they strode. The further down the block they came to thinner roads, with again blood red brick building complexes. Terracotta tiles stacked like scales, capped the crown. Windows seals were distinct with striped red and white bricks, and inlaid were cast steel barricades. They once were a symbol of a greater livelier time, but since the war, the bricks became more symbolic that homely.

They could see a brick archway with a metal park sign, and above was a partially brick but mostly wooden bridgeway with people above looking down with finely made dresses and masks. It led to a building above the arch itself.

"Litus?" And he looked at her, "do . . . Do you trust her? Do you think she betrayed us?"

He shook his head, "if she lied once, could she lie twice?"

And again Litus shook his head, he did not know why, but he did.

The entrance of the park was a large garden of hedges and flowers and tall plants. The flowers were of red and black petals.

There were small patches of fruit larger than Jane had even seen, and hedges shaped like benches. On the right clearing into a sandy embankment was the small river of Pelite flowing through a tall aqueduct embedded in the ground. The water was clear, but the level was low.

A hundred or so feet up the river, behind a wall of tall thickets of trees, was a large wide bridge with a wooden building atop it. Jane noticed it when climbing down a cast steel ladder embedded in the stone of the aqueduct.

She read it, but didn't shrug it off. She pointed out the bridge and said, "over there what do you think that's for?"

Litus shrugged, *I don't know,* and it showed in his posture.

They had started to head back with the pitcher filled with a strange anxiety shaking in their steps. Past the hedges were two soldiers with sabers at their sides, positioned at the sides of the arches. They were lucky when they arrived when the soldiers were rotating duty. They politely trickled out of those soldiers' sight, and Jane said, "I don't think we'll be able to just walk by, they could ask us who we were. Or would arrest us for no reason. We could fight and win easily, or subdue them subtly."

He shook his head, and pointed to other people in the gardens. "They'd rather want us caught."

Jane looked around the park, and saw on the other side a mirror of the garden. With buildings built up against the walls, and a stairway made of romantic stone leading up to the buildings atop the wall.

Litus wrote in the dirt, "wait."

"Wait what, for them to rotate? It could be hours. Besides, the longer we're here, the more likely they'll ask questions, or kill us. No, that bridge, we can cross it, and easily come back. Look, there's no guards there."

The entrance of the bridge far down the river was held in a strange forest of overgrown and unkempt trees. As they quietly and subtly entered and pushed through all of the thickets, there in plain view was a simple bridge without rails, and windowless. Above the second half-floor was the roof of simply stacked clay tiles. From outside-in they heard small thumps in a rhythm, and as they walked closer to those walls, they heard the sound of a sand-like substance being poured in the water below.

In the wall there was a massive door with a smaller door embedded, but both were locked or stuck. The building was unconventionally wider than the bridge itself, and off to the right side they climbed a wooden staircase to the second floor door, and still the sound of small thumps that permeated through the wall.

Jane whispered to Litus, "I don't want to see what's through there," she glanced up, "the roof is low, and surely sturdy?"

Litus leaped up grabbing the ledge of the roof. On top of the roof, he grasped his hand out. The roof started to shift; she took his hand, but as Litus started to pull her up the shingles shattered under his weight. Crashing through, he fell and crashed to the first wooden floor, and Jane fell back onto the landing.

Litus was surrounded by shattered barrels, and a coarse white powder. It smelled somewhat like hay or wheat. And he was stuck on a platform above the water, with openings, and a . . . a thing. It was a twelve foot tall beast, with charred porous skin like a sponge or coal stretched over it's bulbous, and brawny figure like stretched leather. Horns like sheep of the same charred characteristic protruded from the sides of the thing's head, and it's shaped like a gargoyle. Equipped their hands were knife-like fingers, and they gripped the barrel of that powder.

The giant gargoyle threw the empty barrel down, finding out with it's dull eyes, what fell from the ceiling. The ground vibrated after each step; Litus tried to get up. The beast saw with his own grotesque eyes the shadow that lay. As the beast drew close, it towered over Litus. He drew out a sword and tried to thrust forward. The beast silently groveled, and quickly moved forward. Swinging its leg, and kicking Litus into the wall. Jane gasped but it wasn't audible under the wood splintering.

Jane got up from the landing, and opened the door above. Inside against the walls were stacks of barrels, and broad walkways which wrapped around the walls below. She could see them from above as the gargoyle monster slowly and threateningly stalked towards Litus' body. "Get up," she whispered.

She weaved between the barrels which were stored there. The dust which settled on the surface was thick and stuck to her hands. She grunted trying to push the barrel directly over the beast. It glared up, and tried to reach for Jane with its tall hands. And she gave one last strong shove, and the barrel fell and thrashed over the gargoyle's head, splitting the barrel in many pieces and sending bits flying.

Litus eventually got up, and found his footing. He held the sword, and while the gargoyle did appear staggered, he quickly thrusted the blade into its leg, giving it a shock of more pain. Litus jumped back into the wall, when the monster recoiled with a swing. Smashing barrels in the way. Litus kept weaving out of the way while the powder crowded the air.

As that powder singed as it floated, it didn't appear to affect the gargoyle whatsoever. This powder was his exercise, and he was accustomed to it. He raised a barrel high above his head, and launched it like it was merely a stone. By nearly the last second, Litus jumped out of the way. It passed by him with a stream of white dust until it crashed and puffed a cloud soaring high.

The white powder exhausted up and onto the second floor. Jane backed away as it happened, but still it singed her eyes and breath. She coughed with a sickening flem, and tried covering her nose and face with the cloth of her sleeve. She fell back as the flood drifted towards her, but just as quickly as it entered it fell with a heavy density. But a few seconds lost in a fight is a grave mistake. The crash of a barrel, brought her back towards the edge. She saw the gargoyle below her heave with great force a barrel across the room. Litus dodged it, splinters exploded around him.

She ran above where the gargoyle stood, in attempts to drop another barrel. It jumped high, trying to bring Jane down, but instead a barrel came crashing down on the gargoyle's own head, and again a powdery white dust cloud spread around the beast.

The beast turned and shot up, reaching for a barrel to throw. Litus ran with his blade out ready to strike through the covering cloud. As the beast raised a barrel high, a grotesque slice ran down its arm. It thrashed around, and vibrated the bridge until the dust danced on the surface of the floor. Litus thrustred again and made another gash upon the gargoyle. And the monster – with fuming vitriol – rammed Litus into the wall, and crashed while doing so. The gargoyle stood stationary, before falling back into the water.

Litus kept a handle of his sword as the beast fell back, revealing the black and red ooze drenched blade which dribbled onto the ground and bubbled with contact of the powder. Jane came down from the ladder, and stood next to Litus. All went silent as they looked around the building and truly wondered what it really was. "People drink that water, that powder, what is it?"

Litus came to a barrel, the side had painted on said nothing, but attached to the top was a small parchment. He turned the paper to Jane; his blood stained hands now partially smeared the label.

"Corrosive tonic, barrel one seventy-third. Water cleaner – slash – royal root concentrate?"

"Royal root concentrate," again, she murmured, "what does that mean? What does this do?" She took a second to think, "does Lady Thinithe know? About this?"

They exited through the large bay door's smaller door, and tried to act somewhat naturally. *Is this drug poisoning their minds? Are the nobles and the soldiers drinking this water?* At that thought, they could peer out and see an incoming group of soldiers seemingly mesmerized by the fresh bleeding body in the river aqueduct.

They quickly dashed across the small forest, as they again watched a series of soldiers in a marching line come through the park side opposing them. In the garden parks there weren't any people to blend in with, just a field of red flowers with the end being that decorated staircase. Behind them, from inside the bridge, shouting ensued, and soldiers passed onto the other side.

They ran upstairs, and people dressed in elegant garbs began gathering around the windows of the hall. They looked out and murmured at the river and the beast that drowned. Dust fell off their clothes as they shimmied through the crowds. Soldiers' yells could be heard still through the tall windows. They tried to find someway out, but were ultimately pushed to a hall less packed, with a trail that now loosely followed.

They walked down what felt like a maze of halls, before finding stairs that led down, and out onto the thin city streets. Litus looked around, trying to find some landmark that made sense, and when he finally found one he brushed himself off and walked. "You're not going to her, are you?"

He felt an urge push him further. And he ran up the streets, as soldiers passed by him, with horses, saws, and giant woven bags.

The next street weren't multihomed buildings, but those now familiar walls. And near the end, was the home of Lady Thinithe. A murder of royal watchmen crowded the door and with sabers in hands, as they broke down the door. "She betrayed us!" Jane said, "don't go."

She grabbed his hand, but he didn't go. There he saw those soldiers grab onto servants, and forced them out with a blade to their back. Jane peered over, and recoiled just as quickly, "she betrayed us," she said quietly, and her eyes not blinking, "why would she do this?"

Around the corner to great horror, Litus watched what continued to transpire. At that moment Lady Thinithe was pulled by her neck, onto the cobblestone ground. The grandson Simon was with the rest. The watchmen commanded by a man with a head higher who openly held no sword barked at the woman. He spoke words unintelligible to them, from where they stood.

Jane pulled on his arm. "Go! "We need to go! Before they find us. Litus?" She said, but Litus wasn't ready to go.

He reached into the void, and jumped the guards from behind with a blade to the back of the neck. He quickly twisted the blade to the first, and then the second, and a third man ran away blowing a whistle which pierced their ears.

Lady Thinithe laid on the ground blue and bruised, and possibly dead. Jane to Litus pushing him to the ground, "what are you doing? Run. Run!"

Litus jumped on foot after the whistle blower, and Jane inevitably followed.

The tower of black, the tower of watchmen, could be seen above the buildings in front of them. The watchman pushed away commoners wherever he went, and blew his whistle every few steps. He drew a heave of attention onto the two from people around. The powder had by now fully disappeared from his cloak, but the small regiment of soldiers were still on pursuit.

Jane grabbed Litus' hand, yanking him to stop, and said, "there is no turning back now."

The buildings block by block, and the streets began to widen. And up ahead they could see the castle walls and towers of castle Renoi, in a glittering white and red brick with tall purple banners hanging from all around.

"Stop!" Jane yelled at him, "stop this!" And he stopped.

"Look over there, that tall black tower. Do you know what that is? They carted me there, and . . . did things to me. Now you're running directly there. What do you think will happen?"

Litus looked over, and the watchman was nearly gone from his sight. All there were were the tall brick buildings around them. The walls around some noble houses, the castles and spires of another landmark. But that tower of featureless black basalt was the center. He saw that watchman reach within shouting distance of the only gated entrance in sight, which was kept by a duo of halberd equipped guards.

"Run, go hide down the alley, I just got an idea."

When the guards came marching in a fury, Jane approached them, she told them in such a tone that spoke of fright, and inside she was afraid, "that thief ran down the street, I saw it after he stole my purity. I believe he went down the alley on the far right there, maybe the third or forth so."

The guards and the watchmen pounced with angry stomps forward. Jane kept ten or twenty feet back, then fell into that first alley on the right where Litus sat behind a crate and chair. She whispered to him in a tone of complete fury, "why in all of the lord's cries, would you fucking go, why? You could have killed yourself, then you run straight after the prison. Why? Beyond that gate under the ground is that . . . dungeon, why?"

Litus had taken out his paper to write. Jane had already begun walking away, she checked her corners and continued. Litus followed. They ran past the street and in the alley across. "We need to find a way out of this city, or escape those following us. If we went by ship it would be an easier way out, but we just have to find docking and a merchant or fairy sailor who would let us aboard."

"I had to," was written on the paper, she was silent. *I had to?*

Chapter Seventeen:

There were watchmen after them, following what trace was left by those corrosive crumbs. The watchmen didn't know which street they were on, or if they were in a building or alley, but they were sweeping the city.

To their east a salt smell in the air appeared to be floating from the coast line. It was only a few blocks down, but near was that black prison tower. It loomed over with a gloomish cloud, like the sky. There were watchmen and guards strewn around, because of that tower, and the high nobility's hired thugs. It seemed that as long as they looked greater than peasants, they weren't immediately poised as traitors.

They left to find an open general store. The morning was still upon them, and the air was a cool crisp. In this case what seemed open by a lit lantern, was a standard inn. With a standard name in these parts, "the Crowned Crane inn."

They walked in viewing the interior. Inside a slew of benched tables coursed with fatty foods, and sugary fodder, and at those tables were men of many forms, statures, and what little coins were around. Some would call it homely, others poor. Only one or two were most likely criminals, all the rest something worse: blind loyalty. They interacted with only the innkeeper – who manned the front – since by that time he would have a chance of alerting the watchmen. The city would be looking for long gone fugitives. The innkeeper was sitting upright at his desk while brushing off any speck that may have fallen, and all with a proud smile atop his face. "What can I get for you?" He said in a grand voice, "bed? I have soft warm beds, along with a two meal course. Breakfast and supper. All for a quarter of a silver a night, and one full silver a week."

He didn't have a mask on his face, but he had one on the wall above, and it was an especially decorated mask. "No no, we aren't looking for bedding, I just need some guidance," Jane said looking at that mask.

"Guidance, huh, on what? Your psyche, your budgeting, how long you plan to stay with us?" He clapped his hands together.

"We aren't looking to stay, we're passing by to ask for guidance."

"Guidance?" He said, "guidance. Hmm," he murmured, "come sit, sit. The benches are warm and so is the fireplace. I'll have a good fine woman tend to your needs, for I have other things to deal with, so please sit. Come sit."

"We just need to know where the docks are."

"No, sit. Sit," he said assuredly with that everlasting grin on his face.

They eventually sat down in the benches, and a large bosomed woman brought Litus a pint, and Jane a goblet. As quickly as she accommodated them, she had disappeared, and stolen the gaze of many around. Litus played with the mug, swirling it around, while Jane refused to touch that goblet. Eventually when the woman returned – with a sway in her step – she leaned down, and said, "why're you letting the dust drink?"

"We just want to know where the docks are?"

"For voyage, at this time of year? You'd have better luck than if the queen herself walked through the door. Are you foreigners? Don't you know what is happening soon?"

Litus looked around, and Jane said with caution, "no, I don't. What's happening?"

"The queen's ball! Oh what excitement! You haven't heard of it, what a shell you live under. I guess you two are some, some foreigners?"

"Well we're not, well, foreigners."

"You're not? With the way you walk? Where are you from then?"

"South of here."

"South? I didn't think there was anything down there," and she chuckled, "after such a long traversal, you should take a drink and rest too."

"Please, could you tell us where the docks are, and we'll be out of your hair."

"Oh no, dears, you're not in my hair. Honestly far from it. If I may ask, where are yall heading?"

"Well this city is just a small stop, and we'll be heading away soon."

"I think you two are quite interesting."

Jane didn't speak, and the woman continued while swaying slightly, "if you're going far, wherever it is. I think you might need a bed, just for the night, and I can assure you I can get you a discount for your stay."

"Alright then," Jane sat, and like Litus, played with the goblet, and said, "where is the dock, if I ask?"

"Well, they are east of here, follow down the street, and along the block up north, then you'll see the coast. Most merchants and navy ships are docked these recent weeks. But in about a week they'll be open for us normal folk. Now if you wait here, I will be back in a moment."

But as Litus and Jane left their seats, and headed out, the man at front, said in a loud bassy voice, "wait I need your names."

"Names?"

"Yes."

"We don't know how to spell it, but I can get a spelling for you soon."

He gave them a queer look, but quickly accepted, and then went about his workings dealing with his actual guests. But the moment Litus and Jane left the door, they walked as swiftly as they could and they could first hear a commotion through the walls, and then they could see through a window in the side, both the woman and that man running and watching them run away, and looked with snake eyes.

They walked down the street, eyeing every alley, and building. Once a woman opened a window to let dust out of a carpet. Eventually the sea mist hit their senses, when the smell of salt stained the air. The streets were wider, most were twice in width, and they could see the incoming many many men and merchants with their goods going elsewhere.

Chapter Eighteen:

The docks were manned every inch, with sailors, sellers, and strong men too. Carrying crates of fruit, and jewelry, or other high commodity goods like exotic salted meats. Nearly all of the ships carried two flags, the flag of the queen and another of three wavy colors: blue, yellow, and beige. "Those sailors, not the ones in black, the tanned ones in white, I'm certain they're from Hule."

Litus and Jane walked to ships here and there, hoping to meet with their captains. The strong men and sailors cussed them out, for being in their way, but they persisted.

Litus pointed to a ship with less activity at dock, and Jane said, "hopefully they'll let us board.

They walked up to who they believed was the captain who sat at a table outside tallying down on paper, in fine robes, and a mask pendant rather than one around his face, and said, "look at all those ships, my lord. What kind of ball is this?"

The supposed captain looked at them both surprised, but also relieved, and he said with a grin, "that," as he waved his hand all around what was in sight, "and costly."

"Are you the captain of this ship?"

His face strangely soured, "captain, no. That's a misused title for anyone who isn't manning a sail or cleaning. I'm the quartermaster. I deal with everything that doesn't deal with directing the ship, or leading the men. And why do you come to me, are you looking for trade?"

"Where are you traveling to, after this?"

"Excuse me," he asked leerily, "are you the royal captain, you don't look so, do you. Be off beggar! Thief!"

"No you misunderstand, we want to seek a voyage out. Can you accompany us?"

He looked up from his chair with an eyebrow raised. "You want to take up my time which is quite important right now, and delay much riches for possible voyage out?"

Litus nodded, and Jane said, "yes."

Then the quartermaster took a firm good look at their clothing, and then again at her facial features. "Well my fair lady," he looked down at his document, "I currently won't have room aboard food now, but later when this ship is empty I can rent you a room or two. Depending on the coin you must have, I will charge little for you and your praise."

Jane pinched for her pouch of coin, and put it down on the table, "may I?" He asked. The quartermaster lifted it up a few times, Litus then snatched up the pouch which dumbstruck the man, "what do you thi-"

"Where are you sailing?"

"Where, well, this ship is set to voyage to the city of Breen, up north."

Litus put the pouch down, and then in a posthumous-like tone he wrote down on his document, and said, "welcome aboard miss . . . "

"Just, Lady, for now."

"So be it, Lady and her . . . banker."

A sailor relayed, and the captain was told about the sudden inclusion on deck, and they escorted Litus and Jane to a cozy little room underdeck with some thin beds. *This is too good to be true?* Litus thought, and he readied to draw from the void, just in case.

But time went and passed, nothing came of disturbances. Jane had noticed Litus in reach for his sword for quite a while, "I'm nervous too. What if they were to bring us in front of those soldiers?"

Jane's hands seemed to shiver. "I think there's a draft," she looked outside, and all there were was legions of soldiers, and she said, "will it be all over?"

He took her hand with both of his, and she said. "With all this running, I haven't had time to think about what has happened. I can't believe what they did to Lady Thinithe. They beat her, right in front of her grandson. I'm sorry Litus, I'm sorry."

Litus forgave her with a nod, and she quickly said after, "I really hope the road to the city isn't as cruel as now."

They could hear only the sound of the waves crashing against the hull, making the ship rock slightly. " Before I met you all I had in life was living alone with the possessions of my passed mother. About every week or so, I would take a trip to Deinde, and buy food or supplies. I had always heard about Tolk, but never met him until that day. Eventually I decided to protect myself by my late fathers sword until it dulled, that's when I met the smith. I hope he survived the fire that day. And the guards have always been serious about their duties, it annoyed me back then, but now I'm glad they were so committed to protecting everyone. So I guess my annoyance helped them get attacked, that's what it seemed like. I hope you are that prophet, because I don't know anymore."

Litus listened and responded with his eyes, but wished he could truly respond back. The lack of voice is the lack of time. He could write down his feelings and thoughts, but it could never convey the same temper he could wish for. For a moment there was silence, besides all the muted outside. A stomach grumble took the air. "Maybe we shouldn't have been so hasty at the inn, do you want to come and retrieve what sort of food may be on this ship?"

He obliged, and they left those quarters. They went further below deck where they stored food, it was mainly crates of hardtack, salt, limes, and wine. Of course they snatched up a little of all. Jane led Litus onto the deck, and she ate some of what she nabbed. Out there scrambling on the docks were a series of sailors, all accounting for the cost and goods for the royal ball.

Coming to the ship was a troop of sailors all donned with similar gear to that of the watchmen and royal guards, but instead they wore black. On their surcoats were silver embroidering of another even older royal symbol. It was of two curved blades interconnected, without hilts or guards, just the blades. Leading the troop was a man with a confident step of experience. He was adorned with a decorated silver saber, and a velvet black tricorn hat.

Each step from his boots was audible from the docks. He walked with a sort of disconcert about the opinions around himself, and to everyone he seemed higher. He came to the quartermaster and he asked, "you sir, the quartermaster?"

The quartermaster in a quick movement shot up straight and without waver, he said, "yes, yes, I'm the quartermaster do you ask for our charts?"

"Why would I not? Give them to me."

The quartermaster then gave him the document that contained the goods acquired and anything to do with the ship. "Twelve barrels of hard cheese wheels, thirteen casks of Lumoi red wine, two crates of pink salt, and your sailor count is twelve, not including the captain or yourself. How does that make sixteen passengers? What is this lady and banker you have written here?"

"Well, these two, a noble lady and her banker came asking for a voyage. And they paid for their space on the ship. There's nothing wrong with that?"

"Nothing wrong with that? Nothing wrong with it? This is the time of a great royal ball, what noble would want to leave at such a musing event?"

"I believe I did ask them, but they refused to say."

"If they refused to stay for the ball as nobles, some great nobles, what noble Lady would disgrace the queen like that. Don't you say that's strange and suspicious?"

"Well, Yes captain."

"Excuse yourself when making wrongful accusations, I'm not some low quabling captain, I'm a commodore. I in good graces took place in the limited supply of captains in the capitol. But get your ranks right unless you want to get deposed by your crew."

"Yes commodore, they are inside. If you mean to see them."

The commodore and a few of his men walked onto deck. Hands on their swords, while the commodore himself with calm hands went on his search.

Litus and Jane had looked over the deck to see dozens of armed sailors. They ran to their quarters, and they knew there was no escape, except by voice. So when the commodore and his men arrived, Jane greeted him, and the commodore the same. "Heard there was a noble lady aboard, now I find one above just nobility, you must be the daughter of a duchess. Is that correct?"

"A duchess, no. I'm just a noble lady. Awaiting great sailing," Jane followed trying not to attract too much attention. The aura of power given was persistent, and poignant.

"Yes yes. Noble lady, as I was expressing to your quartermaster, why would anyone of your seatings want to leave on the coming occasion of the ball? Especially with, well, a banker?" He eyed Litus casually.

"Banker, no, that quartermaster is jesting, he's my personal guard."

He snapped his finger just as casually as breathing, and the sailors took them by their arms. "Lying on official documents, especially when it deals with the royal navy, and the crown herself, is a cruel crime, and now you say it's a comic, a jest. The queen doesn't rule with jests."

"Put me down," Jane yelled out before having her face snuffed with a bag. And Litus fought back, but due to the small space and the impossibility of escape, and was forced to surrender, *just for now.*

They were split up, Litus was carted towards the black stone tower, and Jane was escorted by the commodore someplace else. Her cell wasn't filled with grease and blood covered stone that the cells under the tower had. Neither did her cell have a lack of light from the sun or candle. She was in a home far bigger and more extravagant than Lady Thinithe's. Her hands were in chains behind her back, and she stood in the middle of a hall. Sitting quite comfortably close to her was the commodore himself. He held his hand out and was given the key by one of his own guards. Then with just a subtle wave of his hand, they left.

Jane tried to read her situation, all she thought was that she was being used, *he thinks I'm a noble woman, and if I say who I really am, I'll be sent to the gallows. With Litus.* She went to talk but was cut off almost instantly by the commodore, "greetings miss . . . Lady, I haven't heard your name yet, have we. If I give mine formally I ask the same for you. I'm commodore Tylock, I'm second commodore in the Royal Navy, and leading the import's for the royal ball. Now I ask for your . . . formal introduction."

"Where am I?"

"Here, now what is the name of your face?"

"K- Kate," she pushed out.

"Kate? Well Lady Kate, be it you wonder where your banker has gone?"

"You took him to that prison, under the ground, devoid of light. Then you plan to send him and me to the gallows. Would you?"

"Would I, no no. being so close to the crown with actions as cruel as the common foot soldier, would never prove anything of position. Besides he's not under the corrections tower, but atop it. He's more of use to me – with his strange appearance – than you realize. But there is something I want from you more, that you might . . . will want too," he got up from his chair, and unlocked Jane's chains, but still he gripped her hand behind her back, "don't tense up on me, running or fighting won't be happening now. There's more of me than you, but what I want is a negotiation, more and less . . . essentially."

He released his grip over Jane, she didn't run, but stood still over his chilly presence. He went back to his chair, and sat comfortably. "He's not in any harm but yours, if you act like an animal."

"What do you really want?"

He sighed and looked at her face, "to rise in rank through nobility. Easy isn't it?"

"You couldn't muster up the courage to ask some woman to a dance, did you?"

"Are you not some nobility then?"

Jane tried to answer, but he interrupted, "no, of course, you have the nobel traits, but the attitude is unfamiliar. And hands calloused too. No prideful woman would have the hands of a soldier. But you have noble descent clear to all, you've heard that remark since you've been here, which mostly hasn't been long, since you tried to flee the ball by ship in the center of the merchant's influx."

"So what? . . . You plan to show off to me to raise in rank."

He didn't say anything in return, but smirked. "Now about the other part. You won't run because you know that if you do, he will be tried, and well tied. I am an honest man to my word, so under supervision I'll let you visit this man of yours, and then you'll see that you need me, won't you?"

"Bring me to Litus, bring me to him!"

He left his chair, and got up close to Jane, "now now, I say the other part in which I need you. You need to be in fashion for the ball, and I'll personally teach you. The manners, and movement, along with the eating habits, and false modesty. that is why you're here, and not well there," he pointed behind him to a massive window which looked onto that tower in the distance, "now I'll do the honorable thing," he clapped loudly and the doors were sprung open by his guards, "bring her to the prisoners cell, and then back here."

The guards grabbed her by her arms, and she watched commodore Tylock stand, and look out the window, and then the doors were shut by the guards. And they were silent when they shut.

She was escorted by guards there. They didn't bring her in chains, for if seen by nobility at the ball, there would be eyeing and rumouring amongst the crowd and royalty. The tower from the ground was immense, even though it was Jane's second meeting, it was still completely impossibly tall.

The immense wooden doors led to a round room, ahead was a stone spiral stairway, both leading up and down. Jane knew what was concealed down stairs, and Litus knew too from Jane's day on gallows row.

They treaded through the stairwell, with echoing of their steps being the only audible noise. Jane was thinking, *Is this some trap?* The guards brought her to his cell.

Litus was sitting on his bed looking out a porthole. It was a cruel jest to have no bars in the windowsill. They almost expected prisoners to jump down the five fights to death. Jane pushed past the guard, and got to ground expecting the worst. But to her surprise, Litus had not looked beaten, or stripped, but it was as though all they did was escort him to the cell. "Litus are alright, have they hurt you?" She expressed deeply.

Litus shook his head – Jane was relieved – and she grew even more suspicious of Tylock's motives than before. "The commodore is using us for negotiations to raise the lord's ladder, and become great nobility. And he intends to use me, for It seems . . . courting other nobles, and he's planning for you to stay here, to keep me," she came closer to the cell, and whispered, "his promises are in question, I don't know if he will free you, but I have to try anyhow."

Litus understood, but inside he still planned escape, only if it were true Jane would be the sacrifice instead of her. Litus watched Jane depart and leave past the window of the cell. Then all was silence, no guards to be seen, but heard they were there just out of sight. But in the real sense Litus was alone.

Chapter Nineteen:

Jane was escorted back to the palace-like home of Commodore Tylock, there she walked into an introduction of what a lady should look to be. There was a maid without a mask, and with fair skin too. In comparison to Jane, she looked more a maiden, "now I see you envy," Tylock said in a mocking tone, "she will be your servant, to help you in your journey to be beautiful and lady-like. Those war scars will disappear with your calluses. Now go with her, my dear Lady Kate."

She was escorted to a bathroom, with a full porcelain tub. Suds clinged the rim. To Jane the water was scorching hot, she had to wait a minute or two till her skin absorbed the heat. As she bathed, and was helped by her servant, the thinnest of that white powder fell from her skin, along with some dirt, and other stains on her skin. The soap that was used was quite strong, but not horrid smelling, or or burned her skin. Her servant had grabbed a bucket and began washing her hair, and brushing out the numerous dreads. "Look how dirty your hair was, it's quite fine. Like cut quartz. You've been blessed, for hair like this. Now I don't want to intrude on my lord's command, but do you really be of noble birth?"

"No, my mother was a common woman, and my father was a soldier from here."

"You should at least convince me you're noble born, before convincing the ones at the ball. Now are you really of noble birth?"

"Yes, I was born here twenty three years ago, mother a Lady of a great house, and my father general of the royal standing army."

"That's better, but you look younger, like eighteen or nineteen, rather than twenty three, and you also didn't name which house you're born into."

"Well I don't know of many great houses, but I didn't not lie about my age."

"For being a woman of low born, you have quite a fair figure," she noted.

She had the clothes that Jane had washed, and remarked by their quality, "the embroidering is good, but not for what the commodore expects. Greater than what some peasants would have."

"I haven't asked your name, I'm . . . well . . . Kate."

"Stop saying that, a noble woman should always know which words they'll say before she says them," she nudged out the rest of the dreads and marveled at the innate quality of Jane's hair, "my name doesn't matter much, but if I'm commanded to, than I'm Roswell."

After, Jane was escorted by Miss Roswell into that hall of nothing but the table and Tylock. He had dropped his navy regalia in favor of a fine silk shirt, with ballooned sleeves. He looked onto Jane with great appeal and pride. Sitting to his side was a small man, with a fine mustache. He had a kind face, without suspicion, and he also had on a mannequin rack a beautiful dress, and next to him a grand display of garments.

The first dress was unwaveringly beautiful, and his face showed greedy pride. The embroidery of the edges were tightened but not fragile. The cloth too was denser, and the stitching was smaller than a flea. She was urged to try the expensive dress on by Tylock, "it's very, very tight," Jane said while trying to adjust.

"Tailor," Tylock beckoned, and then came to Jane, "your shoulders are too broad to be a fine lady. We'll get those changed."

"My shoulders? Why would the nobility care whether or not I have strong shoulders?"

"In subtlety, my dear dear Kate," he hissed like a snake, "they'll subtly judge you, whether they focus on your figure or not, they'll know. They'll talk amongst themselves, and I," he was right in her ear whispering, "won't let that happen."

He backed away letting the tailor do his due diligence. With a pair of sharp fabric scissors, and a needle and pin, he went to work and accidentally prodded her skin. He noted along with his customizing of this dress, as though Jane were to become a frequent customer. The information included her measurement, from waist, and bust, to what color he likes to look at her in.

After the tailor fitted the dress and other clothes to Jane, he pardoned himself, left, and Tylock had everyone leave. Except for Jane and himself. "What are you planning? You've bought and had me fit into multiple dressings, and your servant girl keeps wanting me to act ladylike before the ball"

"How could you be a lady, when you aren't one. Now if some noble were to peer out their window seeing some wench who I parade as my noble beauty, they would think I'm a fraud. And what would result from that is there," he said pointing out the window towards the tower, "remember?"

Jane remained silent.

"Cheer up, supper is soon, you'll dine with me my dear. My beautiful dear."

Not long after he escorted Jane himself, to a beautiful smaller dining room. This room was surrounded by sconces with warm candles. The table was already set before they entered. "I'll make your plate my noble lady," and he did so filling small portions of bird with gatherings of small vegetables, and himself he didn't make a plate. "Go on, you're my guest, and I must insist you eat before the night falls. Go on," he held a glass.

Jane was hungry indeed, but before she could try the food, she instinctively saw the test start. She went for her glass, and raised it.

Tylock insisted, "you haven't won some tourney have you, lower your glass," and Jane did so, then he poured her a glass of red wine, "goes with roasted duck, doesn't it?"

Jane sipped it, the sweet flavors were almost sickening, but soon she craved it. The meal was slow, Jane would prod at her food, and Tylock would look and take a sip of his glass. The wine level dropped very slowly. Jane took his casual drinking that she was failing his test. As she tested the glass, for a reason unknown to her, she had the wine every time he raised his. Eventually she was beyond tipsy and ready to fall further down the rabbit hole. And when Jane inevitably drank all the wine in her glass, did she then notice his glass. "You haven't been drinking, why?"

Tylock raised his glass up. "Oh Kate, of twenty three, and calloused. What will I ever do with you? But Kate isn't your name, but I see that it is not necessary yet, is it? Come on," he poured her a glass, his was almost full, "not yet."

"Kate is my name," she said with a slight giggle, "that's what my parents name me so."

"No, no low born peasant woman would try to make the world think her daughter was a noble lady with a name like Katheryn. No your name isn't Kate, it's some common name to hide you from the nobles isn't it," he gave a small giggle too, "and that's why you were evading, or escaping this ball. To get away from the nobles isn't it?"

"What?" She said, "why would that matter? No," her words began to slur

"I guess it doesn't anymore, just a fun scenario or what not."

He got up from his chair, and ran a stringed bell for servants to bring Jane to her room and the night fell. She awoke with a hangover that cracked her skull that entire morning. When she had gotten out of bed, it frightened her how the servants were there immediately to dress her. They sat her down and pampered her face with light amounts of makeup. Jane had never bought nor worn any makeup prior, so it felt quite alien for her.

Then off to the table in the great hall, where she saw Tylock sitting in his chair waiting for her arrival. "My dear, Kate. here have a seat," he said with a great emphasis while reaching to pull her seat out, and in. he clapped his hands, and a small team of cooks brought in some trays of silver plated food, "now my dear, how splendid you look, come have a meal for the morning," he grabbed a bottle and pointed it towards Jane.

"I'm not drinking that, you fucking creep. You won't trick me into drunkenness, or anything anymore!"

He stood adjacent, looking down unblinking, and muttered, "chilled soda."

"Chilled soda?" He reached for her glass, and poured one out. The clear liquid fizzed and popped, "what is it?"

"It's a fizzy drink. Try it," he said while sliding the glass towards Jane who looked on with suspicion, he then took it back, and with a quick swig took half the glass. He then pushed the glass back to Jane who carefully sipped the fizzy drink.

After that breakfast, she was then escorted to the bathtub where she was cleaned with flowery soap by her servant. Her skin on her fingertips were softened and wrinkled like a tangerine. She was dressed again in a different, but still elegant dress, and that took half an hour to do. "Do I need a change of clothes after every meal?"

"No, no no," the servant exclaimed, "you've made those previous clothes dirty, it's offensive to address others in any form, including in presence, with dirty clothes. It's rude, and let alone filthy."

"I haven't been in that suit for an hour, how could it of been dirty already, and nobles wouldn't know it of been dirty either."

"Noble lords, and ladies don't and will never have the eye for tools and their sharpness, or love for their fellow man. In pubs or town halls. But what they do have as a gift is the eye of poverty. You need to start acting like a lady, or others will look down on you, instead of at you."

She was allowed to leave under surveillance towards the black tower to visit Litus. She knew that the longer she spent with Litus the longer others would look down upon her, and start to recognize her, so she kept her visit brief. *Why does it have to be so short?*

The rest of the day after descending the stone stairs of the black keep, were almost the same as the night prior, except to a finer detail. Then it was decided by her servant what clothes were heavy enough in layers, and how to eat foods cleaner. Jane looked down at her utensils, grabbing the small fork, and politely said, "why do these forks matter? And why is this one cold?"

"It's the right fork for your meal, why would a stone mason use a sword for masonry?"

"It's just a fork, and a waste of iron."

"Why would a noble woman care about it, if you could afford it, it's yours."

The doors were opened by the guards, and Tylock came through, beside Jane he sat himself, in those chairs of cast iron and cloth. He wore a blouse of black and gold, with cuffs of red, and black trousers with gold lines down the leg. He put his black leather coat, with the naval flag sewn on the breast pocket, on the chair, and forcefully dropped his tricorn hat on the table away from the food. He held out his hand to Jane. She reluctantly gave her hand to him, and there he calmly and firmly observed her hands, feeling her palms.

"Much fairer my dear, no sword in hand, nothing in hand. Much better," Jane wanted to respond, but didn't want to reveal any more information about herself that she hasn't shown through her movements. "My dear Kate, you look so worrisome, what's on your mind?"

"You, and your incessantly need to make me your noble lady."

"I could tell, I shouldn't be able to, because those noble lords and ladies will be able to tell even better so. No, you need to remember to act like a lady, for now, if you want whatever that pacifistic wraith of yours to survive the morning, that is. Now," he clapped his hands, and a servant came to prepare their meal, while Jane tried to keep a blank face. And while they were in the middle of eating together, Tylock observed her face, and informed her, "better."

After dining, he clapped his hands, and told her, "my dear, Kate, sleep well," and then she was escorted by a servant to the room Jane had been occupying, and was redressed in light night wear.

The morning was quite the same as the previous. Jane complained about getting dressed only for a morning meal, and then was held bathed by her servant with floral lye soap. She was allowed to visit Litus but kept her visit brief like the day before. Litus looked almost the same, but his eyes were dilated.

When escorted by guards, she was told to face forward, and look down onto others. And when she refused at first, she was hit in the stomach. The pain was great, and caused her to gasp, but the guard simply put his hand over her mouth to silence her voice.

The rest of that day she refused to speak, even during their supper. All he did was pour Jane a cup of wine, and himself, he refused to speak. His eyes peered through a mask, and they forced Jane to drink from that cup. Finally at the end of the dinner service Tylock spoke up, "now what a bore you are, can't utter in conversation? Did you switch out with your mute friend? Miss Kate," he said like a snake, "this tantrum of yours isn't hurting me you see, only your acquaintance, who's suffering up there. Only you can save him, you see. Oh, but you already know this game. The basic rules that is. You better act like the nobility you aren't, tomorrow, or else, well I wouldn't say. Professional matters aren't for the supper table," he got up to leave, and all he said before leaving the room with those eyes peering at her, was, "have a royal slumber, my dear."

That next mourning, Jane awoke after a slumber of thoughts of never leaving Tylock's side. Or never able to leave his side. That is his face will be that which she sees on her deathbed. The rest of her life, used for his progression, and Litus locked in that tower never to be seen by her again. For in her dream she wasn't permitted to.

Her servant jumped into her room, the second Jane's eyes opened, and the whole charade began once more. She was dressed in a blue sun dress, with black flowers embroidered all along the fabric. When she was escorted to the hall for breakfast, she found Tylock sitting in the same cast iron chair he normally was found in, but his shirt was quite different, it was on the same shade of blue as hers. On the breast pocket was a single embroidered black flower. "Good morning, my dear," he exclaimed, "what a chance your beauty is here. And matching mine as well," he rose to get her chair, and insisted, "sit sit my dear, we have great things coming these next days, of a dance that is. And we need to make time out of the schedule to do so. My schedule is unfortunately busy dealing with those greedy merchant ships, and disciplining those disciples. But fortunately yours is perfectly replaceable. Just to find a slot."

"What time during the morning, or later?"

"My morning time is when we – together – need to make this happen."

"And you're taking away my visits with Litus, isn't it."

"Now that's a perfect time to do so, but I'm not a harsh man, I'll let you visit him today, but only for a brief visit, we have more important things."

She held a silent and fake smile, Tylock noticed, and said, "there, there, my dear, my good dear Kate. oh how you've improved, and such a great influence am I."

"You always were so great," she said, trying to stroke his ego, while subsequently peering down at him with mimicking viperous eyes.

He clapped his hands together, and their breakfast was brought in. He simply started eating, while ushering her to do the same. Of course she did so, while appearing as much of a lady as Tylock liked.

When he finished eating, he clapped his hands and some servant had ushered in to escort the food away, for the service was over. Jane was perplexed by this, because she hadn't eaten nearly as much as Tylock, but didn't want to say a word. Then her servant came to her, and she was brought to the bathing room. Again in the floral scented soap, her hands were scrubbed with a coarse sponge, and a cleaning utensil carved from bone. The servant when scrubbing her hands was particularly amazed by the change. "My lady, your hands have become so much fairer, and paler, and not only that but your palms are so much smoother. Beautiful you've become as of these few days. Only a lady of nobility could reclaim such beauty so quickly."

"I'm not nobleborn, you know that."

"It's a slow process, but it surely shows, my lady."

Again she was allowed to visit Litus, but even briefer than before. The look of Litus's cloak was almost darker, and bluer. And his eyes like shattered glass. In her mind Litus was being drowned by the cell, and whatever they've been doing to him. And the guards posted outside on either side, were silent and pretended to be some stoic statue.

Jane kept her face forward, and looked down onto others who may pass by. When she returned to the manor of the commodore, she was welcomed to dance. There was a small quartet performing a small lullaby-like piece in the other end of the hall. The long table and iron chairs were at the far side, along the wall. Tylock's clothes mirrored that of Jane's dress. His hand was held out, with his palm asking for hers.

"I've never danced before," she watched him with daggers.

"It's alright my dear madame, dancing is like a duel. For it takes two, and is art. You've dueled before, so don't fear, embrace it."

Her hand reluctantly took his, and he swept her in. Jane was like a steel beam, her movements creaked like a rusty spring. Tylock only continued with more emphasis on his movements, in order to force hers. But after a half hour of attempted dancing, Jane's joints felt inflamed. Tylock sounded disappointed, "how much have you failed, Lady what? Kate? No! And now with this much failure I've seen, how could you try?"

"To try at what, dancing? Being a Lady you'd like to show? What, trying to save my companion."

"Ah yes a companion to a peasant girl, with no name, and no place here. How would you begin to of thought, traveling here, bumpkin? And what would your 'companion' have to offer you, or you it. Some sex, some money, how be it?"

"He's saved my life, and giving my sword to him is my debt."

"Debt? Debt!" He laughed hysterically, "what girl, what fool you are. This honor of debt you hold has certainly helped your 'friend's' rotting, and you living with catering, and servants, and nobility. You hypocrite. Either you are playing me a fool, under my own nose, or you are quite possibly the most foolish girl alive. Honor," he cackled at her, "I'd bet for any peasant living under the gray sky, they would live a gray life. Not of pure evil, but neither of pure holiness, but you stand against the nature of everything. Bold and stupid you are, bold, stupid, and terrible at following orders. Get out," a servant escorted her to her chambers, and there she spent the rest of that day. She received her lunch at the door, and supper too.

But that put a thought in her mind, *when this is over will I go with him, where he goes. My debt will be repaid, but still. This wasn't for honor, no isn't. I will save him from that tower, I will do as he says, and then I will return to . . . where? I don't even have anywhere to go. There is no place for me, not here, neither Diende either. I know Litus would let me stay by his side, I don't know why, and still I don't know who he really is, but I hope, I hope for something good to happen for once.* Jane started to pray to the god she had only recently heard of: Selziar. She prayed to this god, and asked for escape, both for herself and Litus.

She wept in the sanctuary of this haven of flowers painted and perfectly human. A voice spoke to her inside her mind, *Dreams are dreams.*

"Is this a dream?"

It is.

"What's over there?"

Reality. It's being held with rope and chain, climb those ropes to see truth. It is known, already.

In a strange way, when Jane awoke, she vowed to take control of the rest of their time together, through a smaller subtler way. She didn't question which vibrant combination of colors were brought to her, or her caked face in powder. In their breakfast period, Tylock looked almost comical with Jane's new perceivable aura. "A good night's rest seems the cure to insanity it seems. You are almost perfectly noble my dear Lady . . . Lady."

He knew when I lied before, will he know again? And Jane said, "grace."

He smiled showing his front teeth, "not quite it."

Jane's face fell, and she uttered, "Jane. My lord."

"But I'm no lord, you see. A navy man that is, but with that kind of speech, I'll be one soon enough. If you speak like that there, they may give me lands. Those real nobles, maybe the queen herself. My Lady Jane. Now be the great noble you are, and harvest what is owed."

Afterwards, she was escorted to the bath, like always. She smelled the room and asked, "different soap?"

"Not at all, my lady."

"It doesn't smell as strong though."

"Does it?"

Jane brushed it to the side, as it wasn't worth wasting energy for.

After washing up, and having her makeup re-applied, she then was dressed in a white ball gown, with a skirt that wasn't too wide, or skinny. When she entered, the hall was draped in thin linens, drowning out some of the sky. Was there always a candle chandelier? She couldn't remember. It wasn't endorned with crustaceous jewels – of various carats – made of cast bronze and a hard dark wood. On each arm were a tall white candle, letting down a soft warm light on the immovable ground.

Tylock beckoned Jane, with his outstretched hand. She took hold, and immediately was drifted along by Tylock. "Now just keep hold, feel the movements with grace."

She was so close to him, but still tried to keep any distance greater than none. She fell forward with their movement. He moved with a sour sort of elegance with his forceful grasp. After only a few stumbling moments, Jane had caught herself and understood what being at the ball would possibly be. She flew with grace, and drifted along the wood lacquered floor. For nearly an hour went, Tylock almost seemed broken with exhaustion, but then to subvert her expectation once more. He just let out a chuckle when Jane expected more perspiration pulsing on his skin. It was a phlegmy throat chuckle, like that of a sick man. "Perfect, oh so perfect, oh lovely, finally finally finally. Just like that, that will show those royal skanks," he laughed, "my dear, you have given me a gift, and after less than a week, I took in a peasant and was blessed with a grand noble lady and lands, oh lands galore," he let out a pant, a drop of hot wax dripped onto the ground, and when Tylock gazed up he noticed the candles were near gone, he exclaimed before departing, "now my dear fetch me a servant to snuff out those candles, and for you, your dripped in sweat, go wash up."

He waved his head back like he was given a slight disappointment from a child and left, and those tall doors closing, was as loud as an old man falling. And as so, Jane went around the almost maze-like halls, and searched for the female servant who helped Jane wash herself, would snuff the candles, but naught. She snuffed the candles, and Jane bathed herself for once, and it was weird not being in someone's constant gaze.

Outside were many soldiers, and soon the kitchen staff came too. With many crates of all types of food and a crate of wine too. She wanted to leave, maybe she could, but she didn't. Eventually Tylock himself came in, his stern face showed neither wrinkles, nor flushness, and his suit was quite the same. His face was blank, like a mask. When he peered unto Jane, he remasked his truth.

That night, when all the same were coming again, she was asked in low tones, "who snuffed the candles?"

"Me," Jane replied with some form of confusion.

"You aren't my servant, you aren't capable of being a servant, your hands are too brittle for their important work, now why would you snuff candles ment for a servant, meaning to discontinue their service I see," he sat and silently sipped his wine, "a true noble recognizes their property is below them, and uses their tools effectively. Remember that in royalty, they're called subjects.

"But let's raise these drapes more. You may not be noble, but you strangely look noble. So now if I may, my lady. Where did you come from? I've just been dying to ask."

"Since you've abducted me?" She wanted to say, but instead, she said, "south of here. Why?"

"Just my growing intrigue, it seems."

The rest of that night was dimmed, the souls drifted as though there weren't some conspiracy occurring. That supper was the same, small conversation, a mask of happiness, over her own tense internal expression. Just before she departed to her quarters and bed, Tylock had motioned her over, and muttered quietly but potently, "tomorrow is our day. Keep that face, I like it more."

She awoke with sweat beaded all across her forehead, and a sense of anguish shaking her nerves. If only she could remember that dream, whatever it may be. It keeps a loom of fear strung to her soul. Once again the moment her eyes peered, a servant was already on Jane's toes. She was ripped out of bed, and put in a poppy embroidered white sundress. Presented with breakfast with Tylock, and after bathed with that faint floral soap. For an hour or two they danced to a small ensemble, she felt the moves mastered by now. Tylock was right, it was like a sword fight. Before the sky dimmed, the gates to the castle would be opened for nobles and men of high ranks.

She was dressed in a thinner ball gown, of stunning red, and crafted with a fabric that shimmered like fire. It wasn't some dress that stretched out the width of a doorway, or gateway, but it more closely clung to her sides than out.

The sky was dimming, the shops and homes kept lanterns lit, and castle Renoi was draped in lines of long candles in glass bulbs, and banner drapes of gold, purple, and black.

Chapter Twenty:

The cell from Litus' perspective was cold and dark, void of natural light, except that which came from the deathly window. Every pestering minute was the same. Emptiness, and the cold draft too. The guards only breathed, they didn't change out, they stood there like statues. Maybe they were statues with a breath whistle breathing wind. Maybe he should escape, maybe the ground is higher than it looked. Maybe so, maybe not.

The day had fallen, the night had risen, the cell was largely the same, except darker. Litus noticed the first movement out of the cell since Jane had been there, a few hours ago. The guards rotated and new ones took their place, as breathing statues. The night fell to midnight, and moonlight's cold piercing wave bounced throughout the cell.

The two were swords in hand. Both long thin bladed, and both grasped their handles with one grip. Their faces were covered in a flesh of bleached tone. Their bodies were dressed in form fitting figures of blood red. They were fighters of flesh and bone. Their swords held out before them, ready for their blades to cross.

He was only a spectator. Even then, with these twin fighters, he could tell who was the superior, and who was the inferior. Their fight ended before it began, the inferior was cut down the torso, with limb falling. He wanted to stop the fight, but his body was frozen in place. He blinked and the swords crossed again, the inferior assembled again, and fell apart too. But the blood that erupted from the inferior never came back. Each time the inferior was reassembled, he was slower. The fight ended with the inferior stabbing itself, and both combatants falling into death.

The light of a lantern pierced the ambiance and awoken Litus. The guard with a tray of gray food, telling him to eat and wake. Litus looked at the food, it was like ash on the tray, and in return he tossed it out the window, and heard the tray crash to the ground.

That morning had remained the same from the other. Alone, with the breathing of guards, and the empty dusty cell too.

The sky had lightened towards midday, when Jane had come by again, and asked, "are you okay?"

Litus nodded so.

"I hope you are safe in here, are you?"

Litus nodded again.

"I'm sorry for being brief, but I need of leave. Goodbye for now."

Litus again watched Jane leave going down the stairs, and all was quiet. In some respects it was now quieter than before, because the void of sound was filled for a second, and once it was gone, it truly felt gone. The midday's light fell again to darkness, and the statues rotated once again. Their breath had been the only thing he heard. But he remarked on how they looked at him, with fear, great fear.

In a tunnel of stone and stalagmites. Sat a boat on a fake river, with two occupants. One held a lantern, whose light broke off after the boat departed, and the other was someone he could see through their eyes.

They spoke of things and murmurs that were not heard, and the light shone a cloak of shadows and weaves of nothing. And a face of shadows, and eyes of nothing. He peered down into the water –

what little light reflected back – and what he saw was a cloaked figure. Faceless, nothing. He looked back, and saw through the one with the lantern, or maybe a third figure, or none.

The next morning was the same as the previous two – Jane visited once more – with fairer skin. She again asked the same questions, with the same responses. The soft blanketed moonlight fell to his cell with frost. The night was there.

All he felt was the crashing of sounds and the incoming flash of light and splinters. Fire . . . fire . . . fire. Tt enveloped him as the water rose, or he fell. The planks came crashing towards, and blood. Blood filled the cloud above him. It was deafeningly loud. He was being thrown around, cradled in the arms of others, and cradled in his arms was a silver twine rod. He kept this twine like a mother to child. The bubbles of air coming from and to, there was wood and sand.

And then he awoke, drenched in thought. He would. And almost instantly Jane was there with fairer skin and dress, and the day was already mid through. The moon rose, and the walls and ground burned him with how quick they froze over. The silence stood over for only a second.

He saw through a glass dome above, a beautiful woman in blood red, and blond. She had been taken in hand with a man dressed even finer than her. Tall sharp leather boots tapped the floor. They twirled in tandem, he saw her eyes, rubies they were. Her movements were refined, but his were polished. His face stern with the smallest flake of smugness. Her face was stern, but with a face of suspicion. For some reason he wanted to shout down a ladder, and her escape.

But he awoke.

Jane had been peering in, she continued to look fairer than last. She looked quite worrisome of Litus, she asked him again, "are you okay?"

He didn't even respond, time felt so quick in the ambiance, but Jane followed up after waiting, "I'm sure, but you may need to escape, the commodore I don't know if Tylock will let me leave the following days. Please if I can't escape you must," she then quickly departed.

Litus watched her descend, and once she wasn't there, a chill took the air. The guards flashed, and the breathing was only a drone.

He saw through the eyes of a familiar stranger. He crossed streets in the shadows. With knives in hand he embarked the stone walls around the castle. He dropped down in the middle of hedges of many angles and directions, but this stranger knew which way to run under moonlight. He ran taking the right and left, under shadow and mist. In a large garden he ran past the pond, dogs and ducks sitting idly. Through the second entrance on the far right he went, and again turned where he needed to be. Out of the hedge maze, and through the castle's back door he went.

When he awoke he tried to remember the details of that dream particularly. The castle looked to be Renoi. He looked out the window to be sure, it seemed so. It was past midday, Jane wasn't waiting for him by the bars. The guards, though, were the same statues as before. He looked back out the window, down on the ground. The fall would be great, but the need to shave down the black tock side with a knife felt greater. The crucial blade which could be tried against the cold.

The chill came, and with it night again.

Over the balcony he saw a young woman in red, and an old woman in gold. Their swords held out, waiting for the first strike, the crowd circled around them. They struck and parried every few sways. Then he saw them neck to neck, and blade to blade. Parrying and sticking, again and again. At last with that final strike, fire erupted the crowd, and enveloped everything including himself.

By the time he had awoken the sky had already started to fade, and the cold breath of the moon was coming too. To him the guards may or may not have rotated yet, but certainty was beyond action. He came to the window seeing the lights of the city shine and the castle in the distance shown brighter with candles of carnival. Down he peered out of the window. He could not see the ground or anybody patrolling. He looked back for the guards, in case this one chance they began peering over, and they didn't. Out of his cloak he drew his knives, and embarked downward. Dropping and stabbing the walls; the cold winds tried to cast him away, but Litus kept his grip upon the knife embedded.

Slowly as he descended the ground became more visible, seeing only the outline of the ground. Later the small shimmers of rain that cast the stones. Then before he purposely dropped, he could see the grout lines between each stone.

When he landed, you could hear the clatter of his plate boots. But before he could let some guards or watchmen spot him he ran towards the castle onward. He threw off his blue cloak and threw it into the void, rather than let a lead propagate, and it was replaced with his wraithlike black.

He slid in the shadows, neither passerby or rat saw him. Racing down the block, and past boulevards. The few streets he would have to pass were filled with drunkards, and jesters buying attention for coin or laughs. He walked down a longer way so as to not draw attention in this dire situation.

And it was down a dingy dark alley which he first met the boulevard from which the castle stood. With its stone walls and pillars, light, and more galore. But guards rotated the grounds in groups of two. One candle bearer, and other halberd, but they both carried steel. And he could see the second rotation a few hundred feet back. His speed would have to be between their passing, and quiet too. As soon as the first were passed the alleyway he sat at, Litus ran while staying under the cover of night. He quickly grabbed at his knife and readied his climb, but as he tried to stick the knife into the bricks it deflected, and then again the grout. The siege walls stood still, unable to be torn down by knife. The stones were merely scratched by the knife trying to insert between the bricks.

The soldiers were encroaching so close. Litus in fear of failing Jane, began to grasp the grout between the large stone bricks and began to climb. In those small dents he pulled and threw himself upwards, catching the next cracks as he went.

From halfway up the wall, the sound of multiple footsteps became far more audible than Litus would like. He scrambled to get ahead, throwing himself up, but it was at a miscalculation that Litus didn't reach the next crack. He slipped, and before he could fall to the bottom he grasped the crack from below. His boots kicked the wall and the soldiers from close drew suspension. "Check it," one said from behind.

The lantern man drew his light up the street and between the trees to see what's past. Between them were only so few trees. Litus jumped up grabbing the grout above, they searched through the low leaves. They drew up another, and the light hit the next. And he could hear their breathing and walking as though it were against his ear, and knew if he didn't throw himself as high as he could and over the wall, it would be settled. But though he came far from where he was, there still was the top he needed to climb. As the lantern's light began to climb above, Litus threw himself over once more, and the light missed him.

He landed on soft well trimmed grass, and surrounded by the hedge maze he dreamt of. And like in his dream he began walking through trying to remember where he had went. It was clear as day at first. The only problem that stood was the darkness of the maze, but not so much, since the cell attuned his eyes towards a darker habitat. His hearing grew tenfold, and he could hear a pin fall on a needle of grass.

It was a footstep he heard that made him stop and draw his blade. Litus looked around his surroundings, but to naught. There was a foot soldier, or something close though, but he crept forward, hearing the surroundings close in. He followed his memory as closely as possible, and it was still clear to his mind. Going forward, later right, then left, forward, and so on, and so forth.

He turned a corner and ahead before he could enter the pond and park in that dream. There he saw a creature, something. It was not a soldier, or human for that matter, but it also wasn't anything like himself: something wraith-like.

This creature's tar-like skin reflected what little light that was given off by the moon. It's limbs were long and lanky, the muscle detail was inconsistent. It stood on four legs, with no arms, and no feet but spears. The body was almost skeletal, and it's face wore the current fashion.

Litus felt a needle run through him. Only that this thing was the queen's guard dog. Litus knew that if he weren't to go through the park, and confront it, or head around, he might never save Jane. so he snuck around trying to not beacon any sounds, hearing the footsteps thump the ground.

He crept his way around and towards the opening to the far right like in his dream, but as he was entering, the thing had crept out and snuffed out like a doghound. It was just the same as the creature in the center of the park. It crept along on all fours, until it saw Litus there on the ground.

Litus rolled back dodging the spikes that pierced the bleeding ground. Before that beast could strike again, Litus drew out his sword and readied himself. That beast reigned high on its back legs, before smacking the ground where he had stood. And he jumped to the side and swung at the beast's leg. It stumbled forward in a high pitched squeal, and Litus drew his sword past the beast, ending the thrashing completely.

But from behind faintly Litus could hear thumping drawing closer. It beat like his heart, faster and faster. Litus retrieved his sword from the carcass, and turned to face fate. The spike-like limb was thrusted down over Litus, but snagged his cloak before he could dodge. It reared its head down, Litus could see balls of opaque glass behind that mask. Before it could strike again, Litus cut his own cloak, which sent fragments of ash blooming upward. A great piercing squeal erupted out of the beast. It roared with a violent thrashing. And Litus dodged the now quicker and more erratic monster's beatings. In every chance Litus deflected the hard-steel legs, as though it were the blade of a sword, or the shaft of a spear. It continued its chanting of piercing squeals, and Litus knew he had to end the bashing, before it grew attention. But the beast only became even more angry as he resisted its death spikes. He saw a small opportunity for victory, and swung towards its legs, but the beast saw its predecessors fall, and jumped back.

It snarled with a great fury, and rushed towards Litus throwing its legs down into the ground where he stood. Litus rolled underneath the legs, and caused confusion with the creature, tripping it in its execution attempt. He quickly rose and drew his sword through the body once more. Thick sludge was stuck to the sword blade.

He dashed away though the maze until it ended with the tall walls of the keep as a barrier. Under the cover of darkness, he ran like a thief. In the back – through a servants door – there was a small mudroom with a wooden stairwell, and a door in front with a circular window. He peered through and witnessed a grand ball of fat nobles and beautiful nobles, garbed in dresses worth more than most homes. The queen's guards were stationed all around the hall. They stood still as statues, with swords on their side, and spikes on poles. Litus journeyed up, and from the next floor he could see near the balcony were stationed guards, but not soldiers.

Chapter Twenty-One:

The gates of the castle were cast of iron with silver inlay around the thick support beams. All along the castle were long drapes of purple, gold, and silver. The silver was caught under a dampened sky and reflected black almost black. On flag posts spread around the high stone wall were flagstaffs with the rich flapping flags of Rientonem, with the royal shield and crest embroidered onto.

A series of halberds lined the walls, standing stoic and still. Nobles and high ranked military men were dressed without a speck of dust sprinkled on their dress. Tylock greeted his superiors with a bow, and equals, a formal handshake. All wore thin masks of porcelain, inlaid with lapis, silver, and gold. To Jane, there seemed an eternity of greeting to nobles of social ranking, with superfluous wealth.

High above there was a stained glass mural of three deities which showed no light from where they stood, and it's then they knew the ball had truly commenced.

Tylock with other officers, and nobles of social rank were led from ballroom to ballroom to the court where the throne was.

There lay long tables, trimming the side walls, and in the corner were the band of dustless musicians, with their shining brass tools.

Soon the first dance would begin. The band slowly built the music, and the nobles commenced at the near same time. "This air is wrong," Jane said so quietly it was inaudible.

The music that played was a small waltz, finely danceable, but silent to others. It was no small wonder that those nobles jumped into dance with the sound of such subtlety. Jane in quick reaction took Tylocks hands and began to dance the waltz the same as the others. Tylock muttered after taking a breath, "slow, but not much has been seen yet, you need to cut like a hidden knife. They must not know of their cuts, until they bleed."

From the second balcony looking down were some nobles, but most royal guards men. Though they were almost invisible to Jane compared to some few men among them. Cloaked figures of red, and black. *Who are they?* And she was ushered away. Their faces were mostly covered, but they were human, just suspicious. Not in the sense that they didn't belong, simply because in one quick viewing they were talking amongst a guard, and a noble next.

The tempo slowed, and with it all the movement until they all ended on a quiet decline. It was then when a series of chefs came from the kitchens and plated the tables on the sides with delicacies. Shrimp cocktail, and large spiced lamb. A large fish was plated on ice with tart lemons, and lettuce. A bucket of ice on the side had long forks made of bronze. Waiters dressed in black garbs, carried trays of wine, and beer, and some chilled champagne too. And all came with many of each.

A man came to them with a certain light in his eyes, of staleness, and presented a tray, with fogged coupe glasses of champagne. Tylock grabbed one for himself and one for his lady, and they drank while watching the crowd around, dine, and talk, not knowing what, but knowing it's not about flowers and art. At least the commonality was to lift the mask to eat or drink. But the mask didn't draw some wandering eyes on Jane, it was her hair.

They wore robes of red, and black, but he couldn't see their faces – for they looked down at the crowd, such the same as the soldiers. There were rooms, or door to rooms, along the wall behind those at the railings. There were no stairs leading downstairs, and if there were stairs, most likely nobles and servants would be occupying those steps. For a wraith was a bead of oil in the ocean. So with the sound of those talking, and muttering he didn't have to worry about sound, but only sight.

He came to the closest door – and upon peering in – there were only cabinets full of mopping and dusting supplies. The next was a room of numerous stacked beds, and cabinets too. A disguise was what he sought, and he went through the servants' belongings. Picking out garments that fit, and before leaving he took a hat from one drawer, and the mask of another servant. He was dressed like a chef, and in fact rumbling through all their belongings he only found kitchenware clothes. *Now where are the chefs, to disguise with?*

He left and came to the next door, which opened to a library, and one of many dining rooms that were connected together. Litus walked through, and there were no eyes to hide from. Escaping through the other side were a similar balcony, with those creepy robed men who overlooked others. The stairwell hung on the side, cluttered with clumsy and drowsy drunks of the new money nobles.

Litus peered over every now and then to glimpse down, looking for Jane. He feared that same scenario happening, like in that dream. *Could it be that dream?* Maybe he could jump from the railing onto the crystal chandelier hanging from a polished brass chain. That would break his fall when crashing down, but those were just passing thoughts.

Instead Litus simply tried to squeeze by, down and through the crowd, but at every gap were demands. "You chef boy, you scullion, bring me the vintage, and keep the bottle," and from another from under their breath, "stupid servant, forgot his own job," and Litus stood stumbling when, a much larger man, dressed in fine silks, a tall military coat of black and silver, and a tricorn hat appeared demanding alcohol in a drunken state. It didn't reflect at first, until he took closer notice at the man's coat, a naval officer. He didn't know the indicators of rank, but didn't want to take guesses. He took a look around, ignoring the officer, in possible sight of Jane, "what are you doing in the way, no trays of cheese, or wine in goblets? Go, you, or I'll call the guards over to fix this," he choked in a drunken roar.

Litus nodded, and proceeded to retreat, but then did he notice not a noble or soldier descending but one of these red robed figures. Litus tried to remain semi stoic – through a stumbling march – and balanced like a servant should be. Of no matter could those looking eyes, those predatory eyes, escape him.

The entrance into the chamber ahead, was obstructed with two guards, with coats of a silver or gray tunic. The metallic nature shifted in the lamplight. He knew that ahead there was a door to the kitchen, but only had to reach it. Litus strutted up to the guards, they clashed their halberds together. Silently they sequentially stared Litus up and down.

Litus glanced over his shoulder, gathering passing glances from where that red robe was supposed to be. Without having those guards notice, he tried to get a better look, but couldn't.

The sheer scraping sound of two halberds unlocking took back his attention. He quickly passed through, the nobles behind him grumbled, and winced when the halberds closed behind. Litus turned and there he saw no red robe, beside the cavalry officers in red, and the few nobles who wore red.

Ahead was another set of royal guards dawned with halberds, only letting in the true nobles, and supremely high ranked officers. And he could tell by the garb of the ladies dressed in ball gowns – laced with silver or gold, or other rich material that stretched a foot or two past her hips of mostly red and blue fabrics – that they were most likely the nobility. And if the commodore and Jane were in any room it would be that room of elegance. But he needed something to be able to enter, so he looked to a table for a silver platter.

The previous set of guards had thought that this servant had gone to procure another platter of gimmick food for the guests. But still watched him when he went towards the kitchen, and showed a squinting eye when Litus looked around instead. *I don't see her, and those guards are looking at me.*

Litus walked through the unlocked kitchen door, and headed through only to find no chefs there to gather food. The kitchen walls and tables were thrashed, like all the chefs had struggled out the door. There were plates smashed with food smeared on the ground, and the air smelled strangely.

Litus noticed further down into the kitchen, through a different room of almost complete darkness, was a single candle – left on a shelf – holding that flickering light. Down damp wooden steps into the dark cellar, Litus walked, and then he felt the pin needles.

A man in a great red military coat, and a high noble lord were talking almost out of ear shot from Jane. Certain vowels and quiet words blended with the similar chatting from all around the gala, but of that was heard, "how would a queen's man such as yourself, take on the rumors emerging from Hule?"

Some time later with just glimpses, she overheard this same couple reply with, "they barely pay taxes to begin with, most don't. Calling them the back of the kingdom is false. They're a wholly different kingdom really."

"Mostly true, but you must see our opportunity, owning a whole new trade in the name of the holy queen. Paying tribute to the queen."

The last she heard them speak, was about the arms they would need to conquest the Hueglinies people, and which side to join, and one of the men simply said, "why stand when we could sit."

Tylock could sense the obvious political discourse around Jane, and pointed out to her, "fools I tell you, from their toes down to their brain. They haven't a clue about the world other than their yards."

"What's happening in Hule?"

"Not some revolution, the Hueglinies people are perfectly happy being subjected with the kingdom, simply because they do what their best suited for, trading, for far less. There hasn't been any ship of tax collectors in nearly a hundred years. No intelligent fool would risk out right civil-war for a worse deal."

"Do the Hueglinies feel this same attitude?"

"Seeing as Hule has never caused conflict with the kingdom, and made the kingdom massive income. If I wasn't a commodore, I'd be a Hule merchant."

Tylock guided her around introducing her to the noblemen he had known, and built ties with previously. Here he spotted a certain man whom he knew personally, which most other noble lords hadn't. "Lord Pelille, duke of the Flumen, great southern lord of Hule. Have your wares paid greatly?"

"Now what matter would that be by Tylock? And not introducing this fine one first. And what be you, dear lady of the south east?"

"Quite perceptive, but not totally correct, this is my lady Jane."

The noble took Jane's palm with his own dark skinned hand, and took a short kiss on the back of her's. "The pleasure is mine," he took a good look at Jane's eyes through the mask, "you are correct, Tylock, north eastern, those beautiful ruby eyes could only be noble. Have you been to Hule before, my dear? For it is quite beautiful during the winter months. Gives great leisures to graze the dunes, and colored canyons without the fear of heat."

Jane replied, trying to speak in a curious and knowledgeable noble-like speech, "I haven't actually, but I have heard a great many deals about the people and wares that come from there."

"Shall we speak later, duke, I have great tales to spread."

"We shall. So long Tylock, for short that it was."

Tylock both slowly drifted Jane away, but also quickly did so. It was a strange feeling, mostly fueled by some nervousness. "He put a pin through you, did you notice?"

"What do you mean, I didn't say anything," she whispered back.

"You said very little, that is, he put you in a trap unable to escape."

"What will happen?"

"In all meanings, nothing that concerns you now, and won't hurt you in the future. But it is my problem that I seek to solve."

The next dance had begun with a similar waltz from the musicians before, but instead the piece was slightly faster, and the notes were a bit brighter. The great lords and ladies swung from side to side, not vigorously, but sudo passionately. In the background there was still that murmuring, and political scheming coming from all, but were separated by their lack of endurance. The high ranked officers such as Tylock, didn't get that exhaustion, or at least not longingly.

After the dance concluded, Tylock had again pointed out the discourse that seemed so easily obvious. "Oh to be the eye of the court. You see their eyes, their gazing?"

"What do you mean, are they looking at me, do I need to talk about politics some?"

"In only a blink do they peer at you, and your body, glistening rather than stinking of sweat. Their envious and glutinous gaze, want what they can't have. You are an enemy to them, yes, but also a jewel."

She knew the words to be hollow, but that the shell was made of truth. It was a cold truth, but one that centered her, in quite possibly the worst way. But there was also the sense of pride, from having some high lords envy the peasant.

That pride soon fell wayside, when from the chanting of horns in unison, came a small league of guards, and they led the high monarch of this land. The court went silent, not even the sounds of the guards mail, and plate armor scraping together, could mask out those haunting reverberating footsteps of the queen. And they stepped slowly, but assuredly over everyone else. A wave crashed through the court. Some fear pierced them all, in a strange alien way. In the equal stun of silence, the radiance of her beauty caught Jane by surprise. Her dress looked like that of dragon scales, with gold pressed into a flowery pattern. The red was rich and auburn when it glistened in the candlelight. It wasn't a ball gown of sorts, but it was still quite beautiful and intricate.

Her own guard all wore a two handed fauchen with handles of bronze and red satin, wrapped with a twisted gold, or bronze wire. Jane couldn't see most of the scabbard, except its purple gloss, and gold and silver inlays. Across their shoulders were striped capes of red and purple. There were no men behind those suits of steel, at least not anymore, they were just men of death. Conditioned to obey. Conditioned by someone, or something. They marched with halberds, pushing them up and down with each step of theirs, and the queens.

The throne was the centerpiece of the palace, and most certainly this converted court too. The queen peered over them all while standing with her back to the throne, and then once she sat down, the guards set their halberd down, giving one syncopated pound into the stone ground. Her hair was white as silver, and her mask was the same. Only a short moment later, she tore off the mask and set it down on the arm of the chair, and the sound of it clinking on the throne echoed through the halls. Many of the nobles stuttered to respond, and eventually mostly all of them raised to take off their masks, but the queen made no gesture to show it was right, and the confusion stayed in those walls. And the nobles and military men tried not to gaze like an uncivilized peasant. Her face – though aged twice and a half of Jane's age – still looked quite young. Her lips and eyes were red as blood, and so were Jane's.

In almost a flash all he saw were that red coat of the cultists. And what he felt was almost the feeling of revenge and anger, but not quite. All of these emotions were forfeit except that of fear. *How can I escape without causing a scene, or I have to kill this monster quickly. Either way it's now or never.* Litus drew his sword from his torso. At first strike he, thrusted into the red, and then again, but to his surprise its figure caught into a flame, and was subsequently snuffed. Like a wisp of shadows, or an imagine of the past. Again from behind the mage appeared, drawing a wand from his sleeve. Litus moved in once more to close the distance, but again when the blade reached the cultist all that emerged was a plume of smoke. Those pins and needles only grew the longer he kept in the cellar. They were sticking in his back, but he also felt a dragging, or pulling from his shirt. It forced him back, before he was put on the ground, and looking down on him was the semi-covered face of this cultist with his wand face to face.

Litus tried releasing himself from the grasp, but that very moment a small sun was at the tip of the wand. Casting a small light outward; more significant than any candle. Though it wasn't lighter than a lantern, but it all seemed so purposeful. A normal face of a man was embedded in that hood, with the eyes of something cryptic, and in his bloodless pale face, he hissed, "not wraith, nor man, and even not reaper," he aimed the light at Litus' eyes, "what are you?" He rasped.

The sun on the end of the wand tip grew angry, with flares of white encircling around, swelling and growling with a candlestick. Litus shifted and looked around, the sword was right next to his hand. "No no," he chortled with a rasp while sliding the sword back with his foot, "now speak it! What will you be?" And he thrust the wand closer to his face.

From out of his torso, Litus thrust the knife he had into the cultist's leg. Who roared in pain and shock, before accidentally releasing the sun into the cellar wine. In a massive blinding flash of white, where no sound was present, and all the sound from the room disintegrated. Complete silence, and complete light was all which was. And when the sound had returned, so did only some of the darkness.

A shallow liquid started to flood the floor, and a dank stench of wine polluted the air, with a white powder that was stored in a normal looking barrel.

It was again face to face with this robed man, and in the greater darkness. The pins and needles were scattered all around Litus' body, his vision went with that explosion. All in the darkness he saw was the gray border of his sight. But in this, Litus' hearing was intact. Around were the sounds of sloshing footsteps. Footsteps of an assassin, and they were as quiet as a mouse. He heard them all around. In a blink, they were to his left, but not now to his right. Which way he couldn't tell, even worse without sight. Litus could tell that the footsteps were slower. Creaking wood filled the room, and Litus now knew where the cultists were. He turned around with the knife still in hand. There was the sound of enveloping, a combustion starting. A flame in the room of darkness, from a different wand, and a knife thrown.

The hall was silent, no nobles would want to have been one to have spoken over the queen: the ruling monarch. Out of the split crowd, there were the sharp poignant steps of Tylock. All turned to him with either fear for his life, or hatred for his supposed superior presence taken from the queen, and some were just cross to be crossed. Even the guards who were appointed the queen, flicked their eyes with bemusement and trepidation to Tylock as he marched forward. Jane didn't know what to think of this, but knew no matter what, she was in trouble. She looked around the court for some exit, but all were barred by the soldiers, and their steel.

"My grace. If I may interrupt you, I have brought a gift for you. And the realm among us," he said while emphasizing his hands; the queen was still, but didn't object, "by great honor, your grace. The realm, the great kingdom has been without the continuation of power, and rule for decades. Even after the searches from the ships and footmen, and the rewards put out by the crown. None had come with a solution, but now myself along with my officers. We have brought a real solution to the future of our kingdom, and to keep it from fracturing in the long future."

She looked through him not even paying a mention of spec, and said, "and what's that, an early secession, or what, my crown, my throne, my castle?" Her voice was cold and stern, moderate in volume, but was a blocking wall too.

Her personal guard shifted their pose to him, and with a single stroke armed their halberds towards him.

But Tylock had planned this too; he didn't break a sweat. "No, no, my grace, I'm a true queen's man, and a high ranked officer of the royal navy too. I don't intend on seizing the throne with a silly rebellion," He turned to the nobles behind him, while within walking distance of the queen, "I've already said it, and I've brought a gift," he elegantly held his hand out while taking slow steps luring Jane towards.

What would showing off your hack "lady" do to impress the queen, and what does he mean by gift. She felt a suspicion, and wanted to run, but the eyes of Tylock, and the nobles cast at her kept her frozen. And under this pressure, she forced her composure, and stepped forward taking Tylock's hand. He gently lifted her mask away, and announced, "my grace, I bring your long lost heir. Princess Garnette of the royal house of Renoi."

Litus stood in the pool of wine, his feet soaked. He looked at the body, his knife embedded in the man's skull. Blood spewed out. Still grasping in his now rigamortis ridden hands, were the fire wand he had attempted to engulf Litus with. It was a considerably more robust and nicer wand than the southern cultist quickly made and kept. Red cherry wood with hand marks were worn in the shaft. *That magic, that ball of fire, that couldn't have come from this, that light.*

He knelt down and checked the sleeve of the dead man, and inside was another wand. And this wand was made of a fine white birch, with wide pores around the smooth wood stock, and he knew it well, when a small sun was inches from his eyes. The weight amused him. It was heavy and dense. *Much heavier than a normal birch stick at the same size.* Litus almost shivered thinking about the light it brought, how that power erupted. *How much is left. I won't use it unless I have to.*

Away he stored the fire wand into the void, and cast out a small marble sized orb of light. The light pierced the wall of stone, and the dirty wine on the floor. And before when Litus had worried where his sword was, in the light he saw it clearer than day. Wine stuck to the blade and hilt like old rotten sweets.

The cultist's robes didn't have a blood stain, or wouldn't have shown it because of its red color. And it was that red robe that left the cellar, the cultists body fell into the wine, and floated silently and naked.

Jane's face was revealed and the queen with her nobles, gazed into her deep red eyes, like it were a mirror, or an oil painting. *The heir, the lost princess, what a joke, no one could believe such a idiotic lie, but what will they do to me now!?*

The queen refused to believe her daughter would be presented in front of court like some sidewall wench, but the nobles saw through less delusion, because Jane looked exactly like the monarch from younger days. Her hair only emphasized this further. Jane knew not what to expect, but the faces of nearly a hundred or more nobles gawking, made her uncomfortable, less so than the queen, and Tylock. *I'm not the daughter of her. You lied to me, my death will be in your hands,* she thought, but could not bear to say.

Her haunting voice brought a daft cold draft through the hall, "do you seek to insult the intelligence of the crown, and her subjects, Commodore Tylock?" She waited for both Tylock's and Jane's eyes, cunning and fear, "for twenty two years neither the army or navy, nor the rewards of gold could find my lost daughter, but you seem to show her here now? But only now she's right in my court. You must be expecting such greatness to single handedly find her."

"I have already found greatness in doing such a deed. Now I see you rest well knowing the kingdom is saved, doesn't it?"

She rose from her seat, and again her footsteps reigned the law. She passed by Tylock, and lightly grabbed Jane's hands, feeling them, knowing them. She still talked to commodore Tylock in a cold dialog, "a good queen's man you are? Don't you feel embarrassed by your mount of evidence you don't have. On behalf of the navy and the crown herself too. I can admit she is subtly different from my younger ages, but she had to be the forgotten daughter of a proud noble lord, isn't it. And now you wish my pardon for successes from the womb of another woman."

"I do not mean that, my grace."

"Then how should I reward your coercion of some other lord's spawn, and proclaiming her as mine, of my dear lost daughter?"

"She was neither raised by the servants of lords, nor the bastard daughter too, she grew up a common woman. And within a week she was transformed into the grace I present you here today, now she rivals your beauty, simply because she is your descendant. Her noble genes are the same as yours. And she is twenty three as well. Your grace."

"You say it as though your certainty is greater than my intelligence. If only then will my throne split," but what she saw were the eyes of Jane, and a light of recognition twinkled, and fell into hatred as she stepped back putting space between them, *I have to run, maybe they'll just take Tylock's head,* "so now you've been brought to unite my kingdom against me, you will not take my crown with her blood or yours. I don't intend to lose my throne after death, and I shall cast your noble ruse away. It will be by my hand that this so-called daughter of mine is brought into justice, of the true law of my hands, and you all will regret your temptation and greed of usurping my throne," they did not know how, but she drew and held the point of a sword towards Jane.

A sword was thrown, sliding across the ground, and Jane picked up the blade. Litus from above the balcony heard naught, but saw that man, Tylock, kept his arm outstretched blocking Jane from the queen's blade. His other, on the pommel of his side. *I have to get down there, Jane will die if I don't and the queen will cause it.*

Tylock kept his hand on the pommel, but refused to raise his steel against the queen. Litus couldn't think when he saw the queen play with her food, she slashed at Tylock's hand, her own commodore, and he didn't refute this. Blood dripped onto the marble floor, and still Tylock kept Jane away, with fire behind those eyes. *The sword, Jane, take it! Behind you.* Litus watched Tylock and Jane retreat when encroached upon by the queen's playful swipes.

I need to get down there, Jane I'll be there, and end this cruelty.

"I will not fight, I will not raise my blade onto you."

"Now you refuse orders, what soldier are you?" She swiped at him, "and you, pick it up, pick up that blade!"

I'm no princess nor some puppet for their political games. If I kill Tylock, will she free me? No, of course she won't, she want's to draw blood, the look on her face says it so. The sword was only a few steps behind her. She turned to look where it lay, and was only a half second from being swiped by the queen's blade.

Tylock still refused his hand to draw on that blade. His black coat now had cuts across his arms, and blood stained his silk white shirt underneath. The pain and anger was across his face, and he looked to the nobles in a plea to gain their support.

"What now, Tylock, afraid to show your plan to the queen, such a queen's man, willing to die for my throne, but not on your hill.

Come on unsheathe your blade, swordsman. How willing are you to die for the state?"

A ring of steel on steel, and a trail of sparks emerged when the blades touched.

Jane's blade met the queen's, and from the court below, Litus could hear the shifting of platemail. The king's guard's halberds were shifted around the circle of the three, and snuffed out unwanted nobles. The roar of the shocked crowd reverberated through the walls of the court. Shaking the dust off the golden bronze chandelier.

Litus looked around in a deep panic, *I need to go back down now, what am I doing, there's no way around, those doors can be broken. Glass shattered.* But around the corner running up were the reds. They burnished their white birch wands. A dozen suns were a bright burning white. With so much power behind the sun the size of a finger tip. That fear only grew, and tension more so. *Do they know I'm not them?*

Then almost immediately, he knew, when they raised their wands towards him, and their light dimmed, or it seemed it retracted. Litus saw beyond the railings as he thrusted over landing on the chandelier. The crashing of a thousand glass teardrops, light scattering about, and the golden bronze shook like a cymbal. The explosion of thirteen suns set out a burning light that erased all else.

The sparks were thrown onto her hand, which wouldn't have stung much before, but now bit into her skin. Jane felt the heft of the sword biting into her hands. They were wrought with pain, and blood, no calluses or gloves protected her now fair fingers. But that hadn't stopped Jane from trying to deflect that attack, to then attack. But it was intercepted, "you won't bring a blade against the queen," Tylock uttered with his sword extended.

"Who's side are you on Tylock?" Jane yelled.

"Her crown first and foremost."

"You bleed for this county, you usurp the throne, what mind have you made up, commodore?" The queen barked while striking upward towards him. He blocked the blade, swinging it away from his side.

"You are using me, for your gain, and what have you got for it?"

"I'm serving the crown, but now we're past the point of no return."

Jane swung the blade from the floor to the sky, Tylock blocked it, and the queen went forward blade towards Jane who quickly retracted her blade to deflect what strike came. And whenever the blade came to Tylock he only blocked and backed off, refusing to fight any further.

The queen found an advantage on Jane, parried Jane's block, and struck a block from Tylock. Her face was mad with anger, stepped back, with her sword raised high. In a blizzard of flurries, strikes came towards Jane and Tylock. They sweat to block the strikes and to parry. Sparks flew with each strike, either burning in the air, or on skin.

One noble or soldier spoke up, "these horrors, how could you mercilessly filet us!"

The queen looked over, not knowing which noble uttered a breath. For that brief moment, Jane used to push back the queen, sword collision, Tylock stunned. The ringing of steel was resonating in the hall with flashes of diamond light.

Sputtering and piercing chirping. Parry and block and swing and retreat. The pattern called, Tylock brought his steel in and intercepted theirs, locking them. The queen stepped back, and Jane did the same. The queen dropped her blade, while Jane rose above, and Tylock eyed both. "What have you resolved to, fighting like -" his voice was cut off, everything was cut off, light from above blinded all. With the heat of a furnace and the unbound power of the sun, they all looked away.

The thousand shatters of the crystal glass, and brass arms breaking the marble floor below filled the void, and stung ears with a piercing stagger. Some of the guards tumbled, and fell over with the explosion.

Tylock rose, and sheathed his sword. Dust scattered half the circle. All Tylock knew was that the queen must have been dead. In reality of now knowing it he tried to mend Jane's perception of him. *He put a blade against me, and kept me as a pet, I won't be his puppet anymore.* When offered a hand, she refused, "get away from me. You hold me bound no more."

Tylock turned to the king's guard who now stood and with his hand on his pommel, he said, "you've heard your queen, I'll be gone, and return with hand to clean this holy mess," and they let him; half his shirt now soaked in blood, the other white, but all were bound by confusion and fear.

Jane looked up toward the chandelier. Litus stood atop, and jumped from above, and they looked at him, silent. *He's alive, he's okay. And again, it's happened.* Litus looked around, Jane was in an elegant dress now cut. Guards stood around halberds forward, Litus drew out a sword. Kept it up, and the knights and reds looked at him. Jane stood, collecting the sword. Jane uttered to him in a relieved tone, "you're safe."

The king's guard looked around almost confused, their supposed heir welcomed Litus from the chandelier, and they muttered under their breath, "wraith?"

It was soon quelled with the settled dust, and the now standing queen. She looked to squash a viperous bug. Each halberd was brought back down, in a shift of metal crowded the hall, and so did the gasps of fat nobles. *They're going to put our heads on the end of spears. I'm done being used as a doll, I'm not the puppet heir, and she isn't my mother. No one would want a mother so cruel. What would forcing me onto the throne serve for him?*

Litus' sword had confronted the other. Steel glistened and sparked, and swirled in a flurry of parries, and attack. Litus swung from below, rising high, and that got blocked by a spinning blade that leveled the field. The queen though seemed too weary, but that was a false mask. Litus thrusted the point again and again, swinging away with an intentional fury, but all it took was one strike precisely made, a swing and parry, and the queen threw out his sword. She raised her sword high, swung with a superior slash. Blood rushed across the floor. Jane cut the queen down her torso, cleaving flesh away like a guillotine. The queen's white flesh shifted as it fell, and Jane threw her sword down, and came to Litus.

The gold threads of that dress filled with blood. The captain of the king's guard shouted, "get those queen slayers!" But as they ran to Litus and Jane, the reds above cast levee walls of flames which encircled those two.

The entire court was filled with the red light from those flames, and the nobles tried to run from the flame which soon tried to engulf them. And the tall walls of fire spread out pushing the nobles and soldiers further back.

The heat induction swirled like a tornado, and all came into one point. From her corpse, came a maggot-like movement. A squirming, and hissing of a monstrous thing emerged, crying. Litus and Jane looked around, up the balcony, and at the guard, until their eyes met the queen. Out of the torn skin, came that thing. A monstrous flesh bat. With stripes of black and white, and the head of a bird with a beak of flesh. That parasite grew to twice the size of the queen, and then some.

With a force of attention, the reds withdrew, and in a voice that sounded like the queen's with a hiss of a snake, the flesh bat spoke, "heat, and Flame. For many a year, since the last king I have been encased, but now I've been removed of this skin. Oh how this air singes, the feel of pain again, and all you've gifted me Tylock, wherever you are. And now you, the daughter, and the man of shadow, will pay for your sight. I'll first gut your companion, and dice him, until he fits in a bottle of wine, all the blood will ferment into an alcohol, and the meat, into a smoked jerky I'll serve to my personal cabinet. And you, my dear daughter, will be the new queen to present such meat and wine," the queen's parasite then bent down gripping her sword in her talons.

"You'll drink loyalty, and dull steel; the sentence of tenfold livings will be within, and that will be your fall. In the wings of fire, and temptation of god, chaos is all that shall cross paths. You look at me like I'm some great beast, but I'm right here, daughter. And you shall meet this power deep deep within."

With a high screech and beating of slimy wings, the parasite queen took flight. The open razors of the black nail talons had thrust down towards Jane. She jumped back, the claw scratching the marble stone below, and Jane swung her blade towards the mass which was the torso. The parasite quickly blocked, and parried getting blocked by Jane again, before disengaging.

Litus drew his sword, and circled around to her back, jumping into a downward slash. It had only scratched the monster when it withdrew, leaving Litus open for a slice heading sideways. He blocked a strike while moving around, trying to find a blindspot.

Jane was in the other blindspot, she approached like a fox, taking the chance given by Litus, and thrust her sword into its side, or at least attempting to. With a great force and beat of wind, brought by wings, both Litus and Jane were pushed back. Jane had the top of her dress torn, a stream of blood dripped into the threads. She only backed away, without noise to give. With pain surfacing, she tried to suppress it mentally. The blade rose high, and with a large wide swing, she tore the steel through the soft stripped flesh.

Litus grasped his sword tight, and with an upwards swing going into a stab, he pierced the parasite's leg, a black ooze dribbled, and hissed when it struck the ground. Steel whipped around, the blade nearly decapitating him, but only grazed his robe. He braced the impact with the flat of his blade. A great wave of sparks flooded all he could see. In the white haze, and smoke screen, he was pulled by the talons. Gripping his robe. Jostling him.

Jane attempted to hobble the bat, but only swiped air. It flapped its slime soaked wings, gaining heights way above her. *She's going to kill him!*

Their blades were interlocked, he was thrusted high, before being dropped to the ground. And in that free fall he saw the fire glistened steel above, pointed down. Time seemed to slow, and in that moment he reached for the wand which destroyed the cellar. At that point he drew a sun the size of a fist, and it burned so bright with streams of fire encircled it. Swallowing and pulsating. Time stopped the moment he threw the sun. He fell further, the light stayed put. And all he could see was a brightness, until the tip of her sword peered through. And the second after, everything was stained. The sound of all was gone. Everything was thrown into an image, but that blade stayed in his vision.

The nobles, and dressed officers were escorted by the king's guard, who were directed by Tylock and other high ranked men when the fire had spread even further. The higher ranked officers tried to argue against him, but Tylock put a sword to their throats and some of his personal men arrested them. The nobles couldn't care, and neither did the high merchants of Hule. With sweat beading from their foreheads, they had red faces, and pale hands.

A vacuum sucked the fire, and made the fire spread further throughout the castle. Tylock understood this, and directed a few men to round up the servants, cooks and their scullions, and any children and any castle alchemists on grounds.

Tylock went out as the smoke started to accumulate. His hand against his arm, smothering his wound. Running up with buckets and wheelbarrows of water, were the sailors under Tylock's direct command. A line of men stormed in, going against the grain. They ran until the fire was present, even with the water they brought couldn't quench it all. Steam cut through the smoke, forming dew on the ceiling. Ahead were the first court, the one without the throne. Men left and returned with water ready to throw. Tylock heard from outside an explosion, from high above a plume of fire erupted and shattered the glass window. "Jane," he muttered under his breath, before returning to command.

It just narrowly missed his eye, and embedded in the marble ground. "Where are you shrew!" And she looked down, "ah," she said while attempting to upend the stuck sword.

Litus' mind had gone into a faze of fuzz, and wavered on. His head focused, and clear once more, and in time for the talon's of the deeply inflamed beast. He moved his head to the side, dodging the talons sharp points, and all the while reaching for his sword which still gripped in his hand. But all that was pulled was a shard on a handle.

They were both in an awful bind. Brandishing her sword forward, she ran towards and swung up the side. A large gash the size she gave the queen before was there again, but this monster has new flesh. It dug in and oozed, poured through, and bubbled awfully. While smoke and shrieking floated above a hiss of steel. The parasite, with a scratch of stone swung out the blade towards Jane, and broke her guard, throwing her to the ground.

Litus gripped the handle, the shard made him quiver only a moment. *What can I do now, use this heavy knife, I have to use something, I have that firewand now.* And so he did, reaching forth in the void. He sent a plume of fire vollying through the hall searing the greasy sweat that beaded on its skin. He sent a succession of fire; a volleying fire enough to destroy the beast. But instead, the grease dripped off in flight.

Jane leaned away from the incoming fire, and fearfully looked at Litus, *Too close for my liking, what was that, who threw that fire,* and she saw him, *Litus, it's broken, your sword.* She kept her sword up, and ran to the monster who was flying towards Litus.

Weaving through the ceiling waves of smoke as the arrows of fire shoot through, the talons emerge. Litus threw down a wall of fire, a standing shifting wave of flame in front of him, and it kept the beast away for a quiet moment. With a knife in one hand and shard another; they interlocked in a cross ready for something.

Wine burned and drove Jane away from the flame which danced against the crystal shards. She watched it drive a maddening hole through the now thick, black smoke that suffocated the ceiling of the castle, and still Jane sought it so, to protect Litus, or try to. With blade forward again, she ran. Passing shards, and dwindling fires and erupting flames. Now all between were the waves of flame.

Litus stood in between the wall and wave. Almost cooking in his cocoon. He looked around waiting for the talons to strike, but when it hadn't, he thought, *Jane.* Litus wanted to escape but with the wave still great, he was pinned. And for moments, he expected something. His knives both together. Without fuel for the fire, the magic started to dissipate into the air. The wave began to crash. It was then when the black ash talons broke through the thin fire wall. He was put to the ground, while stabbing what he could. The red robe was torn off completely, letting Litus escape away. Still brandishing the blades, he guarded himself. They parried and slashed at the queen's sword. He was pushed closer to that flame. With all of his might he pushed, and kept pushing until his feet stopped sliding. He pushed, and the parasite was falling back. Their swords met, parrying the blade, and rolling away from the grip of talons. With a parry and blade roll, he made the parasite drop their sword, but instead of being subdued with an unwinnable situation and killed, the parasite grabbed onto Litus, once the sword dropped. He was strangled into the air. Thrashing, and trying to break free. "You won't escape now, wraith!"

Jane watched him in it's grasp. *In god's hell,* she swore. Without thinking Jane took a piece of glass, and threw it up at the beast. And then another, and it gashed in the fleshy wing, drawing a dripping of blood. Litus however was dropped, landing hard, on the bronze chandelier, a cloud of smoke trailed.

He trudged through the hall of nothing. Complete darkness enveloped everything. Not even the air filled that space, there was only him. For an eternity he walked, no matter which way, was the same. But that was all until it appeared. A door of stone, and silver inscriptions. Inlaid with silver was a symbol of an eye, a sword, and blood. There wasn't a handle, but that wasn't needed. It opened slowly, silently. Inside the world – not built by hands of men, or trees, and with stone not from the ground – was a great court. He could tell its greatness by a certain ambiance. The smell of the air, and the temperance too.

He walked through the door, and overlooked the court. Those below may not have seen him, but he saw them. One man was dressed lavishly, in silks that shined and glistened. Half his head was draped in fiery unruly hair, and the other side was rotten, burned, and with hair white and silken strait. Half his face was covered in a mask of white porcelain, inlaid with runes of silver, and jewels of red. The other man sitting was almost normal in comparison, or at least familiar. It was a man of shadows, without constraint form, not lines could be drawn. Made of nothing but shadow, *is that me? Who is that man sitting across from me?* Though he could not see his face, or any eyes, all there shown, was shadows.

The two men seemed motionless, but were exceptionally not. Though he couldn't perceive what they say, he could tell they were arguing, bickering, and yelling. And neither could win, against each other. They were equals, complete equals. *Who sits in the third seat?*

At the round table there weren't two seats, there were in fact three. One for Keroth, one for Mortith, and one for Selziar.

He felt the stone railings as he walked past. Across the room there was another door. It may lead down to the court or somewhere else. He watched the round, as he walked. The pillars of stone block every here and there. Eventually both figures were gone from the table, where they went, he didn't know. The door was made of birch wood, with an old natural finish. Stepping through, was a corridor filled with massive gray stone pillars filling the aeon of space provided. The door was gone, and all was now this. And again he walked through the dark hall, but this time he felt more uncertain. There were pins and needles that sprinkled his body, his skin. And it felt everywhere, except there.

He kept walking, the pain was now centered behind him, and he ran. He looked back, and what he saw was a figure enveloped in shadow, *was it the man at the round, himself? Or maybe it was the other one, with the mask?* He couldn't tell. He just kept running.

Needles dug into his flesh, drawing blood. His feet were being torn away, bit by bit. Ashes and blood fell from him. Until there ahead he could see there was a sword. It didn't shine with hope or fear, warmth or cold. His being torn to its last bits, grasping the handle, his hand was all that was left.

Jane kept her sword up, encircling the fallen parasite, while ready to guard as well. From behind she took a slash and stab at the beast, before it got up. It's claws brandished, and in an attempt to grab Jane's blade with a snap. She retreated back while keeping her sword in a guard. Deflecting the taps and grabs. "Daughter dear, stop fighting. I'm not your enemy, we fight for the same lord."

"I'm not your daughter, I watched my mother die in the snow, you aren't her. You aren't human, you're a bug, you're a parasite, you're evil. And all of you in this kingdom have tried to kill me, I won't give you my body, I won't give you my death," and Jane went into a strike, she bobbed her head around every talon strike.

She got close and sunk her blade into the wet flesh of its torso. The parasite shrieked in hissing pain, which pierced her ear, but then was transformed into boiling hatred. Jumping back towards Litus, the parasite went. She snatched the elegant sword up, gripping it firmly. And decided to take Litus hostage as a sort of shield. "It seems you care about this wraith of yours dearly, my dearest daughter. Don't you mind if I reciprocate the love? Ah your lovely eyes, I had eyes like those, until you cut them off me. And my hair, you took that away from me. So why don't I take this away from you," and she pierced Litus' body with the sword, and a cry came from Jane which shook the court. The queen's sword was dripped in clouds of red ash.

She ran to him, in a rage of great winds, Jane matched steel for steel. She couldn't care for the sparks; she treated it as though it weren't there. And the parasite laughed in a haunting act, she threw Litus' body aside. The ash swirled around, following their blades. Jane began her strike from above, and redirected it around slashing high. Jane attacked with a great force; sweat beaded on her face. Parry and block and attack, from high and low, push back and forward. The ash followed, the blood flowed. The sparks splashed on the ground. Jane pushed closer once more, and again in a cyclone she twirled the tip, disarming the blade from the claw. The sword was cast aside. But the parasite knew this, she grappled on the steel Jane carried, twisted it, and quickly disarmed her. It fell towards the other blade, and the touch of the blades sparked and popped.

Jane tried to back away, the fear drove the parasite closer. She twisted around Jane like a snake. "A younger, far prettier body, why don't you be mine, the wealth and power, all you have to do is surrender yourself my princess, or you could succeed and breathe the clean fresh air."

She pushed, and heaved trying to escape the grasp, but couldn't, "by the blood of gods, these fires will burn until all the stones are ash, and the ceiling has crashed down, and then we will both be dead. Your blood and mine."

A blood that he hadn't known before, but it didn't bind him. In a flash he stood far above the queen's parasite, watching down. Time within the entire hall seemed to stop, the fire was cold, and he both was in control and not. The queen looked up at him and muttered, "I shall bring you back down once more, little wraith-"

"Death."

Wall of fire that stood behind them was extinguished; a thrust of wind pulled the rest of the fire closer. He raised the sword high up, slashing down to his feet, and it was all over. The monster, it's talon feet, and all things around were severed; except for Jane, who fell to the ground, and crawled away from the reef of blood. The corpse hissed and began dissolving away.

Litus stood still, the tall blade aligned with his eyes. Clear of blood, and shown no warmth or coldness. The crossguard was long and thin, with square hooks at the end of each quillon. He gripped the red leather handle with both hands, not bending the silver braided wire that looped around. The diamond pommel pointed to the ground, and it too showed no temperature. Then once he completely regained control of his mind, the blade broke off back into the small shard. With the rest disappearing into ash. The hilt stayed what it became.

Jane picked up the queen's sword which slid next to her. Litus walked over to her, and she tried to say something, but there was nothing she could say, or think of. It was all a blur. She eventually tried to think of something, "are you okay," and he nodded, "we need to go. Here," and she gave him the falchion.

He put the thinly bladed two handed falchion into the void along with the knife, and the shard. Litus embraced her giving a full heavy hug, and she said in a calm voice, "so this is how I die it seems."

The smoke and fire still spread, so their true reunion was broken shortly. Litus rose, and went for Jane who looked at the sword on the ground with its long and thin profile, even the set of quillons which cornered the blade, were thin bronze. The sparks came from the enchantment on the blade, nothing too strong, but still burned them. On the hip on the husk of the body which was the queen,

Jane stole one last thing, a scabbard and her life.

Embers fell from the burning curtains and portraits of the dead. Litus took Jane's hand as they ran towards an exit. *The kitchen door. No, it's locked.* The window of the door showed flames which cracked the glass. The floor started to seep a wine slurry which spread quickly into a lake of fire. As they passed through the burning halls, smoke caught in their breath, queasing a grinding cough. The collapsing cage of stone; the beams crashing down behind and around them. The screams of nobles were ever present now, Litus saw guards stationed around the second main hall, they were organizing the incoming sailors with buckets of water, and anyone left to escape the fire.

"Look there, as long as we cover our face, they won't realize. The soldiers don't have the eye of a noble, and the nobles only look after their own blood and skin," Jane muttered and moaned when the exhaustion and pain finally broke in.

Jane collapsed on the ground coughing. Her face was pale, bloodless. She clearly couldn't stand anymore. "If you die because of me, I won't forgive you; leave me, you're the prophet. He was right, Tolk, you really are the chosen one."

Litus shook his head, instead he carried her on his back. He brunted the force, and pushed on "My debt is only growing," she said, but didn't speak, but that didn't matter.

Just like Jane said, they didn't care to point out the faces of everyone, just as long as people were leaving Renoi alive. A crew of men carried their buckets of water, and wheelbarrows of water, and another brought buckets of sand, and wheelbarrows of sand.

They were under the black skies, with streams of smoke leading up combining into one large cloud of exhaust. Fire was present in the windows much brighter than candle light in the homes across the cobblestone road.

The sound of crackling was ever present instead of silence. Litus was running past to the speed of his heart, pushing and weaving around those in the way. But when he saw Tylocks face he stopped for a moment, "don't ever stop," and she saw him too, "keep going, if he sees us, I don't know what will happen, but something will. If I could walk I would have kicked his knee in."

They pursued further until they were out of the castle ground, and along with other streams of noble lords and the troop of water bearers heading to the dock yards. They were in the distance far ahead, when they heard a yell from behind, "Garnette, Princess Garnette?"

Did they see us? They both thought as they ran to the side of a wall, semi masked by the shadow of the trees, "what are you doing," she whispered, and before she could follow up, Litus pulled out the blue robe which he carried, and draped it over her.

The shouting for Jane's name was still present, but their presence seemed absent at least, but that fear still lingered.

There were legions of ships, half were the navy, the rest belonged to the nobles, and the wealthy merchants of Hule. further up the docks in a bend was a single ship, a naval vessel, but it was smaller, with sharper sails, disconnected from all the other ships. Even near that ship, there wasn't any heavy crowding. It seemed all too safe. Far too safe.

The sails rang high, and the world was shifting further, when those two were heading towards that ship, the moaning and pain of the red swelling along their arms and necks. Burns, and gashes visible on all in the crowds.

A series of naval vessels had departed their post and formed a line around the coast keeping order in disorderly chaotic times. But that may have been an intention of some, but surely not completely the orchestrator of it: Tylock. "That ship is a naval vessel the same, they fly the same flags, we should be able to go through, right?"

They boarded the lone ship, remaining under the cover of darkness and ambiguity of recognition. Litus unhooked the tie rope, the ship shook when regaining center buoyancy. They set sail away from the line and passed the burning castle. They looked on as hundreds or thousands of soldiers gathered to spray sand and water into the walls, hoping to end it sooner.

In a swirl of clouds, forming an ever thick whirlpool of thunder striking in the distance. Rain drumming down, coming closer than wanted. The tides rose, and waves crashed. A vortex of storms greater than storms. Litus was stuck to the wheel, trying to keep the ship away. *First a fire, then a storm, we will survive this, and we have to.* There was a faint trace of something, smelling metallic or of static.

What is this smell? Lightning struck to the side of the ship, it was a bright flash of white, and a crash loud and gone quickly. The smell of static lingered in the air. Litus had fallen on his back, and the wheel started spinning without control.

Jane was stirring undercover, the water rising to the window lines. The strike of lightning made her scream out of an immediate fear and panic. Red plasma still hung in the air, when she painfully hobbled to Litus, getting drenched in the rain. "Better to die in the rain than by fire," and the storm only grew closer and stronger, as they voyaged onward, without control of the sails, and stuck where they sat.

Chapter Twenty-Two:

The shy waves crashed just a turn away. "What do you say we do with it, whatever it is?"

"What do you mean, it's a wraith! Ya kill it!"

"I've never seen one of them, but ya sure?"

"Ya I'm sure, that's what those rangers said to look out for. Let's end it quickly."

"But that was months ago, are you sure it were this? Looks a bit sad. Don't it?"

"Don't pity a demon, that's how it eats your soul!"

"Eating who's soul, may that be? Certainly, not from an angel of death."

"My holiness, you don't mean that do you?"

"I do indeed, in great studies can you discern the difference from afar."

"But, their horns aren't there, shouldn't he have horns?"

"Horns? What ya mean, a death bringer is just be as much a curse as any wraith."

"How would ya know, you haven't seen em both."

"By praying to the gods, they forgive this talk of cruelty. I will not see an angel murdered by my own brethren. Now help me carry him back, get him a bed out of this rotten cloak, and rusted steel."

"She's awake," the voice of a timid bedmaid ushered, "inform the duke."

Jane awoke in a wide bed, with a great window overlooking the beach, and a gathering of priests, servants, and other onlookers circled around the frame. She jumped back against the backboard. "Where am I?" She asked.

"In the home of Duke Eiger, my lady," a servant said.

Clamoring through the door, bringing heads towards, was the large Duke Eiger. A trough of sweat was beaded on his flushed face, but mostly beaded his forehead. "My fair lady, we haven't believed you'd wake. I heard what occurred that night from days past. How terrible, but with an open wound in the lake, would be the doom of many stranded survivors."

"Doom? Where are we? Where's Litus?"

"Calm my lady, you are in my hands now, in the castle of Lakeholm. Who is this Litus you speak of?" A sudden realization came, "your lord, by my god's mercy, I'll send men to go search for his body. What did he look like, so we could help?"

"No, he is no lord," she paused, "no, he is my personal guard. Now you make me fear he's gone."

"In all sense he may be, but nonetheless, I'll send a man; the ship wreckage was grave, especially one of the late queen's vessels."

Jane was horribly surprised to hear, but tried to keep her eyes non expressive. "Will you find him?"

"What does he look like?" He grumbled, "this guard of yours."

"Pastor Kreshen, he's awake, the angel is awokened!"

"Calm calm, from a cold lake he came from, and an abrupt shove he shouldn't get. We have prayed for his safety, and have been rewarded, by which god, I know not, but by all three I would assume."

"Aren't there only two?"

"There seems to be, in my house, but in the heart of our land of the living and heavens of the dead, it tis the domain of all of us and the three gods. Each has a great purpose," he lectured on with a sort of love in his heart not present with most.

"Oh my words have rushed away at what's current and important. My name is Kreshen, Pastor Kreshen," he said to Litus, "may I have your name in return?"

Litus reached into the void searching for the pad of parchment and began writing just his name, "Litus."

The priest took a mental note, "so it seems you can not speak. Then your name is more a curse. Do you know who gave you it?"

"Yes," he scribbled quickly, "Jane"

"That is unfortunate, I don't know this Jane. But do you know where she is?" The pastor looked to Litus, and said, "if you survived that infamous shipwreck. Your Jane may have survived it too. But in the grave heed, pray for her. I'm sorry for your loss, and I'll pray for you as well, death or Mortith's loving hands, she may be with."

"We don't know if he's a reaper yet," whispered in his ear.

"Ah yes, you are right, let's know now," out of his breast pocket he drew a thin silver rod, "follow this light."

Light, it's light! If this idiot keeps that light burning, it'll explode, and bring the ceiling down on us.

"I see you're disturbed son, and that you've seen light magic before, from enchantments?"

Litus' stress didn't leave, but he did nod. "I know the power that it brings, and what it can do. And the balance of nothing and something. It is a danger in the hands of those who misuse it. For now I cast only a simple light, as controllable as keeping a pebble in the palm of your hand."

He slowly waved the wand from here to there. He cast a small light from its tip only the size of a pinky finger tip. It was such a casual gesture, it had been as though practiced through decades. Though the gray hairs on the side of his head didn't indicate great old age. The top of his head was still a short swaft of tar black hair.

"So you really can't speak, can you?" He got a quick response, "nevertheless, do you know what a wraith is" Litus looked down and remembered, *everyone I've met, call me the terror and a wraith, but I've never seen one,* "terrible things, in the arms of the gods, and heavenly beings may you be protected from their sight. But now I ask if you know of Reapers?" *I've been called one, a death angel, but I don't truly know,* he nodded. "You were found robed in black, and with rusted out armored gloves and boots. Many of the townsfolk when they saw you, were scared of you. They thought of you as a wraith. It's a tragic thing, being called a wraith. But I didn't see you as one. I believed you as a death angel. And I still do know, but still. You don't have the horns of a reaper, nor the wrath of a wraith. And these grounds would harm a wraith," he paused to scratch his face, "reapers have been known to break horns before. But no horns in total are different. Looking like a being of a void is also different. From most of the gods we have, Mortith is generally depicted as a black death. A being of shadow, a void which light doesn't pass through. Which roams the fields and homes of the dying and returns their soul to the realm of the dead," he chuckled a bit, "though I'm not calling you Mortith, because he doesn't roam the lands of the living, our world, our realm. His domain is the dead, same as Keroth's and Selziar's is the living. But still you do look like him, and that ability to pull things from the void," he gave a breath, and said, "I'm sorry. I seem to have talked your ear off, I apologize. I'm a man of faith and teaching, and I like to teach these simple lessons, wherever I can."

"If you're saying he isn't a wraith or a Reaper, then what is, Pastor Kreshen?"

He sat down thinking, while scratching his chin, "come here Tiamon, look at his face and his eyes."

"What is it?" Litus looked confused, but had a thread of an idea which this could lead to, because Tiamon were Malkin.

"In my travels I've heard of an idea, or a faith from your peoples around – not just the continent, but around – the world. Do you know it?"

"Yes, but that were just a fairy tale, a story told to young litters to sleep well."

"Look, young one."

Tiamon held a hard stare at Litus keeping his mind open, "you don't mean that do you? A being like him is a mythos, it is, it is. I don't know. How is he standing here in front of us? Oh, I should be ashamed of my ignorance."

"You did no harm my son. But yes, I do mean it. He is that prophesied being. Or at least that's our best idea. It's either that or the god of Death is in our presence now," Tiamon began to pray, "your eyes appeared to shine. You've known of this tale, this prophecy?" Litus nodded, "do you believe in it? Believe in this prophecy."

Litus remembered Tolk, and thought about that sword he pulled from the gray pillared hall, and he nodded.

"I remember being clothed in a blue cloak, do you know where it is?"

"Was it a gift? Nevermind. Well it were marred beyond mending. My tailors on the castle grounds said it was beyond saving. I can have one made in its image, exactly, multiple for you, but before that what did your guard look like?"

If I tell a half lie I may be able to trick him, "he wore a cloak the same as mine, less embroidered but with the same color. He wore it when the ship crashed, that was the last I saw him. If he survived then that cloak would most likely be destroyed the same as mine, I can't recall any features on his face. But he wore a sword without a sheath."

"You care for him but haven't seen his face?"

"Under his hood a shadow covered most of his face, but he had purple eyes which showed through the dark. He was my guard, not my friend. I haven't seen his face."

"On your body we found a sword in a sheath, I'm assuming it was yours then," Jane nodded, "well it's a beautiful sword, a good queen's lady you are – bless her soul – I have men working on it in the armory. It was severely damaged in the crash, rust started tainting the blade, and that sheath is rotted out now. Though purple dye is expensive, I acquired a nice red dye to stain the wood and leather hilt."

"Why are you treating me so nicely, ever since I awoke – and I guess before then – you have been very nice to me. Why?"

"Do I need a reason to help a fellow noble lady, especially one who sailed under the royal navy flag, and the dress you wore – beautiful as it be – was also marred beyond mending. But you must have been at the terrible terrible ball a few days ago. The chaos it brought, awful, truly awful."

Jane looked down at the garb she was wearing, it felt sufficiently worse than what she was wearing at the ball. *This dress is like a potato sack, so scratchy, not even worthy for a servant . . . what am I thinking, this is a finer dress than what I had before Porcelania.*

"One of my servants made a dress for you, or maybe a few, while you slept."

"So they took my measurements while I slept?"

"Seems so. Why don't you get dressed, I'll be back later."

First leaving the great room was the duke, then followed by his male servants, and then the priests, and then a woman came streaming through with a few dresses of immaculate quality. First they put over her a white dress with gray and gold embroidery, but it seemed to not fit her very well. "It's a bit tight," she muttered, and the tailor woman shrugged, "especially in the cups," and the tailor woman pulled a marked ribbon from her sleeve and threw it around Jane to get a better measurement.

The next dress was a bright blue thin ball gown similar to the one she wore at the ball, but less constricting. The bell of the dress protruded further than she was expecting, causing her to almost fall from a snag on a chair. But once she got to a clear point in the middle of the room – a haze of light cast on the blue – Jane realized that the heft and thickness of the fabric had become a great strain on her shoulders. "The color and cloth is smooth and rich, but it hurts my shoulders," *If I talk like a noble then they'll think of me as one.*

The third and last dress that was shown, was almost like a ball gown, but was much lighter. It was almost reminiscent of that dress she wore before the crash. It was black like charcoal with red embroidery of two slashes interlocked. It was a symbol of the house of Renoi. *These symbols, they're from the queen aren't they. Does he know I killed the queen and is he sending guards to kill me? I have to act carefully and calmly, maybe he doesn't actually know?* She began to sweat a bit, but it only showed on her face. "You're sweating dear," the tailor spoke up, "have you gone ill, dear lady?"

"No, no I just haven't seen a dress of such great qualities. It fits very well. Especially in the chest area. I like it very much, but what about this symbol, isn't it the queen's crest?"

"That's good because the duke asked for those symbols which I protested. I believed only the royals and her men should wear that herald, but what the duke asks, I stitch."

Does he too think I'm the queen's heir, her daughter, how did this rumor spread so quickly. Damn you Tylock.

Litus and Kreshen left the church on a walk which the pastor thought could help him. Litus realized that the church was the grandest building within the town, and the castle Lakeholm didn't count. But the church was only a wooden structure on an old stone foundation. with one large spire, and a stained glass symbol. An eye in the center, a sword with scales at the end of each quillon, and blood dripped from the eye and blade. Litus peered up at the symbol, in awe of it, but for a reason he couldn't discern. "This church, though not as old as this symbol, or myself for that matter, is one of the oldest in the north east. It's a shame, more people could use community and prayer, but to them they think praying is useless with one the gods missing. They think that praying to the other two would bring up an earthquake and kill us all, but I think not. To me even if Selziar's body has left these lands, his soul is still quite present. I guess that's why when having that stained glass made, I used that symbol. Justice will always be present, even if it isn't not potent enough to tell."

Over his clothes he draped a gray half cloak, "even with your cloak of shade, do you still feel cold, or get cold? It will be winter soon, that's all I ask about. But when you travel through Hule you might completely miss the snowfall. Well maybe not the mountain tops, but conveniently there's a mountain pass straight through. Carved by the river."

Litus drew attention from the townspeople who already saw him, and others who saw a man of shadow – although cloaked in black – and first thought of a wraith. He felt uncomfortable, *they're all staring at me, even though I'm not what they think, they still see me as a wraith.* He felt alone, Jane was gone, and she was the only one who cared. His eyes showed it, more than he would like to let on. People gave those looks of disgust and fear, all because of Litus. He tried to withdraw into the void, all until the pastor put his hand on Litus' shoulder. "They fear you because of their ignorance, it's only natural. They use what they know to understand the world. What limited world that is, they just want safety. They won't lay a finger on you, as long as you're with me."

The church was in the center of the town, and was as stated the oldest building of the town. Not that the town didn't exist before, but that from the chaos of the times, it is the current oldest standing building. All of the houses were built of beams and plaster canvases. With a slick wax-like coating against the walls. And a spiral dome of wood and clay tiles. But even with all these precautions, most homes were ready to fall over.

They walked past the homes of new, shops of old, and people of grimace. They would shudder in disgust, those few who were faithful would pray with a hand symbol. One hand touching one shoulder, second the other shoulder, and the final, their forehead. The priest took no mind, or appeared to not look so, he kept a face of confidence and courage which helped mend those first impressions of the onlookers. Moments later while Litus followed Kreshen, a draft of salty wind appeared against their winds. The short brisk wind beat against the coast, and they came to the docks, and most of them were made of freshly cut lumber, while the older docks were being mended by dockmen. They stopped, and Kreshen said,"Come, let's stand and watch the waves and birds for a moment."

And for that moment of near five or ten, maybe even fifteen or twenty minutes they watched the wave crash lightly. Birds swam on the surface, waving up and down with the water. The calming sense of the sea, and the stillness which Litus hadn't felt ever, made him feel something new, *what am I? If I'm some chosen one, why am I this chosen one? Is my purpose just to kill? And I let Jane come to her death. Why did I let her stay with me? It's my fault she's dead. I couldn't save Tolk or Lady Thinithe or Rouvel. They had me-.*

Kreshen put his hand onto Litus' shoulder saying, "it's okay my son. I'm here for you. It's okay to fear for her, it's not your fault. It's not your fault," he continued to look at the subtle overlapping waves, he let out a short cough, and said after, "I know what you must be thinking, feeling, about being this prophetic hero of sorts. I couldn't know how to feel about being this hero, but I know how it feels to be unsure of your purpose. That's why I became a priest. I knew my abilities could've been used to help those, though they may not feel it. I still care about all of us, but you have a greater purpose than most, far greater. I can help you, through all the trials and tribulations. That is if you decide to fight. It's your choice, the world will turn the same for a thousand years more, and people will live and die the same as those now. But you can change that, you could restore some safety and reassurance to the people around us, and everyone everywhere," he paused to look at Litus who was watching him as well, "are there anyone in your passing who you cared about, or care about you?"

Litus pulled out the paper and wrote down Jane's name, along with some other names: Rouvel, Tolk, and Lady Thinithe. "What happened to them?" Kreshen asked, *they're dead.*

He tried to write it down, but his hand shook, "death comes, to here and there, and when times seem unfair just always try to take a step forward. Just keep walking. And don't fear death so quickly. He's a kinder soul than most would know. Their lives were laid for you, and you should keep moving forward. That's what I believe."

And they stared into the lake water for a moment more, before departing the docks. As they came further away from the shore, the winds and smell of salt lessened. And still the people stared, on the west side of town, they seemed to stare more impudently. There was a small store district of the town, which would seem quite surprising, but it was quite a large town – especially compared to Diende and

Demorte combined. But otherwise what seemed out of the ordinary most was a semi paved street of cobblestone, and gravel. Mostly gravel, and on the side of the streets were irrigation like tunnels which most likely led the water away, but some carried all the way to crops. The faint smell of both burnt and cooked bread streamed the road, and Kreshen followed. "You must be starving, you haven't eaten since the wreckage. Or longer than that. Now this bread may not be as great as what's served on silver platters in Porcelania, but for some small town like this, it will do."

Litus tried following Kreshen inside the bakery – which had a small cafe-like dining area with loaves of gray bread on wooden stands – but was forced out when a man behind the counter yelled to him, "get out thieven, we don't accept the likes of wraiths or things that look like yer."

"Calm, my son," Pastor Kreshen said, "he is with me, he wouldn't cause harm to anyone here, because he isn't a wraith."

"Don't matter, don't like him, don't want him in my shop. He'll have to wait out for ya."

"Alright then," he went to Litus, "I'm sorry son, but you'll have to wait out for a moment, it'll be a short time. Only for a short time."

Litus waited out like what was said. Every few seconds or later a man or woman would like expected stare, sneer, and depart quickly. The clouds twisted above, small thundering trickled far away. A child had walked up to Litus, sad and clearly upset. He in turn was quite surprised, no one had just walked up to Litus besides a few exceptions. Especially a child that be. The child clung to Litus' leg sobbing. *What's wrong he wanted to say,* but was beaten to the punch when the child spoke up, "Mr Death, my mum is sick. You can help her? You can help her."

He didn't know what to do, he couldn't comfort the child with words like how Kreshen comforted him. All he did was bend down to the child's height, and gave him a hug. That was all he thought.

"Get away! Get away wraith! Get away from my son!"

A man came running up with a broom handle ready to swing at him, "let go of my son! You will not get him! You won't kill him!"

Litus let go of the boy, who ran away towards a pale thin woman who was his mother. The father kept a distance with the length of the pole before going to strike. Kreshen bolted out of the door, a loaf of bread between his arms, and he yelled, "by the grace of the gods, what do you think you're doing!"

"The wraith had my child!"

"He is no wraith, you just attacked an angel, leave, so may Selziar forgive your crimes against others."

"He ain't human! Get the fuck out of here! Child killer!" The father left before leaving with his wife and son, clearly distraught. With tears and fear streamed down his face.

It had been thirty minutes since being garbed in the black dress. Most of the servants beside a few kept with her, mainly to make sure she didn't collapse and die. Jane had only peered out the window looking down at the rest of the keep and the beach below, and further in the distance at the town which looked like a speck from her distance away.

"I am going out to take a breath of fresher air, if you mean to keep me safe you are allowed to stay with me. If not, then don't."

The castle walls were made of a white stone, like a pale granite. Unlike Renoi, this was less a series of connected courts, and more of a real battle ready fort. It didn't mean it wasn't furnished for lords, especially dukes, but it wasn't as grand as Renoi, which Jane had become infamously and quickly accustomed to.

She had begun to ask questions, such as where she could allocate food, and wine to drown out the fear of Litus' possible death. When the night sky started to show, she was asked by a servant – who followed her the entirety of Jane's travel through the castle's grounds – to return to her chambers cause night is coming soon.

There was candle light which lightly emanated from the frost glass window on the other side of the tower. *What are they going to do to me? No, they're going to kill me. Could I escape? Maybe, I saw a few exits, or escapes, but they have horses, and the stable is far away from the gates. I couldn't capture a horse and escape, nor could I run without. I must hope they won't kill me. All these nobles, their murderous gaze. All but Lady Thinithe were evil. Hope, please.*

Inside the dark room, only illuminated with the light of a single candle held from a candelabra by the duke. Besides him were a man with a great long beard of gray and black, with a saber concealed to his side, a black leather coat draped over his shoulders, and a tricorn hat of the same black leather hung on his head. "You seemed to have a lovely walk through my walls, my lady. How does it compare?"

"What are you doing? Do you plan to kill me with this man's blade? Don't want blood on your hands?"

"Blood? Heavens no, I don't want blood, but I do want the truth, and the entirety of the truth. And this man isn't some hired thug, or guard I keep to push away peasants or political opponents, or whatnot. No, this man is my truth wizard."

"Truth wizard?" The term was ignorant to her, but was easily able to put together what it entailed, "I have done nothing to say, but the truth, duke."

"I could tell, but you haven't said all I want, which is the whole truth and more. You have evaded questions I have wanted, and now my time is coming to a close. I would rather make this whole procedure walk smoothly."

"Fine, ask away."

The truth wizard stood high, his sharp eyes looking through Jane, one hidden hand behind his back, and the other resting on his pommel. In a sickly cough he said, "you won't move, you won't lie. I will know, if you try both. Do you understand?"

His eyes creeped her out, "yes."

"That was true," he stepped back into the shadow and let the duke ask his questions.

"Now," he began a cough, "were you ship wrecked?"

"Yes, isn't that so obvious now?"

"It's true."

"I'm breaking in the glove. Now, when I said to stay for I would return, did you not stay?"

"No, but I didn't -"

"Truth."

"I don't want excuses, all I want is truth or false. Now, you were at the royal ball?"

"Yes."

"Truth."

"How much longer will this be?"

"Not much longer, my lady. Do you know a man, a commodore named Tylock?"

"How could that be important?" *Has he heard of this from other nobles?*

The man took a step from the shadows, drawing an inch of the blade from the scabbard, "answer, girl," his sickly tone withdrew into the shadow.

"Yes, I do know him."

"Truth."

"You are his pawn, of sorts, or maybe more accurately his puppet?"

"No, absolutely not!"

"Truth"

The duke scratched his face, thinking, "and you killed the queen?"

I thought I did, but that thing, that stripped parasite was the queen, wasn't she? I don't what to say. "No?"

"No? What do you mean no, did you kill our queen or not? Hundreds of men and women saw you."

"No!" Jane exclaimed.

The duke turned to his truth wizard, expecting an easy answer. "It's complicated. It's rare when truth meets somewhere in the middle, "he said something faint that couldn't be heard, but it was a murmur of frustration.

"What is it then?"

"Hmm, closer to the truth, my Grace. You may want to ask differently."

"Then you killed the queen?"

"She tried to kill me! It was the only thing I could do."

"Truth."

"So she attacked you. Alright, and I have only one more question, then your sentence will be made. Are you Garnette Renoi?"

"No, my name is Jane. I'm not your puppet, and I'm not Tylock's puppet, and I'm not anyone's puppet."

"The first was a lie, but the rest was the truth."

"What do you mean? A truth or a lie. Is she Garnette or not! Who is she bound to?"

"Her name isn't Jane, but her real name is Garnette Renoi, daughter heir to the throne of Rientonem. Your lord. And she spoke truly at the last puppet remarks."

"Answer once, only a yes or a no, are you Garnette Renoi?"

"No!"

"A lie."

"That's not true, I'm not the daughter to the throne, you will not force me."

"It is true though she doesn't know it."

"Do you believe your name is Jane?"

"Yes!?" She yelled with disbelief.

"Truth."

"Then this sentence is adjourned, come," he said to the truth wizard as he departed the room with all the other guards and female servants after. *What do they want with me, I need to leave.*

Jane went to the door, it wasn't locked, but guards were posted outside.

It were a cold morning, Jane looked down onto the shores, the sea comforted her even if it failed to kill her twice. *What are they going to do with me? I don't want to die, I don't want to. I'm not the heir, I've been thrown into this fucking game of theirs. It's all a game, and Tylock made me the center. He convinced the court like a child of parlor tricks.* In the distance she saw a vibrating and shifting speck, it looked like a ship. She couldn't see the sails, but she made a grave thought of what it could be. She went to one of the guards close by, "what is that ship in the distance? . . Ser?"

He went to another guard, one with a scoped looking glass. "A royal navy vessel. My lady."

"A royal navy vessel?" She repeated under her breath, she looked up to the guards men, "I need to meet with Duke Eiger. Now! This is important."

The guards looked confused, but listened to the lady's commands, and as the duke said, she was the queen. Though that was both impossible and unlikely. It was treated so, but she had known her real mother, and her death too.

Two guards escorted Jane to the duke's quarters, he had been sitting at a table – eating a flank steak – when to his surprise, he was disrupted. "What is the meaning of this, why have you brought her to my dining quarters."

"Her grace ordered us to."

"Rumors spread fast," he said under his breath, "how many men know of this? Of her position?"

"I don't know, but us and maybe . . . Almost all the men on this flank of the keep knows."

"By god's grace, this wasn't meant to be some low man's rumor, inform the guard to keep silent. Now. And if they don't know, inform them it's a drill."

"What is it, your grace, Garnette?"

They all have gone mad, have they caught a disease? I'm not the queen, I don't want to be that. The image of the parasite coming from the queen's flesh still persisted, but she kept her composure and went with it, "I need to leave, duke."

"Leave? Now? To where? The castle of ashes?"

"It's the Royal Navy, there here, they're clearly after me."

"It was Tylock who found you, and presented you in front of Queen Mary as her heir. Was proven so, you killed her-"

"She tried to kill me! It was self defense, and still I didn't kill the queen."

"Is that so? Is that surely so, it doesn't matter, besides that you are the actual heir to the throne, and in the wake of chaos, the man who brought you the crown has taken reins of the navy."

"He what!? What do you mean? Don't you see, he was only using me to gain fame, and lands."

"So? I would try to win favor with the queen, and was rewarded with a lake."

"The queen was not my mother, but a . . . a thing, a parasite controlling her from the beginning. I saw it crawl from her body. Like a maggot, you haven't seen this like I have. She was helped by these red robed cultists, who threw fire at us and the nobles, and also her own guard. The kingdom is a mass plot by a cult. I don't know why, but it is. This kingdom is ruled by monsters."

"Is that so? Is that very so? You have lied to me before. But fine I have an easy solution to all this chaos, and madness. Come have a guard get Darien, my truth wizard here. So we can settle this business."

"They sail here, and will arrive in only a few hours, if not less than that."

"You still think I will give you an escape from the throne, your people, because you don't like Tylock? And of this parasite nonsense, get him. If you are true about this, I'll give you supplies and men to travel away and we will solve this diplomacy."

It was only a short moment later, Jane had told the guards to hurry. And Darien was thrust before both Jane and the duke. "Your grace, and lord, you have an urgent need for me, what will it be?"

"What you told me, Garnette, is it true?"

"Yes."

"My lord this is true, but what is it?"

"All of it?"

"Yes," Jane said wearily.

"True as well my lord, what is happening?" He said with a cold hard face.

"In a sense," the duke paused his eyes became pin holes, and sweat beaded on his forehead, "war."

The duke bolted up, he was followed by two of his trusted guards, Jane, and Darien. He peered from the battlements high up, and from a spyglass, "damn," he muttered, "they've docked, one ship here, another at Terbien. You'll have to hide, and then we'll make your escape. To Esty, the rangers there will keep you safe."

They came to Jane's quarters. He yelled at the guards to get some handmaidens, and her clothes. "For now you'll hide and be disguised, both will work, but only one won't. For all we know a navy man who saw you at the ball could be aboard those ships, let alone Tylock."

The handmaidens and servants came in with a trunk which would fit on the back of a horse, and they undressed Jane and inside the chest they first put fit her dresses – including the black and red embroidered she began to favor folded inside. The other dresses were tailored to hopefully a better size. As well as the other clothes were another pair of boots, dress slippers, and food. Hardtack made a section of the food, but some limes were packed and a loaf of bread or two. "What about my sword?" Jane asked.

"On the same horse as this chest, the scabbard and sword will be on its side," she was told by a servant.

"Now get her dressed like you all: a servant woman," and he left with the rest of the guard.

It was a flight of time, pouring out of the flask. Not enough time in the world, but when they realized the dress's chest didn't fit Jane's, the tailor woman started to take apart the cloth and restitch. To hopefully fit, it wasn't snug, not even a smidge. But it would have to do, for the navy crew in their black and silver tabards, came through the castle's gates.

It was the next day, Pastor Kreshen awoke Litus early in the morning. He informed him that the service was beginning soon. In the rows of wooden benches sat maybe a dozen people, he didn't dare sit with them. The ceremony wasn't very long, the few people who sat had looked more cheerful and happy than the rest of those in the world, but it was a hollow happiness, not like watching a child grow to become a great man, or the feeling of finding a gold coin in a pile of hay on the ground. And this little joy faded the moment the bread giving ceremony was over. Kreshen sent Tiamon to the bakers, though it was mid-morning for more. And the baker was most likely still getting his goods together again. But Kreshen asked Tiamon to gather mainly the cheap bread.

About an hour later, Tiamon came through the side entrance of the church. "You won't believe who's here."

"Who?"

"The Royal Navy, and with two ships. What do you think the occasion is."

"Are you sure it's them? Usually anything about the crown moving is passed on to her lords, and Pastors, and rumors from everyone else."

"Well I saw the ships, from yonder, they were just leaving the river."

"Did you hear any rumor about this, because I haven't been informed of anything."

"Not about the navy, but people are saying the queen is dead."

"Please don't speak such blasphemy so lightly. The queen is still young, she hasn't passed on yet."

"No father, she was said to have been killed."

"Well if that's the case, then it's just a rumor first and foremost."

Litus overheard this last bit, from walking in, he immediately felt a cold sweat. "Welcome, Litus, I have bread if you'd like."

He shook his head, they had this same conversation the previous day prior, and Litus wrote down that he couldn't eat, but Kreshen said it didn't matter. "You're shaking, have you caught a cold?"

He shook his head, "what is it?"

Tiamon blurted in, "Litus have you heard these rumors? The queen has passed, and the naval ships are here. Two of them at least."

Litus pulled paper and wrote, "the queen's Ships?"

"Well, yes," Kreshen said, "wait, that ship wreck wasn't its flag the . . . " And he looked at Litus immediately, seeing his answer, "a ship searching through the wreckage maybe, really only because of its flag, or maybe who was aboard. Who was onboard who could warrant a search like this?"

On the paper, he pointed to Jane's name, and then himself. "What are you a pirate? You stole the ship?" Kreshen looked at his eyes, "no, no. Were you forced to? Steal that ship, both of you?"

He nodded, "do you believe you have committed sin my son?"

Pirating a ship from Tylock, and that parasite thing, I have not sinned, I did what was right. And he shook his head. "I know I don't know the full story of what you've done, hopefully piracy was the worst offense – if that – but I must support you. Morality and honesty is more important than the law of the living."

Tiamon said, "if you escape now you might escape their searchers, and I'll help you. It's my people's prophecy, I have to help."

"And you will, but you are inexperienced. This world is gravely terrible. I don't want you to have to experience it."

"The world is always terrible, but this is something I can do. I'll learn about the world."

"This isn't a matter of curiosity, but of fate. You will experience what this world offers, but not now. You're too young to deal with it now. You will stay here, people need help, they need prayer and hope. If we were both gone it would be hopeless."

"Why are you leaving? The people need you, they need faith."

"They do, both from me and you. I have the experience of this world, and we must do what we can, for that is what we must."

"What do we pack? Not much till they come here. But I'll find sacks to fill. Clothes, bread, any dried food we have. A lantern, two."

"We will have time to pack, but not now. If the naval men find that the Pastor of the church has disappeared the day they landed, escorting a cloak of shadow. They'll come after us, and I fear what they will do to you. Litus, we'll hide you under their noses, and then we'll pack and leave at nightfall."

She and the servants made their way down to the grounds, where the kitchen stood, and stables were, and also where a tall bushy faced man with a combed blonde mustache stood in that familiar black uniform. He strode in as though he owned the keep, and stomped his feet into the dirt until the duke had arrived. "You stomp your feet on my grounds as though you own this keep, captain."

"Do you forget rank duke, I'm the commodore of this ship. I lead them, not you."

"I know rank quite well, but it seems you have raised quite quickly and recently. Or am I mistaken? Lucerne," he added on with a pause, "Commodore Lucerne."

"It was through my bravery and strong leadership that I was promoted. It was through great strength and hardship, my hardship."

"And about that hardship? Tell me about it later, will you?"

"Great, I'll tell you. Great."

Lucerne put his foot on the ground and made a spin towards his naval men coming through. The duke's face remained stoic, but his eyes were like the fierce dragon's, and he yelled, "and why do you commodore these men into my walls? What have you the right?"

"What right does the Crown have to her lands?"

"We both know of the queen's passing. Now I ask again what right do you have to invade my lands?"

Darien stood off to the side along with Jane, and the other servants; listening while appearing to work, or at least Jane and Darien did. "You heard that one, but did you know of the new queen? Right before the old queen passed, we found the heir to the throne. That is also a reason for my . . . accelerated promotion."

"You mean to tell me you found the queen's daughter, her heir!? After twenty or more years, you found her?"

"I won't give myself credit, but I will say the navy is in great times now."

"So this is an order from her grace herself. The new crown I mean."

"Yes, and what we seek you to ask is the queen's murderer. They took the wrecked ship off in the distance back there."

A servant woman whispered to Jane, "you need some soot on your face, and sweat in your palms. To become a servant woman, or to look like one."

They both went to the kitchens, Jane's garb had almost immediately become dirty with flour and spices of different sorts of gunk from around the kitchen and cellar. After so long without work like this, her face became pale and flushed with sweat, and within the women, they worked harder for their collective fear of the navy men.

Barging through the door were two men with that same black tunic. They were scruffy men, their honor drowned long ago. "We are doin a routine check," he emphasized, "now show all of ye in the room. The cellar too."

They all formed a line as quickly as they could, dying down the fire in the stove to not burn down the kitchen. And those with rusty joints getting out of position struggled and made everyone sweat, "speed it up, so you women don't disturb my time," he yelled.

And they put their palms on short sword pommels. Gripping the poorly cast bronze end, and the sailor who was shouting kept shouting, "in line! In a straight line!"

He examined each scullion boy, each cook, each servant, all the women and men, and once he got to Jane he looked at her, and continued on. It was when he came to a big burly man, who looked like he could carry a barrel of wine in arm, and drew out his sword. "Now a man like you could have cleaved through the queen, a great swordsman I heard. True?" His smile stretched across his face.

But before the cellar man could respond, the sailor slashed at his hand, cutting it off leaving a bloody soaking stump and muttered, "no, ye aren't a swordsman, with only one hand," and they left laughing.

The day went on, they heard some shrieks of mothers, and yelling of men. Each time Kreshen would pray for their safety. Sorting through the food, clothes, candles, and cradles for children now empty, and beds for the sick, and other such things. They went through with what the church had to offer in terms of hiding spaces, along with supplies to make their trek.

In the kitchens they had the new bread which they knew would be packed. It was a matter of finding some lantern staffs for when they're out of sight of the town. Tiamon had asked if the light he emits from that silver rod would work better than a lantern constantly being filled with oil, or candles. And in response Kreshen said, "to survive our travels through Mulder, we've got to sleep on our toes, and walk lightly, I'm not sure if I'll have the strength to constantly be conjuring light."

"If we aren't packing why would we be looking through the church for things to pack? Aren't we doing the opposite?"

"No, we are just doing a little bit of fall cleaning before winter. Or you could say we are just figuring out what to give back to the community, which you should. We are finding things to pack, and places to hide, so when we do leave, we can do it faster."

Up the stairs they found a little crawlspace. It were dark inside and looked concealed if you were to put something small in front of it.

Litus crawled through, it was completely dark, "now inside if need does come, there is a latch which opens up through the roof. Try it, don't want it to stick when the need to escape comes."

"How would he get down from the roof, if that's the case?"

"Hopefully it won't be."

Litus couldn't find it, there was no handle, nor a gap in the wood paneled wall. He peered his head back through and shrugged, "I know that there is a door in there, I haven't used it, or seen it in. I don't remember how many years, maybe it were last when it was built. Let me see."

He pulled out his silver twig, and a light – like a small candle flame – that lit the small cavern, and emitted no heat. "Here," he said rubbing his fingers on the panel, he pushed hard, but it didn't open, "I guess those decades really do something."

This time he shoved the panel, and it popped open cracking some of the shingles off. "There," he said, a little bit of sweat beading on his hands, "the rooftops, it was meant for cleaning off the tiles, but luckily rain and birds do a good job of cleaning up twigs and leaves."

The day began to grow dimmer. Light began to fade from the sky, and soon with the oncoming invasion of searchers looking for Litus were coming to the church's grounds. "Now we're going to let them into the church to search, it's not the best option we have, but if they find nothing they'll stay away from these grounds."

"Even if they find him, he could claim sanctuary, and they couldn't lay a finger on him."

"They would commit a crime Litus didn't cause, and force him out. Over the will of the gods, and the sanctity of the church. If we don't let them search, they'll search from outside, and then they'll storm in. whether we like it or not. Sanctuary only goes so far."

Kreshen had watched them from outside, sitting on the church's creaky wooden steps. There were about five men who approached, palms on their pommels, and on their black tunics were splotches of a hard wet sheet of fabric. "You are pastor Kreshen?" The leader of the men said.

"I am, are you men of the faithful as well as sailors?"

"Me? No," he said, "not now, but from orders of the crown, I have need to search this town for certain people."

"Well I can help your search if need be, can you inform me of their details?"

"In Fact I could not, it's unfortunate; directions from the navy high admiral himself. Now if you'll step aside, we have to search each building in this town."

"Let me open the door for you."

Kreshen heaved the door open, sweat was on his face more than it should have. When the men walked in, they were blinded by the light reflected from the stained glass. "Augh," they grunted, "why is it so bright in here, it is near night."

"Oh it's all the candlelight streaming off the stained glass. It keeps the church alive until it's true night. I can have the candles snuffed if it will help."

"And bring darkness into the hall, I think not, keep the candles alight pastor."

The bright blinding light kept on. Kreshen led the men past the praying hall, and the three men followed. He told them what each room was. On the direct left was a spiral staircase that led upstairs. Further ahead to the left there was a storage room on the left, and the kitchen on the right. And at the end of the kitchen, lead to a small cellar going further down, and a bedroom with many beds.

"Continue," he said grimacely.

The priest then led them up, and the stairs creaked with every other step. "Now up here we have mostly storage rooms, closets too. As well as some accommodations for myself, and my apprentice too, and also a separate prayer room for those who need a prayer in private. I'll give you time there if you want."

"Is this all?'

"Yes, yes it is, found what you needed?"

"No." He roared, "we'll go through every nook and cranny until we are satisfied until we've found nothing or something."

They began to tear apart every room they came through. Throwing cabinets to the floor, and smashing flower pots on the ground. Kreshen had been shocked, but after a while he came to his long forgotten senses. *In the name of the gods, and the voice of the queen, what right do they have to do this to a church!?* The lights of the candles started to dim greatly, and the light that had appeared up top was now much less bright.

"Bloody dark, those candles are nearly out. Oh night is almost here."

They continued to rummage through, the lead man was breaking through a storage room, the largest one on the second floor. They were in the same room with the hidden closet that Litus hid in. "How much shit do you have in here! Get in here," he yelled to another sailor.

They tore apart this room, throwing old beds to their sides. Folded clothes, and spare wooden supports were scattered on the floor. They almost stopped when the other man spotted a small cloth pull on the floor, the fabric almost blended in with the wood floor. The leadman went to Kreshen, pulling him up with one hand, "tell me what's behind that door!"

"It's a storage closet, built when the church was built, whenever it was. Today we have little use of it. Search it if you want, we don't store anything there."

"Search it!" He growled at his men.

They yanked open the little door, but of course they couldn't see anything inside. There was nothing but shadow. The lead pushed Kreshen down, and came over with a lantern, his face filled with rage. When he put the lantern light in, there was nothing, just wood panels. He checked the sides for a secret door, "if you're hiding one door, there's another."

He banged his hands on the sides, but for nothing. There was no door, revealed. He crawled back out, his face flushed red, and gargled, "I've had enough. Searched all this for nothing."

He slowly left, the men started to gather back. Downstairs two more men came back from the storage rooms, kitchen, and bed rooms. All five left with salt on their brow. Blinded again by the light, after being exposed to the absence of such. When they closed the door, Kreshen let out a breath, Tiamon in an angry scowl, and Litus watched – from the roof – the men leave and gather up to go raid another house.

Chapter Twenty-Three:

The church was ransacked, dismembered, and disgraced. Kreshen was tired, taking a seat on the only thing that wasn't thrown, and it was a small stool. Litus knocked on the panel, it had gotten stuck, which was as much a mild inconvenience, as it was his savior. Well that and pushing the secret door wedged it to a point where it got stuck. Litus pounded on after a while, cracking a shingle in the process, he felt shocked and embarrassed, and decided to leave it a mystery and to hopefully not be uncovered. It took both the weary Kreshen, and the young Tiamon to open the hatch, and Litus walked through blending in with the shadows.

"They're gone at last," sighed Kreshen, still wiping sweat from his brow, "while we gather our supplies together, we might as well put the pieces back together. It'll take an hour and a half to fix the twenty minutes of destruction."

They pulled the cabinets up, and the beds on their feet. The shattered clay pots of plants were swept up and away – but the plants themselves would have to be dealt with at a different time. In the kitchen, their loaves of bread clearly had a bite taken out of them, and then stabbed as though Litus was hiding in the loaf. All the shattered dishes were swept up, the non-broken ones sorted through. These men didn't cause as much damage to the kitchen and cellar as they could have, or maybe the man who did this job was lazy. Either way is was a relief, dealing with this mess rather than the upstairs jungle.

They had gathered their supplies, consisting of the cutaway chunks of the man bitten bread, a handful or more of candles. Lanterns with oil, as well as lantern poles. Extra clothes for Kreshen, a bottle of ink and paper; Litus had begun to use the same piece of paper and point to words to get through. They both carried water bottles wrapped in leather, with a leather strap. Litus hadn't the need for it, but Kreshen in a dizziness forgot that Litus couldn't eat or drink. Otherwise, Kreshen kept a small chest – with a leather strap that wrapped it on his waist – and had items which Litus hadn't known he had, or didn't see him put in. It wasn't a large chest, merely the size of a large ale mug, or maybe only twice that.

Before leaving through the back of the church, he met Tiamon at eye level, and said, "the people here still need faith. I know you can give that to them. And if they ask where I went, say I had need to speak to other churches on the navy's arrival and actions," and before he closed the door he said, "goodbye," and they left behind the church.

Litus watched one corner, and Kreshen watched the other, his eyes weren't as good as Litus' but his experience was most certainly greater. It showed, too. They were both clothed in dark shadows weaved into cloaks – Kreshen's was wearing more of a dark gray cloak. The cobblestone circle which held the big buildings of brick and plaster, and the church itself in its center was gone. And now the gravel roads became dirt paths. It felt like it was a good indication of distance, and as they went their feet became more and more disguised in shadow.

The lights from wooden lanterns stood on sconces above the doorways. Usually near that light was where most people's only window was. Even though most also had a shutter covering the glass, to Litus and Kreshen it was another threat to their rapid departure.

Litus had begun to take a turn when he was stopped, Kreshen's arm grasped Litus' chest, and he whispered, "not that way, the black coats roam there. Come follow."

He passed into a deep shadow, the entrances of homes didn't seem to exist here. The alleyways between thick rows of homes were completely drenched in darkness, and they could barely see anything in front of them. They jumped barrels of salt, and wine that was in their way, and they jumped past scythes and rakes too. And a stray light from late hung lanterns hung over them. The roars of men fighting could be heard from afar, before being suppressed with sweat, blood, and steel. They made sure to not make noise, and be not seen, but opportunity has its chances, and when a boy saw them pass through, he gave a shout, "men in the alleyway, men in the alley!"

"Quicker," Kreshen barked, as they left the alleyway, and entered another across the street, "we must not be seen at the stable."

The stable, are we stealing horses, wouldn't that draw more attention? And just ahead out of the dark alleyway and across the dirt road, there was a stable yard on the outskirts of town. With its shingle roof, and bare beams holding together a red horse barn.

Litus stopped him, not wanting him to steal a horse, and not wanting to bring attention, though he didn't say it, and the light wasn't potent enough to write, but Kreshen seemed to know what Litus was thinking, and he pulled from his chest a purse. "We aren't stealing horses, my son," as he jingled the purse.

Far past the town in the distance they sought, was a wall of fog. Kreshen alone knocked on the door. The door had been painted either red or brown many years ago, but was now showing the bare wood under, and it was dented and scraped by who knows what. A minute passed and he went to lightly knock again. The door was opened by a large man, with a large red head, and a lengthy graying beard. He scratched at his pants, and yawned asking, "your holiness, why? Why are you here at this time of day? Are you conducting night sermons now?" He gazed down properly looking at Kreshen outstretched hand as he held a purse of money, "why's that?"

"I need to depart quickly. I will buy two horses from you. I have enough to pay, I can assure you I have enough coin," as he jingled the purse.

"It's not a matter of coinage, pastor, it's a matter of timing. You have need of steeds the same time as when the navy is searching the town. Now I respect you, your holiness, but if I sell you horses, I could be in trouble with the crown, the navy I mean. I don't know why you must leave, but anyway I can't sell you my horses."

"It is a matter of great importance, you see."

"But of what importance? If I may ask, your holiness?"

Kreshen said with faded breath, "those navy men destroyed the hall, the side room, and the kitchen. They marred it beyond reason, and they attacked me too. By the church I must heed a warning to the duke. If you let me ride today, I should be able to arrive in the morning. Those men are using the past queen's name for their desolation to the gods. It isn't right. Can you sell me the horses? Like I said, there is great need for them, for your church and for others, I need to give warning," he repeated his words to give a greater emphasis on the dire stakes.

The stableman almost seemed convinced by Kreshen, but still had his own concern, "I don't doubt your reasons, pastor. I heard from the baker and blacksmith east of here, that the navy men beat their children, and destroyed their wares, setting fire to hay on the ground. And they burnt their feet smoldering the flame. I want to sell you horses, and I think I will, but why two?"

"One for myself, and another for the duke himself, or the priest of the keep Diamon."

"They have their own stable, don't ey?"

"Yes that is true, but I can assure them more urgently, leaving much sooner, they won't have a reason to wake and feed and saddle their own horses, when mine are ready."

"Alright I understand what you inquired, come in, I'll get dressed."

They looked over the horses, Kreshen had paid with a handful of silver coins for a gray and black steed. " Now they are both the largest, fastest, and healthiest steeds in my barn," The gray steed, like Kreshen, made consistently quieter grunts and neighing; otherwise, the black steed was completely quiet. Only the sound of breathing, and the clopping of hooves could indicate the horse was there.

Litus stood in the fog far off from the town, blending in the shadows. He was met by Kreshen mounted on a gray horse, while carrying the reins of the black steed. "Have you ever ridden a horse, Litus?"

He shook his head, "won't take long, but could be dangerous. Here let's saddle you up on her first."

Litus' presence had initially shook the horse with visible intangible fear, and the horse also was too afraid to bolt Litus off, so instead the horse just stood there shaking. Litus ran his dark hands through the black hair of the horse. Soothing, calming her, she began to shake less. She felt less pressure than before. "You've gotten her to start to trust you, don't forget she has a soul just the same as you. The way you treat her, she'll treat you. So be kind, and she'll be kind too."

For twenty minutes they rode east before circling around to turn north towards the ranger's keep in Esty. They hadn't decided to go further north from there on to the simple border town of Bert, but they would make that final decision in Esty. As they rode on, Litus' mare gilded across the fields, smoothing her steps, as they became more antiquated.

Even with their lanterns raised high on staffs, the light could only pierce so far into that fog wall. It was almost peaceful, they trotted through, climbing high hills, and passing through the wet grass plains, and even with the thought still lingered of the navy men mounted and riding towards them, it was almost serene.

Litus dove into thought, *If Jane is alive, if she really is. I hope she can forgive me for abandoning her, if she lives, hopefully it won't be short lived by my presence. Nothing good has happened with my presence. Hopefully my presence isn't the doom of us all.*

It had been an hour of riding, or maybe an hour and a half. Their steeds were clumsy and merely trotting their paths, and Kreshen spoke up before dismounting, "this is far enough away, and dark enough as well. I can't see anything besides the light our lanterns are giving off, and that's not much. Here I'll help you dismount," and did so, "we could have a small fire here, I have some tinder to use for heat, and enough light to ward off wolves or other wildlife. Don't want to see a red fox come for your things. They pass bad luck, not that I'm superstitious, but I'll pray for none."

Litus reached down, removing rocks and other small things from the ground before he laid on his back. His long dark shadow hair – which emitted no light – was put back in his hood. *Have I always had hair? I can't remember.*

The small kindle bloomed like a rare flower in these lands. *I wish she was safe, I wish she was alive. If only I, if only I went alone. Alone. Pastor Kreshen had a better life, or will have a better life without my interference.* It twinkled – the flame – it danced gracefully and beautifully, but as well as differently and horrifically. It never swayed the same twice. The slight breeze, and the sheen of mist and rainfall from the air and ground never snuffed it. It never stayed put. Always flipping and flowing, but it were still a small flame, and only that. *I can't leave him here, at night, but I can't let him go to his death because of me. If I have to fight chaos, I'll do it alone, no one else will fall because of me. No one.*

Chapter Twenty-Four:

"If he wants a party for his rampage through my keep and people, then I'll give him dinner alright. Be my simple guard."

The navy men – mostly Lucerne – had forced Eiger to throw them a little party, before they departed. The night drew closer, the sky had become a pinkish purple canvas diffused by the gray. Many people simultaneously thought of that sky, how there weren't many like it, you could find years between skies like that. But for the duke – and his men – they hadn't time to consider what nature could behold. They had a man named Lucerne in their way.

Duke Eiger commanded servants to turn his hall into dining quarters, a large table for the high men. Then a series of long tables for the low men, and one at the end of the room for half of the servants. The kitchen staff had been a heat and flurry of chefs and scullions rushing here and there to produce food for all the sailors, and staff within the keep. The fires roared, pigs roasted on spits, rows of chickens too. One chef was fed up with all the spits being taken, he tried dangling a raw chicken over fire with two metal forks. But what was most back breaking was the cellar men. There was more erratic flour, spice and salt in the air than moisture. Duke Eiger sat at the front, beaconing over a man to grab a certain casket of cold wine.

It had been a long while till Lucerne sat next to Eiger, as though he were his best mate. "My duke, now that the food seems to finally be coming out from the fire, I have a great need for this party. And a great thanks to you."

"You don't have a need for a party, you just wanted a party, and I'm willing to accept that."

"Then there's no fuss," he went to drink from his goblet, "gosh, there's nothing in my cup," he grabbed a servant's attention, "bring me wine and the bottle. And pour it for me too."

"Yes, yes," the duke broke in, "bring the strong one, the special vintage my great great grandfather had stored. I see this as a particularly important day for gambling."

A low candle light flooded the hall, They both smoked an oak-scented tobacco from their pipes. The duke had a modest ash pipe, it was clearly made to smoke with it ingrained with soot. But he looked at Lucerne's pipe. The stem was nearly twice the length of Eiger's. And the wood smelled like it was freshly carved, the chamber didn't contain any ash, nor did soot even graze the pipe.

"The sea must break them more than they rust steel?" The duke asked.

"Especially when the ocean mist salt seeps into the leaf and ruins the puff."

"Mud too," he said before puffing lightly, "in trenches and the blood of other men and horses. But here, take a drink with me, to war!"

Not caring about what Eiger said, Lucerne roared as well, "to War!" He said while spilling a drop of wine on his chest; he drank the entire goblet, "very strong, very strong."

"Yes, but good, the taste is very good. Put's vigor in your body, hair on your chest, blood in your body."

"Yes, yes. I agree, it's great. Very different from what I've had in the capitol, but good I'll say."

"Then another round of good old wine, from my great great grandfather. To wine!"

And again Lucerne matched him and drank the entire goblet again, "to wine!"

"You and your men will eat my food, ransack my people, and drink my wine. To Wine!" He said, taking a sip of his goblet, and it was finally empty now.

"To Wine!" And down another goblet went.

"To the crown!" He said, not even drinking from his goblet.

"To the crown!" He finished another cup.

The duke reached over to the bottle, tipping the heel towards Lucerne, "come my guest finish the bottle, it's an important honor of having her crown's own commodore here. To the crown!"

He burped, and filled his goblet with the last of the wine, he roared, "to the crown!" And finished the goblet in one swig.

Duke Eiger sat up to begin eating, they hadn't dined yet, and he wanted to burn the alcohol in him quickly. He dined on roasted chicken and corn. Hearty meals for a complicated night, and it was soon going to become more complicated. Darien had returned, and perched behind the duke, looking like only a swordsman. He paced behind the duke. He gripped the pommel with his gloved hands, and he gripped tight. His furrowed brows looked around, but only subtly, and mainly towards Lucerne. *A drunk man is a man who will only listen to impulse, instead of patience.*

"Now as a guest under my house, my family, and roof. You should be expected to be a guest, and me the lord of the house. We will both follow these rules. Like I said, my role is the lord, and you my guest."

Lucerne nodded in agreement. Eiger continued, "outside of my lands I am ignorant of the rest of the kingdom. But you not only as my guest, do know what is occurring in the world. And especially as a great navy man. You surely have seen the world. Will you help me understand what's happening in it?"

He looked up at him, and with a long pause he opened his mouth and muttered, "I would, but no."

"No! Now you are contradicting yourself with what you told me directly earlier. You lie to me under my roof?"

"I would not lie, especially to a duke in his own home. But you on the other hand, raise your voice to your great guest, and a commodore for her crown's navy? Hmm!?"

"It wouldn't be her crown yet, within my life I have witnessed the death of the previous king, and the crowning of the late queen. That was within a period of more than a week. A week. And the navy acts singularly. And what would the navy have to do with our queen's murderer? Wouldn't it be more of my domain rather than the navy's?"

"Don't be foolish, my lord, duke. This is of concern of murder, and the murder of the queen. More so, that's a great concern of mine. And my priority."

"You call me a fool on my land, drinking my wine, and under my roof! You're out of line commodore."

"I have no line. And I don't need one. My men can keep this keep, you've let them."

"And I have yours. How would the queen herself respond to an out of line commodore capturing a duke's land, under no authority? Or more so, what if I tell your superior officer, Tylock?"

"Pah," he stifled, "you only joke, you're a funny man Eiger, duke I mean."

"I may be stuck in this keep of mine, but I can tell when the kingdom is shifting. Now tell me – you all knowing great one – I gave you wine and food and shelter. Could you give me some news?"

"I really shouldn't but you are a kind one, a kind man," he belched, "let me tell you a secret, I want to be in this with you together. The army is in shambles. Unlike us in the navy, we got ourselves together after the queen's death, and the burning of Renoi. We are strong compared to those seasick land dwellers. Those men have no leader behind them, we could buy their arms for cheap. For silver, or even less, copper. They want to be led, they just don't have the courage to do it themselves."

I should thrash this man – this man baby – what experience does he have with leading, or fighting? This isn't leading, he got drunk off of my invitation. And he thinks it is an invasion. I really want to thrash him, but his stupidity will do that to himself. He thought to himself more before responding, *If the army really is in shambles, will they get reunited or would other lords be able to buy their support? I already have a higher lead. I have the real queen's support. I can destroy the tyrant running the navy, unite the army, and restore the monarchy. I'll gain lands, and wealth, but it'll be independent from chance.* "Buying loyalty for cheap you say, for your hatred of the army, they would surely hate your sailors the same, but me I have no grudges towards either. No hate. I can sway their opinions, and make the crown stronger."

"Let's make the crown stronger, friend."

"Bring us more wine," Eiger said to Darien, who in return whispered in his ear, and said out loud, "the strong wine, correct?"

"Yes. the strong stuff."

Darien went alone, he hid in the shadows of the keep. Hidden nooks only known to those of old knowledge of the castle herself, and not every person would want to know about the castle, and her history. Lucerne and the duke had continued their half drunk, and wasted arguing. *That young fish orders me to fish up stream, while he gets flushed from a single glass. And his men, following a fool such as he, makes them greater fools. Being bought by a baby.*

A third of the ship's men dined and drank with the duke – though not at the same table. A third were out among the castle; some of that third on the grounds, some pursuing more hidden needs, or hidden goals. The last third, were keeping the ship, and guarding it with steel. All three were invaders to the duke's lands, but that middle third were particularly dangerous.

Through the ghost halls, Darien crept. He was older compared to the other guards of the keep, but he still walked without worry, only caution. The maidservants mostly hadn't known about these halls, so in return they built up with spiders and webs, dust, and damp puddles. Not every man would or could be able to roam these halls. There was only a few feet between the walls, more so there was a faint sound. You would hear only when silence was sound. A whispering within the cracks of the stone sediment.

He opened a door, out of a painting in a golden gilded frame. He had come to the other end of the keep, checking both ends of the living hallway. *I'll check the duke's quarters, then the queen's room. If my men aren't there, they won't be either.* He prayed the three points. *If they find anything, I'll pray to Mortith for my deeds, if they don't then Selziar, and if they find me, I'll pray to Gruel.*

He stalked through, putting his ear to the duke's door. For a minute he waited. For the slightest hint of a murmur. For the footsteps of an assassin, or the espionage of a traitor. He heard nothing, but a breathing. Was it a draft of air, or a man.

Darien came back to the painting, and with a quick head check, he snuck through. The ghost hall wrapped around the duke's quarters, and then some before being cut off by old rubble from a time long gone. Not even old man Darien knew what had laid beyond. Nor will he today, or in the foreseeable future. He stood by the wooden door in the stone. Waiting in the dark. He couldn't hear much, but he was waiting for a certain sound. A purposeful sound. His breath was slow and cold, he felt the air enter his lungs, his chest pulse. *The click, they've left. Now it's a matter of who.* He slowly opened the door, on the other side were stones cut thinly from the same rock from the rest of the castle.

Inside he felt a warmth in the air, but to all discretion. Nothing was different with the room, nothing except the heat. *I can't make an accusation of tampering from this, the stuffy air. Wait.* It was a little snag or pull of a rug. A tiny little bump. It was not there before, and now it was. Darien left the room checking the brass door handle for damages. Not once in decades had a guard, or Duke Eiger, or even his personal servant scratched the door lock. The handle, but not the lock.

He relocked the duke's door, and continued on. By going to check the queen's room. They had packed her belongings away, but if he saw someone, or if a man would enter that room, high up in a tower. *There'd be a traitor among the servants, and a wheedling is in order.*

That tower in particular hadn't any ghost halls to creep through. There were only the shadows and footsteps to hide in and away. He scoured through. From the balcony he stood on, he could see sharply up at anyone's shadow walking to her room, and looking down on the bailey, he saw the queen and a small posse of servants looking busy. Hiding her in the lion's den was the best solution they had, while this unknown assailant roamed the halls.

In the light of a torch he saw just the shadowy figure emerge. It was only for a second, and he ran. Darien picked his pace up, enough to not point out himself among the navy, or even to the people of the keep. Even Eiger. His seemingly plain clothes stood out to no-one. It couldn't, a dark gray was duller than dirt, but perfect for what Darien was: a loyal servant.

Sweat beaded on his face, his hands close to his blade. His beaten leather boots stripped away for his thick wool socks instead. Silence, close to it. Up the stairs at the end of the hall, and into the south most tower, he rose up. He passed the battlements, watching ever closer. And watching for this figure. This shadow. This threat. He continued his pursuit, running in the dark across the walkway. The tallest tower, the north most tower, in the spire. He entered, ascending the spiral. This time he gripped the handle firmly. The door was broken open. *Intruder! Where, where are they!* He thrusted open the door. There was only the ambiance of darkness, and vale of light that pinpointed spots in the room. He looked around. Within the dark it all seemed normal, but he could feel eyes on him. He could sense a presence.

"Pour me a glass, servant,"Lucerne said, holding out his goblet.

"I forget, why are you here? It was asking for my help in searching out this murderer?"

He glared to the duke, "her crown's navy doesn't need help, but cooperation."

"Yes, that was right. You searched among my people, and ate my food, and drank my wine. Will you have to leave this morning?"

"Yes, yes, my duke. The navy has a great need for finding this murderer."

"And so much coin, taxes I mean."

"And you wouldn't lead a search for the murderer of the past queen?"

"I would. Personally."

"This time, oh these dear growing times, are great indeed. But for splitting reasons. The fear of Hule, and the north and south disconnecting are grave. It's happening, I'll tell you. The queen bonded the kingdom herself. And now with the dysfunctional army, putting their own ideas into practice. I fear for a secession. That's why the navy has to bind together what makes this kingdom good. Empty what tries against it, and fill in that hole with glue. And how about you, are you the leg of the chair, or are you a termite?"

"I know who I support, and it's not the queen per say, but the ruler of the house of Renoi. The royal family. Although the lead of the royal family is the queen. I represent more than the people. I believe in loyalty."

"That's good, very good. I agree with you. But obviously from a navy's perspective. If I go, you'll go with me friendo. To unify, and strengthen the army," he giggled out of his flushed face.

The duke watched Darien enter from a side door, many besides the eldest kitchen staff used. A drop of sweat released from his face. Falling on his lap. Darien's face was paler than it had been. There was an almost indistinguishable cut on his arm. But to a searching eye – such as the duke's – it was clear a sharp small blade had cut through the truth wizard's coat. But it didn't stagger him. And from, the small red stain on his pommel, who attacked him, couldn't twice.

Darien came to the duke's side and whispered in his ear about what he found. The duke pondered in thought, before ushering him to continue their plan. *One door picked, and the other broken.*   He returned back to Lucerne who poured himself another glass, and he stated, "how could you maintain all of your troops while on the sea? I assume that since Tylock had sent you here – to a duke – he would send you towards the other parts of the kingdom, such as Hule. There's no reasonable way to communicate to your soldiers to complete your responsibilities. I, on the other hand, have a full court, and castle. And lands, and food. Perfect for an army. Your's would be an investment into our army. Your share would be a word towards the army. While I will be in command of this army more often, you won't have the burdens an army causes. Such as accommodation, food, steeds, and steel. Your command, when commanded, will be the same as mine, or in their eyes greater. How about this deal?"

"The command of an army, without the determinants of one. So when I fail my duty, which obviously wouldn't happen, you would be the scapegoat?"

"Most likely. If I'm the one around giving orders. They'll see me as their dysfunctional leader, and like you stated, they need a strong leader. Do they not?"

"Oh they need a great one."

Then do you accept my deal?"

"I . . . I accept."

Around the stables, were a small gathering of five men, along with the stable boys. There weren't enough men to properly protect the queen, but it was the maximum they could afford to not draw attention to themselves. Together – to the center of town, at the church's grounds – seven would ride out, and after that they would ride out with six.

I saw the queen in the bailey earlier, most likely they put her in the kitchens. Hard work for her, but seems to have worked well. Darien took the ghost halls till he was close to the kitchen. He opened the door, looking around. Till he came to the servants, where he ordered a group which included Jane to come with him. *If I bring one with me, they'll know, but a whole posse, it'll seem like I'm not escorting the queen, hopefully.* He brought them into the dark halls talking as though disciplining the women, and waving his fingers. "You all return back to the kitchens, don't tell the sailors of her disappearance. If they ask, say nothing. Gaslight them if you must. Just keep your story the same."

They all left, he took her hand as they entered the ghost halls. The painting they passed through closed with no sound. In the lantern light Jane looked around, in awe of what she saw. "These secret halls. How did I not see?"

"See," he whispered, "if I didn't open up the door, would you have known? No. is this the only ghost hall? No as well. The secret only seems obvious, cause you know the secret now."

The night dawned on, men at their posts including both the navy men and the duke's men were both exhausted. Under only the diffused light of the moon. Darien led the queen's fellowship out of the west end of the keep. Furthest away from the coast. They made sure to keep riding west for a long while, until any glimmer of sight was easily interpreted as night flies.

The cool wind brushed on their faces. In the distance they could see the midnight mists emerge. They all felt a sense of fear. The five men feared the urban legends: the beings of the dark plains. While Darien feared someone following them. It was obvious how careful he was, but the duke had only so much of an idea from his position.

Jane was sitting in a pool of fear, but it had been so long since this fear had been settled that now she felt mostly rage. A semi-subtle rage, and this fire fueled her to press forward. She didn't want to be their queen, and she certainly didn't want to be in this situation, but she was stuck and had to walk the line. A shivering arrow struck her with the coldness of the halls.

They carried on through the night which no longer lent any light. Darien commanded all to slow, Jane needed help convincing her steed to obey. He directed them all to light their lanterns, and they continued passing through the rising and falling waves of dirt and grass.

Jane didn't have the light to properly see the sword. Not once had she seen this sword that drew her, she called it hers. Not by the fact it was an enchanted sword, which came by rare. Even during the Baker revolution, she had only known of it by the talk of others from Deinde. *That cult killed Tolk, and all my people, my friends. The entire town, destroyed. That parasite has to be their work. They destroyed Litus. I'll kill them, I'll kill all of them. I may not be the actual queen, and many will realize that, but I'll raise an army to kill all of those cultists, and Tylock too. They took everything from me, my home, my people, my friends.*

She drew from the scabbard the heirloom blade. It was both long and thin, but also curved in like a leaf. She swung the blade around only a bit to not spook her mare, and resheathed it. But Jane also noticed that the scabbard didn't just hold a sword, but also a stone, and a little dagger. It seemed to emulate the heirloom sword, but it wasn't enchanted. Not even Darien – some wizard – could enchant it. But the cultists could, and they wouldn't do it for her. They'd only do it for a parasite.

As the morning started to rise, and the sky was a blanket of orange and yellow, they brisked through a field of wheat. It was still wet from that storm a few days ago, and the light seemed to bounce off the hay, and began scattering it in the wisps of wind.

Their horses put hooves in the dirt as they drew closer. The grass began to thin, and homes and smaller farms were all around. The dirt paths became harder, from the constant leveling and flattening of footsteps. Eventually after that, they walked onto gravel paths, and the horses kicked the small stones as they trotted. By mid morning they had come to the cobblestone paths of the church. The stained glass symbol which glowed with the new daylight, drew their dropping eyes. They dismounted in front of those white wooden steps.

Chapter Twenty-Five:

The dunes of the white sands blew as the night sky guarded and led him further. Those grains threw against his eyes and face, but still he pushed further for the doors of sandstone. The chains around her hands rustled in the wind, the dry sands kernels embedding between the iron and skin. Torch fire emblazoned the red shifting sands around them pushing in a new hue. Fire emblazoned the temple of chaos, or red hot uncertainty. The black sack was over her head, its coarse wire texture cut at her cheeks. They looked flushed, from a first look, but that was only the scratching of the wool disguising her fear. She stayed quiet.

The back of his red robe dragged against the sand, and that too was embedding kernels into the weave. He grabbed more of the chain pulling her, and she lost her footing. "Get up," he yelled, "get Up!" While yanking the chain up, forcing her on her feet. She could feel his warmth, or lack of. It wasn't a man under that robe, but a skeleton reanimated. A being of living and death. Luring her, bringing her. Did she know? Maybe not, maybe so. Who were they, she didn't know.

Past the dust clouds – to the temple of blood and ashes – were a dark hallway that led deep below, under a cathedral of hate and fire. A roaring chant of thousands and thousands sounded the stairway down. With walls of porcelain, and pillars of redstone holding the sandstone and salt dome high. A gathering of heat, and suffering, a church of hell and magic fire. The rattling chains only added to the orchestra of screams; the harmony and timbre of the screams melded in the soup.

Cages hanging on massive sconces and chains of iron, held the skeletal remains of the still breathing living and the old dead. The women were stripped of their clothes. Torn off with clumsy daggers. There was the rotting carcass of an oldman. His skin was partially burned off, and dripped to the bottom of the cage like wax. All their skin was smeared with soot and dirt, with traces of blood from knives and nails.

And down once more, they drew. Even though they walked down, they arrived above. They entered the chamber. The pope of this church stood on the stage of the procession. From his fingertips he emitted the heat, and a stream of black smoke which moved into runes readable by none. His robe was red the same, but lavishly decorum of gold stripes, and embroidery of death. His head was that of a deer skull, the antlers tipped with crystalized blood and made of gold. He stood above all, and even from above they saw him tower.

He walked to the procession, he was part of this trial. This holy order. Flames rose with each step closer to the holy pope. He stood nine feet taller than him and his chained woman. He pulled the chains, when she stopped to try and make sense of the senseless. The red demons – on either side of the carpeted arena – prodded with their forks at her legs. Those little cuts looked like mouse bites in cheese. A small dribble of blood made a small demon jump from his seat to lick the sweet fondant.

Once they were within reach – with a roar of demons cloaked in red – the bronze and bone clawed pope grabbed the girl. He played with her, like a cat plays with a bird or mouse. He spoke in a language and tone which made the surface dwellers cringe, and recoil with pain. He put her upon a x-shaped crucifix. Her arms tied above her head, and legs spread apart.

He didn't know where, but he was thrown aback when the pope drew out a staff of soot covered pine. Once he reclaimed the ground which he stood on, he was drawn in with another sensation. It was a sickly sweet scent, it smelled like a smoking forest. It was full of ash, and the dank smell of burnt sugar too. But it didn't just draw him in, it drew all in. It was a sort of hivemind of attention. A craving desire being born into this world.

The Pope drew a spear of soot from the end of his staff and collected the attention being cast towards him. It was a birthing. Everyone started to convulse, with a shimmer of light burning and shaking around them all. A vacuum of power is sipping away from their minds, and hearts, love and hate. But it took their attention and desired more. Power. The power of minds, of words, of the lands, and the magic inside us all.

Half of all being deprived, had burst into flames. And they laughed. He laughed. They all laughed a hearty laugh, as they burned to nothing but ash. And that flowed from them towards the newborn. An orb of crystal began forming around both the stripped flesh of the baby-like thing and the woman, who in return began fusing with the monster. Her skin burst aflame all the clothes that surrounded her, and for only a moment could he see her face, but not recognize her. He knew her, or at least he thought he did. Her skin was bleeding into stripes of black and white, pure as snow, and black as soot. That was all he saw, the crystal took her in a cocoon. And put her in a motionless coma. He looked at the Pope, and the Pope did the same to him. He had no face under that mask, but showed eyes of partial red, not red like blood, but like a mimic fire. It danced, around him, it danced. There were flames all around, and the smoke drifted upwards. Ash and blood, ash and blood.

"Wake up," he yelled down above him, "please wake up!"

Litus was bolted up, his hood fell to his back, letting his shadow-like hair flow too. "I've been trying to wake you for ten minutes. You were shaking violently in your sleep. What's wrong, what did you dream?"

He looked at his hands, he felt as though he still carried the chains. *What was that? That dream, what was it? I can't remember. I have to deal with that, the dream. If I have to continue, I must forgive and forget her.* "It'll be alright friend, you can move forward, I know you can. You must."

He pulled from the void the shard. He did not know exactly why he did, but he grabbed the hilt holding the stable crossguard to the level of his eyes. Those square hooks were meant for something, but he did not know what. "Why do you carry a broken sword with you? Do you plan to fight like Ser Bywin the strong?"

Litus gave him a stare of curiosity, for he hadn't heard of this man before. He stored the sword in the void; he had the feeling the shard would be useful some other time. "Ah, Ser Bywin was one of the best fighters I've ever met. He died nearly half a century ago, and was a really harsh man, but he could fight for his life and then some. He could fight anyone, and win. Forgive my blasphemy, but he died in his sleep, because death couldn't take him while he was awake. But he generally fought with restrictions to himself. And now as his name becomes legend, any would-be sword fighter has tried the same. With blunter blades, and crossguards that stab your wrist."

The morning sky was crisp like an apple, and cold like the river Bleue. But soon it would be striking their face like needles from the pine from Mulder. For another storm was approaching. It were the infant children of the one days prior during the royal ball. The string fell off the ball of yarn. Just a string, but a great force still. But from their sight it was hours away, if it didn't move away such as the course of nature might.

They packed their loose belongings, which was mostly a lantern, and bits of uneaten food away. They mounted their mares, however this time, Litus was more assured with his horse, and the horse had clearly felt the same for him. She kept him on with the first bumps of rock, and he petted her reassuredly. After he forgot to do so, she blew air from her snout.

The morning plains were flat for the part currently, which helped the horses break in their gallop and walk. They trodden north for many miles, a dozen miles at that. They rode up and down short hills, and past a field of corn and grain, and also other crops. They could see in the great distance on small mountains the outskirts of the forest of Mulder. And unfortunately for them, that is where they headed. It drove chills and goosebumps through their arms and backs thinking.

Kreshen pulled through up ahead, to see what lay further on. He had a sense for something, but he didn't know just what that was. In Front of them was the steepest hill within miles of here. Kreshen rode around the side till he was past the hill, and what he saw made him dismount for a moment. Litus followed him, and once trotting to where he was, he too dismounted and stood next to him.

Kreshen looked back and forth at the plains that led ahead. It was all swamps, horrible marshes. Where they stood was the last stretch of solid ground. The grass was trimmed around where they stood, almost funneling them through the swamp. "The swamp will end, the plains are less aggressive than the forest, and less proud than the Haut range. We'll go around, after a break. Let the horses rest for now."

They parted their belongings on the ground, Kreshen was sharpening a knife with a wet-stone whilst saying, "have you ever roamed the plains before?"

He looked up for Litus to give a response, he hadn't really. Litus was very familiar with the forest of Mulder, and the oceans he had a lick of terror for, but the plains were alien. He shook his head respectably, "they're not as cruel as the world around us, and to be completely honest, the plains are more of a comic than the mountains, or forests, and seas. They seem to be playing a joke on us with this marsh, but we'll get around. They wouldn't play with us for long."

He took out a small bundle of sticks, an old kettle and a set of cups. Before Litus could reach in the void for the fire wand to light a fire for tea, Kreshen beat him to the punch. He looked confused. *How did he light the fire so quickly?* He looked with this bewilderment towards the pastor, and all he responded with was warming his hands by the fire.

A small breeze brought over a chilling wind that broke through their clothes. And eventually both of them were huddled by the fire, warming their hands. Kreshen poured a cup of the tea, making sure to not drink the loose leaf, and gripped the cup with both of his cold hands. The horses were brazing and grazing – eating grass as they went – before returning to the two, ready to depart once more. The horses were very well disciplined.

The salt of the sea crashed and beaded in the air, as the sails gripped the wind and cut through the waves. He looked out the window in the cabin of the ship, writing letters and planning with a series of different maps and letters from high lords, and duke's of Hule and some of the east too. He received a letter from Duke Pelille's ship a few days ahead, "congrats on the great promotion, Tylock, but now that you've become the great head of the Navy I must ask you to reconsider this game. The military enforcement of my people. Your people are not mine, I'll grant you welcome to my home, only if your sailors don't follow. I can find your traitors in my men by my own skimming eyes. If this displeases you, then let it. Your friendship is great, so don't tarnish it like a flame to a pewter cup. Your loyal queen's man, Duke Pelille."

Tylock gripped the letter in his fist, "how could he not understand, this is a matter graver than him. Far larger than him and his governance," in the bottom drawer of his desk was a bottle of a deep red booze – it had a sickly sweet smell – and he poured himself one, while placing his boots over the desk.

My queen is missing, I have gained much, but lost plenty. I gave her greatness, and she threw it all away. I hope she hears this thanks in Hule, for offing the old queen. The wretched mother. He drank the shot, only one, and recorked the bottle away. An officer was let in by two guards, he was clearly high ranked if not the captain of the ship. He tapped his boots together and announced himself to the admiral. Tylock in return slowly and proudly brought his feet off the desk, and leaning in his chair with a wave of his hand beaconed the officer to sit. "What do you report, captain?"

"The twin cities have been uncooperating in letting us dock. What do we do, grand admiral?"

"What we do is dock. They are subjects of the crown, and they will loyally be subjected to the crown. If they deny us, we have the right to fight back. Will they start a civil war without the moral grounds, or political grounds, or even the militaristic grounds. They are just children who have to be punished for their misdoings. We will dock, we'll make sure of that."

"And sir, if I may?"

"Go on," Tylock beckoned while sitting back up to continue his planning, sorting through certain highly detailed maps, "go on!"

Well sir, why do you think the queen's kidnapper and mother killer brought her to the twins? And what about the average folks of the twins?"

"That's a matter of greater concern than you, and don't go asking your commodore, he'll be scrubbing barnacles off the hull, if that's the case, and you with him. Now I do need your commodore, I need his attention on dealing with this crisis, we need those in power in the twins to be felled, not the people."

He clicked his boots together, and left the cabin. The captain's perspiration stained the wood top. Tylock took a leather strap and rolled some of the maps. He grabbed a much larger map, a heavy map made of wood strips strung together and a large parchment stitched on top. The commodore came in and helped Tylock unroll the map onto the desk, it barely fit, and they ended up moving two desks together to fit the massive map.

"Admiral Tylock Sir, you asked for me?"

"I did indeed, I need minds in this matter, valuable minds, and eyes for strategy."

"Strategy, in what? Aren't we hunting an assailant who kidnapped the queen?"

Tylock subtly looked towards the door, and exclaimed to the commodore, "you kid in these times. Great things are happening. We are saving our queen, and strengthening the kingdom as a whole, while weeding out the weak, and replacing it with the strong. Those who are willing to put effort into leading and being a great man. A loyal man at that. Won't deny this progress?"

"No I don't deny it? Deny what progress? Seating the queen on her throne is only going to strengthen the kingdom, and after that I could retire," he said stroking his gray beard.

"Oh it will, it certainly will. But nethertheless, my orders come from the good of the realm. And you will obey them," he opened the top drawer from his desk and sprawled on the map a series of chess pieces. Each ship was a black pawn. Tylock made an idea as to where to put the black queen, "here, she's headed to Hule most likely."

"And . . . And you're so certain?"

"More certain than you. It's only a matter of how she'll get there. And we know she may or may not have boarded a ship the day of the ball. But of what I know, is she's not a posh princess who wouldn't let some puddle get in the way of what she wanted. In a sense she's as scheming as a viper paired with a hawk. We'll be the one to free her from the cage, and throw away the key."

"If she took the ship, it would be a month's sail around the south bend, and a half more the north bend. We could catch her with our vessels easily. That depends on which vessel she took."

"Her majesty's personal ship."

"She still hasn't the experience to navigate, we could find her either way."

"Either way it'll happen, because it's not a matter of catching up to her; it's a matter of catching her. If that makes sense."

"We'll go around, no matter how long it takes. This bog only lasts so long."

They both mounted on their mares. There was a slightly greater wind once on horseback, it wasn't noticeable by their skin, but the sound was subtle. It rang like a high pitched doorbell in an orchestra. If you listened for it, you would find it. But it wasn't a bell, it was a long thin weave of the wind. Their trotting was only pulling the knots in these threads, and shoe marks in the grass.

For an hour or two they treaded the green. The long grass was folded in half dropping their cold sweat into the ground. The rolls of the plains were like kneaded dough. Plump in certain points, and dipped in other plots, and there were flats here and there as well. The screen of little water drops were being cut by the knives.

For miles they rode, and still the bog remained to the left a hundred feet away, and every mile or two they would come to a wall of fog. Each bend and hill was like the one past them, and another further on was the one they were passing now. Kreshen stopped his mare, Litus followed suit, "these really are cruel times, when the plains decide to stop a priest and the hero of prophet through," he prayed while growling at the ground, he turned to Litus and muttered, "we must either stop, or go through the marshes. Wait out the world, or play their game. This is your quest, you should make the decision."

Litus turned his head around the plains and the swamp, coming to a conclusion. *I will not be some mouse for cats to play with. We'll deal with it now.* He turned and pointed to the marshes, Kreshen let out a sharp exhale from his nose, and muttered, "so it is."

Kreshen turned his mare, and both were not ready for the mud. Litus took the reins forward and went. Kreshen followed behind. They marched through the green, the short grass funneling them towards the wetlands. Their horse hooves plodded into the marsh, pulling wet clumps of moss and grass with it. Ripples danced around the patches of grass.

For an hour already they drudged through the stink and filth that unearthed with churning the muddy water, but that wasn't the worst of times; that draft of wind turned back into their face. Now it was stronger, and most certainly more present to them. Especially Litus who's hood had been pulled off his head, letting his hair drag with the wind. So now it was wet, windy, and cold.

"You're the chosen one, but I don't think you've chosen the most comfortable walk," he grumbled as a piece of mud was flung high between them plopping into the water.

Even though it was closer to midnight than night, the hue of the sky dipped, as though a storm were coming soon. Kreshen looked to the sky only to grumble more. A sediment layer drifted over the surface of water made of small wisps of smoke or mist. They both slowed their gallop, their horses breathing easier than before. Kreshen wanted to say something, but prayed the three points instead. Not thinking of an explanation for this.

Litus reached through the void and pulled out the two handed falchion and while holding the reins, he held the sword to the side, and with the coming of the mists, it surrounded them, and engulfed their view. Even the forested hills in the distance were gone, and soon after, in front a cut in the mist wall had appeared. Similar to the short grass, but this time, it didn't feel optional.

Cold fronts spun and weaved through them, pushing and pulling warmth and cover. Their hoods flew away, having to be pulled back tight. Kreshen prayed the three points again. As the mist drifted over like a ghost in a manor, it came to them. Slowly encircling. But it wasn't a shove, it was the boundary. They reared their horses before picking their pace up, before the mist fully took them. It moved slowly, but surrounded them quickly.

The flittering strings of cold winds talked in their heads. Of honor, of death, of chaos, of justice. They ran furlong across the mud; it was almost a surprise they didn't slip at any moment. The horses were in control for as much as they possibly could. The hallway was thinning the further they went. Litus put away the falchion and reached through the void for the fire wand. He pulled it, gripping the wooden shaft tight. And kept the end outstretched in front, in case there were attackers ahead.

"I don't know what this is, why this is I mean. But keep going. Keep moving forward. If there's people at the end of this, if we have to fight them. It'll be a better outcome than being stuck in this fog. So don't stop; keep moving forward. You have to keep going further even if I can't."

Don't be an idiot, Litus felt, but couldn't say. They just kept trodding forward. Even with their horses wheezing and the water below losing the life it contained, now was a gray water.

Far ahead they could see a breaking in the walls. Past was a door of shadow, it was a hole in the white mists, but that didn't stop the fog behind them pushing them further and further ahead. They passed a furlong more, the gray waters punching up in the air. Mud flailed from the horse shoes, and they walked furlong until they could see past the outline of that door. From their perspective it was a building, in the middle of a marsh. But stone grounds were better than muddy waters. They traveled one more furlong, and at its end they pierced through the door. Shooting through the hole and onto the ground once more. It was a bridge. A stone bridge.

The ground was flat except below the bridge was a deep trench filled with water and mud, and stretched into far reaches of fog around. Standing on the bridge was a figure, with old chainmail, and was leaning on a scythe. The figure was a knight with a tunic made of a fabric of woad, or dreads of the same flowers being embroidered on the cloth.

They took steps closer. The figure handled the scythe with both hands, and swept its blade through the air. Moments later with a wave of pressure – blades of grass were cut below – like a shock wave in the ground. Their horses backed up, Litus's horse nearly took him off, and again the knight swung their scythe. A ripple of air spooked the horses, and Litus was bolted off his steed this turn. His breath was taken, but it was softened ground that caught him, and he had survived worse. Far worse. Litus picked himself up, the horse ran off away, but remained within the walls.

The knight stood resting on the shaft of the scythe. A sound of wind flowed through like a cackle. *Was the knight laughing?* He fought two strangers with the power of an enchanted scythe, and then threw them off their horses. *He laughed at our falling.* The knight held out his hand beckoning the shadowy figure to fight.

Litus stayed still, and kept his wand raised. The knight put his green gloved hands on the handles of the scythe, slowly and menacingly, and drew back to strike. But Litus struck first. He threw fire at the knight, and in return received a torrent of wind. They spiraled together, rising high before breaking away into the sky thirty or so feet above.

Once the tornado had decayed away where Litus could see through. He again saw the knight leaning on his scythe beckoning Litus forward. Kreshen had taken the reins of both horses and looked on as Litus began to approach the knight. He didn't know who the knight could be loyal too, or even why there was a bridge in the middle of nowhere. But he knew that knight was a force to be reckoned with. And not just because of the enchanted scythe. *Why a scythe, of all tools. A scythe?*

Litus had readied to cast more fire, and the knight put his hands on the scythe once more, and drew it back. *I can't lose fire, for a fight like this.* He put the wand away, and searched in the void pulling out the falchion once more. He gripped strongly, but not tightly. Walked forward, with the blade further than him. The knight stretched his fingers as Litus approached, and gripped the handles with his green hands. He hadn't a sword on him, just the scythe.

He ran up the bridge, Litus took a swipe at the green knight. He swung from high up striking across. The knight backed up and caught the blade with a shifting between his blade and the joint. The knight pulled Litus by the sword's friction. He untwisted the blade, turning it towards Litus begging him to go back. But from Litus' perspective it wasn't a plea but a grave force. Litus dropped the sword, it rang as it hit the stone below. The knight kicked the blade towards him, waiting for him to pick it up.

Kreshen watched from behind. In his younger days he could fight, but he wasn't that man anymore. Neither gun ho, a fighter, nor as naive as he was when he was younger. Kreshen drew his horse further, dismounted, and with his fingers raised in front of him.

Litus went into a guard, leading ahead, and he only needed to move slightly to cover all his sides. Litus shifted from side to side while guarded, taking jabs sporadically, to try and catch the knight off guard. Only plucking flowers off his chest at most. That wisp of air which sounded like a chuckle was emitted once more. Litus didn't fear it, or hate it, he feared it. This knight hadn't taken the duel like it's a fight till death.

Kreshen reached with one hand around his back, his fingers forward. He came closer to the bridge. It was like a wave of pressure was pushing him back, an intensity, fear. He was paces away from the stone, it was almost instantly when a massive wave pushed him back with a force which caused his head to fall first. Hitting a hidden rock in the ground, Kreshen fell unconscious.

Litus looked back hearing the pastor fall. Within that blink of an eye, the scythe blade was wrapping around his neck. He only had a split second to drop, not letting the scythe reach him. While backing away he blocked the shifting blade and lunged forward for a stab. The knight backed away and gently guarded with the haft of the stock between his hands. He twisted the end without blade in a retort. And with a quick recoil, the knight threw the blade around towards Litus.

He backed up, bringing the tip down. With that clang of steels, he brought it back up with the parry of rust bits falling off the scythe blade. He returned the blade, and thrust it forward. The scythe pushed the sword blade down, getting locked again. But Litus didn't wait for the knight to twist the blade. He kicked the knight, drawing the sword's blade back into control. Kreshen still lay on the ground unconscious.

Between the knight and shadow, there were stings of steel tapping with each block and parry. The grass knight swung his scythe low to keep from his face, and that is what would seem the most effective a scythe could be, but in the hands of man it were more dangerous than a spear, sword, or bow in a normal soldier's.

Those cold strikes kept repeating faster. Both of them made moves to try and tire the other out with predictable moves. They each expected to study the enemy with, more than deliver that killing blow, but it didn't keep the knight from playing games. He held Litus back away, there were only a few targeted attacks. The knight backed away, and used a wave of wind to push back the shadow.

They were on opposite sides of the bridge. Litus went to quickly check the priest, there was no blood on the back of his head, and he seemed to gain consciousness. He was dreary from the tumble, but was able to somewhat recollect his thoughts. He reached for his back, and pulled a dagger out. It was only sharpened on one, because on the spine were barbs. Litus took the sword breaker from the priest, who quickly fell back unconscious without a word. A gust of wind sheared the grass blade around them, and another cut a gash in Litus' cloak. Which moments later began to reweave itself.

Litus went in head strong. The sword breaker in his left hand, the falchion in his right. The knight eyed him and the dagger. His bone fingers gripping the handles tighter. They met in the center. Litus brought his edge from the low up, but feinted the sword instead twisting the edge into the knight's hands. And even when Litus cut the man's hand, shearing off the pinky and third finger of his right hand, the bone was dry. There was no blood in this man, but there was a skeleton. The foliage skin had rewoven around the cut, sealing the skin. Litus realized they were both monsters, the fear and bane of men. He truly did feel it.

The scythe had swept vertically up and met Litus' shoulder. While trying to back away, he only pulled his shoulder against the blade more. Litus – with great pain – lunged and drove the blade quickly forward. The scythe came and he swiped the dagger's teeth into the curved blade, locking it. Litus reared back, pulling the knight to him. He had taken the sword, and tried to cut at his opponent's hand. But he hadn't the leverage. The grass knight kicked Litus, withdrawing the dagger's teeth from the scythe blade. They returned swipes with parries and blocks, and retreated away from each other.

The knight backed away, throwing horizontal swipes pulling back to his hip. He rounded the movement into his side, and prepared a long attack. Litus felt the pins in his front, and needed to end it swiftly. He rushed up the knight's boundaries. Getting met with a blow of wind and steel. The long rusted scythe blade twisted at the joint in a horizontal gesture moving up with the sharp spike-like end coming towards his jaw. And Litus blocked with his sword raised high, the dagger clutching quickly, and Litus redirected his block into a blow cutting through the grass knight's old mail. He took the blade out, and before the knight could make some final double death blow, Litus swung the blade, beheading the knight.

It was a duel to the death. One left dead, and the other wounded. Litus, upon putting his blade away, went to Kreshen to reawaken him. And again to his pleasure, the pastor awoke quickly, but not easily. "You're alive, thank goodness. I wasn't much help, maybe the years have gone long on me. Though it doesn't tell, it certainly shows. That knight was no knight at all was he. Not even a man. I realized it eventually, but he was of this land, more than any lord or house. He is a plain's knight. You have the liberty of being a rare man to fight, survive, and kill a plain's knight. But I don't think you're the bragging type, are you? You don't say anything about yourself, it's all done with action," he chuckled and asked, "can you help me up, and get me some water, please?"

Once Kreshen was up and able to walk – without a searing headache nailing his head – he observed the corpse, and checked the position of the sun. Litus had wondered about the scythe, and with so much, threw it into the void, with everything else. The green grass-like skin began to wither away into the ground. The bones of some unlucky farmer or soldier stayed, but the mail would rust away with the moisture of air and rain. The mist walls which once stood high for a near hour had started to dissipate, and the sky too started to fall. They had already left the bridge traveling till true dark, and they camped. Litus found the scythe easy for cutting a circle for their fire, and bedding. Kreshen slept hard, and Litus too under the sky of no stars.

Chapter Twenty-Six:

Jane, Darien, and their men stood in the mud room that led into the abbey. Jane noticed that Darien had a strange look on his face, he questioned something about the church as though there were something apparently wrong. "Stay here, we'll stay the night. I just need a word from the Pastor . . . If he is even here tonight."

Jane moved to the abbey hall to sit and wait with the four other men. One dealt with the horses, the other with the church.

Darien walked through the kitchen, thinking of the old church the way a man does to an old battlefield. Sitting on a stool was the young adult malkin eating a salted fish. "If I remember, you're Tiamon?"

"Father Darien? Is that you, such a strange time to come, a weird day that is."

"Now I never thought Kreshen would keep the church in such a sorry state, where is he?"

"He left after the navy arrived. They did this to the church. Did they do the same thing at the keep?"

"Somewhat. The duke wouldn't have let his castle be stomped around the same as what happened here, but the navy found blindspots. But I ask again where Kreshen is. Where did he go?"

"He left not so long ago. He told me that he was going to heed the warning to the other churches. He has a responsibility. Why are you here father Darien?"

"I need accommodations for the people I brought here. They're waiting in the abbey. They also need space in the stables. You haven't kept any for a long while, so you wouldn't mind, would you?"

"No, the use of the stables are for everyone, from the people of the town, or the keep. But you aren't staying here, for the night?"

"I too have a responsibility. Not the same as Kreshen, but in a sense, quite similar," before he left, he asked Tiamon, "if he's gone, who will run the church? You?"

"I have been under his wing for a while now, I can and will lead the church while the Pastor is away."

"I only wish I could have seen him, asked for a sermon, is he still near, you said he hadn't left long ago. I knew him for a while, the navy must have committed such blasphemy that caused Kreshen to flee unprepared. Around this town are only three churches, the one in the keep, the one at the rangers keep, and in Bert too. Unless he wants to cross the river. I may see him and ask him myself, my accomplices may see him too, and you will start telling the full truth."

"In the house of the gods, you tell me I lie?" Tiamon said calmly, "I've done nothing but tell the truth."

"Not the full truth, you've known me better than to not say everything," Darien had the sword on his side, but knew his restrictions and didn't put his palms on the pommel. He stood still with his arms crossed.

"The Pastor told me he left to warn the other churches of what the navy has done. That's all. Father, I can make room for our guests, and give them food, and they can precipitate with the sermons, if they'd like to, but I would not be questioned about the actions of our Pastor while under the gods roof. Under his roof."

"Alright, I won't ask, I'll keep faith in this church untainted. Just the sudden change in leadership shifted me. I'll be leaving, and like I said they are in the abbey. Gods be with us, Tiamon, gods be with us," he prayed the three points, and left the kitchen. Tiamon took another bite of his fish.

Kreshen, I've known you for a while, I wouldn't think that you've left the church in younger hands even for hurricanes. What would the navy have done to cause such an immediate leave. I couldn't be that, what are you running from Kreshen?

Darien returned to the group and was followed shortly after by Tiamon; he introduced them all, and made his departure. "I'll be returning to the keep, my position to the duke is important. You must understand."

"And my position isn't, I thought you were here to protect me?"

"No, if I was your protection I wouldn't have brought five other men with me. No, they are your protection."

"What if I order it, what would you do then?"

"And what throne do you sit on, what laws have you written, and which guards are in your control? You have enough protection from these men, and the sanctuary of the church grounds, you're safer in many respects than the duke, that's why I must leave now to return to his side," he tipped the brim of his hat and exited through the door they entered before bolting onto his horse, leaving urgently.

Tiamon didn't want to ask questions or receive any, and when any came to him he either referred to what Darien or Kreshen told him, or he just refused to answer whatsoever. He had offered them the cracks of bread which he spent time breaking away, as well as wine from the cellar, and fish as well. As they ate he dimmed the lights of the church one by one until the church was dark except from sconces on the wall which held still burning candles inside a chimney globe. He brought them the men to their rooms, and Jane to a separate room. Which had some of the men in rotation guard the doors. *Why would the great lord want to hide a lady here? I'll let them stay, but I won't be an accomplice, just a kindly priest of the church. Bless the gods.* And he prayed.

There was a sword hanging in the middle of the fog. She could only tell what it was with the faint glimmer of moon light. The ground below could have been a field of grass, or a court of polished stone. It could've even been a marsh, but the sky showed no light on it. She hovered only slightly above the ground. Wasn't quite like flying but it felt like walking on an unmoving surface. A disconnect from the world below, and people there too. If there were any.

That sword hung from a string of air, which caused it to spin slowly. She felt the presence of eyes staring at her, hundreds of eyes, but when she turned to confront them. They weren't there. But she still felt that presence, she was so sure, but could her own eyes lie? *I'm not crazy, there are people out there. Or things watching me. It's the cult they've found me. Isn't it?* "You will die for what you've done. I'll kill all you cultists. All of you!"

For long moments there wasn't anything, just a breath-like wind. "You use this name to enmasse a militia, for revenge. You are it, yet you can't conceive to believe it. Are you the queen now, Jane?"

His voice boomed like hearing a calm man yell, she turned to see this man stand in the shadows. Only the occasional draft of light illuminated his figure along with the swords, but not enough to give detail, "and you think you are in the moral right? These men will die for you, will you rule for them? Will you care for them?"

"Yes, I will, after I get away from the navy, and I'll find and destroy the cult that haunts us."

"Us? Yes, us. But still you plan to hold these men, however you gather to this name you proclaim yourself hypocritically. You lie for murder. For murder on a grand scale. Genocide is what that's called."

His figure disappeared, she felt a hands grasp her shoulder, "no you wouldn't cause a genocide," his soft voice emphasized, "with the power you'd have, you'd lead wars. So go ahead. Steal that power. You can use that power better than most. Lead a war of superior morality."

I'm not stealing power. "So you say this power isn't yours but you take it."

"How did you-"

"Why do you take it? To kill all who stand in your way, you thief, you'll cause the holocaust that history remembers forever. You'll kill us all, in genocide we're the same. And I'll guide you for who you shall be, and will be, Garnette. That church bed can't save you."

His hand and spirit disappeared with a laugh that echoed his departure, and she saw the sword continue to spin in the darkness.

She awoke in the middle of the early day, the cold air stirred with the seasons. Sweat beaded on her face, and chest and dribbled down her breasts and hands. She looked out the window, the dark sky had lingered, and she felt the slow lingering of time for once. *Just a dream, a horrible dream. I'm not going to lead men to die, I'm not. I'm just over-reacting, it was just a dream.*

The soft morning light was a dew of sap leaving the pores in trees. It oozed, and crystalized in the early cold. And by mid-day the sap would soften again, and flow mercilessly. The Navy's men were still searching the town, but now the ship at the keep would sail away, and they would help accelerate the search elsewhere.

The men and Jane were up early. When that dew still was stiff, and the only person who saw them leave was Tiamon during an early sermon. He didn't bother them – for he was scared what the sailors would do to the church after they searched it normally. A shiver ran through his fur, it was quite obvious when all the hairs around his arms, and around his large yellow eyes sprung up like goosebumps.

They had looks from the older people as they rode through the town hall. Jane for certain hadn't liked the attention, and was lucky when she decided that the blue cloak would be best in hiding her. She was told otherwise by her guards, saying the bright blue dye would have men stare, but Jane argued that her hair and eyes were more likely to draw attention. They reluctantly grumbled with agreement, and stayed silent. Though as they rode, they heard mostly talk about a group of men and a woman riding out.

They heard an old couple come to their own conclusion of them being some sort of spies to use their magic eyes that the normal navy men hadn't. It was just a small rumor, made partially from what the navy had done here, but it wasn't the end. There was a blacksmith who had begun his day by heating his forge up, and for a split second he looked up and saw the fellowship trotting by. The ground turned from cobblestone to gravel. He muttered under his breath, "stupid children gonna get us in trouble," he hacked a small morning sickness, and continued waiting for his forge to heat.

They trotted by at a semi-fast, semi-slow pace. Trying to escape the town, and the sight of people from their windows, on the ground, or even passing by. The next sermon only attracted a few regulars who stared for only a moment at Jane and her guards. "First the sailor men, and now the Lord Eiger sends men too. I'll pray to Selziar to end this chaos," an old woman said.

It had been near twenty until they passed on dirt roads. It was another ten or twenty minutes until they reached the outskirts of town, and passed a stable marking the end border of the town's buildings. A strange man looked at her and then the rest of them, and he prayed for the three points and quickly ran inside. "Why did he do that?" Jaune asked.

"He's praying, have you never been to church, you never pray?" Another one of the men said, in a gruff voice.

"Not really, I don't feel like asking favors to a god of death, and the other chaos. Gives me shivers. I don't like it. We continue riding, and don't stare at the people here. We don't want them thinking beyond what is expected."

The grass flats waved while the troupe cut through the light wind. In the far distance was a spiraling of dark clouds. As they traveled towards it, Jane asked Jaune, "those storm clouds, shouldn't we be concerned about them?"

"Most likely by the time we were over there, the storm should end; we should be more scared of the navy dogs. I know I am."

"They're more bark than bite," the guard's man named Barrett interjected in a gruff voice, "they're all children in their fathers clothes."

Then all the guardsmen nodded together, somewhat reminding Jane of the guards from the town of Diende, and she felt a sort of emptiness inside. *I could have saved him, I could have saved them too, the guards of Diende, Tolk, Thinthe, it's all my fault.*

One of the younger men looked at her, and said, "I know it's a hard time, with all the threats and running happening, but you're free now. Look around you there's nothing but open fields."

"You don't get it," Jane murmured.

"I may not, but still, it won't be harder than it's been."

"Don't curse us, damnit," the other gruff guard Garland said.

"What's your name?"

"Me, I'm Garland, that boy, well, we call him Pinky. Like a baby mouse."

The plains had started to waiver, flowing higher and lower, but not to any great extent. But over many hours of pushing, it showed with their mares beginning to breathe harder. They had rode from mid-morning to mid-day. Jaune was very certain that no one was following them, but Garland protested it, saying, "any skilled man can weave a garb of grass and hide in these hills."

"You paranoid twat," Barrett interrupted, "if someone could find us here, they would have bound all of us the moment we stepped outside Lakeholm."

"I'd rather be safer than sorry."

"And I'd rather sleep light, and live."

It was near the sundown, the keep was being kept together with the sleep deprived servants and guards. Darien's return turned some heads, who didn't even notice that he'd left. Darien in return had a stern face. He strode through the castle grounds with a hand on the handle of his sword. He gripped tight as he came to the duke's chambers. There were two of his men posted at either end of the door. "Is he inside?" Darien asked.

They nodded truthfully, and he said, "open the doors," and they did so to the outrage voice of the duke yelling, "I'll have your heads, you blubbering fools, it's by my-"

Darien strode through waiting for the doors to close, and the duke's expression changed immediately. "Does the wheat grow well?"

"It does indeed."

"A good harvest, indeed. And how strong are the incoming winds?"

"Safe and certain for now."

"Alright, by a week's time, you must find me a man who can keep the keep, in order. A strong man, but even more so, a reasonable man."

"I'd tell Pastor Kreshen, but he's gone from the church."

"Gone? When? Why? Never mind about him, you'll need to find your next best man, we're boarding ships to the capitol."

"You'll need me for truth telling, or battle?"

"Both, I'll need you for both," and he was sitting by his desk handwriting a note which won't exist soon.

He poured pewter colored wax over an envelope and stamped with his house: a crest and shield of a ship with the sails looking like harps. On his crest, the ship was placed over a sea of cornflower, and above the sprawling plains of rye grass.

"Now what's happened to the Pastor?"

"His apprentice Tiamon had told me, 'he said he was going to warn other churches' he told the truth, but not the whole truth. I don't know what it was about for certain, but the navy was a part of it."

"I haven't heard anything of what they did down south. What did you see?"

"Terror, there was complete terror among the people's faces. Pots were smashed, they even rampaged through the church. Looking for something, or someone. We went under their nose, completely undetected. My men are guarding her, they'll keep her safe if they're found, or attacked, they'll return the favor."

"And you're certain?"

"I am, your grace."

"This would be time to pray for their safety, but if the wrong god reaches them, they'll either get swept in a thunderstorm, or a harvest of death. But now we must start our arrangements. I want to first bring fifty men with me. Enough to make a presence, not an invasion. My servants will be mine, and about two dozen will board with us, on a different ship. A fifth of the grain, a third of the horses, and half the armorers. I will not have all my steel be worked by men I've no records of, or knowledge of loyalty to me. Remember you can't trust a lord, even myself, but one who coattails off the crown is a man worse than untrustworthy. I may not trust them, but I'll force them to stay within walls. If they try to jump over, well they won't."

"How much gold do you plan to bring with you?"

"Half."

"Half, My grace!?"

"Yes, half, I can buy sellswords, but they'll betray me to the higher bidder. And I'm certain I'm not the only duke, or lord offered this position. But with this half, and Lucerne's half I'll have an army greater than anyone else, and moral grounds to use them."

"But now that the army has been split, they've already been bought out, by the lords in Porcelania."

"They have some men," he waved the envelope, "he has more, and isn't a noble lord."

"And what makes you think this man won't betray you? Especially since you're building an army for yourself."

"He won't, don't forget I'll put walls around all these lords and him. And no this army isn't for me, it's for our queen when she takes the throne."

"This chaos hasn't begun yet, but I think this little wave will pass over us. For we are strong, and they are new and their foundation soft."

"Are you really sure? Every day, more and more ships sit around us. I would leave before too long if I were you."

"Bah," he spat, "those cockles don't have it in their bones and pale blood. Nah, I don't see a need to be worried."

"Why are the navy here, anyways?"

"Why should I know? We're subjects too."

"What are the chances they aren't our navy? Those damn island freaks!"

"They lost one war, another won't hurt me."

"Still a lot of ships."

"Bah, weak wood, weak men."

"Yeah, how will they board? They don't know anything. Nothing! They are absolutely delusional and know nothing! They'll meet your right hook."

"If they get off their damned boats, that is."

"Heh," he pulled a pipe from his coat, and a bud of tobacco, "even the other side of the docks?"

"I . . . I don't know."

"Nah, I don't think so. How would an entire fleet go unnoticed by the entire navy, and be able to surround us. No, those weak bastards are wealthy pirates or those weak eastern islander maniacs."

Their food had been brought to them on a wooden tray, and the waiter had a fine mustache which brushed lightly in the outside wind. With it they were passed a little cup of spirits, and the two men clinked their glasses and drank. Quickly after the waiter held out a piece of paper, and said, "here is your bill. If you need me, call for me."

"Wait!" one of the men exclaimed, "this isn't right!?"

"What's wrong?"

"Look at this, why is this so much?"

"Money changes, what else can I say?"

"No, it's those ships, it has to be."

"We aren't savages, we can't be letting those toy-boats convince us we're to eat our heart out."

They were interjected with a sack of coins smashing on the table, and a man saying, "Lord's grace."

They both peevishly and confusedly stared, while the man simply walked away.

On the other side of the courtyard he came to another sitting, and eating a small meal. "My grace. Out here on your own?"

"You know I'm not your grace."

"But the son does hold that title, or he will."

"I'll be your grace, when I do, but for now, I want to eat in peace knowing we aren't about to be stormed by ourselves."

"You should be in the safety of the keep."

"You also shouldn't give food to a seagull," he sneered.

His light armor clinked with his heavy sighing. He pulled a chair, and whistled while calling for a serviceman, and he said, "bring me a small goblet of something light, and whatever scrap others order," and the man nodded and swiftly strolled away.

"Are these going to be the last days?"

"Quite possibly, but not before my cup is empty."

"I guess, don't stop drinking."

"I will eventually, and by that time I won't be able to swing a sword, so there must come a time to take the risk and deal with this all."

"That should be my fathers doing."

"Not just here, I assume."

"What do you mean?"

"There's this air, something about it is wrong. It blows the wrong way."

"You don't say."

"There's a chaotic discrepancy again. In the air."

"Is there a fire nearby? I think I smell a fire."

He sat up, looking behind him. In the distance there was a fire which broke out in a house, and its smoke had carried its way over. The little goblet was firmly planted on the table, and he took it up and quickly planted it back down, empty.

"Get up."

"I'm not finished, and well. I'm your lord."

"Not a wink ago you were, now get up, or die."

"Fine," he said reluctantly while looking out to the fire and then to the people, "are we able to help them, those in the house fire?"

"I don't know. Frankly, I can't put you in that danger."

"What if there's a child in there?"

"There could be, there could also be no-one in there. It's none of our business."

"Here, it's my father's business."

"You are a lord when it's best suited, and a civilian too. You must stop this childish behavior, and get to safety."

"I'm not trying to be both."

"Let's not ponder on these things; there's time to think elsewhere, somewhere safer."

"They might die!?"

"A Lot more will die soon, if . . . look," and he pulled the young lord to his shoulder, pointing his head out to the docks in the distance, "they, the shipmen, decide to take the shores. Or!" And he pulled the lord around, "if they like the gold in your pockets, and meat on your bones. A siege is a siege."

"But-" he interrupted with a shush, "fine, take me back."

They crossed into the dark where commoners may not have known even if it lived under their noses. And through a tunnel below the surface he led the young lord. The light of a single candle illuminated the fleetful two of them. Until he stopped at a small alcove which held a ladder in the loose stone. "What's over there?" And he pointed to the end of the tunnel.

"An outlet, it was used sometime ago during the last war. It's not a place many know about, yet."

Chapter Twenty-Seven:

The storm clouds growled in the far distance, closer than before, but still days away. Hopefully it drifted away, and missed them, or only heavily dropped in precipitation. Litus and Kreshen awoke in the early morning with the cold winds blowing harder still. The land of the plains itself had begun to flatten out with large hills in the far distance. Kreshen prayed for a long while, Litus thought it was about the weather, or the travel today. He bucked, and they rode further.

A few short hours passed with the winds pushing back; Litus when waking pulled his cloak hood tight so as to not constantly throw it off his head, and it was difficult to pull his hood back over due to his now long straight hair. Even as the sky began to lighten, the ground still seemed bleak and barely green. In the distance the short mountains looked flatly purple with their bottoms covered by the sprawling hills and trenches of the thunder plains.

The horses were well accustomed to the sound of thunder, even close by. But Litus in particular had only started to get acclimated with the sound. So when he heard an explosion in the sky, he had instinctually both looked for it, and shuddered.

"It's just thunder you're looking for. You'll only hear it. Lightning is what you pray doesn't fall on you. Pray to Selziar as much as Keroth, so that he has the bolt only to drive fear rather than death. You should pray to Mortith as well."

Still for thirty minutes the winds had bellowed, tears balled on the mare's eyes as they tried to look forward. But the wind in a quick turn slowed to a point where it had almost felt like there wasn't any wind at all. "Come let's run quickly while we aren't slowed so much," and they rode faster.

The sky had risen and fallen, and the winds had over the period of time pulsated in intensity. Ranging from a light trickle, to the speed in which a weary man is pushed back. Litus had felt those pins and needles, and had become more attentive, but after a few seconds with no one in their surroundings, he thought *My hands are so cold that I'm confusing the chill with danger.*

They stopped for the night when the wind chill had pierced through their clothes without mending in sight. Kreshen layed out more of the bundle of sticks he carried, but didn't light them. Around them all, including the horses was a faint shimmer, like the wobble of light seen from things far away. "I'll exhaust myself by starting the fire myself. These past few days have been the last time I exercised. Can you light the fire for me Litus," and he did so.

Litus felt a faint image of the forest, but it wasn't a picture but more a span of the forest over hundreds of years over the span of infinity. All the time at once, all the position of the world which Mulder encompassed, at every point in time it ever existed.

They awoke to dread, the chill winds taking all heat from their skin. The fire completely burnt away, Kreshen was awake before Litus, and was seen eating salted beef jerky with a chunk of bread cut with a cleaned sharp edge of the swordbreaker. "I don't see today getting better than now," he took a swig of water, "you looked unwell, did you sleep well my son?"

Litus didn't know what to think, all he felt was confused, and it showed in his eyes. Kreshen noted this with a simple nod and said, "these are confusing times."

They passed through small rivers, which were too small to map out, and depending on the time of year, may not exist anymore. Though the size the river currently was, could be a source of water for a small house, or two even smaller homes. The current ran north, and so they ended up following along. For thirty minutes they rode, before they encountered a dead mulled field which once grew most likely wheat and vegetables. "Do you see any cop left? Any fruit or vegetable?"

There was only some tall grass and dandelions which penetrated the grazing field. No wheat, maize, nor any tomatoes or vegetables. All that remained besides the tilled earth was wooden posts to help crops grow. but still there was nothing. They let their mares eat what tall grass they could, and soon fell upon the one house in question: *Could they let us stay the night?*

On weathered and unpainted boards of wood were holes and teeth marks from rodents, and on the door which stood ajar was a blackish red crystal splattered on. Both men feared what could be inside. Would it be another plains knight, or maybe a shadowspawn lingered from Mulder. But for Kreshen, he feared most of all behind those walls would be a wraith. Even thinking of the word, those true shadows reborn made him shudder. Litus had heard of these beings from almost every walk of life he encountered them – from the queen to the common people across the land. But never did he see one of these men, who was supposed to look like himself.

I don't want to see what's inside, but if someone is in danger. Litus began to walk to the door, Kreshen marked out to him, "I'll go too," as he prayed.

Litus walked first, sword raised forward, and Kreshen had a lantern in front of him. But there wasn't anyone. Not a single living soul, and with the light, no shadow occupied space in corners or elsewhere. There was a body on the ground, it was of a man, or used to be. His body already mostly decayed, and wrought a pungent deathly smell. But they didn't notice the smell, just the cavity in his skull brought by most likely a mace or large rock. Kreshen prayed a short death sermon, and they left. The reward of shelter was not worth tampering with the dead. They both knew that, but Litus felt it inside.

For the rest of that day, the winds stayed small. The still air kept the chill that hit them, but not as hard, not piercing their clothes. They were able to rely on less sticks from the diminishing bundle, and were able to keep their hands warm just from that small fire.

The next day had been worse than the first and second days combined. Those engorged swirling dark pools of cloud fighting a war was closer than they could have liked, and it was only a matter of time when they would ready the great force the storm brought.

"We may have to stop halfway where we could be. We're going to get stuck in the storm; it's too wide to go around."

Through most of the day they pushed through all of the incoming wind, and rain, and the thundering close by. The sky was a dark ooze of swirling moldy and suffocating carpet. Not even the covered lantern light could pierce through all of the droplets of cold rain. But the worst was far more, the chill seeped into their bones, like their bones of ice were scraping with each bump and trot. Their mares were barely audible, but they clearly looked distraught.

They rode for an hour more – which felt three more than that. Until the rain had started to slow, and the sky was more visible. Litus was shivering and tired, but Kreshen was pale as a ghost. He could fall at any moment, and he almost did, but they decided to stop for the day. It was a short ride, but it took so much of them to cut through, dulling their bodies.

Kreshen laid down on the wet ground, Litus took care of their horses, and put them at ease. He built a mound of sticks in the same way Kreshen did. To the best he could remember. He lit it on fire, and the wand grew lighter once more, but not by much. Kreshen had cast the same spell around them all which blocked most of the rain and wind. He said in a croaked voice, "Litus, have you ever heard anything about the Ranger's Guild?"

He shook his head, "in some of my years past, I would give sermons to the rangers there, but now I would assume they would have either become personal guards to some high lord, or the captains and commanders within the castle walls. I haven't been there in a long while, but it's quite a fortress. Larger than the duke's keep. It might be me, now my memory is starting to waiver," he coughed, "in my chest is a letter I mean to give to them when we arrive. If not, then you now know where I keep it. They are some of the proudest men I've ever met, as well as some of the strongest fighters. And of course they're good with the woods, they'll help when they read the letter. Now I only ask you for something, can you fetch me some water, I'm very tired tonight."

And Litus brought him a canister of water, and under the fire heat they camped through the rest of the night. While the true storm drew ever closer.

They began their ride early in the morning, and had snuffed the fire after breakfast. Pinky helped Jane onto her mare, and she looked at the scabbard' sword on the horse's side. She rested her palm against the pommel feeling the cold crown pommel dig into her skin. Within a few days the storm – which hung in the sky faraway – would either be upon them, or would have passed away. "Ah great storms like them always mean a harsher winter."

"What will it matter, we'll be in dry heat by then," Juane said.

"I've got family back in town. I'm gonna miss the winter harvest," Pinky said.

Jane said, "winter's harvest? What's that, a festival?"

"Somewhat, though this castle dweller wouldn't know."

The commonly quiet guard Sam perked up and said, "it's a tradition we have in the town. In my family we would boil down seawater we collected months prior, and sell salt candy. Our neighbors, and other townsmen buy a mug of the hot sweets and spill them on the new snow. You get an entire sheet of salty sweet candy."

Pinky interjected, "it wasn't just sugar, it was also the early snow stopping all the farming. It was a few months break from back breaking work. Though when I became a soldier for the duke even in the snow there was still hard work, just not farming work."

"I don't think I've ever done that. The snow always meant more work in the castle," Jaune said.

"You never thought of sneaking out once?"

"I would be breaking guard and duties for pleasure, I would not become a traitor for so low."

"Ahead," Barrett said, "look at those marshes. And the impassable fog."

"The plains are playing games with us," Garland said.

"We'll continue forward, if the marshes are deep we'll go around."

For nearly ten minutes they went up and down hills till the bog and great fog were right in front of them. "There's horse prints in the mud, two sets, unfortunate fools."

"Unfortunate?" Jaune said.

"What is this, Mulder?" Jane said.

"We're still nearly a week away from that forest," Barrett stated in a gruff voice, "your grace."

"We'll go around," Jane said.

"Your grace, it's just morning mist, passing through will only be as difficult as deep the bog is."

Jaune retorted, "we'll go around!"

For the entire day they rode around the bog, it always stayed a few dozen yards from their left. Later the midday clouds shifted onto dark blankets, and all the men dismounted and the old guards helped Jane dismount. They assembled a tent for Jane, while the rest of them would sleep under the stars. *They don't even let me do my own work. I can assemble my own tent.* Though she still camped in the tent. While the other men sat around a fire they built, cooking some of the food they carried with them. The night was in full and the only man awake was in rotation.

There was a cacophony of abrasive winds striking the flaps of the tent waking Jane in consequence. She stormed out of the tent, to be hit with a chilling wind. They quickly ate morning grub, and packed away, mounting on their mares. The wind in the sky and down to the ground blew hard, being little wisps of needle and thread piercing fabric.

"Why is the wind so strong?"

"The storms usually aren't this bad, we're receiving the end of a hurricane it seems."

"It didn't hit the castle or keep badly. Just the waters, and plains."

"Strange times we've entered," and Garland prayed to Keroth for mercy.

"Why are you praying to Keroth, why not Selziar?" Jane asked.

"My Grace, Selziar's dead, for near a thousand years that is."

"I've been told his body is gone, but his spirit still roams."

Garland breathed heavily, he knew entering sensitive topics with such brash steps could end up poorly. He said with slight stuttering, "well, your grace, I wish that was the case, but Selziar was killed by his brother: the god Keroth. Their virtues clashed and Keroth committed a virtue that forever changed the world. We were plunged into chaos, order is only small spaces, or false promises. I pray to Keroth for good chaos, and hopefully I'll be granted a lucky few weeks. Without anything trying to kill us."

"You know a lot about the world."

"That's why he's always so paranoid," Pinky interjected.

"I will not have any slick talk that divides us," Barrett said.

"Well, well I have always been interested in the way the world ran, that's primarily the reason I became a soldier, to hear more of it. And I'm not paranoid, I'm realistic, look up if you want proof of the chaos," Garland said in his old voice.

For a few hours they rode, climbing hills trotting through tall grass. Little droplets of rain glimmered in the soft light, and fell onto other blades, when pulled by the wind, or stomped with hooves. They passed over small trickles of dried river beds. It indented the ground, which would have been a somewhat passable stream of water for only a little bit of crops. But it most likely would have been used for a greywater stream. The stream ended before anything could have been found. No standing structures, but there was a small village which was nothing but ash. Stones which held roofs high were now tumbled to the ground in this pile of ash.

The daylight slowly faded and was engulfed into the incoming storm. The light sound of thunder ringed faraway being part of the ambiance. The tent again went up, and before any guard could have helped Jane down, she grabbed the pommel of her saddle and dismounted quickly. A few looked at her, especially Barrett. He arched a brow, and simply bowed leaving to finish setting up camp.

The men again sat by the fire telling stories waiting for their salted mutton to cook. "The closer to char the better," Barrett urged.

"You've lost your sense of taste – old man – any longer and it's charcoal," Pinky said.

"Don't call me old, I can still beat up a boar with my fists. And I can beat you with just one finger."

"Alright old man, let's go, I'll put you on your ass."

And immediately once Pinky said that, he was jabbed in the side with Barrett's calloused thumb, and was thrown back on the ground, gasping for breath. "Fine. You old man. You can beat up a boar. But that doesn't mean eating coal isn't strange."

Jane had watched from afar, sorta outcast. *I didn't ask to be treated like a queen, I lost everything for what? This, this loneliness?* Pinky came forward to her holding a wooden plate of salted mutton and a chunk of bread, "it isn't much my grace, but it's all we have," he gave the water canister around his hip to her.

"Thank you," she said, eating alone in her tent.

The winds crashed against the tent rods, causing them to buckle and shift with a small but prominent sound. The early hiss, and gravel feel on their feet really strained them. But still they kept going. They traveled through the thin morning mist; which hung low at the horses feet almost disguising them.

For a myriad of forgetful windy hours, they traveled. The wind in many times had snatched up the hood of Jane's cloak letting her straight blond hair flow in the wind, and a few times caused Pinky and Sam to rubberneck, only to be beaten over the head with Jaune's fist. Jane had laughed a bit at their antics, saying, "you play too much."

"Yes your grace, we'll stop, your grace."

"Stop calling me your grace, it makes me uncomfortable."

"Yes, your . . . my lady."

Jane shook her head, which only caused her hood to fly off again, and again Pinky and Sam got a thrashing.

It was all good and fun, they even started to forget the cruel taste of the cold piercing their skin, until they were reminded of something. It was a lone cabin far to their left. They rode to it. Barrett, Juane, and Garland all noted the fresh set of prints in the wet ground. And Garland said, "someone's been here recently."

They saw the door, and the crystalized black blood that was stuck on. It was open ajar and inside they saw the heavily decayed body of a man.

They sat at a table. The duke in a throne, with Darien to his side, and sitting on a stool was a man in plain clothes, but with a carved face that didn't reveal much emotion. And he sat high and straight, and was strong naturally. His darker toned face hung naturally in the dimmed light. Darien had personally picked the man, and his trust with the man was great, but the duke wasn't going to let even his best man possibly make decisions for his land and people that could end in catastrophe.

The duke tapped his fingers on the table drawing immediate attention from everyone inside. The storm could be seen far away in the distance, thundering striking light and sound through the window with a crash breaking the silence. "You know why you are here?"

"I do," he said in a tight, efficient voice.

"You are one of many men we've been seeking for this . . . position. In my stead you will run the keep, the guard, and procure taxes, and keep the peace of this land."

"Taxes had already been collected, my grace."

"They have, you'll be needing to collect the next few baskets of taxes when the time comes. I don't know who you are, but the leader of my guard has put his trust – my trust – into you. So what experience do you have?"

"For the last fifteen years I had been a cardinal leader of the rangers guild. I had been rising in rank for nearly a decade before that. But before that, I was the son of a pewter craftsman, from out west."

"So you're a Hule man. Do you have experience in manipulation?"

"Yes, and no."

"Kindly explain."

"To be a cardinal leader, you would have been a leader in all ranks before, it's a position second only to the head of the guild. I have used men to concur tasks, in every turn of master and apprentice, to the stone's chores. But the most difficult was nearly ten years ago now, when a whole squad of men were lost in the forest. I had to lead a near thirty man hunt for those missing men. Ended up finding half, the others were dead or missing. Keeping a line of supplies for that half month of searching, while trying to keep more supplies for winter, takes something else.

"And for that no, I don't deal with politics, I deal with work, hard work. If a man is breaking his back for the men sitting, those men aren't men at all. And under my command they weren't men or rangers. They're disgraced."

Darien stood forward, but the duke ushered him back with the raise of a finger. "Running an entire county isn't the same as a guild. Do you think that running this castle will be anywhere the same as the guild?"

"Well with a guild, you only have the members of the guild, and the few servant's who make their way north of here. Running a county clearly takes more care and small actions, but there's more men to do different things. If I can make children into rangers, I can run this castle too."

"This kingdom may need strong men like you, especially here, running my castle and county. Are you ready to take hard decisions? And keep the law and the lawless in check?"

"I am," he said efficiently and strongly.

Chapter Twenty-Eight:

The morning was cold, greatly so. The wind was most of what they heard, and no longer could it be forgotten. Every time they had they thought that they were acclimated to the thrashing the storm gave, and the intensity only grew. It would have felt more comical if it hadn't nearly killed them.

Kreshen slept poorly, he admitted his falsehood of a preemptive death. But he survived the sickness. "I'm sorry Litus, I made you think this is the end. But it's only the beginning. And I realize that we've not entered the storm yet. Just the little waves on its outside. Today," he was almost too afraid to say, "today we're entering the true storm. What we've seen almost this week was not the true storm. Better brace your will better that I."

And Litus watched the sky swirl slowly. It seemed almost serene if it weren't for the hurricane winds that were drifting passed. He pulled his hood tight, and helped Kreshen to his feet. He stretched a minute, and said, "I'll pray to all the gods, each together, and we'll make it through. Don't doubt this one moment, look at me Litus, don't doubt the gods."

If I pray, hopefully it will keep Kreshen going. And Litus prayed the three points too; a second later they mounted and began to ride out. The beads of rain fell on them like being hit with small rocks. Small arrows which struck them like a whip. But still they pulled through.

For half an hour they trudged through. The rain kept the ground soft, causing their hooves to indent in and collect dirt. This caused the mares to slow as they walked the rain riddled plains. Keeping them further behind than they'd wanted. But still they drove on. It was midday, but the telling wasn't possible. It was just the clouds, and still the dirt clung.

"It's their hooves. Dirt is just sticking to their hooves. If we keep pushing so hard, we'll kill the horses. We need to slow down."

Litus reared down, *We need to be out of the storm, not slow down. If the steeds fall, we need to keep going.* Then Litus kept forward, harder now. His mare was becoming disheartened, and ever more scared. Kreshen yelled over the storm with cracks of coughs inserted, "stop Litus, you'll kill your horse, you'll kill yourself. Wait!"

Litus looked back, almost asking Kreshen to keep moving forward, faster so they could escape the storm, before the storm killed them. "Wait!" He yelled again.

Kreshen ran up to Litus, who was keeping the same pace. His horse hissing and screaming with the thunder so much closer. For a few seconds there was a metallic taste in the air, and the feeling of cloth sticking to itself rather than to their skin. In a sudden and violent crashing of light. Purple, blue, and great white outshined their lantern light. And all the darkness was vanquished. But that was gone for a second without sound. A deep ringing, a high pitched hiss.

Litus was forced to stop, his mare was ready to run, but didn't buck him off. Kreshen rode up next to Litus, hands over his ears and arm over his eyes. And Litus could see a bright white. Everything looked bleached in gray light.

There was a tinge of desolation in his growl, "don't you know what you're doing, my son! You are trying to kill yourself and your horse. Damn you."

He was in complete disbelief. "Litus," he said in a disappointed way, "I've not feared much in this life. The world is living just the same as us, but if what the old Malkin people say is true, you are a hero. This prophecy of yours so parts the sky, and rids this world of terror, and I've vowed to you. I've vowed to you! You're trying to part a tree with a dull axe, and you're trying so desperately hard to do so, but you can't, and if you kill yourself before it has begun, then you have done the world a horrible deed, and you'd disappoint all who may hope. That is what I fear, failure. I will not have you fail today. Even if you kill me."

Litus took his gaze away, *this is a storm, a hurricane. I have the strength to go, let me do it.* Kreshen moved his horse around, "look at me, Litus. When I fall, it will be a priest who falls, you will fall all the faintest sliver of hope with it. That storm is just a storm, we fear it the same as we fear sickness. It passes. You have the strength to knock down a thousand trees, you have to sharpen your axe first."

Take time to sharpen my axe? I'll take time once the storm passes. He's not understanding the danger we're in. At any moment, anything can happen. It will happen. It must.

He stood in the middle of the void now. It was warm, surprisingly so. There was nothing but him, darkness was nothing, and he floated like it was a pool of salty water. But it didn't feel wet. It felt like nothing, but that didn't remove the fact that it was warm and quiet and empty of everything. It was so quiet all he could hear was the static in his ears.

Now within the pool he felt a complete absence of needles jabbing into his skin. Had he gotten used to the feel of being pricked?

For hours and hours, maybe days, he drifted through this pool. Over that time it transcended and descended into the craters of a milky orb. And hours later from the black ness of the void above the white, was a blanket of gray. The image of the hole, and the many holes scattered around the surface were distinct, with lines and ridges. But he saw it as a flat plain before he could see the dimensions.

In the sky, it really was a sky, he could see depth and hue within the gray. Less so the same pure gray that showed before, but now with hints of blue and green. Brighter lines across a crest were whiter. Then the picture zoned back. There was an entire picture. An entire world. In a sea of pins and lights from the outer void. And Litus picked his head up, and saw the ridges of impact made from things. The collisions of things long past. But at the same time it happened at the same time as collisions a hundred years in the future, or five hundreds years in the future. Or even the events when all that is seen is gone, however long that may be.

The end wasn't the twinkle of other times, but a slow decay and diminish. Until all had left from here, and everyone was dead. Time was a painting, the entirety of it, all at once.

He took steps around the crater, until he walked far over the ridge and onto the flat surface. Litus had forgotten about temperature, the warmth was nothing, there was no cold, no heat. It was just him watching from the celestial body at the flat present being examined in almost real time. Before he realized, he had walked the entirety of the celestial body's surface a billion times. It was the world that they walked on; he stood on the moon. The pale yellow dust being picked from his kicks. The world turned half a revolution and showed the swirling of masses, of great smoky clouds battling for the sky. Their flamberge swords gripping each other, and with each interlock running bringing flashes of smoke and bolts of lightning.

Even with their screaming and parley, there was still a hole in the complete center of their bickering. A sanctuary, a safe haven. A great triumph, but horrid tribulation. This was the world we walked on, and somewhere down below was Litus and Kreshen. They were traveling, and they were for certain in the warzone of storms and winds.

They trudged through the mud, and hills, and rain, and fog. And through this bog they were arguing. Kreshen had clearly engulfed his disappointment into rage. And Litus could watch himself nearly break Kreshen's back.

The powder from the moon's surface began to melt, and combine into a clay sphere, and the void began gaining mass of a black dirt. And all of this extended to the world far away. The clouds fell into a ball of dirt, shaping into a mass of fire and blood. It fell apart into two spheres which became two different planets, and they were sucking each other's blood, like a vampire.

The ground below fell apart, all crumbled into dust, and burned up into ash. Fluttering away in a sea of storms. Being sucked into a new void. The being of dirt shaped and shifted into a being with a true form. Slender and tall, being seen through a foggy glass disk. Half his face was engulfed in flame, being burned into a crisp. The other half was laughing a hideous but loving laugh, and he looked down on them all, and his eyes pierced through the ground leaving a hole in the ground. As the being faded from the void, leaving it behind. But what remained was Litus and that laugh.

He blinked his eyes, he was on horseback, and Kreshen was talking to himself thinking he was being heard. His voice was like gravel. A deep burring and bickering. Litus looked around, Kreshen was following from right behind. He gave a strange look to Litus who hadn't looked around for a few hours now. Litus stopped in his place, forgetting his place in the world. He felt like a lifetime had passed, and in a sense it had. He saw the eye of the storm, and the world which would become. Kreshen was right. They were bound for safe haven within the storm, but only if they slowed their pace to acclimate to the climate. Litus gave a nod to Kreshen, and Kreshen returned the nod slowly while changing his face from angry to confused. "What is it?"

Litus pointed forward to the storm, *the eyes of the storm is close.* He watched the storm swirl and somehow he knew what Litus meant with just the point of his finger. The winds and rain beat on, they progressed forward until the night sky fell, and they made camp. "But please, for the sake of others, you have to slow down, and think of your actions before you make them," Litus nodded, and the day ended.

The morning started like the nights prior, heavy with rain, and heavy with wind. It pulled hoods, and the flaps of clothes. You could only know what's ahead of you with one eye ajar. "Do you want to hear a fisherman's tale about storms?"

Kreshen wasn't able to see if Litus had nodded or not, so he decided to tell away instead. "Long ago, maybe twenty or thirty years back I met a fisher setting out to sail in a storm. I had asked him before he left 'why would you go sailing, you should head in, and hope it dies down before attempting to sail,' I thought the man was a bit crazy from previous interactions with this man, but I didn't stop him then. If I were there now I would have, but back then I was a rougher grit. I let the man sail away, while I made barricades over the windows. And over the windows of the homes around the church. I was trying to help all I could, before the storm reached us. By the time the storm – the hurricane – hit the town, I had almost completely forgotten about him not from hate, but from stress. And when I did remember, all I could do was pray for him. It was two days later, he was alone on his small ship, and he had caught enough fish to feed the entire town for half a month," He paused for some breaths, and said after, "so if we survive this, the future will be good and fair. Hopefully."

It was almost comical, on time thunder roared, and lightning struck. The rain beaded cups of water with each drop, and the lightning broke the ground below like a boxer. "We're getting closer to the eye of the storm. We can make it, just a bit further."

They were coming from the bottom of a hill, once dressed in fine grass of emerald green. Now all the moon-like craters scattered around the mound, and mud sloped the side. A vale of mist emerged within the thinner droplets. Precipitated into a shroud of uncertainty. And the hill's peak was only a single peak in an entire hill range, a crescent shaped crest that formed a wide wall that was in their way.

"Up the hill, we can make it if we try," they pushed and heaved up. They dismounted their steeds, taking weight off their backs. They marched up. Litus slipped back when the slick mud threw his feet from the ground. "We're almost there!"

A massive bolt of lightning struck down, flitters of electricity lingered above. Forcing them to pause for the brief moment. Litus looked around them all, concerned, Kreshen spoke up, "are you all right?"

Litus picked himself up, and continued. Through the muddy pool they slowly rose the hills, and gritted their feet in the ground to not fall down. For thirty minutes they passed through this filth, the mud clinging to their boots, and rain poured. As they journey closer, the storm only grew stronger. The eye of the storm was protected by the mercenary winds, and they guard with poison. Great poison which uprooted the trees from the ground, and the skin from the fruit of the hills. They would then take the meat and distribute it further. And all of the land was flattened for the army of the sky. This was a siege against the skin of the ground. And Litus and Kreshen were being pulled apart in the midst of the battle. The soldiers of grass were being swept away. The sailors of rain were decapitated by the blades of grass. The bloodshed dripped down the fields. Painted brown with dirt. The woad paint imprinted in the ground. The blue water floating above the brown. The signals of birds spying on the keeps in the back.

But the plains weren't winning this skirmish. Through thick and thin, the blood and ash rained down with each bolt of lightning throwing down the fire of possible victory. And when all was dissipated in the world, there was the crater left. Trenches were dug in the ground, filled with the waste runoff of old blood. Patches of moss stood above water, watching the two men march their way through. Each poke and stab of the hurricane winds parried and blocked. Replied with the throwing of rocks and mineral pellets. Catapulted into the sky exploding the pockets of rain as they fell. Litus and Kreshen would be covered in the blood of this warfare, pulling with the weight of a bolder their lives. And as they dragged this stone with chains, the blood caked on the rusting metal and porous surface of the stone.

The fire roared even higher. Thunder exploded at their feet. The skirmishes of soldiers on either side grinning as they attempt an easy kill. With each slice and parry of their bladed grass, and rupture of the sky. The heating of the plasmic ridden air. And the cold of the icy rain – which now drenched their dress in the frost heave of the deathly ill. But even as the stresses grabbed and stuck on. Their shoulders being bitten and slashed at. Their faces were nearly unrecognizable from the refugees of the wars of man. This was not a war of man; this is just a battle in a long standing war. The battle of the plains. The trenches tripping their steps. The dark light blackening the water drowned the sky. But they had to continue. Their mares were screaming in pain. Their hooves were cemented in the blocks of congealed blood. Lightning struck close by. Litus and Kreshen both heaved to free their horse. And with the few remaining strength of the hearts, they pulled free the hoove.

The world was seeming to close in on itself, but through a faint glimmer of light they knew their place. It was a league away. They drifted through the grim. Soldiers were being swept away to rot in the trenches. Rain poured like buckets of coarse stones, and wrought iron spikes. And they continued. It was only twenty feet away. With each agonizing step they groaned with pain, but that couldn't stop them. Not man, or shadow, or their horses too. The footmen even as they tried could not stop their pursuit. And it all ended, when they passed through. Into the eye of the storm, and it was beautiful. The air was sweet with clarity, and dry too. Above they could see the sky in blue. Far above they were the first people in a thousand years to see the blue and orange sky for what it was. In the eye of the storm.

Chapter Twenty-Nine:

The morning was crisp with a blossom of the cold welcoming in the near-winter weather. The sky showed a bluish hue to the clouds that hung above. In the great abode of wind, the storm they were reaching was only a few days away – the true storm that was. They were only in the outer folds of the hurricane. The closer they came, the less so they would want to enter the deep harsh rains that preceded them. However much they didn't want to go, they had to, and that's what they told themselves. So to the younger of the men – being Pinky, and Sam – they seemed more to drift towards the storm – and castle beyond that – than they had ever really pushed their feet on the ground.

Jane was quiet, and was absently connected from the men who were there to guard her. *Why can't they treat me like they treat each other?*

Jane pulled her horse towards Jaune – who was leading the group. Jaune appeared surprised by the queen appearing right by him, "your gra- . . . My Lady, what is it? Is there something wrong?"

"No there isn't, I just want to speak with others for once."

Even though Jane clearly didn't act like a royal figure, her title put a frog in Jaune's throat. "What would you like to talk about?" His face felt hot with anxiety.

"How did you come to lead this party?"

"Well," he shifted in his saddle, "the guard master Darien had made me the lead in this . . . party. That's what we'll call it."

"Isn't he a truth wizard?"

"Yes, he is, but a man can hold more than one title. In his case there's two: guard master, and truth wizard."

"And father," Garland said, "don't say titles if you don't include them all. He's a holy man after all. Don't know if it's a sin, but I for one won't be the one finding out."

"Do you also believe in vampires?" Jaune said.

"Don't disrespect your elders. Especially when all they care about is saving your skin."

Jane let out a bit of a chuckle, and Pinky pulled forward, "what are we talking about?"

"Paranoia," Jaune said.

"I'm not paranoid, and I don't believe in vampires. I believe in reality. True reality, and what hides behind the veil of shadows and such."

Pinky with a cheeky grin on his face said, "vampires, what do you believe in wraiths next?" The next needle of cold winds blew through their clothes, chilling their bones.

Garland's face fell, and his features became stone. "Now listen up. You don't ever speak so lightly of wraiths again, do you understand?" His eyes were pin needles.

"I was just . . . just trying to make you guys laugh."

"No, you won't do that again, especially around the queen."

"Alright, I'm sorry."

Garland kept his eyes on him, and Pinky withdrew back leaving the front of the party quiet and empty. The day drifted by slowly. The patches of grass blew in the winds in unison. Jane was quiet and deep in thought, such as the people back in Diende. *Why now? Why do they still linger in my mind, they're gone, and that's that. If I think of them, these guards will fall next.* There was so much, all gone. And her face remained empty of emotion. She no longer tried to hide, it now felt somewhat natural.

They made camp in the flatlands while dark resided. They knew making camp on the top of a hill would have been greater than the flats, but they had to make do with what they had. The winds weren't as strong as they had been while riding the hills, but it still was present. In this case though it helped them bring up the high blaze sooner. Jane had been in the circle with them warming her bones by the fire. *If I had worn one of those dresses the noble women had at the ball I may not be cold with all those layers.* She gripped all the loose fabric from the black gown. Hoping it would store some of that heat.

All the men remained silent in her presence, and it was very apparently so. "Every other night, you all talk about everything there is to talk about, why not tonight?"

All the men looked at her, but dared not to glare. "Well my lady, we didn't mean to disturb you."

"No no, I want to join you all."

"You do!? Well I have an idea," Garland said, "you all think of me as paranoid, but I know better, for I have a story to prove the strangeness of this world."

"Tell away," Jane ushered.

"By this year, this story is close to thirty years old. I was half my age I'm currently, maybe more so, I more or less forget how old I am, I guess. I have to have my son remind me. But for this It doesn't matter so much. This all started in a dream. Dreams are hard to remember, but this one was different, I remember it the same I remember my children's faces. I was riding to the abandoned city of Neit, it had been abandoned for nearly fifty to seventy years at this point. Today I don't know if any of these lands have reclaimed lands there, or if it's all been taken by the forest by now."

"Another taken by Mulder?"

"No no, this city wasn't even in this country. Far north from here, and west from the Haute mountains. In the little kingdoms, or little republic, whatever they call themselves. But the close forest of Bor de Mer, is cursed almost just the same as this," he pointed north to the distance, "and in this dream, days had passed traveling to, and passing over old bridges over the witch finger rivers. And a few days later, I passed with people I hadn't known entering the abandoned city I had never been to before. The buildings were high, very high. The tallest I've ever seen. I know, I saw this before they fell – it would have been a worldly sight today – but by then the buildings were all decayed. We were searching for something, in a dream you just don't know why you do things, you just do them. And after a day of searching with nothing, we as a group decided to make camp. I woke up – in my dream – to the sound of fire, and burning. I cursed to the god Keroth," Jane paid closer attention, "for the chaos he brought me. And I bolted up. Sword drawn, holding it out in front of me. I still heard this burning fire, and smelt smoke, but I hadn't seen either. I walked out the hold we were in, and for ages and ages I walked under the moonlight. When I look back at it, I imagined what the clear sky would have looked like: just black with pure white circles in the sky. I came to a courtyard, where the fiery smell and sound was. And there was a great bonfire. Bigger than I'd ever seen. And standing in front was this woman. The most beautiful woman I'd ever seen. Her face was only visible by her outline. Her figure was visible from the thin vale-like dress she wore."

A handful of the guards had looked at Jane, waiting for the queen's disapproval, but instead they found a face deeply intrigued. She broke away from her focus on Garland, and looked at the guards, "what?"

"Oh nothing," Garland muttered, "this dream had ended with us looking at each other. Her skin was cast black by the bright light, but her eyes. Her deep violet eyes pierced me, and then I woke up."

"Was this woman someone you knew, I knew someone who had purple eyes, though they weren't a woman."

"I never knew this woman, and I'd never seen anyone else with violet eyes before or since. For months I kept having this dream. Every night. Over time I started to know the people in my dreams, their features, their names, even their fears. But the woman with those violet eyes, my dream would end before I could even speak a word to her. All I knew about her was her eyes and fire. A few more months had passed, and by the end of the harvest season, I decided to leave, going north to be a sellsword. That's what I did to keep paying for the long voyage. I just had to go to this abandoned city. If I were an older man, like I am now, I would simply ask a wizard, or anyone to help soothe my dreams – if they could. Just something before wasting such a long time for what would likely be nothing. But I was so much younger, and dumber too, like you two," and he laughed at Pinky and Sam, and once his chuckle ended, he said, "for about a month and a half of sailing, I eventually made it up river to the castle of Leus, and convinced the lord with my great charisma, nah, I'll be real, he probably pitied me. A deranged young man journeying to a city that was supposed to be abandoned. I had found out it was no longer abandoned, and for some reason I didn't believe anyone who said so. How could this city have people? I dreamt that it was completely empty. But when I left, for some reason this lord gave me a troupe of people going for tax collecting or something like that. Their faces were the exact same as from my dream. I must have creeped them out knowing exactly everything about them. From the way they laughed, and their faces of disgust. Oh they were so confused by how I knew who they were. And so was I."

"So did your dream tell the future?" Pinky broke in stuttering.

"That is a good question, how I said it it seemed so, but I'm no conjurer. I guess I would have to say yes, but it all became true once I decided to make this dream true. It's like a two edged sword. Was it meant to happen, or did I make it happen? Maybe it's one, both, neither. But otherwise, we had traveled for nearly a week, passing that same bridge, just like it happened in the dream. Everything that I dreamt happened in reality. When I was young I thought that since the city was populated, the dream wasn't perfect," he let out a cough, there was a chill that passed through the air again, "when we arrived there, to my surprise, there really were people in this town. More than just a dozen who tried to seek refuge or find homes, but the entire city was filled with people. At Least what I saw of it was. I had searched the towns, to my company's disapproval, but hey I was young, and I was confused, and I was stupid too. There was one person in the city who I was looking for. But after the entire day I gave up searching. My company and myself stayed in the inn. To say they were mad would be an understatement. To them there was no reason to stay here, and that the lord was an idiot for being affiliated with me. That night was the first night in which I dreamt anything different."

"Now that I think about it, you've never told us this story before," chimed Pinky, while Sam looked with arched eyebrows.

"I'm telling a special secret story to our important lady here. I felt it was fitting."

"Well this story is sorta scaring me Garland," said Pinky.

"So you're the paranoid one now!" Garland chuckled.

"No you still are," all the other guards said together.

Garland shook his head, "anyway, the dream," his voice was smooth, and quiet. All their attention was to his voice. Not the sound of the fire crackling, nor the wind bustling was audible, "it was a poem, I could not see the woman who was saying it to me, but she whispered it in my ear, her arm caressed mine like she laid in bed behind me."

The casks keep what the flame burns
The scales tip, and the world turns

I am death the angel of souls
I am the fire which brightly burns
I am the peace that never speaks
I am the time which slips away

The red rain will fall
Look into my eyes
The red rain will fall
Out of this dream ridden mind

"During that last verse I heard the same sounds that emanate from the camp here tonight. I woke up, a fierce sweat drenched the clothes I wore. I ran out, barely dressed except for the sword at my hip. In the same courtyard there was that woman cast in shadow, with purple eyes. This time I saw another being. It was the fire itself. In my dream that fire was simply a bonfire, a large one, but it was just a bonfire. Here it was different. The city itself was on fire. I yelled out to the woman, but not even my voice could be heard over that blaze. She walked through the blaze, completely untouched. And I never saw her again. The fire encircled the city, completely destroying it and all who lived inside. I don't know how many survived, but I was lucky.

And since then I ask myself many questions. Did the woman warn me of the fire, did she cause it? I simply don't know."

"Is this true?" Jane asked.

"When I look back, I can't remember if her eyes were really purple, or red. But to me, it can't be anything but real, cause I don't know what else it could be."

As the hours passed further into the night the fire slowly died, the winds blew harder with the storm approaching ever closer. Jane was again alone in her tent, the wind beating against the side flaps. *A shadowy woman with purple eyes, almost like Litus. How could that story be real, it sounds too much like a story. Too much to be true. But could it? My dream, those red eyes, what about him?* The chills ran through her, urging Jane to wrap herself and break for sleep, but like most nights she thought of the recent past. *I never even was able to talk to him, he didn't even have a face to see. It's all my fault. All of this. And now I have to run this kingdom; this insanity. It doesn't even make sense. That truth wizard was clearly too old for his position. And the duke too, and Tylock especially. He put me in this mess, he's the reason Litus is dead, and I will return that favor someday.* The winds eventually subsided as she fell asleep, all but the chill.

The bones in her body were cold. Winter was coming sooner than they'd like. The image of the moon pondered Jane in those final moments, that yellow orb.

The fire was just hot coals at this point, Garland was mounted guard and Pinky was awake to ask him more questions about the story. Twenty or so minutes had passed since Jane fell, and now because of his supposedly quiet whispering, she was now awake. Those fleeting moments of annoyance fell away with an interest for more of that story. "Pinky, Pinky, get some sleep, you'll want it in a few hours when you're next post."

"Fine, but who was that woman, who do you think she really is?"

He gave the quietest laugh he could muster, "I don't know. That's the truth of it, Peter."

"And you're paranoid."

"Fine if I accept I can be paranoid – however reasonable it is. But will you go to sleep?" Pinky nodded, and Garland said, "I am reasonably paranoid. Now you better go off to sleep."

They were both silent, except for the sound of thin metal scraping. She could hear Garland shush Pinky and there were those fleeting moments of silence that hung and lingered far too long. But it all broke with a boom of a voice, "get back, go protect the queen," he barked at Pinky, and yelled to them all, "wraith! Wake up all you, a wraith attacks in the night!"

Jane looked out of the tent, her heart beat in her chest. *Wraith, they're real? No, no, he's just paranoid. How could it be?*

It was only a few seconds; Garland met the shadow rider's blade with his own. Garland was on the low ground, raising the blade upwards. The rider pushed him back with the strength of his black horse, and long saber. Garland had successfully blocked each swing, but wasn't able to find an opportunity to advance. So he tried turning around the rider, with better positioning. The rider jumped from his steeds back. Blade flailing in the air, opposing all strikes coming in. the rider directly pushed Garland back. It was a fight of lightning strikes and pouncing parries. The blocks were stopping an unstoppable force.

Jane's weary eyes were too slow to register their attacks. She watched by peering her head outside while Pinky ran up to her, sword in his hand, "my lady, we must go. It isn't safe."

"Where did the wraith come from?" She demanded, *so that's what they look like. I lied to Litus about them, but there's one here.* There was a yelling coming from Garland, they looked to. He had a massive slice down his arm, severing the jerkin which protected him. Pinky barked, "we must go now!"

"Aren't you going to save him, Garland."

"I'm here to save you!"

"Go save him, I order it."

Pinky looked between the two with resistance, but it was an order. Pinky ran towards the wraith sword raised forward. He yelled, "down you shadow!"

The wraith in a split second interlocked their blades. He grabbed control, forcing Pinky's blade to fall to the ground, with a coating of fresh blood, and a left hand too. Pinky grabbed his new stump, and screamed in pain. The wraith went to sever more, walking close to the young man crawling on the ground. The soft light of the moon shone harshly on the wraith's blade as he twisted back towards the weary Garland. The wraith intercepted the attack. And again they were match for match. Their blades met high, and parried low. The ring of each attack growing louder. "Go to the queen you fool!"

It was over already. The wraith's blade was sheathed, before Jaune, Sam, and Barrett could arrive. Jane stood behind them all. The little light glaring off the blood, Garland on the ground, sword in his hand, and he was dying. Jaune and Barrett went running to the wraith, but the shadow rider was already gone. There sat no hooves, only blood.

Sam and the white faced Pinky stood over Garland's body, Jane was right behind them, and when he spoke you couldn't easily tell it apart from the wind, "the woman, I know, I know now," his eyes went gray, and Garland breathed his last.

Jane watched his face draw pale, and his lips turn orange. The blood from his chest pooled on the ground below. They were all motionless, Pinky was in immense pain, and when Jaune returned, he watched them all. Barrett immediately broke in, "put your stump in the coals. Now! You have to cauterize it. One death is enough tonight," he looked at Garland, he looked as though he could cry, but refused to.

"Pack your things, and wake the horses, we ride tonight, and we don't stop."

"What, are we going to leave Garland's body?" Jane said.

"Your grace, your life has just been threatened. Garland has done his duty, and now we must leave."

"But-"

"The storm is ahead, and the ground is cold. I'm here to lead you to safety. We leave now, and only now!"

They packed up quickly; there wasn't any time to snuff the coals. As they left they all drew their eyes on Garland's body one last time.

With the rising winds – while on angry steeds – they pushed through the harsher and harsher storm threads in a weave of insanity. The only light was that of one lantern, and the moon itself. It was a low burning candle, because the further they rode, the more and more dried river beds were in the way. *If they didn't follow me, Garland would be in the castle still alive. His children would have a father, and Pinky a mentor and hand. No matter where I go, everyone dies around me.* She kept her palms on the pommels of her sword, and saddle. *With this, no-one else needs to die because of me. With this blade, I can kill all who try.*

Chapter Thirty:

The docks of the keep were busy with progress of packing ships, and it would only be for these few days left until they would leave for the castle of the queen. There was a team of thirty men taking grain and packing it into barrels for shipping. The seamstresses were patching all old uniforms and garbs possible, as well as making flags for the duke's ships and the flag bearers. The guards were sharpening their halberds, their swords, the pike heads were stored in crates, leather jerkins mended, or made, and the few steel men were polishing their plate to make real shiny before they disembarked in just a few days.

Eiger stood by watching the crews pack and load the few ships he wanted to depart. These three were only a quarter of his ships. Though they were his largest vessels, and were designed for war rather than cargo. This was a concern to the shipyard master who questioned the duke's decision, "these ships aren't meant for cargo, they're meant for combat. You mean to fill these till they burst of grain. Enough to feed an army. Do you plan to bring the rest of the castle with you?"

Eiger gave a short chuckle, "I see in the near future the possibility of losing ships. So I see it as more of a reassurance of bringing really strong ones, they're harder to sink."

"Do you mean to start a conflict with the crown?"

"No, no I don't want to start a conflict, and neither will the crown against me. I know that for certain. We'll have these vessels in the docks just outside the queen's keep. And if there's any navy ships, I'll find a way to remove them."

"Having the navy start this conflict is just as bad?" He patted the hull of one of the ships in question, "she could only fare so much against another of her sister vessels."

"They're my ships. If I need to sink one for greater outcomes I will."

The shipmaster gripped his tunic with a strong hand and looked pale, "you wouldn't dare sink her, it would be the same as drowning my wife and child!"

Eiger gave the man a small look, "I don't want to if I can, but might if I need. No reason to fret, if it does occur you won't even be there to see. You'll be maintaining the rest of the yard while I'm gone. How much has been loaded?"

"I'd say near all of it, but ya still need a day or two to load the rest. The grain should be done by today, midday closer it be. So I'd say we should be on time for your schedule, my grace."

Duke Eiger nodded, and began to return back to the castle grounds. There were pigeons flying above carrying notes tied to their legs. He looked on with curiosity, but remained stoic to the others around. The gates opened with a trough of soldiers getting their gear in check. And servants rushing around cleaning and serving food as seen fit. While Eiger was rushing to get to the dovecote tower. He was met by Darien in his jerkin holding the letter.

"Where's it from, what does it say?"

"Lucerne has left Porcelania."

"Already? Has he acquired any sort of man power?"

"He has purchased sellswords and such. Mercenaries make up his army."

"Alright, why has he left?"

"The notes don't say here," Eiger took a few slithers of notes, "these are from Lucerne, all of them?" He shuffled the papers, "he openly admits to buying mercenaries. Why? I wish you could tell if this were true or not."

"He may believe you would think this was a great leap forward; to him acquiring men was acquiring men. The more manpower the better."

"Men are men, but mercenaries are loyal to the one who pays the most. While loyalty to lords is greater. I thought a man of his rank could wrangle low nobles at least."

"Do you think he did this on purpose because of your deal?"

"I don't know, he was quite drunk when making that deal. We'll have certainty when we arrive at least. We'll figure it out the more information we gather as we get it. The information I want, though, is where Lucerne went."

"In the notes it doesn't state where the mercenaries are either. If they went with him."

"They'll most likely be in Porcelania, it would be a waste of a deal to make if he decided to break it less than a week later. And if that's the case, I'll hold that above him, high above him. A duke's power is far greater than his commodore position."

"But if he gets the upper hand? He has the power of the royal navy."

"He has access to the power given to him by I'd assume this Tylock fellow."

"The new grand admiral?"

"Precisely, any notes about him?"

"Not much that I've seen, not even where he's gone, the man has kept his trail small. I don't know why though. Maybe assassination attempts?"

"Well he has ascended quickly. He took the position, and I don't know if I believe it completely from Lucerne, but the entire navy united to one cause, to one person."

"Attempts on his life from the previous admirals, maybe?"

"Someone's after him, he wouldn't know it's us yet, hopefully not. Lucerne is what can either make or break this. So we better be like Tylock, keep an eye on our back, and then we back stab him. Power is potential. And we have great potential."

The streets were dusted with litters of hay here and there, but mostly it was covered in the soot and shreds of wood and grits of steel. But it mattered not when all were squashed under the heavy heel of Tylock's boots. The only slightly unmarked door on the right led to a large brick manor, in which the navy command occupied for the time. There was a plume of smoke rising from the chimneys of the manor, as well as some of the occupied homes around. An officer who strode next to Tylock carried a scribe-pen and noted down words for other officers somewhere else; maybe Porcelania, maybe the city name Hule, or it could be to the city across the water: Fer.

His boots made a click against the hardwood floors, even the officers who followed weren't as audible. The chandeliers that hung above were covered in layers of dust. Blinds were cut and thrown off the curtain rods. He entered a hall with a large oblong table of hard mahogany, and stone faced men. They roared his welcome, all garbed in clean tailored navy uniforms. They were the Navy High Command. None a man – besides the armed guards or servants – were a rank lower than a captain, and with a second glance Tylock didn't see if there were any captains. That made for better chances for success. He gathered the one empty chair left for him. The seat at the penultimate of the table. He gathered himself so – placing a long leather jacket on its back – before seating. His black hair blended in with the black of the jacket. One of the navy men opened, and said, "Grand Admiral Tylock, as you can see we were able to seat ourselves on the entirety of Ser, though the city across is grinding our pleas away."

Tylock regarded slowly, "we aren't giving pleas. We're demanding on behalf of the crown that they give up their ports. When they send more birds, Commodore Barwyn, and they say we don't have access to their docks, we'll know we will have access."

"You mean to wage war against our own people. You would be starting a civil war."

"Our own people want us to dock – they don't know it yet – with those lords, and public officials in the way. They've turned these great cities to dirt, and need to be resuscitated by the crown. And they're harbinging a fugitive: the queen slayer," Tylock said.

"We've told them that," an admiral said, "they haven't listened."

"If we attack the shores with men, we would be at a disadvantage, and we would have citizen militias against us. Loyal to their lords and civil officers."

A plethora of the command began a small bickering about how to handle the city, but when the wooden chair legs from Tylock's seat rubbed against the hardwood floor, it squealed and suppressed the choir. He gripped the ears of the chair with black leather gloves. "We are not invading their land. We are not attacking civilians. And we are going to dock. Whether those traitorous men restrict the law or not. We'll surround them, no ship's in or out. The large vessels will interrupt fishing as well, and lastly we'll fly in droves and droves of pamphlets with doves and pigeons and any bird we can catch."

The Admiral Broarch – who sat next to Tylock – gave him an odd eye, and a raised brow, "so you mean to tell, what, all the lords and city council members a book of surrender notices, or do you mean to tell all the men in the city of theirs to surrender? I don't see how giving them papers to wipe their ass during a siege, leads to our victory. Would you care to detail us in how we are to aid from this?"

He gave a gruff sigh, "we're giving them a common enemy. Those without moral standing, lawful standing, are against the crown, and no remorse for the church, and religion. I can see in the near future, fighting and massacring their brothers. Bloodshed being made, but not by any of our men. Not a red speck on their garbs. The people will decide their fate, and when they make it, we must reward them for that."

"Reward them," a man said with a chuckle, "you're speaking politics rather than battle tactics."

"All battles are politics. Just on an individual scale. But when our battles are won by the people, they expect something. And to their victories they will. Their victories are our victories. Have men send letters, and encircle the island with ships."

A small officer spoke up with concern, "most people are illiterate, how will they read these letters?"

"Those who are literate will read to those who aren't. Next."

An admiral from the other side of the hall spoke up, his breath waving his mustache, "for the materials of the letters, where do you say we procure these? The locals here?"

"If we make a debt to the people of this city, they'll be stuck with us, and be bound to the crown knowing they think they have power."

A few faceless men made slight chuckles, before covering their mouth from search-full eyes. "Is there anything else this meeting has to bring up? Particular to churches and cults?"

"I wouldn't fret over that cult, they are a small fanatical group. Ones who are keen on the east's favoring of the dead god," Broarch said.

"Even a small mouse who hides from cats, can still chew the foundation till it falls and destroys everything," Tylock stood walking towards the tall draped window behind his seat. He pulled the blinds letting in the fading orange daylight flood in, "starting here, and moving west we'll need to change the church from one sept who worships all, to individual churches all funded by the crown. A church for the dead, a church for Selziar, and a church for Keroth the chaos god. And hopefully some of these cultists will become priests."

"So you want to turn these anarchists into what? State backed anarchists?"

"No, they will be the state backed faithful."

He clutched his stump of sticky black blood. Garland hung over his shoulder berating the young man. He slumped on horseback, while Jaune, Barrett, and queen Garnet stared at him with pits and eyes of pure fire. There was a sound of a dog squealing and raven cawing and the sound of the hurricane burring a glistening of sharp needles of ice and lantern oil fire. It was only when a sharp and quick trot of invisible horse hooves, had reared to him, with a long saber which reached down to the ground from horse back that he knew a wraith was there. He reached for his sword – while the spirit of Garland hung with him – but there was no hand, both his arms were capped with stumps covered in blood. The long curved saber was glistened with fresh blood on old blood, and all he could feel was a cold and wet sensation in his chest. His white robe was now stitched with red fibrous strings welding the serration which was made. He went to clutch his bleeding chest, but there was no touch, no fingers. Nothing but their stares, of fire and blood, and blood and ash.

In the dark wells of rain and wind, Pinky found himself awake and slumped on the neck of his mare, and the horse was trying to keep the young man from falling. He looked to his fellow riders, to faces cold as ice, and dark as night.

Chapter Thirty-One:

The night fell, the stars above and the moonlight shone through the gaping hole in the storm. It was quiet, the only noise came from the crackle of the dry firewood embers, and the sleeping murmurings of their mares, and the heavy breathing of Kreshen and the wind walls that protected them from outside. Litus watched the warmth of the embers radiate. The blades of grass slightly twisted and bowed in the light waves of air which passed through. Dots of orange plumed high into the sky blending in with the stars.

Their clothes and belongings were strewn across the ground set to dry. The small branches damp or drenched from the army of rain were placed closer to the heat. And since both Kreshen and Litus sat just a few feet from the flames, they were being warmed and dried as well.

"When I was younger, I used to look into the sky at night, and imagine what's beyond there. I thought there was a world beyond ours which the gods were from, or that it's where they sit to watch us all. I used to believe that the moon was a cup of milk, or a ball of some hard cheese. But now I really see it. The stars seem so far away, and now that I get to see them. For some time when I was older, I used to believe there weren't any stars, I had never seen any, and knew I would never, and I'd say that deep down inside I didn't believe there were stars, or a world outside our realms where the gods watched us. They seemed to exist in their own space away from people, in their own god towers. But now I don't know anymore. Look at it all. This is just a pinpoint of what's outside, but there's so much we don't see. Let's just hope the Malkin people's prophecy is true. I'd like to see the sky again tomorrow. For much of my life I've heard that the cause of the forever clouded sky was from the invasion of the chaos god's soldiers. I hope that once you fulfill the prophecy we can see this again. We just need to check."

Litus' face showed his concern. Kreshen said, "this is why we're going to the Ranger's Guild. They work fast, and it's less than a ferry. They don't report any traveler to the crown or duchy either. Since the navy is after you, it's the best way to get to Hule," still Litus' face had a question, *If I'm not, then many fell for nothing.*

He pulled out the map he absconded from the magic shipwreck. He pointed to the city of Atreau, and looked to Kreshen. "You know already, but do you know that Atreau is embedded in the mountain? From my years of traveling I've known that that town has a great Malkin community. Up in the mountains. We'd know more about this prophecy from them than by young Tiamon. Who knows, when we get there, there might be more prophecies to do before we travel to Tisden. Maybe one of them will help reverse the sky, so everyone could see the stars like we see them now. Oh how great would that be."

The fire burned low for a while later, the stars still showed their bright light with the radiance of the passing moon. The grass blew in the small winds still, and the hurricane spun around them, the battle of dirt and sky was going to be upon them at the break of day. It was the only night which was free of rain, wind, and mud.

They packed their bags tight, wrapping their bundles in tarps of blankets, trying to keep their wrappings of sticks dry. They lit their candle lanterns, and took the reins in one hand, holding the lantern pole with their other. They stepped through the glass wall of fog and the suspended arrows of water reflecting the fragments of light bleeding from the sky above back at them, and the small flickered candles made the light scatter around.

The ground took most of this punishment from the trotting shoed horses, and the volley of perpetual thundering. It was the ultimate vendetta, both sides angry with the escapees. The army of dirt tried to sunder their forces of mud bared with arms. The cavalry encircled their position, with the pondering of the great triumph of the invaders of this war. The trinity of war: man versus the sky and ground.

Kreshen prayed to the gods, all three, and instead of praying the three points he prayed to each individual gods. Muttering under his breath as the fire-fight was still anew. The light of their candles twinkled in the new shed blood of mud and grass, and rain and sky. The commander of the skies was throwing electrical tridents down, passing near the violently scared mares. Kreshen looked up at the sky, and in the lightning light he thought he saw this figure. He didn't know what to think of this thing. Not knowing if it was a god. The only god who could command so much static building hatred and war: Keroth and Gruel. In the swelled pits that were eyes, shown a red gas illuminated with the same bolts before being thrown down. Litus looked up at this creature too, *I feel like I've seen it before, but what is it, just some clouds? Or someone?* But after a great attack of light – which left craters a foot deep were spurred on the flats – the figure disappeared.

It had transpired over an hour or more of travel. Time shifted about unevenly and slowly as they swam through the mud and rocks, but as they proceeded, the heavy rain and mud turned colder and churned. They treaded out of rain and into great fog. The ground below was stiff, it wasn't a sluggish mud, but their mares almost couldn't resist showing some desperate sign of amusement and tranquility. *Nothing that could come from this fog as thick as I've seen before, could match the fury and terror that was the hurricane. We must be so close to an actual peace, and actual safety. Feel's strange, is something going to succeed? I can't be; there's always something new. There always is.*

The tension in the air grew with the ever growing hurricane, and the fear of wraiths, the thought brought a blood pumping feel in their chests. Pinky especially was distraught. He lost a hand and a mentor, and no matter how hard he tried to hide it, it showed. But Jane felt something else completely. *How many will die because of me? Everyone around me will die, why? Because they think I'm the queen? How has everyone believed this? I didn't start this, but I'm living with these consequences. If they put me on the throne how many will die because of me, my presence?* She kept a palm on her sword hilt, she felt the crown dig into her palm.

For hours they rode, the growing rain pulled and pushed hard against their skin, and eyes. Their minds were being stretched like a sweater caught in a river of loose twigs. Everyone of them, including their mares. "Your grace, you have to ride faster, we need to get to clearer lands before the night has finished," Barrett muttered, "Pinky you failed once to guard the queen, you need now to follow orders. Let that stump be your lesson boy."

Pinky gripped the sword hilt, trying to keep the reins in his elbow. There was a dark dread smeared across his face, "I tried to save him, I could have saved him. It wouldn't have been difficult, two on one. We had better odds."

"It's a wraith! Have you no mind for these matters? To know what comes in the dark! In a blink of an eye the shadow would have killed her! He ordered you to protect her, not stand and wallow and stutter about. This isn't some camping trip, this is a matter of the entire fucking kingdom. Have you no sense!?"

Jane looked at them all, *I need to tell them, if I don't they'll, I don't know, but they need to stop following me. Besides, I can protect myself, alone.* They rode for a little while longer, Jane slowed only slightly, Jaune spoke, "my lady you must ride faster, it's not safe out in the open."

"No. No, I am not the queen. I am not the heir, and I'm not anyone. I don't want more death. So stop following me. I'm not the queen. I ordered Pinky-"

"Pinky didn't lose a hand, and Garland didn't lose his life protecting a common peasant?" Barrett said, "so you're not the queen, our queen. Do you mean to give pity for death by making it meaningless?"

"No, no!"

"Then what do you mean, my . . . what would you call yourself now! Because no matter what you think, you are the queen, Garland is dead, and our orders from the duke are to keep you safe. If it weren't for the crown and throne you own, you'd have died to that dark steel blade instead. Now stop sulking. Ride peasant!"

"Peasant?"

"If you say you aren't the queen then you aren't, and we won't treat you like one. We'll treat you like how the noble treat the lower men.

"Now keep riding, if that wraith attacks again and we lose another man or two, I'd rather be closer to the guild than to stand my own ground."

Jane clutched her fist directed towards Barrett and Jaune, but was simultaneously in conflict over them being right, and picking ideas not meant. She kept it buried inside, and let the rain strike between the jail bars around her heart. And that wind still roared. And no matter what the hand won't return to its socket, and the body won't walk again.

The thundering grew to an exponential size. It made the storm they traveled through hours before seem like a light hike. Further ahead they could see the blinding white lights strike down a mile ahead or so. The rain pounded hammers into the skin and reins. The mud burrowed deep keeping the moisture to their disadvantage. The five of them were forced to slow, but it didn't stop their progression forward. Whether they liked it or not, they'd have to keep moving forward.

With each step they came closer to the mine field of divots left to smolder in the rain from the explosions of pure bright light. A strike from the heavens to punish the land, and to punish them for surviving the wraiths attack. Out of the black entangled clouds of chaos rained down a serpent of more light. Suddenly their horses tried to jump, and Jane almost fell off. The cold water darts pierced their clothes, and the chill of agony was all they kept as tokens. Another lightning bolt rained down only a dozen feet away from Jane making all the sound around turn to a single toned hiss. She covered her ear and temple a white light blurring her vision. She was again nearly thrown off her horse. She clutched tightly to the pommel of her saddle, and wrapped reins. Jane was thrown up with a kick and nearly fell until she was caught by Jaune. "Stay on your saddle, from now on every hand needed, one less, we'll have one less man."

Through the thick of thunder and break of sweat and blood they pushed and pushed ever further through the storm of storms. And even when they were spreading their souls thin over all the breadth of ground, they still pushed further. The night turned to sunrise and the sunrise rose higher, and from the pitch black the sky was now a dark dripping light of rain.

At the end of the storm was a wall of fog and mist, and quiet ambiance. But even with this seemingly quiet embrace of sanctuary they didn't stop or slow down. They only rode faster. The less loose lightning diffused the fog into a single mute light for those moments, and broke up the quiet motions of race.

For a while it was just this same loop of riding, and the only difference was the lightning being further and further away. Until at one moment all they could sense from the lightning was a small crackle of sound, and a flicker of light. They rode through the day and only stopped to have food, and to give their mares legs some rest. After, they departed once more.

It was soon when the night sky rolled over that the drifted from the thin fog into a clear chill of sky commenced, but soon while they traveled they discovered a small flickering set of lights some acres ahead. Pinky looked closer, "are those the . . . the wraiths?"

"Wraiths? There's more than one?" Barrett asked cautiously.

"We don't know if they're wraiths yet, but if there are two or more, we have to either stop, or run in a different direction. We'd have to add another day or two away from the guild."

"If we can see them, could they see us?" Pinky said.

"What if there's more behind us? To set up a trap," Sam added.

Barrett said, "we still don't know if these riders ahead are wraiths. If not, we may be able to give help in return for more hands. Seeing as we're two short."

"But is it worth the risk?" Jaune vexed.

If we're out here for any longer we could be attacked again, but if they're wraiths would we have been able to see them? "You don't see a wraith until they attack, right?" Jane asked, "I've never heard of a story about wraiths needing lanterns or candles. My real mother told me that wraiths can see in the dark. They don't need to carry candles or lanterns. These riders ahead are not wraiths."

"And you're so sure?" Barrett asked.

"It could be a trap?" Sam said worryingly.

"It could be, but I've never heard much of wraiths setting up traps. But I've also never heard of survivors of wraith ambushes.

There's plenty of time for them to get a lantern, such as the dead man's cabin from a few days ago," said Jaune.

"What do you suppose we do, Jaune?" Asked Barrett.

"We should go to them," Jane said.

"But is it worth the risk?"

"How close are we to the guild?" Jane asked.

Jaune thought for a second, "about three to four days away, you think that the guild's men would ride this close."

"Maybe the duke sent a pigeon?" Barrett said, "if we could survive the storm maybe a legion of pigeons could too. The duke would do something this large for the safety of the crown."

"We'll ride to them, but be ready for blood."

They snuffed all their lights except for one, and for some time they rode closer, and closer to those ahead. They stalked them, keeping even their mares dead silent, and they crept slowly, closer and slow. Pinky whispered to himself, "if you are a wraith, I'll take your hand and gut you. Just you see."

He was shushed by Barrett, and Jane thought, *I hope these idiotic riders aren't wraiths.* She gripped the handle pulling about an inch of the blade. Small dribbles of rain began to fall, the clouds were thick with tears. They came closer and closer over a near half hour of stalking. Thunder shimmered closer, a loud rumble stalked Jane and the guards. Her hood was saturated with the cold rain. She pulled the steel further from the scabbard. *Don't be wraiths.* A bolt of lightning struck many miles behind them, but the boom it sounded was close, and the light it emitted was wide reaching. The rider who blended in the dark ground turned around, all that Jane could see were his bright purple eyes. Quickly after the riders snuffed their lanterns and trotted faster. Jaune snuffed the lantern, yelling, "trap it's a trap!"

Purple eyes, it can't be! He's alive!? She tapped her heels against the side of her horse, gripping the reins with both hands. The quick shift threw her hood off, rain hit her face, and dripped down her long hair. She came closer, their war horses were clearly faster then the riders ahead. The rest were trying to catch up to Jane, yelling at her to slow down, to stay together, and muttering loudly to themselves. But she didn't hear, or really bother. What she saw was the friend she thought she lost, within reach. No matter how fast their horses were, they couldn't out run a warhorse. "Litus!" She yelled, but it wasn't loud enough.

She came closer, and closer, *why can't you slow down. Litus you fool!* "Litus!" She kept yelling.

From behind Jaune rode up, "you fucking idiot, I won't let the queen kill herself on my watch. Stop! Wraith!"

"He's no wraith!" She yelled in protest, and heeled her mare's side and roared faster.

She was within thirty or so feet of them, and she could see in the glint of moonlight a silver saber, and she yelled once more, "Litus!" And he looked back; his eyes were wide in shock.

Litus stopped his mare, Kreshen yelled from ahead, "you can't face them by yourself there's too many!"

Jane reared her mare to stop, the weight of the rain pulled her along. Jaune came barreling by sword swinging towards Litus. He parried the blade not letting a scratch land on his dark mare. Jaune yelled to Jane, "get away, it's the wraith!"

Their blades swung and parried, in great forces and metallic squeals. Litus was clearly the faster dueler, he swung again and again, barely Jaune could keep up his sword in a block, he growled, "is this the best you can do wraith!"

Kreshen rode forward, and a ball of light was on the end of his finger. "Stop this by the grasp of the gods. Stop this fighting!"

Litus with one last swing, twisted his blade forward, throwing up Jaune's blade. Putting his sword back, Litus came down, and Jane did the same. They embraced together. The rest of the guards came swords out, with the sharp tip pointed towards Litus and Jane. Kreshen raised his hand high, the blinding light on his finger tip grasped the attention of the guards. Pinky was the first to look, "Father Kreshen? What are you doing with a wraith? Get away from that wraith!"

"A wraith? No. A wraith wouldn't grasp someone like that. A wraith would have killed us all by . . . by now. Litus is no wraith. Why are you all here, we've done nothing to warrant being followed, though I don't know how you did follow us. Has the navy sent you all? We are just heading to the rangers guild and that's it."

Jaune dropped down from his horse to pick up his sword, "well, we seem to seek the same exact thing."

"And what do you think we are seeking? We've nothing to say, and nothing to tell."

"We both seek refuge from a storm, and horses to carry us there," he said like an order, "and hot food to cook and eat. And you have dry wood."

Chapter Thirty-Two:

The storm turned south, and it's dark tendrils came first. His leather boots were dry in the closed halls of stone, but they were quickly subjected to the rained on mud and the slush of wet hay which was spread on the ground to absorb some of that moisture. Eiger was met by Darien who kept his hands on the pommel of his sword, and Darien said only one thing, "the ships are ready."

They trotted down on horseback, and the rain persisted still, now only coming down harder. He boarded the first ship in the harbor which would leave. His steps were loud and drew eyes from his sailors as he passed to the quartermasters room, which had a slight chill from not being lit by any candles. By a wave of his hand, two men went around the room to light all the candles, and the room now flickered here and there with the warm orange light of the candles, and the cold patterings of rain and the sight of blue and gray clouds outside the large window at the back of the vessel. Eiger sat at the large table with a sizable map of the world sprawled over with large ornate weights keeping the map from rolling up. Darien sat to his side.

When the ships first departed with a large boom and retraction of anchors, and eventually stopped their chaotic rocking, the quartermaster came through the door. "Have we lost any men?" Eiger said sarcastically.

"We haven't, but we have begun to sail again without any problems, besides the rain."

"I'll pray we don't find this rain up north."

"It might rain, but that hurricane seems to have gone west."

"Then we only have to deal with one storm then."

"And what storm is that?"

"The capital storm is a storm of great importance to either avoid, or be on the right side of morality and history for, and we currently have an advantage. If truth be told, what is known is true."

Darien spoke up, "there's been no further word of Lucerne, my lord."

"When we arrive, we're to get the black tower in our control. And we'll send watchmen to him. The tower is the only sort of civilization in that city, and we'll not have them land in Tylock's hands. If I get their power, I'll be able to get the small lords men, and work up to get the higher lords men too."

The tower was the last sense of order left, and was also the last branch of the army mostly together. *I just need time to build power, and if Lucerne were smart he'd be there to keep me in check.* "I want to know where Lucerne is, I want to know what Lucerne is doing, and I want to know what men he already took."

Darien said, "and if he isn't in Porcelania?'

"That gives us both an advantage and disadvantage. If he starts a conflict, it will come fast. And hopefully his command is as great as his negotiations. If not, I want men, and I want the tower, and I won't back down."

On the rough sea-seen table, were old candles which lifted their warm gaze upon the commodore's face, but barely missed the other man on the other side. Only his worn brown hands were seen, with scars from blades and burns from sliding rope, and calluses making his palms pale. Lucerne rocked his chair, and crossed his arms. Trying to show some control through his lounging, and Lucerne was stout to believe that this would enforce not only his grip on others, but tried to make his opponent think that he had the might and will of the entire Royal navy behind him. "It's only a matter of time and price. So I think we should discuss the price over some classic pirate rum. The cold old stuff is stored below deck."

"Rum? So you've seen for yer self what we keep low?" And before Lucerne could bring the feet of his chair to the floor, he said, "we ain't got rum, we've got whiskey."

"Whiskey is good too, send a man to get us a bottle or two."

The man raised a hand, and with a gruff a sailor went out to grab two bottles of whiskey from the cold cellar. "So it's about price, that's what you say?"

"It is about price, and it's only a matter of time."

"Before what? You gain conscription into your navy? Not the Royal Navy of the Rientonem throne?"

"The throne has been fragmented since the passing of the late great queen. The navy remains strong, and to keep the peace we need men, good men, strong men, and experienced men. You would claim a large command, and your men would have command of their own ships, or troops."

"So yer aren't buying a fleet, yer buying men to move at yer whims. Am I correct?"

"That is one possibility, but at this time you'd be part of a fleet, under my control. You'd be paid well, and fairly."

"But why? Again why do you seek us, rather than yer own people?"

"Because the kingdom is fractured, while the navy holds strong. I have less risk getting hands on deck this way."

He coughed a laugh. "No, that's not it. You could get so many men from the poor south, or hundreds of ready hands from Hule. No I don't think you want us because you need more hands on deck. I think you need hands for a task that requires heavier actions."

"In a sense, yes. I need to bring justice, and need stronger men than I'm provided for."

"Justice? Whose justice? Not the god's, yer gonna carry out yer justice. And you want us to do it?"

"Again, I guess you could call it that."

"You're not taking us for merchants are ye? You want something sharper."

"I do. Can you imagine what my needs are of you?"

There was a shifting throughout the dark cabin. Out of the darkness and into the small light were two glasses and two square shaped bottles of whiskey. The commodore remained in shadow. Lucerne waited for someone – mostly the man to reveal his figure – to pour him the whiskey, but was surprised to receive naught. So reluctantly Lucerne dropped his chair to the ground, and popped the cork and poured a cup. "And you?" He waved the bottle over the second cup, poured reluctantly, sliding the glass the shadow.

"You've said little of how much we're being paid with. I find time to work nice."

Lucerne gave the man a grin, pulling out a purse laying it down gently with his gloved hand, and slid it towards the shadowed commodore. His calloused hands grabbed the purse, audible counting each coin until he stopped. And with a breath he groaned, "this is a lot for a man, Aye for me I would be at your side, unless this is supposed to be split," he gave some time for Lucerne to rebut, but snatched that time back, "no this is the amount for every man I take?"

"No, no no, if you want our hands, our steel, yer gonna need every man paid the same. We're all part of this same vessel. We all work as a team."

"But you're the commodore," Lucerne mocked.

"And I make the commands, and they follow."

"Fine, every ship, every man, every stray cat will be paid the same. Now is this final?"

"You want near a dozen ships, to add to your what two dozen, three dozen. Yer taking gold from the dead queen's hands?"

"For the fate of the kingdom, I do my part."

The ship rocked and the rain dripped on small compartment windows around the cabin letting in their blue night. There was a clink of glass as it tapped the table. The glass slid down the table, stopping short of the bottle. Lucerne finished his glass, and said, "another round?"

"Not now. I want some more information about this."

"About the pay? The plan? The rain? What do you want to know?"

He chortled, "so you are paying us to be your strong men?"

"Yes."

"Because you don't have the hands you want."

"Yes."

"A commodore to another commodore."

"It seems so."

"Not an admiral or politician or lord something. Not anyone higher than yourself?"

Lucerne smirked, "you already figured it out, do I need to answer?"

The man in the shadows didn't respond. He pulled some small kindling up to the flame and that warm light fell on his face as he lit his tobacco pipe. He put out the kindle and the only light was the smoky brushes of leaf burned onto his thick black beard and his dark reddish skin was visible only slightly. And his viper eyes pierced into

Lucerne's. He tossed the purse back, "what you want, you can't get with someone else's money."

"Why wouldn't a pirate want easy money!"

"Easy money, we love easy money, but we aren't pirates, we're privateers, commodore," he puffed the pipe, and cackled.

Crackles of cinder and ash flew high from the heat plume of the campfire. The rain slowed to a halt, but the clouds still were dark and full of hate. The look of beat up men surrounded the light, and showing to each other their scratches, while their backs faced the dark hills. "Kreshen, you are traveling to the guild, why?"

He looked around expecting to see Darien somewhere, but he wasn't. "We're attempting to reach other churches, and to tell the pastors what crimes are being committed against us."

"I've seen it, before we began traveling towards the guild, we stopped by your church."

"I assume Darien was with you?"

"He was, how do you know?"

"I've known that man long enough. Did Tiamon show you some hospitality?"

"He's a kind fellow. Your church is in good hands."

Kreshen nodded, scratching his face. Jane remarked watching Jaune and Kreshen speak. "We saw what happened to your church, it was just like what happened to the castle."

"What tyrant took control of the navy, and why make us ordinary people suffer, " he shifted to look at the woman in their party, and said, "I believe you are this Jane I've heard about."

"Father Kreshen, this is Queen Garnette."

"Yes, father," Jane said over him.

After fleeting moments of complete dumbstruck awe, he regained some composure, and said, "Litus spoke . . . wrote about you, and I know he always thought about you, my grace," Litus nodded, "we thought you had died, and we especially didn't know you were the monarch."

"I thought the same, but to Litus. I thought that everyone . . . I thought that he just," she stopped, thinking.

"There's dark times, and there's light times. You have to keep pushing forward till you find those times."

Nothing good has ever happened to me. Litus has been my only light, and if he stays with me, he'll die for good. There is no good times, they would have come by then. "I live only in darkness. Since I was born, and now it only grows worse. I don't think I'll ever see this 'light' you speak of."

"Then I'll pray for it."

"Pray to who? The dead god?"

"The gods don't die, the foundation of the dirt is of the three virtues: death, chaos, and balance."

"I live with death, and chaos. There's been no balance, no hope, only death. I would pray, but what good would that do?"

"Have you ever tried it, my grace?"

Have I ever tried not living in misery! "Why would you ever say that!?"

"I'm sorry for upsetting you, your grace."

"And stop calling me your grace."

They stared at the two of them, Litus included, and later it faded just the same as the fire. The night rolled through and sleep came as a blanket. Jane stayed up thinking, before she too fell asleep.

They rode out in the early morning, trying to remember and forget about the dread of wraiths, and their new numbers didn't give them any confidence. They hadn't spoken of Garland to Kreshen, and neither did he see Pinky's missing hand, not yet at least. So when they began their ride he peered at his fellow riders, and saw Pinky's hand. Over the hills and tall grass, he asked Pinky about what happened. Reluctantly Pinky spoke with him, and the day drifted on, and quivered when Pinky had to recollect that event so close but infinitely far away. During his telling, Pinky looked over his shoulder expecting to see Garland there, but he wasn't. Kreshen looked down at his hand, the reins, looking at everything, but nothing in particular. Kreshen knew the feeling, he knew it all too well.

"So you all kept riding through the night, until you caught up to us."

Barrett chimed in, "forgot you were out here father Kreshen. This storm has caused harm, and death, but we account for worse, and expect worse."

"And what if you end up better than before, or find some paradise?"

"It won't."

"So do you pray for balance, or pray for luck?"

"I don't have time to pray. Wraiths roam the field waiting for some sorry fool to waste their time waiting for a response. I fight, or I die, there's no time for religion."

They kept riding through the plains, the clouds splotched wet here and there, and the forest outline was gradually getting larger, but at glances here and there it didn't appear so. It felt just out of reach.

Kreshen drifted towards Litus' mare, "we're out of the storm, and going into fire," Litus looked at him, "not with the guild, past it, and past the forest. You can't place certainty in which you don't know grows. The lightning road is treacherous to say so. For decades the road has gone unprotected. The only safety you find comes from the armed merchants and the rangers on the other side. From the last I've been across the stretch, the thieves had only started to make their domain. By now there must be gangs of thieves, with moves that they know work."

Litus drew out his sword, with a flourish, trying to downplay such fear. "Even if we get the first attack, they would have numbers, given if they were in gangs," Litus withdrew the sword and drew out the scythe, "now that might do it."

Jane came snickering, "you'd kill them here and there, but with a scythe?"

Kreshen said, "it's an enchanted scythe. It conjures and controls the winds. It pulls and pushes and also cuts like a scythe."

"Who would enchant a scythe? Wouldn't anything else be better?"

"There are other weapons and things that would be more useful in war, swords, spears, arrows."

"A nice halberd," Barrett butted in.

"Yes a halberd, or just a wand. But a scythe can do very well what weapons can't. You could clear a field of hay or corn in minutes rather than hours. To the best of my knowledge you can't mend magic. It does its due until it runs through."

"Well," Jane said, "where did you get it, Litus?"

"From a small battle over an empty bridge," Kreshen said while Litus nodded.

For some time they continued to ride. The day became afternoon, and the winds brushed the slopes. Earth tilled with each track of horse shoes. "We haven't stopped in a while, we should let the mares rest, and our legs stretch for a minute."

"We can't," Jaune said calmly.

"Why? We've been riding for a long while, we all need a break, especially you five. If you'd like, I can brew some tea."

"I'm sorry father, but we won't stop, not while the wraiths roam these fields."

"My son, it's folly. If you wish for danger, it will come. And if being 'prepared' for a fight means that you're willing to lose sleep, and kill your horse. You won't survive when a wraith does return."

Jaune's hand rested on the saddle pommel and he said after a few moments, "we'll break for now, but don't plan to stay long, and no tea."

They stopped near night break. Kreshen liked to stretch his legs after a long ride on horseback. There was a chorus of cracks heard from the stiffness of necks, and backs of almost all the riders besides Litus. They rode on further in a slightly better mood, which wasn't wholly visible besides Kreshen. The stormless night drew on and for hours they rode on.

There was pain. Fire and pain. In the walls of stone, and the heart of the flames were the cold real taste of salted earth. The campfire bristled with the smell of fatty cooked meats, and a dance of many hues. It shifted from side to side slowly wobbling, twisting its way into an angelic figure. A figure of purity and beauty. A hissing ooze emanates from the ends of the logs. The scent of the rotten ooze mixed and mingled in the emulsion of fat in the air. The water in one frame of time was separated and another it was forcibly mixed until it separated again.

He knew it was himself, he knew without any mirror that it was himself, though he couldn't recall his name. What was his name? *Who am I?* There was the faint sight of other figures – unlike the sole figure in the fire – that were ethereal in nature. They looked familiar. Like skeletons, clothed, but their flesh was somewhat translucent. There were six of these spirits sitting solum thoughts without the light of the flame illuminating their figures. They were motionless, stagnant. Time perceived them differently then he. He was there all of time, there from its beginning, and will be there through fruition. And what he saw was the future. In the glow of the fire, it turned into a ball, with green flame wisping around like the brushing of grass blades. The smoke that billowed had smothered the ball loosely. He tried wafting the smoke away, and it bubbled around, and surrounded him, coddled him. The flame grew deeper, and larger. Each tendril of flame was purely visible, every action happened at the same time. Motionless it stood stretching and absolving all what has been and what will be. He saw into this flame deeper, becoming one with it. He was seeing all of the faces of the world spring around in the flame. From the mountain tribes of Haute, and the ships rocking on the Trecaunte straight. And then he traveled deep, into a great ravine, and there was a castle made of black jeweled crystal with halls of infinite shadow in a pool of something unknown, and unreachable. There was something hanging in the hall, it felt familiar but again unknown. It was something, *I am something different.*

He was thrown out of the flame back again viewing the campfire, the flame shifted from green to a purplish blue hue. The smoke of gross ooze came again protecting the image from onlookers, and still there were seven ghosts, with forms of a translucent aura and skeletons of pristine white bone. He called out to the onlookers, "I want to see further!" But there was no response.

He got back closer to the flame wafting away the smoke, and again the flame grew to over take all of sight. By now it was night, *was the sky blanketed? Both I guess.* The moon hung high in the sky, letting down its blue light on the sands and dunes. He leaped about the endless plains. The mountains were far away, but not as tall as Haute. Houses of unknown shapes were carved into the rockside. Steps went all the way up to the highest structure, which seemed to be a cathedral. He leaped forth, in the figure of pure energy and having light radiate towards fear. A series of malkin dressed in formal religious robes were filled with this light, and they asked him, "what are you?"

"I am what you seek," and as he waited for a response all he got was disappointed faces, which he could hear.

And again he was thrusted out of the fire, and again too it changed hue. This was a flame of shadow, without any smoke, without any ooze. And the onlookers, all one of them looked to him, directly across from him. "Look into the flame, but only for a moment," the figure said, "this is where you seek; this is what you seek; this is who you are."

He peered into the black flame, and in a cave he saw, a deep cave with echo but no sound. He felt the need to speak, just to try, but there was no sound. That soundless void grew into a hissing in his ear. He kept walking through, past a gateway there was a stream of water, purely reflecting the void it sat on.

And then he was ejected. The campfire grew small and the flame was a fuzzy white. The figure outstretched his bony hand, a shortened deer antler. "Of falsehoods you'll meet, you will give and see what was past that gate, with this key," he held out between his bone fingers a black iron key, with an eye on its bow.

Chapter Thirty-Three:

The morning rang with the early frost of winter. Litus awoke with a choke in his gut, wanting

to seek what he saw, to know what it really was. *A flame of green, blue, and black.* In his hand he gripped the black iron key. In the early light he saw the ridges and detail of the key. He put the eye in the key up to the light and he looked through. *Nothing. This key opens that gate, but where is it?*

They had packed their things, sprinkled dirt over the smoldering charred remains. Litus helped Jane up her horse, and he mounted his next to her. Pinky walked up with a certain eagerness in his step, and he said, "we can't ride off yet, we've got things to pack."

"Doesn't look it, Looks like we're all packed up already," Jane said.

"Well besides that, shouldn't he be with Kreshen? To help him mount?"

Litus looked towards Kreshen, who just mounted and began riding up next to Litus. In Fact almost everyone else had begun to mount as well. Pinky's face had started to blush with embarrassment, "well shouldn't Garnette's guard ride with her, not some creepy thing with a sword. And a dark horse."

Litus looked at Pinky, and he said, "are you gonna say anything about it?"

Litus didn't speak, but Jane said, "he can't-"

"He can't refute my claim. I'm your guard, and I should ride next to you for your safety."

Barrett and Jaune rode up, and Jaune said, "you speak as though you're the only guard."

"But he isn't. I don't like that he claims our job, without our vows, and he looks like a wraith."

"He isn't some wraith," Jane protested.

"How do you know? How do you know he isn't trying to grow chummy with us before he kills us in our sleep, cause he's a wraith."

"He's not a wraith," Kreshen said, "son, I know it's been hard since Garland's death, but you can't take that out on Litus. He's not who you seek."

Pinky grabbed his stump. "How do you know?"

Jane said, "he could have killed us last night, but he didn't. He's not a wraith, don't be stupid."

"I'm not stupid. I know who I can't trust, and who I can. I don't want to put your life at risk again. I need to ride next to you. I must be there to protect you."

"Stop being a boy," Barrett said, "with a missing hand, you could never be her personal guard even when she takes the throne."

"Is that so? I will prove it then. I want to duel," he turned to Litus, and said, "get down from your high horse and duel me. Whoever wins will ride next to the queen and be her personal guard."

"Don't try it, I want Litus by my side," Jane said.

"We are your sworn guards," he said, shifting his gaze back to Litus, " Do you accept my duel?"

Litus dismounted and stood across from Pinky. He nodded, "can't even say yes, fine if I get you to speak. I'll make you say surrender."

Pinky stood with his only hand on the handle of his sword, and in as clean a way as possible, he drew his sword. He looked to Litus who didn't appear to have a sword, or a scabbard. "Where's your sword?"

Litus reached into the void, and drew out his sword: the two handed falchion. *Not a fight to the death. So I won't kill him.* Litus stood still, sword to his side. Pinky with his sword raised high, ran to him. Pinky swung from high to low, striking sideways. Litus blocked and with half hold on the blade, pushed back Pinky. He stumbled back and retreated a foot or two back, and tried to keep his sword raised.

Pinky put his sword into a high guard, while Litus began to encircle Pinky; keeping him shifting his position. "Stop playing, and fight me!" Pinky roared before storming forward.

Their blades met here and there in little prodding tests. Litus blocked and parried each swing Pinky made, but didn't attempt a strike. Pinky showed his plans on his face, and went from a side guard and backed to stab. Litus swung his blade around and pushed Pinky's to the side. The tip of Litus's sword grazed Pinky's face, taking a few hairs with it.

Pinky fell back, touching the side of his face to check for blood or cuts or damage. There were none but those few severed hairs. "Stop playing with me!" He said while swinging his sword around, back and forth. Litus was able to dodge the hate fueled rage of steel. One parry ringed and flashed sparks of steel. Not like Jane's sword, but something harder. Their steel flashed with the concavity of check and recheck.

Litus stepped back, from the irrational swings. Pinky too stepped back, and readied another strike, "one has to land."

In a flash, Pinky thrusted the sword towards Litus, but the steel had reverberated in his hands, and the blade was caught by Litus' hands, and pulled away disarming Pinky. Litus pushed him down, and the tip of his blade grazed Pinky's throat. "Fine, then, we'll duel again. And next time, you'll be the one on the ground." And he muttered under his breath, "wraith."

Pinky picked himself up, and went to mount, Sam came up sword in hand, "I want to duel as well," Litus nodded, and Jaune said, "we have places to be! Stop this, we need to leave!"

"In a moment. We should know who is best to defend the queen. And we started with Pinky."

Litus nodded again, and put his sword into a guard. "Just a nice parry," Sam went silent from then on.

Their blades touched and vibrated with each tap to test their reach. They circled each other. At the drop of a feather, they pounced. Sam drew the first strike forward, Litus struck as well, their blades interlocked, but only for a moment. Litus twisted his blade around Sam's and went in for a closing, but Sam raised his sword while retreating a few steps to not be hit.

They began circling once more. Sam reared his blade and extended the blade towards Litus, and he shifted only slightly into a block, but Sam had feigned and the blade turned its way high. Litus had to retreat back to not get snagged or cut.

Barrett and Jaune stood by the side muttering to each other to whether or not stop this folly. Jaune yelled to them, "finish this soon, we need to leave."

Litus flew forward slashing up and to the side. The turf cut from the slash, leaping up, and was parried with one good and small shift of the blade. Sam pushed the blade forward. Pushing Litus back once more.

They kept shifting their stance to prepare for each other's attack, but Litus struck first. With a great swing high leading low, he clawed into Sam's tiresome and trying block. Sam retreated back to push further, and in two strikes, Litus was forced back, and cloak nicked. He kept a guard still but waving.

Litus leaped for an attack, twisting his blade around Sam's and pushing him back further. Sam tried to parry, but was forced only to block. Litus swung again, breaking through the block. In three consecutive blows, Litus stripped the blade from Sam's hands and the fight was over. Sam nodded and retrieved the dropped sword. Litus returned his sword to the void.

"Are you all done? We've lost time from that, you stupid bastards."

"I'm well done, Barrett."

They all mounted their mares, and Litus remained by Jane's side, though for the preceding half hour there was tension still present in the air and each gallop. But eventually it subsided into nothing. And that feeling of nothing stayed.

They rode the high thunder plains – though the thunder was a day or two away. The grass rolled, and the sun sank. They lit a bonfire still having some wood in the roll of sticks left for the next proceeding days. Silent Litus sat only near Jane and Kreshen, because the guards were anxious around him. But he just sat sharpening his sword against a flat rock drenched in rain water. Pinky came to Litus, and in a whisper he spoke, "we'll duel again some other day, and then you'll lose, or you'll die," Litus drew an eye to him. *Then it'll be your death too,* but did not say. The silence drew on, no bug or bird flew above, but the cold light of the moon emanated and spread evenly dark on all the land in sight. Except for the fire they lit.

Chapter Thirty-Four:

"When should we arrive?"

"Tomorrow my lord."

"Good, good. The storm hadn't slowed us. Any word on deck."

"Of what?"

"Concerns, discomforts," Eiger said, "conspiracy."

"None sir."

"That's good. Same with the other ships?"

"I don't know, but I wouldn't doubt it to be fine. Just fine."

The sky was still gray, and the sails still grabbed the threads of wind which would feel almost still to those who weren't sails. Some birds flew far above, almost drifting into the low clouds. They flew weightless and free to be where they'd want to be. For those fluttering moments, it was just that. Until a large bird, an eagle took the small bird in it's sharp grasp. There was a twitter of squeals from the pigeon before it succumbed to the talons.

Jane awoke with fear in her cheeks. They were flushed and sweat accumulated on her back, making her clothes stick. "Another day of travel? I'm getting sick of this. There's calluses on my thighs, and the smell too," she looked to Jaune, "do we have anything to eat?"

"Your highness there's rolls of jerky, and leather of your boots, and the meat of your mare. Which would you like."

"Just give me some jerky then."

Jaune tossed her a cloth wrapped slab of salted pork, and dried hard beef jerky. While Jane tried to chew the meat, father Kreshen came over and sat next to her. "Care for some tea?"

"Sure," she said, and as she looked at Kreshen, she asked, "would you like some of this salted leather?"

"A little wouldn't hurt."

She handed him a strip of the salted pork jerky, and he gave her a small clay cup of loose leaf tea. "It's bitter!" She said, "it's really bitter."

"I'm sorry your grace, I don't have any sugar with me. Neither cream. And If I did have any cream, it would have been churned into butter by now."

"What did I say about calling me 'your grace'? Call me lady at least. I'm not the queen, and I'm getting tired of being called the queen!"

"Well why are all these men – Eiger's men – calling you their queen? For as long as I've known of Eiger, I didn't see him as a con-man, nor easily tricked."

"No, Darien, his truth-sayer wizard man, refused to believe me when I said I wasn't the queen. I was grateful to escape the Navy and Tylock, but I'm not the queen, and I don't want to be."

"Tylock, I don't think I know this man, is he an officer of the navy you knew."

"No, well yes. When Litus and I were trying to escape Porcelania, he caught us, and on the day of the ball, he presented me in front of the queen and her court as her heir. I don't know why, but they believed him. Just because I appear to look like her, and Eiger and Darien assumed that I'm their queen because of some lying magic."

"Well I've also known Darien for a long time too, he was a priest before he became an armed guard for Eiger. He doesn't tell you if your words are true or false, he tells you if your heart and mind are true or false. So even when you are saying you're not the queen, deep down in your heart or mind, and in your blood, you are the heir, and you are the queen."

"How do I know that Darien didn't tell him a lie, or is working for Tylock, or something."

"I guess you don't, no one for certain could know that, but I don't believe he did, so try to keep moving forward. Never plant yourself in doubt, find your truth, and I guess stay within rational reasoning, what seems to be incredible may really be ordinary."

To find my truth?

Eiger sat waiting for food, as the night sky began to fall. On his table was a bottle of spiced wine all the way from Frostwind. He poured a glass himself, and poured another to the commodore. "The night is cold, the food is late, but I'll board Porcelania tomorrow. Have we spotted anything awry? Such as naval ships, pirate ships, anything to look out for?"

"Nay all we've seen were clouds, pigeons, and eagles. What are you concerned about?"

Doors were opened by guards letting in servants with plenty of cooked chickens, and vegetables, and a whole loaf of bread. Eiger turned his attention shortly after back to the commodore, and said, "unrelated variables."

Through the miles of hills to flats, and tall grass, and marsh lands, the sun fell, the moon rose, the chill of blue light was diminished with the warmth of the campfire. By tomorrow or the day after they would hopefully reach the castle: the rangers guild, Esty. They sat and ate – except for Litus – what rations they had, and soon they went to sleep, but Litus was searching for something, for answers. For answers of his dreams, the figures, the flames, the meanings of it all, and who he really was. Was he this prophetical figure of the Malkin. Why were the Malkin mostly the only people who knew about this prophecy? *Am I really meant to kill Keroth?* It was stray, and came from seemingly nowhere, but it found its way into his mind. *Was Tolk right? About this prophecy?*

Kreshen went around to each of the men, and women in this party to console with, to the best he could, and he spent an especially long time with Pinky. But everyone from Jane's company checked their back every half an hour or less. Soon he came back to Litus, and tried to console with the mute shadow. "What's on your mind my son?"

Litus took a few seconds to find something to write in the dirt with, *Dreams, and prophecy.*

"Is that it?" He said calmly, Litus sat for a second and nodded, "nightmares? No. I don't think you'd be very concerned about nightmares, or dreams, if you didn't think they had any real significance. You can't put men in jail, and death can't determine where you stand with dreams. But you are also a prophetic figure, or hero, so there may be something different. Does that deal with both of your problems?"

No, he thought and shook his head. He wrote in the dirt quickly, *Am I it?* "Well, you can think about it, and worry, but you can't know till you do. I knew enough of the Malkin prophecy to realize it, but to confirm it altogether is different. That's the reason we're heading to Hule, there's a malkin church in the mountains where I know for certain we can prove this prophecy. And if you are the knight of justice or what they call this prophetical hero. Then hopefully we can find a way to make it happen."

Litus looked at him confused, "I don't believe once we realize you are this chosen one we'd, or you would just travel to Keroth and slay him. Or what the prophecy says truly. I guess we'll find out on the way, or we'll find once we're in the temple. Does that help?" Litus didn't know yet, but nodded respectively.

For hours he drifted in the dark void, yelling out, *Show me the fire, I need to know more, I need to know more. Show me!*

"You've come alone it seems. In these quarters assassination is possible, but not to escape. So now I wonder what you'll do. Burn every field in search, with those embers catching fields of barley or maize. The flame mimicking the great dragons of long ago. As they dance and burn all the farmers trying to save their crop. Or maybe you'll attempt to light this ship with the magic in your wand or fingers. But no I don't think you will. You find use in me, you need to know my position with the 'crown'. Not my rank, but the fire burns bright with me. And you want to know my temperature. Instead of knowing my temperance. But I'll give you a gift before leaving, that I'm not some immovable wall, nor am I some dainty feather. I am the fire, which finds its way in the small crack to turn to ash and spread more, until I've done what I will. And that is that."

Chapter Thirty-Five:

The sails were high, and the air was clear, the sun shined down and revealed all they would need to see. Behind the carefully planted trees, and small houses in the distance the duke could see the castle: Renoi, and other towers, such as the black tower, and other palaces in the city. *That tower, now that I see it again, only two weeks later, and I feel this dread pierce my chest.* For some time as the city came ever closer, Eiger thought more, *but where's Lucerne? What is that man doing? Shouldn't the Navy have records of where he's been and where he goes? Unless he ran away, without discharge. Where did he go, and what is he planning?*

Eiger returned to his cabin. After half an hour, he could hear the commodore, yelling at the crew about something, and he wondered what it was, which was dampened and muddled by the thick wooden walls that surrounded him. A minute later, by horn and waving of flags until he could hear a sailor yelling back to the ships behind and signal back, "slow down! Low tide! Slow down Low tide!" And he kept repeating the message until it was repeated back with all the ships behind. *How long will this set us back,* he thought, and left his cabin looking for the commodore for an answer.

"We're in low tide, if we don't take this slow, or wait, we could tip a ship or kill a man."

"Don't be irrational, take us there as quickly as possible."

"We're trying my grace, we just can't risk the damage we'd do to the hulls."

"Then have this resolved as quickly as you can."

Eiger retreated back to his cabin — reviewing as many letters he had — trying to plan. Darien stepped in and as always he had a gloved hand on his pommel, and rough garments in case of a sudden attack, but it was his face which showed different, "we should be there by midday at most, and late night at most realistic, my lord. But we won't be able to try unifying today, nor tomorrow, and if plans go flawed the next day or two."

"Well, losing a day won't kill us, while the navy has plenty of days. And what, I need to spend half a week unboarding my ship, and deal with small diplomacies within the castle? But you are my personal guard, and a trained priest. I want you to try and make deals with the churches, the clergy, and some small lords. I was ignorant to believe that low tide wouldn't happen to slow our progression. Even without this set back, it would still take a day or two to unpack the ships."

"Your grace, I think in this important point I should stay by your side as your guard, and leader of the guard. What damning assassin wouldn't try when it would be so easy. You in a quickly assembled study, focusing on keeping to schedule, and a paid assassin would swoop right in, and end it all."

"If you're thinking that I'd be assassinated, or kidnapped, mere days in the city for political reasons, then you shouldn't be alarmed. If I were killed the moment I'd arrive, not even Tylock with all of his napped power could deal with the suspicion and damage he'd cause himself, and his constituents."

"We don't have much on Lucerne, he is missing, and if he could buy off the black tower, then we would be sailing right into a trap of our own making."

"That is a consideration made. I thought I was the paranoid one currently. But you are so much more scared than I," he chuckled with his teeth, "no, I considered it, and I almost immediately threw it away. There's no possible reason for there to be a trap waiting for us in Porcelania, ah it's so close." He remarked for a moment, "but we have nothing to worry about. We are safe to set a trap for the navy, for Tylock, and for Lucerne."

"And what makes you so sure? Logically Lucerne could be sailing to Tylock, or keeping the tower black, or our 'allies' – whoever that may be – silent."

"Simple," Eiger said whilst lighting a tobacco pipe, "Lucerne accepted."

The day rolled, and the tides crashed, and rose high. Eventually letting Eiger sail into the ports of Porcelania, they docked and the duke had Darien drift out into the city to have a first meeting with the clergy, and faithful and believers of the church.

The day was dimming down, Darien had his lantern lit low, and kept low in case of loose ground. He was careful and wanted to know the land better than the dwellers. "Though the church shouldn't be a grave threat as the tower which hung in the sky. Lucerne had every advantage: corruption and information. If he knows, or knew how to use his easily given power, anything was possible. But Lucerne is a conflict for the future soon. The people are now, and the church seems the best influence on them."

He adorned a thin wooden mask — lacquered to look somewhat-like a porcelain mask. And in the dark streets, he went almost completely unnoticed. He was only a few blocks away from the cathedral of the three, when he was stopped by a watchman from the tower, attempting to keep some governance. But the first apparent ruling in the city seemed almost the same as it had weeks prior. That was on the surface. "What's that on your back?"

"A large knife."

"No, that's a sword," he heaved, "you mustn't know of the laws of this city carrying prohibited items in the open."

"But it's on my back, not on my hip. I'd like to continue on, sir, good day," Darien tried to walk away but was stopped once more.

"Not so fast, old man, you don't walk away from me. Why don't we head over there, on the counts of two laws broken."

Darien looked down on the watchmen, and continued to walk away. With a rushed draw, a sword was pointed and just as quickly dropped with a quick and expertly precise slash. Darien rose the blade high and drew it into his scabbard. He reached into his coat, and a note and crest were shown to the watchmen who was gripping his hand. "And I was in the right to protect myself, and in the right to carry this on my back. Good-day."

Darien picked his lantern off the ground, and walked back through the shadows. In the distance was a cathedral of sculpted stone and cement. A large stained glass art of the old trinity was covered in dirt and dust. Darien opened the door, and was in front of a gathering of prayers, and a pastor was giving a sermon.

He sat a few rows from the front, and waited for the pastor to finish his slow and heartless speech. *If I were to tell Kreshen, he should have a crusade against this church. He might be the only man, but the chandelier would finally be dusted.* All the praying people filed out slowly – Darien waited – the dim light faded as candles were being put out, until the last light in the cathedral was the one the pastor held, and the lantern Darien held. "The sermon is over my son."

Darien came to the priest, "I am the personal guard and hand to the duke of the Pagmonila fields, Duke Eiger. Do you have tea?"

"Um . . . um, yes! Let me brew a pot now."

Darien followed close by into the kitchen where he made a seat for himself, while unfolding a paper, "your name?"

"Lazith, sir."

"Your holiness is unmatched in these halls, but do you think it's holier than the whole east coast?"

"Of what? Are you really questioning my holiness?"

"No. I want to know if your holiness matches that of the people?"

"These walls have stood for a thousand years."

"So they have, but are the people as holy as these walls are?"

"So you care for sugar, sir?"

"Thank you. I'll take your normal amount of sugar and the complete truth, father. If you have any?"

"I'm old, what do you want of me?"

"We're similar in that, but I've seen more of the world, and you've stayed in your complacency," he pulled out of his coat pocket a folded piece of paper, and passed it over to the priest, "for a thousand years you, and your predecessors have stayed still, cause you could. Soon that will change, I'm giving you the option to change, before you're forced to. The people need belief or faith, in the gods, and in morals. And they need faith in good people. This won't be the last I visit, and the duke will come to pray here soon, but know of what could come."

"And what's that?"

"Change on a grand scale, but now I must go. Goodbye."

In the distance they could see a clearer outline of the forest, and a speck of stone almost camouflage in the distance, but with a squint could be somewhat seen if only for a moment of hard looking. *Hopefully that's Esty I see. We can quickly gather more supplies and journey through the forest.* The day was still early, and the ride was at least half a day's away. There the incoming winter, and a smell of fire on their clothes they've come accustomed to. There was a flitter of hacking coughs and mild annoyance between riders and mares. There was small bickering, but they didn't want to fight, more so they didn't want to waste their energy so wastefully.

So they rode, and they didn't break for tire, the hours rolled by, and the sun rose, and stilled in the sky for a while. This was the last day of back breaking desolate riding. The brass blades stood still, and crumpled under the horse shoes.

Some time had passed further, Litus drifted into thought. *Our paths will separate again, won't they? And this time for good.* Jane looked over with a smirk on her face, "why so glum, I know you like danger, but you can't fight storms."

We have and survived. It showed in his eyes. "Well the storm was an easy fight, compared to what will follow. The fighting will never end. But together we'll deal with anything that follows or comes."

The cold rain saturated their clothes so that when they rode their heat and sweat made them smell gaudy and rotten. It was a heaving musk they'd come accustomed to, but Kreshen and Litus smelled less.

Pinky's stump had an irritation from the air, and Litus noticed when he forcibly put it between his armpit. Barrett caught a cold, and was hacking a cough, muttering harsh words under his breath. Yet still they rode. Even though now at the finishing line all their terrors felt intensified, with Pinky and Jane looking over their shoulders for wraiths, and Kreshen praying that the rain doesn't fall, and Litus hoped that his mare wouldn't give up or Jane being separated again. *But it will happen eventually.*

The day rolled on and they rode the plains and waving hills, ever closer. Eventually they could see it with certainty. Soon out the castle were riders in dark green garbs. It was only a matter of time when they could see the castle from below, and were met by these riders, four exactly. Pinky's good hand was on the pommel of his sword, and so did Jane and Sam.

They stopped once the oncoming riders were before them. "State your names," a man said with a gruff tone, and a silver star pendant was embroidered on each side of his collar.

Jaune rode forward, and said, "I am Jaune Belheart of Duke Eiger's guard. And you should know the matters of the rest of us from the letter the duke sent you."

"We have, and that deals with it, but Kreshen is that you?"

"It is I, and I have a letter with me explaining my situation too," Kreshen held out the folded letter, "it explains everything clearer than I currently."

"Why don't you try father?"

"Well me and my partner are on a mission west to Hule, the churches are dire."

"And that answers one question, but who is he? The wraithkind? Why is he with you?"

"It's hard to explain, but he's one of the reasons I'm heading west rather than east. He's not a wraith if you're wondering, he would have killed us all before we arrived."

"I already know he ain't some wraith. I've seen em before, fought against em before, was left with this scar," he showed the guards rather than Kreshen, who knew about the scar, "that still doesn't answer why you can't head east. Is this some criminal?"

"If he were, so would I, and an entire race of people, and the queen too. It's of importance that we get through the forest, and go west."

"It wasn't that long ago when we heard of the murder of the queen. You're her heir, you're here, and the killer is traveling with you."

Jane spoke up quickly and loudly, "he did not murder the queen, I did, after she attacked me."

There was a silence for those fleeting moments, Jane's face went red with fear, and her pupils went small. The head ranger in silver said, "what do you mean you killed her, what happened?"

"What are you going to do with me?" Jane said.

"Hopefully nothing, but what happened?"

"Have you heard of commodore Tylock? He proclaimed and revealed me as the heir, and the queen didn't believe him. She decided to fight me to see whether I was her daughter or not, and I won."

"So you killed the queen," he reflected, and he muttered under his breath, "everything has changed huh," he then spoke like he did before, "but you are the queen now, and the guild stands with the duke, and with you. But it's best not to speak of murder for those you just met. Your grace."

"My letter, here."

He dismounted and walked to Kreshen, and once back on horseback he read the letter carefully. "So that's why. But I'm sorry, Kreshen, to find a ranger able to take you through, and a little bit further, you'll have to wait some time. It's still the busy season. But we do have beds and rooms for rent."

"How long?"

"Maybe a month, maybe half that. The merchants come second, after the queen."

"And this," he pointed to the letter, "doesn't?"

"I didn't get to where I am by sitting on my ass and order men around. That's unsustainable. This," Morrosey pointed to the letter, "is chance, I know this, I won't say the word, it's sacred, but it's a slim and risky chance. I won't help you, but I won't deny you as a customer. But don't spread this talk so much. It's a deep risk I'm taking."

"That's why we two will do it. An old priest, and a man of no name and no family. If we fail, we may not fail those who could come after. But still we're in this for the long run."

"So you are."

They rode further. The grayish white walls of the fortress were heavily detailed. Kreshen hadn't been here for a long while, but every time he saw the fortress, the size always gave him awe. *Have they made it larger?* The main gates opened, they crossed a bridge over a trench. Outside of the keep were encampments of many dozens of men, campfires blazing, and men returning with a coney rabbit in each hand.

Kreshen could overhear the young guards talking about the tents and men, "do you think they are rangers?" Pinky asked Sam, and he shrugged and said, "maybe."

"But why are they outside the keep rather than in?"
"Maybe they ran out of room."

"Well look at the castle, it's almost as big as Duke Eiger's, maybe a little bigger. Why can't those men sleep in the castle?"

"Especially with the rain, and soon snow."

"Call it bureaucracy."

They entered the bailey. One side had many stalls of horses, and another had a forge. Troupes of gypsy merchants strode through following a ranger to a concession stand to determine their travel fees and taxes for Mulder. But since they were gypsies they would most likely have to pay more. They would have no other guard than the knife on their belt and the ranger leading them.

The forest gate was just as large as the east gate, and the north gate too. And the inner courtyard was wide and full of space, unlike the duke's keep. But men still walked the battlements, and stood position in the castle towers.

They were led through past small towers, and dozens of smaller buildings of men and some women doing chores or jobs. The inside of the large keep was immaculate, it was prestigious like the castle Renoi, just not as large.

Kreshen walked up and handed Morrosey a small purse of heavy coins. He looked inside, "this will do. Have a servant bring them to rooms."

A series of servant women had taken their belongings, to such gruff, and led them to rooms. The guards were at least put in the same tower as Jane, but not the same floor or as nice rooms as Litus and Kreshen, and especially not as nice as the queen: Jane.

Litus and Kreshen were escorted to a room on a floor, as the servant brought Jane upstairs to her room. Litus sat on a stool by a desk, and was finally comforted with stillness.

Chapter Thirty-Six:

"The kingdom of the heavens transcends all which we are and will be, except the gods who walk among us, and we won't attempt to destroy the laws of the land from which they sought or we'd fight for an unjust cause, an immoral cause, and thy ground shall crumble and oceans dry. Thou who crosses the gods have sinned across the plains of light and must travel through the halls of darkness knowing all who make you, being a pillar that which holds up your spirit. And it is only by those who can destroy those pillars can they see above the sky. Most people will not, or could not break the fundamentals. A series of pillars carved from the bones of gods and wound with threads of silver spirit from the land and lives all around us, binding us to a certainty.

"The sins which are not forgiven when you die will remain in death, but forgiven in rebirth. Rebirth is the start of new. A child is pure and innocent, free of hatred, and sinful thinking. When the world is swallowed by nothingness shall we all rest, such as how it all was before land grew, and rain fell, and the gods walked on the land they created. Then there shall be peace, and solitude," the pastor read.

For an exhaustingly time the pastor read without passion, but with authority. He closed the book with a thump, waking the older patrons who proceeded out of the hall shortly after. But Eiger stayed, brushing off dust from his shoulders. He walked up to the priest who looked both confused and scared. "Duke Eiger, lord of the Pagmonila lands. I presume."

"Yes indeed. I also assume you know why I came."

"He gave me a document. Do you think you can buy a church, and the people? And you question my holiness. Have you no respect?"

"I don't question your holiness, you however can greatly help your people, these people. And it's simple to do so."

"And why should I, what reasons should I change an institution which has stood for a millennium. No, I know that you want to change it? To make it yours."

Eiger began to walk away from the priest, before leaving he pulled out his purse, "things change," he handed him a paper roll of coins, "a tribute to our gods."

"Well is this all you've come to talk about then, my grace?"

"No, I'm also confused."

"And why's that, my grace?"

"I have not received any news following the funeral processions."

"It is a hard subject to deal with the recent loss of our lord, and it's even worse since that horrible night. The funeral was already held, nearly a week after the burning of Renoi. There was no time to grieve, and the navy admiral who held this procession stated, 'we must turn another page in our kingdom, or else a wave shall crash and break these walls from which we've held', and shortly after they put to rest the queen, and the generals of her empty house the day after. And the lords and nobles from afar had their remains sent to their lands, and the lords, nobles, and military men from here were buried on the day after the queen's."

"That is most unfortunate. I . . . I guess I will take my leave, and hopefully the gallows and death don't come soon," and Eiger prayed the three points.

"Do they know?"

"The low servants don't, but her personal ones do. And her guards may depend on the man. Some come from the navy, others were her guard before Queen Mary's death."

"What about the king's guard, the old circle? They were her closest guard, closer than her generals and admirals. Closer than her child."

"Jane didn't even know she was the heir, she refused to believe it too. Whoever is sitting on the throne now, can't be seen. Because if Jane was proclaimed in front of the guard, then once they see whoever is locked away, we'll be able to proclaim Jane. And we'd have leverage against the navy too. Denouncing them from the royalty."

"We can't do that now, and losing an entire navy would cause a civil war, and it'd be a slow suffering. With men who can't sail, and men who can't dock. The most who would suffer are well . . . everyone besides thieves during the ensuing sieges. But what I want to know is if the guard knows if the queen is the actual queen. And if so, we would be in a greater spot than you'd imagine."

"Do you refer to the fact we'd be able to hold it against them? The truth?"

"Yes, but more so what I mean is that we can hold it against the navy, but we can have a series of solutions to our problem in case one or another fails. It's a risk I'm willing to take."

The low-light of the fading day, hung on the overlooking balcony with her own personal servant. Eiger waited with a soft smile pointed across the small table for a bottle and meal. "You were the head servant and maid to her majesty before Garnette?"

Her eyes were without blinking as she took her gaze from the large maze from below, and steadily raised them to the duke. "I was, and still is, her grace's head servant and maid."

"That's good. I must thank you for keeping a room for me and my men, so nice and tidy. After nearly a week of sailing with a near week of sailing a week before that is undoubtedly exhausting. But have you ever been on one of the queen's vessels? Such as her private ship?"

"Yes I have, multiple times, and on other vessels when the queen traveled using her royal navy."

"Her personal vessel, what a beauty, a very nice ship. I saw it before the fire broke out. Much has been rebuilt very quickly."

"Well the fire took place in the main court where the nobles were and where our late queen was found, as well as in the first court kitchen."

"It's a shame the army defected from all this chaos. It shows their character. Very proud of the navy and their men. Would you say so?"

"I would say, yes, I love my queen and her ships very much. I pay plenty of taxes for them."

"That begs a greater question, why aren't they here? With this much ground being tilled, the possibility of piracy or attack from another crown could commence. The ports are currently defenseless"

"I don't know much but a commodore named Lucerne was supposed to be here. Besides that I don't know much, because I'm just a maid."

"I don't mean to rush, but what happened to the circle guard, the king's guard? They saw what happened that night, the fire, surely they must have seen the perpetrators?"

"Um, well the guard has been silent about the fire, and they don't watch the queen anymore."

"They don't, why?"

"Well, that's because they were embarrassed about their failure to protect her. I assume."

"I was hoping to speak with the navy, and possibly use their help with wrangling all the little militias, and meddling lords. Do you know when Lucerne will return, or where he's gone?"

"No, no I don't, I'm just a maid, I don't know much."

"Yes, yes you are," Eiger said after having a glass poured with wine. Knowing that only two sets of eyes were looking at him.

In the early morning with the bitter air biting goosebumps on the duke's arms, he was met with a knock at his chamber door. He sat at his small table on the balcony, and yelled, "who is it?"

One of his servants quietly came in, and addressed the duke, "your grace there's two people. A woman with your breakfast, and a circle guard."

"Let them in, both of them."

She nodded, and opened the chamber doors for the two, and closed after. Eiger sat in his chair with a tray of hearty food. The guard with his helmet in arm, and hand on pommel stared down at the duke. Eiger wondered if the man was there to kill him, arrest him, or was it that maid from the night prior? "Why do you disturb me at this time of day?"

"I wouldn't call this a disturbance."

"What would you call this?"

"Reasoning. I'm here to reason with you."

"About what, and more importantly why at this time of day?"

"Firstly, why are you here?"

"I am here to restore the army for the queen."

"Are you?"

"Do you doubt me, all the money I've spent, all the time I've devoted, how dare you."

He came closer to the duke, "do our cloaks shine red as blood? Does the sky stay blanketed, and the rulers hide behind doors?"

"What?"

"How does a daughter missing for over two decades return by the hand of a commodore on dock duty? And how does a monarch lose a daughter and a king's guard on the same day, and not look for them?"

"What are you saying? It's heresy, while I'm eating breakfast. It's heresy!"

"Stop this, you're here for something different. Yes, yes, I can tell by your piercing eyes, and I want to change it, only differently, to break the eggs in the nest, including the ones you don't know about."

"You're offering me to break my vows to this kingdom and the queen monarch? What if I decide to relay this to the queen, what will you do then?"

"What queen?"

"The one who sits on the throne."

"Does a throne make you a monarch, or does the crown make you a monarch. If the monarch hasn't been seen for weeks, are they really a monarch? And if so, who's running this operation?"

"It would be better if you spoke straight from now on."

The man looked grieved, he placed his helmet on the table. "How did those fires start, do you know that, were you in at that time?"

"I wasn't, but I heard that a candle was left in the cellar, causing the liquor to catch."

"Do you think that the closest people to the queen was her circle guard? No it was a secret league of these wizards, we of the circle guard were told not to look or interact with them. But we knew they were fanatics, and powerful too. But did you know there were two fires?"

"I do."

"They cast fire down surrounding the queen, Tylock and Garnette, and soon this wraith man, with purple eyes dropped on them, but this all happened after that commodore announced the princess. We couldn't protect the queen. And that's when the cellar fire erupted. That wraith, the fires, all started by these robed figures. Did you know that? Cause I saw it. There's another force controlling this kingdom then the person who wears the crown. And the navy is in the game now, do you know how?"

"Tylock," he said slowly.

"No, because after they 'found' the queen, we as her guard were instructed to guard her room every day and night. But we have not seen her, only servants see her, and some diplomats, one from the navy, and another I don't know the name of. We guard what we don't see. That's how."

"How can I believe what you are telling me is true? Why would you be telling me this, altogether?"

"I have very little to gain, I've made vows, for a crown which may not even exist. You were the lesser of multiple evils as I see it."

The streets were grimy and covered in the remnants of man or soot, and a violent crowd throwing glass bottles on the stone ground – with those shards glistening and bouncing in the dim lantern light. There was uncertainty in the streets, tax collectors were sifting through the strewn threads of the crown's cash while the passersby were not even certain who ruled over them anymore.

Darien carried not a sword, but a simple dagger on his back, and a cheap cloak he bought off a street peddler. Under the dagger sheath was a sword breaker, but he would have rather had a sword on his back, but if watchmen or gangs saw his blade, they might just try to rob him, or kill him.

He came to this pub and inn at the bank of the river stone road, and inside were the old gruffs upset with the taxes, and the young not knowing when to stop prodding others and getting bloody noses from thrown hands. On the end of the room was a small pub bar, and behind that was a kitchen of smoke, salt, and fatty meaty smells. There was a cracked glass mirror on the wall covered in grime. But none of it stopped his cold stride to steal a seat. The bartender with an almost clean face – besides a small slice of grime – said to the man, "why so stiff, stone face? You from downtown?"

"No, what do you serve?"

"Slow down, I ain't the merchant kind, speeding through life. We have ale, and warm ale."

"How about a pint," he said, dropping a coin on the counter.

He laid down the cup of warm ale; there was a small murmuring from behind, and a man pulled the seat next to Darien, dropped a coin, and said, "same as him."

"So it is," the bartender said.

"You new here?" Said the stranger.

"Who's asking?"

"Don't be so crass, old man. What's with the getup, you plan to rob the queen?"

"Why do you care what happens to the queen?"

"Nah, she's dead as dirt, but they still run things," he looked at Darien, receiving a grim face, "it was a joke, old man," he said, "where ya from? Never seen you here before."

"Did you sit here just to ask me where I was from?"

The stranger put down his mug, "bit of a bark for an old stray."

"A pungent smell for a thieving cunt."

His face dropped with fire in his eyes burning bright, "you old fuck," he said pulling a knife from his boot, "you'll see who has the cunt."

Darien spit on the floor, "bad ale," and he dropped from his seat, but as he was walking out into the alley to disappear. The stranger followed him, "you don't treat me like that, old man. Do you know who I am? No, I'm gonna teach you." He held the knife to his side, "give me what you have. I think you have more than you're showing. Dressing like that."

"You better put that knife back in your boot, before I do it."

"You better fucking try," he said, rushing Darien.

But Darien stood still, hands behind his back, gripping the dagger in one hand and sword catcher in the other. He just waited for the right time. Darien notched the stranger's blade in the catcher, and he twisted his arm causing the blade to fall from his grip. The stranger came close to grab Darien, giving him a kick to the side. "You like that, ya fuck!"

Darien pushed him back, slashing at his arm. Blood dripped on the cold cobblestone ground. The stranger dropped to the ground trying to grab the knife he dropped. Violently lashing out, the stranger tried to stab Darien, "where are you!"

Darien remained out of reach, *what does that mean?* Out from his side was another man with a broken off plank of wood, but he was using it as a club. He ran swinging at Darien, but this old man simply backed away letting the clubber over extend. Darien put him to the ground with a swift kick to his legs.

"You bastard," the stranger said, getting kicked by the heel of Darien's boot, "where's the rest of you!" *How many is he gonna rally?*

The stranger leaped out the knife forward, but Darien again grabbed it with his sword catcher, and twisted his arm. A man with a knife ran to him, trying to put the blade in Darien's back. But it couldn't penetrate the thick woven layers. Darien twisted, slashing at the man's face, a spew of blood came from his face.

A fourth man with a similar plank of wood ran to him, breaking the plank over Darien's back, causing him to fall to the ground. "Get him!"

Two of the men jumped on him, Darien received a kick to his side multiple times. He grabbed a man's legs, stabbing him through the leg with the dagger. There was a volatile sound, and he fell grabbing his leg letting Darien rise up. He kept his dagger forward, watching his sides.

The stranger came forward trying to tackle him, but Darien dropped low, putting his dagger into the stranger's boot, pulling out a spew of blood. He yelled in pain, "you fuck!" While grabbing his foot.

Darien turned to face the other men; blood dripped from the tip of the dagger. A man with the unbroken club came swinging; it was blocked with the side of his arm, and a grunt. Darien swung back, his hand gripping the dagger tightly made his fist like a reinforced block of stone. He gave the man a swift jab, and a kick to the gut, knocking the man over like a falling giant.

The other men came forward from either side. Attempted stab, and a punch to the gut. Darien took it, swinging even harder. He brought the heel of his boot down on the foot of one man, and brought him down with a knee to the gut, and a grip of iron to the jaw. *Three down.*

He swiftly brought down, last man standing. Darien walked back to the stranger, picking up his sword catcher, and he said, "anymore."

"Fuck you."

Darien held his blade toward the man, "who are you?"

"Fuck you!" He repeated.

Darien got close, keeping the dagger close to the stranger's skin, "who are you?"

"You'll regret threatening me, ya hear, I know people. Men stronger than you, you'll see."

"And who's that?"

"Karaway will get you, he owns this part. He'll see what ya's done to me, and get you. You hear."

"So be it," Darien said, pushing the stranger back, and walking away.

He heard a rustling from behind, and the sound of steel grating on stone for a faint few half seconds. Darien turned, "reminds me," he said, grabbing the stranger's grip, "I do what I say," and he broke the stranger's grasp, freeing the knife, and he put the blade into the stranger's boot. And left.

In a secret room, with low light from outside, stood Tylock waiting for his constituents. Little time passed when each walked in. There were five men who walked through the door, they were all the handpicked admirals and some commodores from the Navy High Command, they sat together at a round table in the inner circle.

"Please take a seat," Tylock said, opening a wooden chest at the front of the table, "this security council, on which is being held, is a requirement to keep the peace and sanctity of the crown. Each one of you – as I see fit – is an important cog, worth high rank and land for which you will keep the peace. And we will fill in for the queen's absence, as we track her down, and return her to power," they all nodded in agreement. "We have many actions to take before we would have that chance, and prosperity to the land. Such as the aftermath of this siege, tying Hule to Porcelania with stronger rope, and the religious zealots. Which will all be dealt with simultaneously."

An admiral that sat on the other side of the table spoke up, "that will stretch our manpower considerably. We would have to pull out of the siege, smugglers would have their chance to keep the siege rain on longer."

"Admiral Perot, I want your fleet out of the siege. We have plenty of ships to secure the border. I'll stay in command here, but you will sail west, we need to secure the southwest from secession."

"What makes you believe that Hule will try to secede? They are in a better position than the east. It would be a better use of my men to try and restore the army in the city. Or to keep the city safe from pirates and such."

"I'll have men dedicated to the city, and that does raise a good point, but I don't see a great need for an entire fleet to disappear to a city I already have control of, when I need control of the wealthy west. In particular, I need the city of Hule."

"What about the army? Our strength is significantly weakened without men on the ground."

"All the lords supply their men to the national army, and since the burning of Renoi, they took back their men, generals deposed and such. I foresee that these petty lords will start skirmishes, but none of them have any real strength to pose any threat to anyone."

"But that won't solve the threat outside forces pose to the capitol currently."

"Once we find the Garnette I'd assume all the lords will return their men to the national army, new generals will be selected, without any secession, but a proper cleanse of all this corruption. But you did raise a point, and so that brings me to you Admiral Broarch."

"Yes, grand admiral," he said, shifting in his chair.

"You will help sort out Porcelania, and to restructure the church, like discussed with the rest of high command. But you'll carry a document detailing how the church will be separated, and why."

"And if there's any uncooperation? Fights, or if one of these rouge lords try to start conflict?"

"For what I know, that is the responsibility of the city's watchmen. If their post is abandoned, it's your command, and responsibility," the admiral nodded.

There was an admiral to his right, with piercing eyes, "you'd rather us do all this, but what about the queen. We placed a dummy on the throne. The king's guard doesn't know it, and they're not meant to watch her, and if they do?"

"They vowed to protect Queen Mary with their lives, and they failed. I'd want them deposed, and sent into castle black."

"What if we never find the queen? What if the real queen dies? What then, do we keep a puppet on the throne?"

"No, we'd find the nearest relative, and if not. We'd keep whoever we put on the throne. We rational men could make sure none could tear the seams of this country."

"You'd risk all that, to hide a mistake."

"It's either us, or them."

"And whose them?"

"Know your place, Admiral Taylor. We will recover the queen alive or dead. And either way, we'd have someone on the throne."

"And what do you have planned for me?"

"You're going to help me deal with our greatest opponents. The zealots I mentioned."

"Those religious fanatics I've heard about."

"Indeed. This is one of the most important deeds we need done."

"To commit murder against the gods faithful."

"No, not at all. We are going to infiltrate a terroristic militia which has infiltrated every sect of this kingdom, and we are going to cleanse it of this tyranny. But we are going to find the most opportune time to cure it. To find the weak belly of these bugs. And to know, we must work with them, know them as our brothers, to infiltrate their ranks as they've done in the navy. And once we strike. We purge them like passing a disease. And like a disease, we'd only be stronger than before. Grow immune to treachery. And we'll pray to the same god as them and win his favor."

"Win his favor?"

"Yes, they reigned for too long. They've grown accustomed to being so stationary in their grasp of power. So our upheaval is only expected, change is what we'll bring. And to them it'll be chaos."

"That's a conspiracy if I've ever heard one. They're the true ones in power? How long have they been in power? How did you gain that title you hold so dear? In one night you claim the title of grand admiral, and supposedly the entire navy?"

"I should have you thrown overboard for saying that, the disrespect," Tylock looked down at the box, he pulled out a glass for each man – including himself, "I met the man who I believe is the pope of the zealots, these cultists. I talked with him. The power he holds is great and true," – and he passed each crystal cup to the men around the table.

"These cups you question, will only exist here, and now. The only power that exists now, is chaos, and death. I have obeyed two virtues that bind the land. And was rewarded. I did what was right and holy. That is why I'm the grand admiral. You question what is questionable. Not what is good."

He pulled a bottle of red wine, and out in each glass he poured the maroon elixir. And himself last. He lifted his glass first, took a sip, and the rest followed. He sat back in his chair, putting the small chest on the ground. He pulled out a wooden pipe, and lit a smoke. On his face flickered the light from the embers, and the strong smoke lingered above them all flowing dormant.

He ordered commodore Erik to the north west, while the rest were by Tylock's side in the meantime.

For a few days following with another gathering of the high command, Tylock finalized the document which would fix the aging sept into a holier system. Admiral Broarch was staged to sail down south to the Capitol, and further on eventually.

He sat at his desk, in the home he took, and drafted notes. Of every person, and the interaction, and the position. But he looked at the notes he wrote for the leader of the cultists. There was very little, it was all in a dream, but even after waking, the dream felt so real. Even remembering, it felt like something in our realm. It felt somewhat strange, somewhat alien. It was intriguing, but ultimately it didn't matter. But still that note lingered, and memory too.

Out of the window he overlooked the city across the water. There was a fire billowing smoke high until it melded with the sky above. Every few glimpses was a faint sound of someone screaming, or maybe it was a bird or another thing. It was all really small.

Tylock stood over it all, with an idea, and a plan, some parts he kept to himself. *Just where are they? Where is the leader? Is he in the city, with full control of the crown? But he must have suspected something from me. How much of Hule does this cult control, if any at all? If they aren't in Porcelania, where would they be? How much shall we burn, before they are singed away?*

Chapter Thirty-Seven:

The warm but ultimately small chamber Litus was stashed in was corrosive. He hadn't been very lonely with the company of Kreshen, and occasionally Jane – who was only afforded so little time – would peep in, even if she hadn't much to say. Outside his cell was the worst of it. For once he felt this hatred, but none wanting to attack, to kill, to rob, none of it. There were no fights in Esty, but the strangeness of looks at him were piercing – similar to how the rangers looked towards those gypsy merchants.

Kreshen came through, holding a small smoking candle with the scent of sage pushing away the stale dust. "Get up, come walk with me son," he said with muted enthusiasm.

Litus followed, and they walked through the work, and halls. He kept his hood well covering his face. But the servants and few rangers walking the halls, and the merchants selling wares within the walls lingered on in curious disgust. "They don't like many things, like any other, but they don't like what they don't know. I think I can say that about everyone."

Where are you bringing me? Are we leaving so soon, we found rangers who could take us? He grew accustomed to Kreshen answering his questions. "The more you learn – even falsehoods – the greater you understand the world that's presented. And repetition may be the key to knowing just a little bit more."

They walked to a cart with a draped bonnet, and a man and malkin sitting by waiting, "greetings you two," Kreshen said, "the gods bless you, I am Father Kreshen, and if you can I'd like to ask you some questions."

The gypsy man spoke first with a grin that strode across his entire jaw, "that's very formal of you Father Kreshen. There's at least one face that doesn't treat me like sick cattle. I go by Sean, or Seran, it doesn't matter much. And what about you," he said looking at Litus with particular interest, "who're you, what're you?"

Kreshen didn't answer but followed up to the malkin, "but mainly I wanted to ask you something – in private – if it may be okay?"

"That's fine; Sean, would you go?" And so he did, disappearing out of the side of their eyes, "do I know either of you; what do you want with me?"

"Me and my companion are traveling south past Mulder, to Atreau, the holy land to the malkin, but I want to know more about their traditions, values, and their prophecies before we make ourselves a fool."

"I can tell you much about our customs, and such. But I want to know something too. Who is he?"

There was no budging it, Litus thought while stepping forward. Pulling down his hood; his long shadowy hair fell. *Every malkin I've met supposedly knows who I am, do you?* "Let's not be rash Litus, we don't want to freak out someone we just . . . "

But Litus and the malkin stared at each other, until something clicked. "You're him!? I've seen this face before – in books, in dreams – it was a prophecy we prayed upon, but never believed in. only hoping. Are you really it? Him?"

"So you're going to help us?"

"Is he?"

"We believe so, but we want to know for sure. That's why we're traveling where we're traveling. But will you help us?"

"I'll answer questions, but if you're wondering if I'll travel with you, I won't. It's either you are or you're not. I have things in my life, and I won't put hope over reality."

"Thank you. I just want to know one more thing if that's alright."

"Now what do you ask?"

"For certain we don't know what the prophecy says, what it means. Do you know, my son?"

"I know what the words mean, but how it was written, well, it's been so many years. But what it generally means, is that a fighter of justice, knight of justice – whatever the name was – would bring balance to a world of uncertainty. Or something like that. That's a line I remember."

"Do you know anything about determining if he is . . . the justice knight?"

"In Atreau there absolutely is, probably in an ancient dusty scroll, but I don't know what it would say. But I assume there is something there."

A man walked up with a pipe and two swords on his hip. He said in a gruff and strong voice, "Pastor Kreshen is that you!? Why are you bothering my clients? Don't you have someone else to preach to? I kid, I kid."

Kreshen turned with a slight amusement, "last time I met you, you were a young man, wanting to become a ranger, and now look at you, you've grown so much."

"You surely aged more than me, you don't look any older than when we last met. But look father, I've become a ranger, I can hardly believe it myself."

"You're not just some ranger, Elliot, I've heard your talent with the blade. You've been given a talent, pray to luck for that, and I hope you've been just with it."

"It's merely practice, father, don't flatter me so much. Besides, this is my last job of the month. Heading away after this. Just have to deal with the money aspects of all this. Really tiresome," he looked down to the malkin, and passed him a scroll which contained the bill, "where's your friend, that gypsy guy?"

"I don't know, couldn't be far."

He pointed at a specific line in the bill, "this is what you owe, and I need you to sign here, and after I need to find that damn gypsy, and do the same. Then you can do whatever the fuck you want, just don't go looking for me, I won't be here."

Kreshen asked, "where are you going?"

"I'm traveling down to Tabier, for a pint, and a night with a beauty, won't be back for maybe two weeks. I like to travel, but I've gotten quite good at it over these years."

"Shall we meet again, bless your day. And could you tell Tiamon my blessings?"

"I can, and god bless you Kreshen. Goodbye for now."

A knight of justice. When Litus had the chance – in the awful room – he wrote down his concern to Kreshen. He wrote with a quick pen, "I've met others before him, and he said the prophecy somewhat differently."

"Then we'll have to see once we walk in the halls of old scrolls penned by cats. What did this other malkin say?"

Litus scribbled down his thoughts, when there came a knock at their door. *Jane? One of the guards? Who is it?* He thought while writing half his thoughts. "Can I come in?" Said a man, who by voice wasn't either Jane or any of her guards. *Who is it?* He reached to grab a sword. But when Kreshen opened that door, the face who peered through was that gypsy man, "Sean was it? Why, if I may ask, why are you here? Would you like a blessing?"

"You know I very much would. Could you give me a quick blessing, my journey here has been more inconvenient than I'd like, but I can see my luck as of recent."

Kreshen prayed the three points – getting a smirk from the gypsy, "for the gods of we, shall all men be one, all hope be one, and all fear be one, and all love by one be true. When we see the sky, and ground, and the dead as one, we shall live with peace, shall we live with the humanity we're born with, and we will die with iron in our grips, and fire in our skin, and from the harbor our bodies will sail-"

"I'm sorry to interrupt you, it was good so far, but I don't pray to the other gods. You're giving praise to all three, when we only pray to one."

"I didn't know that, I don't know much of the gypsy's. I didn't know you prayed to one, which of the three do you pray to?"

"My people, we pray to Gruel. Or what is his name here? For the lord of luck?"

"Oh, well his natural name is Keroth, and I do know of prayers dedicated to his deeds," Kreshen started by praying one point, and in a low voice he spoke, "be not afraid from the heat of a flame, nor be afraid of the passion of the same flame. For each flame is different, and burns bright and true. From every string of uncertainty that you may feel, will or not be changed with a stream of hope, and of transcendence. But those who try to rob the common man of his love, and his opportunity shall be persecuted with a barrier to simple joys."

"I've heard that one before, not the same, but thank you anyways," Kreshen nodded and went to the door, but was cut off, "I'm sorry, but um. Well, I came to ask a question, I didn't get answered earlier. I don't intend to be rude, but what is he?" He said, looking towards Litus.

"I'm sorry to tell you, but that's a private matter. For my companion and I alone."

"Please, I want to know if it's a curse so I can help."

"How would you cure him, if I'm asking? And if you can, how did you learn to cure curses?"

"Through prayer, and practice. My people are dwindling conjurers. We're persecuted, and were taken from our homes. But my people have been practicing exorcism and curing for hundreds of years. I can help if you'll let me."

"Give us a second," and Sean left the room, Kreshen said in a quiet tone, "I know a little about curing, and if what he says is true, then we could get a step closer to realizing if you are it," Litus thought, *if he tries anything I'll give him his treachery back at him, but I don't trust him,* and he shook his head and put the note away, "you can come back, Sean."

"And?"

"We won't do it."

"I need to know. Hmm, what about a trade?"

"A trade? No, we said no."

"No I'll trade you a deep question about me, for what you know I want."

Kreshen looked to Litus and back, "alright, why are you here? Why did you travel here?"

"My people were scattered and our land stolen."

"By who?"

"By thieves, we lived in the town of Pachu, before the raiders came."

"But why here? Where are you going?"

"No more questions."

"No, I'll ask enough questions to equal the weight of our loss. Answer, where are you going?"

"What. Well, fine, I'm heading further east. I need to preserve my people, and our teachings."

"And your travel partner."

"The guild wouldn't let me pass through, because I'm a gypsy, but Carrion, that malkin was able to bargain with the rangers on the other side of Mulder, letting me pass through with them. We were only companions through the forest and that was it. Are you satisfied?"

"Not yet, I have one last question. Why do you need to know who Litus is? How does that help you?"

"It doesn't, it just satisfies my curiosity. And In a way it's a pilgrimage, to know what we didn't before. It's reverential to the children of uncertainty. Does that satisfy you now?" Kreshen nodded and said, "it does."

"Alright then, I'll start," they both looked at Litus – staring at the flames in his eyes, "take off your hood," and reluctantly Litus did, "what do you think he is? Human, or something else?"

"He is a cursed angel of death. His horns, his body stolen, and castrated from himself."

"Then where is it?"

"Deep in the forest, in Mulder, we need the help of rangers. There's not many beings that could strip a reaper of their skin. To cause an angel to fall."

"So, so," he rolled his sleeves up, "have patience, it will take a minute."

"Do you need anything clerical? Burning sage?"

"What purpose would that be? We need passion, not serenity. Light a candle, or that fire place."

The flittery red flames danced in the air, as the heat of the gypsy's hands fell upon the Litus' mind. It put Litus into a sense of ease, a sleep with certain uncertainty.

There were candles, two of them, their light flickering. Nothing else in the void existed except those candles. But he existed, or saw through the eyes of something existing here. And he knew of a name: Litus. He came closer to the flames, observing each deeply. A structure of stone and mortar. It was older than the dust on gravestones. It was most likely a wall, maybe the guard wall connecting the iron gate? Or maybe some castle in the future, but it was something.

He then peered through the next candle flame, and inside was flashes of a pool of water, and took out stone and mortar walls. Two stone walls encased in great flame. *Was this a future of death? For him, for whom?* He pulled his head back, to observe both candles together, and their twinkling little dance.

He bolted up, pushing away the gypsy's hand from his head. "Go," he said in a low scratched voice.

The gypsy backed away from Litus eyes directed at him. "I guess the curse is too strong. I can't do anything about it. If an angel has fallen then what can a mortal man do?"

"What happened?" Kreshen asked.

"You were right, I'll be gone, your holiness," and the gypsy left quickly.

"What happened," Kreshen repeated, "you spoke. You said 'go' what did he do? What did you see?"

Litus tried to speak once more, and with greatest strength but he couldn't muster any word.

Kreshen looked at the fireplace watching the flames dance. He was handed the note Litus started and hid from the gypsy. It read only, "I am to kill the chaos god: Keroth." *But what am I?*

It was the smell that lingered in the air they couldn't get off. Even when all their things were gone, and the entire room skinned, the stench still hung. It was embedded in the stone, and wood beams like hairs on a young man's head.

So for most of the days, the queen's guards were either guarding her room, or making camp outside the castle. Pinky for one liked being outside, it gave him a comfort of solace, and kept his mind off Garland. But when it came time to run his shift, he thought about Garland much more. *I need to be more professional. I won't mope around like a kid. Garland wouldn't like that. Would you?* He pivoted his head expecting a response, before quickly remembering he wasn't there. He just kept a hand on his pommel and stood watch. *What if I can't two hand a sword or use a halberd, I can still fight one handed. I can get better at it. I can adapt, I have to.*

The long table at the top of the tower was carved from an old hard tree a long time ago. Each scratch had a history, each smudge in its lacquer a reason. Strong men poured over the table with wealth and knowing that their position was well guarded and unchanged. That was the same position that the head of the guild: Ranger Morrosey held. And he knew his duty to his duke. To keep her safe from all the searching eyes of the corrupt navy and the clutch of some aggressive religious force, who want her for a reason he didn't know, but didn't challenge their intentions. If they existed or not. But Jane who sat on the other side knew of their existence, their power, and their intentions. And concerning them, she wanted one thing: to escape, and to kill all who took away what she loved. All who threatened her life.

She looked outside observing the clouds, trying to think less about the horrors of that cult. "My grace!" Morrosey said, "I can't let you leave. Out there is a deceitful mass of hate and deceit. I'm doing my part to put you on the throne. Where you belong."

"Well I'm the queen, and I'm ordering you to let me go."

"No, you're not. Do you think titles make the man? Do I run this guild because I'm the head? No. I run this because I do it well. And I'm putting myself in great danger keeping you. So I ask again, do titles make a man?"

"Why do you call me the queen then?"

"Being the queen doesn't give you power, having power is power. And you have no power to be stupid. Eiger is putting himself in grave danger trying to give you power too, so you should be thankful and stay put."

"From what?"

"I can tell just from your face, you're expecting me to say what you already know."

"You may have been told by someone what is out there. But I've seen it. What they've done, what they can do. I'll never be safe here. So before they catch up to this, I need to leave."

"If they, as in the navy, this cult, or even a gang of thieves dare to intrude on these very walls we have copious numbers of plans to follow for your very survival."

"I think you're taking this too lightly. That cult they're everywhere. Can't you see it. They'll find me, and when the fire rages will you keep me here to burn to death?"

"Do you know how many clients we lost to Mulder, how many this year?" Before he let Jane speak, he said, "none, we didn't lose a single soul. It's all because we train for every situation the forest throws at us, and plan for every shortage, and every hostile situation. So don't you dare doubt the advantage you have currently. Cause if you keep crying danger it'll come for you. Whether you like it or not."

Pinky stood outside guarding the door, with a ranger who too was on guard duty. He had the urge to put his ear to the door and hear what commotion they made, but it was that ranger across from him looking with query eyes. Ready to question him, saying "What are ya doing son," and he didn't want to hear it, but instead the ranger said, "why are ya making that strange face for; ya never guarded a door before?"

"No I have, sorry, do you ever wonder what's going on inside?"

"Oh yes. Always, but I always play it off as though I know what I'm doing."

"You do?"

"Yes, every time. If I'm not in the meeting, I'm usually guarding it, like now."

"How easy is it to become a ranger?"

"Now don't take this personally, but with that missing hand, it would be impossible to become a ranger."

"I think I need to become a ranger. I need to be better, so I can protect others."

"Even if you could – which you can't – no ranger will take you as an apprentice, because you are missing a hand. Being a ranger isn't about fighting for those you love, and those you want to protect."

"Then what is it?"

"To tell the truth, it's not as noble, nor is it as poetic as being a guard to a monarch. It's a hard life, but it's not something fit for you."

"How did you . . . "

"The field rangers may not know, but I do."

"Could you help me?"

He thought for a second, and after a minute he said, "I'll have a bonfire outside the walls in a few days."

Chapter Thirty-Eight:

In the bleak shadows of the sky, loomed the incoming storm of night. A ranger was splitting logs, while another was feeding it into the fire. Once the fire was engulfing the flames enough to generously give a heaping of light and heat; men gathered around the kindling. In particular was the fellow Ranger Telemond, as well as two of her grace's guards: old man Barrett, and novice Pinky. With the cold winds – brought from the southern plains into the border edge of the forest kingdom of Mulder – came the changing seasons. Autumn leaves dropped, and soon would be blanketed under heaves of snow. Between then was the cold, the harsh cold winds.

All five of these men were sitting around, and once accustomed to the heat from the fire, began to talk. Telemond stalked their conversation, and knew all he could about Pinky. "I've heard that you want to be one of us?"

"Well I've thought about it for a moment, but honestly I just want to be a better fighter," the young man said.

"I get it, you want to be a better queen's man, and being trained as a ranger will certainly help you in that. But you don't know enough about rangers then you'd like."

"I know plenty enough!"

"That's the same ignorance that got Tamlin Barnsted a hundred years ago."

"What happened to him?"

He gave a small chuckle, the rangers around had a slight grin across their faces, but managed to suppress it for their relaxed stone-like face. "Around a hundred and eighteen years ago now, Barney Barnsted, the head of the rangers guild – at the time – had a child named Tamlin Barnsted, and even though the guild preceded the Barnsted family, he tried to give the guild to his son, like it were some heirloom. That was questionable among the high ranking men, it basically would make him a lord rather than a guild leader. But a hundred something years back, there was a turning point in the guild. Wealth that was. Hoards of wealth from Barney. At this point most had turned their heads on keeping the guild the way it was, and were willing to have it pass down the Barnsted name. But that child, because of this, was never given a normal childhood. He was the absolute bane of all the ground ranger's existence. In many accounts they said this child was given more with less outcomes. Hell I bet kings didn't have it that easy, they had to at least learn politics and ruling and stuff. This kid was given the largest guild in the kingdom, while not knowing how to tie his shoe.

"It all started with a bet with a ranger who was pissed off at this kid, who was now the dull dim age of eighteen. His aging father was becoming worried about the income of the guild in the past few years, as well as realizing his son's growing incompetence. So when this ranger – his name is often forgotten, but he – came to Barney, and he accepted, thinking his son would easily become a good ranger. For he was young when he became the head of the guild. 'Blood is blood,' he thought, 'if I could win this throne, my son only has to do half my work, and he is my son. If I could do it, he could do more with less.'

"Now this kid had started his ranger training about this time of year, winter was just a few weeks away. And this kid thought he could be a full on ranger by this time."

"What was the bet? You never said it?" Pinky said.

"I'm getting to it, young one, don't rush the story," he released a cough, clearing his throat, and continued, "by the end of the next season this kid thought he could become a competent ranger. That was the bet you impatient kid," he gave a good chortle, "that is the bet, do you know how long a ranger trains before they are awarded the title?"

"No I don't."

"And neither did this kid. Though you are certainly smarter, you are listening to this irrelevant old fool. So he thought, he genuinely thought he would be the fastest trained ranger to ever roam these woods, wield a sword, ride atop horseback, and everything else we do. And since the first season was basically over, he had one season to become a ranger."

Pinky's face went hot with small laughter, and so did old Barrett and the rest around the circle. "Now kid, do you know anything about these woods behind us?"

"Well I know they're cursed, and that the merchants of Hule come from the other side."

"Then you certainly knew more than this kid. Because he grew up so close to these woods, he started to forget they were cursed to begin with. Well maybe not forget, but believe he knew better about the woods, because he watched them from the outside. You can't figure out the key to a lock by watching keys go into the lock. You can piece together how the lock turns if you knew how to pick that lock, but that takes talent this kid lacked. He believed he had the key to the forest kingdom all because he was given a shiny sword, and a fresh and sharp falchion.

"For three weeks before making his first expedition to the thick of the forest, he was trained on how to set up a safe camp, as well as simply told how to weave the trails. But he only drowsed through these teachings – it made the ranger who was forced to teach this brat annoyed, and have time for his hobbies. But the kid had child-like desires. The misuse of swords. All he ever wanted was to play with swords. I heard that the most annoyed a ranger got at this kid, was when in combat, he used the sword like a club. Always going on how it was some special trick. A trick he called it. Much to say his palms were soft, and grip weak. And even more, this man-child would then pull out their falchion instead of admit defeat. You know what happened next? That sword was stripped from their stupid hands and they whined about going too hard. It was better too. It really was a waste, they threw away good steel."

"They gave him two swords? Why? Do they want him to lose a hand?" Pinky said, disregarding that he only had one hand.

"We use two swords for multiple reasons. The falchion is good for cutting brush, leather, cloth mostly what isn't metal. The bastard sword is for confrontations; oh there are plenty of them. Got this cut on me leg from the woods," he raised a pant leg to show a long red scar covered in old scabs about the length of a forearm, "you only wish you could see what I did to him. But anyway, another reason is that the falchion is the backup sword. Fights get dirty, and the woods are extra special at fighting dirty. But I guess if you didn't have another blade on yerself after dropping this, you'd not be a good ranger. I wouldn't want to be known as the ranger who raised this man-child."

On his hip was a hidden wooden flask of a strong scented ether. It was refined from the sap of trees, and could strip scale from an iron billet. It was surprising it wasn't seeping through the hulls of the canteen. Pinky was repulsed from the smell, "you don't want a swig kid? Ey it'll clear your gullet of anything stone or metal. So the ranger master to this man-child had elevated him, and the reason? I believe just to get out of his way. The first snow had fallen, marking true winter here. Do you know what makes an apprentice a ranger?"

"Well you talked about being elevated by the ranger master."

"Yes, yes. Every ranger apprentice, when their master thinks it's ready, then we must march through Mulder alone. Don't think this is as easy as walking straight. The forest is-"

"Cursed, I've heard this, but how? Why can't you just walk straight through?"

He unlatched his canteen, and tossed it to Pinky, and said with confidence, "it's easier to get with a woozy head," reluctantly Pinky took a sip of the tree cider, he gasped as it burned his throat, "if you try to walk through the forest, the deep forest that is, you'll be scattered and lost, like a rat in a maze. I've seen with my own eyes a merchant who tried to cross the forest by themselves, and ended up walking straight back without realizing. How we see this is like a knot. This large thick knot of multiple strings, and numerous things. How we find our way is called weaving the shadow. You have to find the right string, and follow its path through. And there's other strings that become obstacles, and you have to weave around those threads. This could mean walking uphill, to end on the bottom of a hill. Or walking around one side of a tree rather than another. The ground which you think is real, isn't. Think of it as a staircase, which when you walk up, you end up walking down."

"What, are the stairs changing shape, or something like that?"

"Asking more questions than Tamlin would have. To be honest, I'm not sure this kid ever knew what the weaving of shadow was, or ever heard of it. He always was told to have fallen asleep in the middle of lessons."

"You've kept saying the same things to draw out this story, can you get on with it?"

"Eager are ya, have some patience, the story doesn't hit as hard without the buildup. You've got to know why, before you know what."

"Everything is always patience this, patience that."

"And for good reason, there's time to act, don't get that wrong, but those are few and far between, you have to wait for the deer to come to you before you hunt, or else the deer will simply run away.

You certainly have that experience already with that missing hand of yers."

Pinky looked at his missing hand in anguish, and said, "alright fine, continue the story."

The elder ranger's stomach had started to grumble in a low rumble, and he clapped his knees, "not after I've got myself some grub to eat. Can't tell the juicy part on an empty stomach. Or else this will cause all the tension to be broken before it arrives."

They broke off, only Pinky and Barrett sat by the fire. They could hear the ranger behind them discussing what they have, what sort of meat, and what was recently hunted. Deer, maybe a husk or three, and the rabbits gone uncounted. Someone would get a thrashing for not counting that. But they came back to the camp with a spit of skinned rabbits, a skinned chicken or two, and a near dozen ears of corn still in its husks.

They poked and prodded the coals, to dance brighter. The embers of flame rose until they completely burned away. They slowly turned the rusty bar of the spit until the first of the rabbits were cooked. They began breaking down the meat with a knife that was – conveniently in its own little scabbard – on their belt loop. One of the rangers replaced the bar with another cooking bar with chickens, and another few rabbits. The spit turned with a rusty squeak, while the meat sizzled over the fire. A few more rangers came with the looming smell, and the sky started to drip down like cooked oil.

"Let's snuff the fire a bit, I want this to be a slow cook."

A ranger left for a new canteen of water, and Telemond slapped his knee. He gripped the leg of a rabbit in one hand and another spread some salt from a spiced tin. The camp light shook and glowed on his face, "Tamlin, after only a month and a half – though it was closer to two – had decided that it were time to pass through the woods. His master raised him, and at the end of that next week he would journey through. He was pushed about much more, than in training before. Funny enough, this was his first time going deep in the woods. I've heard that when he was a child he would wander into the woods alone, and when the rangers found him, he would cry and sob. Then once out of the woods, try to go back inside. Real pain in the rear that one must of been. Though that determination could have been his only redeeming quality. If he only knew how to spend his time better.

"So it began, the first snow of the season fresh on the brown grass. The limbs of trees now hanging low enough to simply walk onto. The winter was burning cold. Wearing multiple layers of socks, as well as a scarf to cover your boot's opening, so the snow didn't seep in, and melt. But what this boy did was he just wore more and more layers. Until he could barely move his joints," he grabbed the canteen back, taking a large swig – wiping his beard – he continued, "now boy, quiet your blabbering, for this tale isn't as fun, as it had been before. We tell this tale as a heeding to those such as yourself. And take this as your first warning."

"First?" Pinky muttered to himself.

"The harsh cold of this new winter was unlike our winters of hallow past. Every turn, rangers and the servants of the keep, and I've also heard that merchants warned that boy, about the dangers of the forest, and all he said was, 'I was born here, I know the forest better than you.' It was midday, the first snow had mostly vanished by then, and the next was a week away, at least. At least! He journeyed out with his fur lined clothes. The two swords, and a pack of supplies. The last anyone ever saw of this boy was the guild crest embroidery on his pack," he grabbed another leg of rabbit, spiced it, and continued, "he had been walking for near an hour, complaining about the sores on his feet from the forest's unnatural terrain. The green moss, and bushes, and the fallen waxy leaves of trees spaced between the evergreens. The light snow which spotted the holes began to diminish the further he walked. What he thought was that he was gaining ground? Oh it wasn't the case. For thirty minutes he walked, and on the ground as he walked were more spots of snow. They piled higher and higher as he drifted. This made Tamlin think those tales of leaving while walking straight were true. So he turned around, to try and trick the forest itself. But as he continued, all he could see were these piles higher and higher than before. He turned around again, and after another thirty minutes he turned in a different direction than before. But still it was all leading him forward, through the trees and growing snow piles. But after another thirty or forty, Tamlin had decided that the forest was playing a trick on him. So instead of turning in endless circles, he decided to just walk forward into this ever growing expanse. The midday had begun to fall to noon, and noon to night. But that couldn't be, plenty of time had passed, but not an entire day yet. Tamlin got scared, he didn't know why, but there was this sense in his gullet that the forest wasn't playing jokes. Not long after it started to snow, with trinkles of snow falling through the forest top. Talmin thought that the rangers who told him that the next snow was a week away were idiots, and didn't consider that time had passed differently. But still he walked. Further and further. The ground became more and more blanketed. But now the snow has covered the entire forest floor. The base of trees, and the bushes, and the small saplings too. His boot prints were left in the ground, but what awed him was that the snow wasn't cold. His feet didn't feel cold, nor were they wet. As the snow began filling the entire air, Tamlin soon quickly realized this wasn't at all snow, it was ash. The thick plumes of falling ash, fell into pillars on the ground creating a sort of prison. Tamlin ran as hard as he could, but the ash still fell. The pillars lined his left and right side, growing high into the trees. It felt like hours, but it was mere minutes that he ran. And soon came the smoke. It looked like the fire here," the smoke and crackle of chicken skin filled the air, "and by some accounts it smelt like chicken too. At least it eventually would. Are ya listening kid?"

Pinky only nodded, "so the kid was walking into this forest of ashes, the pillars rose, and after the smoke came too. From sconces in the walls were torches made from the limbs of trees, and ash that stuck to. They all lined up to lure Tamlin further and further on. The sky had darkened and all the light that lived were the torches. From far behind Tamlin could hear footsteps. Like a heel on flat stone. A click directly behind him. Was one of the rangers there to help, who was it, 'How did they find me?' Tamlin had thought. Somehow Tamlin walked the thread of pure fire, and he now had to walk through the ashes. The further he went, the larger the sound had become. The ash had fallen to shin height now. His footsteps once he made were now filled with buckets of ash. It was all ash, there were no longer any trees, but a palace of ash. And it really was a palace, a whole kingdom, made of ash which now looked very similar to the marble floors of castle Renoi. But these footsteps from far behind didn't stop. Like tapping your fingers on the table. It resonated in this hall. Tamlin spun on his heel while drawing his sword. He waved it in the ash-drenched air. In his timid voice, he said, 'Come out! I hear you! I know you're there! I command you to get out!' but there wasn't anything. Beads of sweat fell and froze on the ground. He turned over and over again, still the creature wasn't there. He faced what he believed was the way he was walking before. But for certain no-one could know. He just ran down the corridor, with his sword waving in the air, cowardly. The ground was cold, everything was cold. There was pain beginning to grow in his feet. Every direction was the same. The pillars of ash were prison bars."

"What happened, with that monster, what happened?"

"It's not gone if that's what you're thinking. For near half an hour, he stumbled through the woods. Still the footsteps sounds were present, but this thing wasn't visible, not yet. Tamlin wasn't attacked, so he decided to slow his stride. He put his sword away, and thought himself safe."

"Why would he put his sword away? That's stupid."

"Remember who we're talking about. Tamlin is as sharp as a broom, and believes himself a knife. But in his misguided persistence, he just kept walking. For a long while he walked, ahead was a new building, made of this ash, and the twisted beams of the old grown trees. It was the court of the forest king. There were tall pale figures, with clothes of nature, and a crown of thorns. His face was shifting like brick walls during quakes. This king's face turned to Tamlin, in a rustic way. He spoke without moving his mouth, in the timbre and tone of a whisper-like winds. 'Why are you here child?' Tamlin put a tight grip on the handle of one of his swords, 'child! Who are you on my land, get out of my way I have things to do!'

"The king whispered slowly, 'So be it.' And a twister of the ash began to engulf all of everything. Tamlin could only see through the stray windows of the tornado the crown on top of this king engulfed in flame, and it all was being drawn closer. Tamlin had begun to run away from the swirling ash and fire. His feet being picked up by the hands of the twister. He yelled from the top of his lungs, but no sound could be heard. His lungs were being drained. And before he could know, his arms and legs no longer were connected to the ground," he paused, taking a long hard swig of the strong tree cider, and he tossed the canteen to Pinky, this time taking two swigs, "helps ya understand less."

"Less? What happened, I want to understand more."

"We all do, but sometimes understanding less is more," Pinky gave a strange look, but Telemond simply said, "in the pool of uncertainty Tamlin floated, naked in this pool, the stars of burden shooting down and burning in the sky. The blanket wrapped existence, and what he saw was this uncertainty. The echoing of bells ringing to a marriage in churches which he'd never seen before. The black sword of a knight of legends buried deep in the soil. It was all of everything, and nothing of courage. Tamlin continued walking through this void. The blue moon rose and the sky shifted on its axis of pseudo symmetry. He was being chased on the ship's stern with the bark, and leaves rustling in the pool. The blue moon shifted."

Pinky started to get woozy while the sound of the fire took all the space of the ambiance, that and the crackle of chicken skin.

"Tamlin kept running, the fires blaze behind him with the pounding of great mountainous drums raging from behind. And from all around the forest walls were the rain of ash and snow again. It all seemed correct, but from behind the pounding grew more. Instead of a drum, it was a trotting from now on. He was drenched in sweat, and melted snow. Ash pasted on his skin. The moon evaporated into red, and the fires were all surrounding, all mighty. Smoke was a knight, without morals, without honor, and didn't believe the tales of hope. With the drug-inducing scents made from the evil of the woods, Tamlin was lost in a maze made for competence to play. The trotting is what stayed above all the color shifting, and world bending chaos. The fire burned into ash, and all was around now was the dirt in the ground, the moss on the base of trees which hung high, and the bushed of small red fruits and green leaves. The hooves of a dark horse reared up at him. The black curve of a sword wavering in the little light afforded to them. The cloak of a wraith shadows all. Tamlin tried drawing his sword, but in backing away fell and the sword dropped to never be recovered. He tried drawing the second, but the blade of the horse rider was quicker. Splattering the blood of fools on the bushes, and filling the dirt with moisture, and roots of trees with soul. He let out one final scream, heard for miles, but he was never found. Not a footstep, nor an account."

"What," Pinky said, clutching himself, and hit the stump where a hand used to reside, "if no one could know what happened then how do you know?"

"All fairy tales are rooted in truth, but all fairy tales are meant for reasons. The warning of what comes with the cursed forest. To ever enter what shouldn't be mistaken and underestimated. All those who try the impossible without making possibilities, will always be lost to time."

The night dawned on, the cider and skin of the chicken and rabbit made the men sitting around telling stories to scare, or make each other laugh continued. But the imagination of someone as old as Pinky being subjected to the insane chaos of the forest was grim to say the least. Even though among the guild members it's just a child fable, the lessons were grave to follow. Especially grave in the forest itself. The fire had snuffed away over hours of sleep, and all that remained were the ash, and the smell of meat.

Chapter Thirty-Nine:

Eiger sat over Darien's bed, as he was getting swabbed with once white pieces of linen by bed maids. He groaned when each piece of fabric was applied and removed. Eiger shifted to the head mistress, "when will he be out?"

"Well he's not too injured, but he's still old."

"Hey," he said, "I'm here, and I heard that."

She turned to him, "it's still true."

"Doesn't mean I like it. Unless you could magically make me a decade or three younger, I don't want to hear it."

Eiger laughed heartily, "I'd like that too," he let the humor slip, before he spoke, "so this lord Karaway rules the low end of the city. Did you find out if there's more lords in this crime ring?"

"I did not."

"We'll find that out soon."

"What day is it?"

"An unfortunate one."

"Alright, then as long as you don't need a sword, I'll do truth sensing."

"Good, that's good."

"I don't think I'll need a sword anyhow. Unlike the streets the castle is supposed to be safe."

The room had the new old ash mixed in with the dust. It hung to the rafters above. Little flakes would fall off, and get crushed under the heel of boots.

Darien grunted while wrapping the bandages around the bruises around his chest. Eiger had already walked away, keeping an image in his stride. In the castle grounds before entering the horse drawn buggy, he prayed as much to justice as to luck.

As the cart rocked, Eiger watched the people on the outside, "do you ever wonder how it all came to this?"

"What's that, my grace?"

"It may seem rude from my perspective, but how it all became unequal. Over there," he pointed far in the distance, "now I haven't ever seen the slums, but I've heard what it's like. In a city with a mass overflow of lords and ladies, there are double or triple of the lower classes. Who live in shacks. Those lucky enough may have found a dropped gold coin in the streets, and could afford livelihood in the better brick. And here I am being drawn into by cart to determine what will happen with their lives. I don't want to bring in religion now, but could there be a god of balance when the world is so imbalanced?"

"What has brought on this thinking, my grace?"

"I guess and assume it comes from the fear of failure."

The streets still looked the same. There were papers cemented to the ground from rain. The great homes of the lords were unwavering in their beauty. But now they put great iron bars around, trying to keep their firm grasp on what they had. But the tower in the distance – whether they liked it or not – still appeared strong.

The buggy slowed and rocked as they pulled by the tower, and the cart door was opened by one of the tower's men. A series of halberds were put in two lines as a man in a bright yellow and black gambeson came to greet the duke. "Welcome, my grace, we've been expecting you."

"As have I, sir Pias"

At a hardwood table, they sat equal distance from a blazing fire, and they sat while food was brought to them. Eiger held a goblet and spoke first, while Darien was only a few feet behind him. "I didn't come here to dine, or necessarily make acquaintances. I have duties to uphold, just as you. That's why I came here."

The head of this organization just kept prodding and ripping the meat from chicken bones, and he said in a groveled tone, "you're saying that as though I don't equally have duties to uphold. But let me break the ice, what are you here for? As you say you're not here to make my acquaintance, but what I know initially is that you seek something not just from me, but from the tower as a whole. That's the given. So your grace, what do you ask for?"

"The tower is the only force in this city and the entire east which has some governance. I seek to reunify the peace of the streets, where children can walk without glass in the feet, and where women can talk to a stranger with no fear. I seek to bring the crime which low lords control to turn to ash, and to bring the throne which sits in the castle Renoi to the power which was held greatly."

"Peace?" He scoffed, "is there not peace already? All crimes which could be committed are under our shadow. The comedy mask was the image our past grace fashioned, but still that image lingers. Or to put it simply, crime is down."

"Has it, well of course her presence hasn't faded out, it hasn't been very long since that day."

"No, but a lot has happened very quickly, so in a sense it seems like an age ago. And still we keep the peace."

"Even in autonomy?"

"Like I said, crime is down, and we keep the laws the past Queen Mary wrote, and when the new Queen Garnette make's proclamations we'll enforce those as well. But we haven't had any word from the queen since her rescue from the navy. Now you're staying in a quarters in the castle and must have met our new monarch? Tell me, is she as beautiful as our last?"

"Yes, very much so you say, but from my short travel through this city, just today, and the travels of my informants too, I can tell that this institution not only doesn't have control over the east, nor the north east, or even the city in terms of protection. There are sleuths of crime, and low meddling lords trying to buy up what share of control they can. You may not believe it, but the tower is weak, and crumbling. It's losing its grip on the governance of the people, and I think you know that too."

Pais put down his utensils, and looked to the fireplace. An old oil painting hung above. Eiger stared at him, before breaking off to look at the painting too, "do you like it my grace? This painting has been there long before I took this seat of power, and I hope. No, I know, it will be there, exactly where it is for long after I retire and die. Do you know what it depicts?" He cutoff before receiving a response, "it's of long lost King Ariston standing on the muddy ruins of a castle long dead. It was an insurrection over two hundred years ago. And from the stone and ash of the castle which stood before, this one was built. It's been a part of this castle almost as long as the castle has stood; it's quite old, but even as the dust builds on its frame, it is inevitable that someone will clean it. Are you trying to clean the painting?" He waited for a response, but none came, "you are right, though I know many in the cabinet will disapprove of me saying, but we are weakened by the sudden loss of the queen, and silence from Garnette is harsh," a slight movement given from Darien told him it was true.

"That's heresy."

"So it is, but I don't see my head being put on any pike any day soon. A little heresy isn't enough to depose me."

"I'm not here to depose you, and I'm not here to rip the foundation from under your feet. I will put a hundred of my own men in your ranks, for a seat in the cabinet and partial control of the actions of the tower. I can clean the streets of the crime that plague us. I have men, but I need cooperation."

"So you want control, or partial control of what the tower does. Alright, but why. What can you do better than me?"

"The land in which I govern – just west of here – in the entire kingdom is the safest, most peaceful, and most profitable per set of hands. Is that not good enough?"

"Running a few towns, villages, and castles aren't as intricate as maintaining the peace of a city. You're coming in as a country bumpkin expecting to make great change. Know your place."

"I know my place quite well, and you admitted so as well. But you keep attacking from the same direction, and expecting a different result. You'll never get it, but I am planning on risking plenty of my resources to achieve it in a new way."

"And what if your plan only escalates this further? With anything new, those grabbing for power will have the chance to seep through the newly paved cracks and be able to break the new foundation that you poured. And I'm not ready to do so. You'll have to show something before I will follow you down this hole."

"These tactics do work, they've been working in the lands I govern, so I suggest you listen to my proposals before you shrug it off."

"If you were any lower man I would deny it, but fine, go ahead, tell me what you plan."

"What happened to the army, and all the unity of the masses, and the lords, they pulled their men out of the kingdom. They put their steel in their scabbards and sheaths. We need a reason for unity. It won't come from one aspect of life. We need lords and their men to have faith, not just in you, but the crown herself."

"Then why doesn't Queen Garnette show herself? I know the people are still attached to the crown – like stated; they still wear their masks."

"Is that because you still enforce it, or do they fear you still enforce it?"

"I don't want to hear this slander, continue or leave."

"The queen isn't in a state to be shown to be around the masses. They won't accept her."

"And why's that?"

"Her own personal guard, the previous king's guard, hasn't seen Garnette since she's been rescued. The absolute pain she faces daily, it's fearsome. It's cruel, and terrifying. If the masses see her, we might just get the opposite of what we want. How would you react to knowing that the kingdom is ruled by a dying woman."

"Is she dying?"

"No, but she's not well. We must not linger on this, we continue."

"Why? Is Garnette sick?"

"It's nothing to worry about for the coming future. So, we should continue."

"You're right, continue," Pias said, prodding his food.

"Though the tower has been weakened, it isn't all powerless. I say with great intelligence and planning we could wrangle small lords back to the crown. Sack those who cause problems, and eventually the tower will have its power back again, and then some. It'll start slow, but grow exponentially, eventually there'll be only two options the lords and masses can take."

"And what's that?"

"Join or die."

"It would work, but I only have one transgression. If your plan fails, it would fail spectacularly and take the tower with you. Like I said, you need to show me the results. And likewise, once the navy returns I could and might ask for their assistance."

Eiger had a sour taste on his tongue from wine Pias brought. But was it poisoned, or was it his idiocy? *The navy is far away from here. And we need to stop this city from cannibalizing itself or worse, the entire east coast.*

That night he sat at a table by himself, in his chambers, and there was a baked chicken, and other things which felt insignificant at the moment. *Do I have the manpower to wrangle multiple lords at once? I might, but the risks are all mine. I have no net to catch my fall. But I still have the church at my disposal. But will faith be enough?*

The light outside had gone away, and the sky was painted with scatterings of covered stars. They were just points of light hidden, diffused, but still there. Eiger could look out from his balcony at the maze in the back of the castle. Its depth was great and complicated. A rotation of guards had come by passing others stationed at the entrance of the maze. He watched their steel halberds shimmer from the faint sources of fire light.

The morning rose, and still he felt a lump in his stomach, a sickness. An uncertainty. And it showed. He prayed regularly. He had considered that the tower and all their watchmen would be out of his grasp, but he assumed it was unlikely they wouldn't accept his offer. Even with so many men offered, he was still denied. He spent the rest of his morning with light anxiety, while he refined his plans without the tower in hand.

The morning bells awakened with a light tone, and repetition of movement, and this image of repetitiveness was a common reality. Darien strode behind the duke, he made sure every man that sat in the cathedral hall didn't suddenly stand to present a knife, or any sharp shiv. But just in case he set men to guard outside.

They sat and waited for the sermon to begin and end. And once it did conclude the duke and the priest spoke together. He listened in, seeking lies and truths.

"Thank you for the sermon, holy father."

"And thank you, my grace. Would you like some bread, it was baked this morning?"

"No, no, I do need something else from you?"

"My grace, what else could you ask of me? I've done what you've asked of me without complaint."

"How many come here, to pray, other lords?"

"Well, low lords come often, high lords less so. And I do know many of them, if you need to know."

"Karaway, Lord Karaway. Have you heard this name?"

"He doesn't come often, but yes I have."

"So you know of him, now how well do you know him?"

"Well he is a charming lord who is always kind, but he doesn't seem like a high lord at all. After my sermon's he will converse with locals around him. And I do not know what of."

Truth, all of it, he thought while tapping his heel. Eiger propped an ear and said, "you speak of these locals? Any recurring faces? Any other lords associated with him?"

"My grace, I do not wish to speak against someone under the ceiling, and above the ground of the gods. It's great heresy, and you will not make me commit great heresy in this holy house."

"You've already spoken so much, in so little."

"Cause I put my foot down now, I will not be your spy or assassinate your grace, I'm a priest. I teach the lessons, and words of the gods. You cannot push me around like a child's wooden doll. I do what I do for the sake of the people, and greater good."

Darien detected this statement and acted accordingly, Eiger responded, "and I do too, we have something in common, we aren't fools who play in the game of larger hands. To succeed in our shared goal, we must work together. Step outside with me for a moment," he put an arm around the priest walking him out of the hold grounds.

Darien began walking towards them shortly after – to not draw too much attention. There was a short-lived shifting among those who stayed in the church. He made sure to keep a keen eye on them. He overheard what came of their conversation. "And you've heard the seemingly insignificant and rudely placed bad mouthing of lord Karaway?"

"That is what I told you, yes."

"And again have you noticed recurring faces of those commoners?"

"Sometimes yes? What is going to happen to Lord Karaway."

"I'm not worried about him, but about the effects of the things around us."

Darien pulled his attention from their talking, because of the increasing rustling from the crowds. He peered at the people, there was a man queerly gazing at him with daggers for eyes, and a dingy work coat covering anything that might be a weapon, or something more inconspicuous. Darien turned away wanting to find the truth further through the dialog. But that rustling and chair squeaks coming from behind were continually distracting. "Quiet down in the hall of the gods."

And the same man who gave him strange looks yelled out, "yer aren't praying either, why don't ya leave!"

"Why are you here?"

"Mind yer own business, old man."

"Quiet, now," he said walking out of a shadowy outskirts of the hall, and once the man saw his face, he quietly sat back down.

It felt strange why the look of his face brought the man down, but it came to him too slowly, when the door shut with a creak. He murmured something under his breath, before running after him. "That man, where did he go?" He said to the guards by the door, "over there," they pointed.

Darien yelled to them, "guard the duke!" As he left.

The man immediately ran down an alleyway trying to keep a mask on his face. He was staggering in his step. "Get away," the man said. "Piss off!" He yelled.

Darien – even in his older years – could at least make do when dealing with fleeing men. As they ran further and further away from the church courtyard, the alleys became tighter, instead of being lit naturally there were candles in boxed lanterns hanging on hooks by doorways and shop signs.

The man quickly grabbed one of the lanterns from up high, and smashed it down. The long melted wax careened to the ground, but the small flickered flame was extinguished before it fell, and it didn't stagger Darien.

They ran underpasses, and through long halls of stone, and soon came into a new part of the city. Of tall brick buildings with many people all sharply dressed in the late fashion of Queen Mary. Their porcelain masks were all perfectly glazed and painted.

The man was pushing through and weaving between people. Darien too was pushing people out of the way to keep up. He followed the stranger through an alley which had a long set of stairs heading upwards. He kept on following the man, leaving from the stairs to an alleyway on the side which could only fit two people with their backs together.

At the first open opportunity the stranger ran from one alley, down stairs, and into a town square, and before Darien could see where he went, the stranger was gone. *Damn,* he thought while observing the square. *Wait, is this?* He walked around trying to find the street and pub. *It looks so different at night. Maybe that was one of his goons?* He thought watching those around, and sweat fell from his brow.

"We're a civilized people, and we have our children to feed. And they!? What do they do!? But do nothing!"

It was a hellish morning. Black oily rain beaded on the windows, if they weren't shattered on the ground already. A pebble was thrown and cracked another window, but still he continued on, "and they don't say anything. They don't do anything!? They are supposed to be the leaders in this city. The duke, the council, the church. They do nothing!"

"If it weren't for those tall ships, I wouldn't have anything to wipe my ass with."

"They haven't even tried to attack us! It's the elites, they're causing this turmoil for not letting them at the docks."

"Yeah, it's their fault. We are suffering for them! They were foolish to try this stunt."

"They don't care about us! We're peasants to them! We aren't peasants!"

"What's stopping us from taking the docks back ourselves?"

"Yeah, what are they going to do to us!? We are the many. With each hand I'll carry a rock and pitchfork, and they'll crumble in their bricks."

"My children, my family are starving because of them."

"They killed my son!"

"They have stores of food in their cellars. Years of food. Just for them! While we starve, they eat to their heart's content!"

"That's it! I can't stand this all. They will be wrung off their food and things. For they have taken our food, our warmth, but they won't take our spirit!"

"You can't take our spirit," some started, and soon the entire hall was yelling, "you can't take our spirit!"

They stormed away, while alcohol dripped, and the light which emanated in the dark came from them. Many dozen flickering lights, where all could see bobbed down the streets letting their smoke trail behind.

"The lord's manor! City lord's manor!" They bellowed out proudly.

"Down the street, at that large one!"

The men shuffled towards the tall building, with only a lantern lighting the city council lords office. He didn't hear or see the crowd building from outside.

It was hard to keep quiet, but the crowd – in their drunken feud – were able to remain out of ear. While the old brick walls leading up reflected very little light back on their faces. Two men guarded the gates with iron bars and spikes on wooden shafts. Even at night they barked at the crowds, while leaning on their staffs, before seeing the eyes of many wolves stretching down the street.

"Get back all you!"

"He's inside!?"

"Get away from this gate, or I'll use force!"

"You and whose army!?"

They drew back before pushing the tips of their weapons through the bars, and prodding at the torch-weld intruders. They grabbed the end with their bloody hands, and the might of many pulled the guards close to the flame. The black soot crawled up his skin, and the other guard dropped his spear and pulled the other guard back. They fell back, as men were climbing the walls. The mob took up the spears against the guards, and drove their torches into the men again.

They saved the spears for a greater purpose. Their combined force easily broke down the door, and sent the flat styled flat crashing down with a thump. A head peered through one of the doors, and slammed shut with a scream as the intruders came in with their torches. The voice screamed. "Guards! Guards! Where are you!?"

A near dozen men quickly ran up the stairs as three to four guards ran down berated by the pursuers. And down it fell and the men took their newly stolen spears and grabbed the screaming woman behind that demolished door.

Another set of men with their barely unsheathed blades quickly thrusted their blades downing a few of them, but the others – in their drunken rage – only grew more vicious. The calloused hands grabbed at the guards from every possible position. They kept stabbing forward. The blood dripped down onto the ground.

"Get away!" Yelled the man at the top.

"Down with the fraud!" They yelled. "Down with the fraud!"

"Why are you doing this!?" But they couldn't hear him.

"Down with the fraud!" They yelled while grabbing his thrashing arms and legs.

They ripped the curtains and clothes from off the walls and bodies, and piled them outfront before tossing a torch and seeing the fire build into a red-hot blaze. The two spear bearers spun around the blaze, before departing the gates with their heads raised high.

Down the road the drunken mass paraded their pillaging. Microscopic embers rose and illuminated the yellowing skin and cartilage. The twinkling light bounced down the street and into the waves. The ships rocked in the distance. They danced down the cobblestones.

They marched further ahead, till they found their eyes on the keep at the top of the hill. Some had fashion new pikes and the crowd went further on. The light behind windows shown on the many enshadowed faces. Again, all was quiet – besides the shuffling of feet and kindling of flame.

Trotting could be heard echoing off walls. Their torch light illuminated the curved white steel. A dozen or more snarling mares broke through their mass. Men fell to the road, and crushed under the flesh and blood. Embers drowned into the heat of the hateful mass, and horsemen kept pushing through the line.

He stormed through the door, his candle pierced through the room flooded with soft moonlight. He held the light to the duke's son, who sat across the window overlooking the city outside. "It's time to go to the cellar, my lord."

He barely responded, and so the guard repeated, "my lord, we need to get you to safety."

But he said in a cold tone, "why?"

"I'm ordered to do so by your father, our lord. Stop crying, and follow me."

"Just stop! Please, just look out there!? They're being attacked!"

"They have come to attack and kill us all, and put your head on a twelve foot pole. Come here!"

"No! Get away from me. I'm perfectly safe here."

A shadow fell past the frame, and said, "I'll be taking this from here on. Go defend the windows soldier."

The soldier stood up straight, and swiftly left the room with a grovel in his step. "They'll be dealt with soon. There Were a dozen or three men, but our steel shines brighter."

"Even dull steel can topple a big old tree."

"Eventually it can, but not in one night. Not without other variables, but otherwise, in a night a lumberjack will break his arms before a tree like you describe would be toppled. Now if you would, please, your father, the lord, the duke, of this land, made an order, and you must follow it too. Come along."

"Fine." The young lord said while getting up from his chair.

Another shadow peered past the frame. An elongated stake fell forward, and drew blood onto the floor. The guard took the blow in the shoulder, and kicked back the intruder dressed in the same crest. "Rat!" He yelled, drawing the blade and slewing the man. "Follow me close, you're not safe anymore."

The lord could see the gate being full of men piled and flames which rose high in pillars. The faces of old women looking down from their windows shown in the dampened light. The children with sunken eyes. The white rays of curved steel shown against the light.

"They've all been destroyed."

"Those outside sure have, but here, well I don't know. And I don't know who below could be after you."

"Or how they got in."

"Yes indeed. We're going where most don't know, besides us, and your lord."

"The hidden tunnel and ladder?" And the guard nodded.

Every wall and window held a guard with a cold face. They held the halberds together, as the two of them walked underneath. Each man they passed kept their gaze averted. The young lord whispered, "are any of them . . . after us?"

"Not right now. You're safe with me. And you're safe under this roof, so don't show your worry."

They went down the corridor, a set of eyes of one man were stuck on the lord's body, and the young lord said, "you! Stop looking at me."

The guard recoiled, and looked away quickly, "sorry, my lord."

They came to a reading quarters far away from the front of the keep. Past a hidden bookshelf door, they went down a ladder into a dark and damp tunnel which echoed their steps, and little else.

"That guard was a spy."

"Possibly, but if they saw you. I don't want to make you weary this time. I'll take you somewhere I know is safe."

"Are you sure?"

"Well . . . Positive."

The clothing they wore were thrown away and replaced with more conservative garbs and hoods which covered their faces. They walked in the dying light of lamp posts towards a strange thicket within the city.

An innocent door with withering paint was opened, and they were greeted by a woman of great stature. The guard gave her a special coin, and she escorted them to the bar while saying, "I'll get your room ready," and she walked away with a sway in her hip.

They talked little over the ensuing hour and night. It was cold, and a draft entered from the window along with other sounds from outside. "Hopefully we'll be able to return in the morning or soon."

Once the day began it had seemed quiet and reserved. They walked down to the bar where the morning customers were getting an early fill. They ate what they could muster before going out. The streets felt different as they walked over the stones. His home in the distance appeared out of smoke, "you don't think that . . . " Dark sprinkles of rain began to drop down.

"It might, but we must get there first to know."

As they walked closer to those grounds, a large rumble came from the ground. "What's that?"

"We have to go, quickly. Go back."

From ahead an ensuing mob three times larger than seen at the gates last night. They tried turning back towards the inn, but from behind another mob had shown their faces. And dark clouds gathered in forces, and the rain muddied the streets and churned with the thousand souls. A thrash of lightning split down the road, forcing the water to steam with roaring heat. And the screams that whistled through the crowd which kept throwing rocks at windows and shattering ground.

Chapter Forty:

For days they waited, for rangers here and there to take their job, but all the rangers were either booked, or on holiday. And It only made Litus more and more exhausted from being jailed to the same room without escape or the excuse of chains to bind him.

There was an office in the castle to sort and try and book a trip through the forest, but after days of trying this blind charade, they really started getting desperate. At one point Litus had wondered if it would be better just to try their luck and leave. For days and days – since they'd been there – they searched through the chanceries for any available ranger. A kind yet bored woman would try and help them with the short time she had before – like the rest of the rangers – would depart on a holiday, but not yet.

Kreshen explained their situation, and in a few moments she went outback to check through some files, and other seemingly mysterious things. Until she came through a short list containing some names of rangers currently on castle grounds. She handed a copy of the list to him, and there it said their names, and where they stayed. It was mostly helpful for those who had rooms in the castle, but for those who camped outside, it would be an endeavor quite more annoying.

The list only had five names which felt slightly discouraging, they hoped that no one else was trying to book in a seemingly poor time. Having to wait precious seconds, when anything could erupt, was a lingering thought at the back of their minds.

The first names they started with were inside the castle. Though there were only two. It was a short walk to the first, and nothing, not after what felt like five minutes of knocking. Just nothing.

The next door was much more promising, since they saw a man – dressed like a ranger, and equipped like a ranger enter. So they came knocking at the door, and for a long minute there was nothing. Not a peep, or sound of breath. "I know you're there," he looked at the name, "Arbaton, I saw you enter your room. I need to travel through Mulder."

For a moment he waited for a response, but only got a sigh from the other side of the door. Kreshen responded, "I am pastor Kreshen, it's rude to ignore a man of the church from his duties."

There were sounds of shifting from the other side of the door until the door opened and Arbaton revealed himself, and he spoke both with hope and worry, "if I knew you were there, Father Kreshen, I would have addressed myself sooner. Until now I've never met you, but have heard greatly of you, Father Kreshen."

"Sing less of praises, I need use of your services."

"Well, father, I can't do that now."

"Why not, it says so on this chart. You're not booked, and not on holiday. Why can't you take this job?"

"I just can't today, nor tomorrow, what other names are on that list of yours, you best seek them instead."

"That is not an answer, why are you so weary to take this job?"

"I'm not weary, I just have priorities and can refuse a job if I want to."

"Why would you? Surely you've heard about my generosity? I will give you more than you ask for."

"No, it's not that, father. I'm supposed to be scheduled for a vacation soon, and taking a job would only delay that further."

"Push? No it should only be delayed as long as the job persists. Or otherwise I'll pray for justification."

"I don't really want prayer – especially to no one – I won't take your job, and that's that."

"You don't understand, I need to cross Mulder. It is dire."

"Again, there are more names on your list, seek them. I'm busy."

Kreshen genuinely looked scathed, he was worried that if he didn't succeed in convincing this ranger, he may have to wait for another month or two. And then he would honestly consider traversing the forest without their talents, but Litus was bored of this bickering that escalated from little. He searched through the void, believing he had something still.

"But even then, taking two, when you," he pointed to Litus, "look eerily like a wraith," his arm was prickled with bumps, "the deep web can hardly account for it, and to take him would cost me more . . . " He was cut off when Litus reached out a pouch of clanking coins, and dropped them at the feet of the ranger.

He bent down – curious of what it was, or how much there was – and with a quick glance, he muttered, "this is a lot, quite a lot. Alright. Fine. I think this can be done. I'll take it for this, if that's what you want."

"Thank you," Kreshen said, his face washing away doubt and anger, "where can I seek knowledge?"

"Oh well, the chancery is where you got that list? It's where you find more, give me some time to file paperwork, and now leave me alone."

"May the gods bless you."

She knocked at the door with a heavy thud, and the recipients immediately believed they knew who was there. Jane stepped through the doorway, and immediately sat next to Litus. "Having to sit and wait for things to happen at the top of the tower is one of the most exhausting and boring things I've ever experienced. But I think I'm getting through to Morrosey. I think in a few days he'll let us go."

Kreshen placed another log in the small fireplace, "we'll be departing soon. Been two and a half weeks, but finally, we've booked it. Especially in the most difficult time of the year."

"Well I guess I'm happy for you two."

Litus looked at her, and Kreshen asked, "what's wrong? Weary of our departure, or that we're leaving so soon?"

"I guess so," she began to feel worse, "I don't think I know."

"Would you like to pray with me?"

"No," she said quickly, "no, I won't," she slowed, "I'm sorry, I just have never been one to pray. I don't really believe in it."

"I see. That's a sad shame."

"Why? No, what am I thinking, you're a priest, and that answers it. I've never been one to pray. Never really had anyone to pray to."

"I can guide you through prayer if you'd like, my lady?"

"As if it would do any good for me. It's not like it could get any better."

"As in the world around you? It's not healthy to think like that, you're being cruel to yourself. You could never heal from self-deprecation."

"What do you mean?"

"Can you think of anything nice to say to yourself?"

"What does this have to do with prayer? I'm not in a depression, or anything. I don't pray, cause I don't see a need to pray.

"And what would I pray for?"

"That's for you to decide. So pray for anything, as long as it touches your heart."

"For something that touches my heart?" She said with a smirk; she looked down at her feet before bringing her eyes up, "how often do your prayers come true?"

"I've seen here and there, but if it does come, then it may have, or may not. We'd only ever truly know if their presence – their body – was in the room with us. And they said so."

"That's not helping your case."

"I hope someday you could reconsider, it never hurts to hope."

But what if it does?

She left shortly after, and tried to simmer her temper. Once she was alone it all came down with her. *Why? We just. Has it been a month already? I thought that. Why?* She went to the fine table in her chamber, a goblet sat on the surface, and an ornate glass flask of a clear liquid next to it. She poured the fuming drink into her crystal goblet, and clawed at the stem. "And Morrosey won't let me leave," *Litus will die, and I won't be able to do anything about it.*

She rested in a hard wooden chair. The arms that contoured her hands were worn and almost glossy to the touch from wear. "Was I the reason his life has been in danger so often?

"But I promised that I'd save him, just once. I can't let him fall. What if I pray this curse away," *What if it doesn't work?* She looked at her goblet, swirling the potent drink in her hand, "if they think I'm their queen, then why can't I stop them from leaving?"

The next day felt strange, Jane woke up with a great headache, and slouched over a chaise chair. Only faintly remembering what she spoke of, but what stood out most was that she wanted Litus to stay.

She in a short time, came to the door of Morrosey's office. Dressed in flowing sculpted bell flowers, of red and black complimenting her pale skin, and glowing long hair. She took time to make her figure appear truly noble. He was dressed the same as he'd always be, a tightly woven gambeson over a gray linen shirt. He looked out his window to check the time of day, "my grace, why are you here so early? I haven't called for you yet."

"I am the queen, and I desire an audience."

"So you do, now that you've disturbed me so, what do you desire?"

"Kreshen and Litus are going to be leaving soon."

"So they've booked an appointment earlier than I'd expected. That's good. But I think I know what you're going to ask, so go ahead and ask. You already know the answer: No."

"Assuming what I'll say, and you're still wrong. They can't leave."

"Pardon?"

"You can't let them go, it's important."

"And how so?"

"They will die, both of them. Where they're going, there is no end, but death."

"Go on."

"They believe they're some prophetical religious being that is destined to kill the gods. They'll walk into a field of death – hoping that through prayer they won't die. They're placing everything on it. I can't see them leave and kill themselves."

He went through a cabinet within reach, and pulled out a letter, "now this is the word of Kreshen, and he outlines what is to occur with him and . . . Litus. I know fully well what they plan to do. I've known Kreshen for quite a long time, and you say this endeavor will kill him most likely, so why should I believe that?"

She thought for a second, and said, "why would they be here, if it weren't the case. And have you ever heard of a faith so close, but you've never heard of it before?"

"Is it new? This faith?"

"No, it's thousands of years old. Most malkin, of old and young, don't believe in this faith, cause it's ridiculous. How can you believe in something with no reason?'

"So he abandoned his people, his church, for this?"
"He left the church to his apprentice. He's been corrupted."

"I've known him for a long long time, and long before I've become the head of this organization. I know he can be headlong, as much as steady, but never have I seen him drop everything without reason. And if what you say is true, I'd hate to stop him, because I'd hate to possibly let him die."

"So will you stop them?"

"There's two ways, either convince them to refund their booking, or convince the ranger who took their offer to drop his job."

"You can't order Kreshen?"

"I'm not a lord, nor am I a ruling monarch, and neither are you," he muttered sourly, "I cannot alone control every ranger to do my bidding. There's rules and regulations, what I do is plan the venture of this guild. I lead it, not force it. There's a great difference you could learn from when you're finally put on the throne."

"Can you at least find out who did it, who took their job?"

"That I can," and he called in a servant to go through the chancery, and find out who.

It was a grueling half hour of waiting for whoever was responsible to arrive. He came in and stood weary, not knowing why he was called to the head of the guild of all people. Not the cardinal, and not the men just below him, but Morrosey was first to speak, "you are the one who booked with Pastor Kreshen of Tabier, and," he looked to Jane for the name.

"Litus," Jane said.

"And Litus?"

He spoke up, swallowing his apparent anxiety, "yes I did."

"Well I've learnt of the recent news that gives me this grave ask of you. Can you cancel it? The booking you made with Pastor Kreshen and Litus, can you cancel it?"

Jane looked at him with weary eyes, and he looked at her confused at who she was, "well I would have, but this is different. I've come upon great rewards with taking this job."

Jane asked, "what can make you break that?"

Arbaton looked at her with confused eyes, "what can you give me?"

Morrosey growled, "you do not know who you speak with."

"Who is she then?"

"Not information you can have. What will you take?"

"What can you give?" He made a proud face thinking he had one over the head of the guild.

Morrosey flipped through some papers and documentation and found a line he liked, "before this job, you were scheduled for a holiday, hmm, today. I'll give you double and all paid for, and you'll have to return the money they gave you."

He reached at his belt for a sack of clinking change, "this? Here take it," he threw the bag onto the table letting the gold and silver coins show.

Morrosey pierced through him with daggers for eyes, "I don't want to see you, get out," he said as he started writing a letter.

Kreshen made his way to the chancery later in the day to see what instructions were set, as well as when they'll depart. He opened the door to the office, and met with the same woman who gave him that list. He – with a plain but assuring face – asked, "I've booked, and I want to know when I'll be departing."

"Sorry, what name did you book under?"

"Kreshen."

For a few minutes she sorted through the paperwork, and when she came back, she said, "I don't have anything under that name yet."

"Oh," he said, "hopefully soon," and he left.

As he walked back to his room, he made mental remarks. *They're never this slow.* So he made a short detour. He came knocking at Arbaton's door, and nothing. Maybe he was out, well it was the only real option now. Unless he was keen on staying silent whenever anyone came knocking, but that seemed quite silly now. That was unless he ran with the money, but even then it would be quite easy to deal with. The rangers guild was professional, some would say more professional than some cities or kingdoms. So he returned to his room.

In the great void he stood, and again he thought he knew he was himself. He drifted through the dark cold fog that was like a layer of sediment on the ground. No matter how hard he tried to push away this fog it stood exactly where it was. The pillars stood where they were supposed to be cutting through everything stretching upward infinitely. He again progressed through this hall of pillars; it happened very often these days. *What days? It only happened today?*

In a flash of heat he was transported to the sun. A desert of sprawling dunes of sand and ice. And the ice boiled into uncertainty. What uncertainty? And as time passed at the same time as everything, a figure unlike himself appeared to come forward. He knew he didn't know this figure, but he also knew that this figure was different from everything else. But what else was he different?

The sky opened – like a stage play's curtain – revealing all the stars viewing them like the audience, and they were the stage play actors. And the other actor knew his lines, and he said in a snake-like hiss, but also in a low rumbling like the shifting of colossal tremors far below the surface, "soon," and he waited for the other to respond.

"Soon where?"

"Here," he said as the dunes blew in the wind and the stars bled showers of light, "here, and now and then and later."

"I don't know it. When?"

"Soon," his figure trailed off in the dust of stars.

Far above in the stars, there was a murmuring of solar flares mimicking him. He did not know which. But he assumed it was he they were talking about.

The water from the ice slivered into a crevice made from a certain dune range. As he walked towards the water snakes, the dunes began to glow and emit a skin melting heat. But he still didn't know who he was, and who he would be. And as he walked closer and closer, the hills melted and purified into beautiful mounds of glass of thousands of colors. And they all pointed towards the center – where all the water snakes combined into a pool, so clear and pristine it seemed like it was crystal – and the light struck under the surface and infinitely reflected into a pure white glow. He looked into the pool and what he saw was odd. The image was a portal into another realm, a strange realm. It didn't mirror life nor death, it was a realm possibly in-between. A hand showed, and the man – now in a different form – said, "are our hands the same? Do we breathe the same breath? Do we bleed the same?"

"No."

"Why?" The man behind the portal asked.

"You are not me, nor are you we."

"I believed I knew what you were was what I thought, was that not?"

"I don't know, but I do know that you are not me. And for myself, I do not know."

"That's strange."

"What is this world?"

"Behind the portal, is a land that ages faster and slower than the waking of the dead."

"So dreaming?"

"No. You are dreaming, and you are living. I am a being of pure thought," he took his hand away and ripples of water reflected a rainbow-like radiance, "you have one final question, what will you ask?"

"Do you know about," and he thought and skewed his words to not entirely reveal it knowing if he talked to who he thought it could be was, "do you know about the destination I'm heading to?"

"You are heading west, through trees and dunes, and you will climb the mountain of Malkin's," the puddle drained into the air with sparkles following with each bead of water.

He was thrown back into the hall of pillars, it felt like home. It faded from the chill of difference from the heat of the glass mounds to the emptiness of the void. He realized he didn't walk into the desert, he was offered an invitation to view the imminent future. And he called this man after the meeting: the silent eye.

He kept walking through the void, feeling the pillar's porous stone. As he walked through the hall, he noticed a being in the distance. It was a dark shadow of a man. But as he kept chasing this figure, it continually and equally escaped him. He thought it was himself, but he believed to make out its face, more specifically, his eyes, or the lack of. The being had no eyes, and features, just the outline of a figure.

He walked to him, and soon they came closer and closer. He knew this figure, recognized him, but couldn't remember where. Where was he from, and where is he from?

It was only a small distance away, when they could notice each other, they listened to each other for someone to speak. "Are you the silent eye? The chronicler I spoke with?"

But in response he received a voice in reverse breaths, "you are not ready."

"For what? Who are you?"

"I am like you."

"You are not, but who are you?"

"You are not ready yet."

For days there'd be nothing. In the chancery where they stored most if not all relevant articles of information, is also where they were supposed to find that ranger: Arbaton. But no matter who they asked, they could reach him. They couldn't find him. No information on when to depart, and what to expect. Nothing.

The next day, Litus came with him, one in search of Arbaton, and Kreshen went to the chancery. He said his concerns but with that specific name, and the responses he got were quite odd. But that may have been his strange arrival, seen with a man who wasn't certain to be a man at all, and a woman who for some reason had a graceful stride. Even still it was Arbaton's name which gave a different response.

The next day, Kreshen again tried to find out anything, absolutely anything about these conspicuous rangers. *We've been told to reach out for anything. I've never seen the guild be this unhelpful, this dysfunctional. I'll let Morrosey know about this ranger.* He would have, but that would be if he didn't have to worry. It was quite tedious to get the same silence day after day. But maybe it was just a repetition of idiocy, so Kreshen backed off for the day.

Again for the next day, Kreshen went through the loop of asking for nearly an hour of anything, but was presented with nothing. For a tempered priest, this caused him to grind his teeth. *Fine then*, he thought as he left the chancery, and he decided to check the bailey for any rangers who he could ask about.

There was one man sharpening his swords, passing the blade over a flat stone repetitively. Another was passing a sword over leather straps, deburring the blade and polishing it. Kreshen walked up, and said, "greetings on this holy day."

"What is so holy about it, if I do ask priest?"

"I guess both everything and nothing. Do either of you know of a ranger named Arbaton?"

They both looked at each other, one shook his head, but the other said, "I know him, or know of him. If you want to know anything about him, it would be better to ask them in the chancery."

"I assumed that, but the problem is, I can't get a straight answer about him, or anything else about what I need to do before we depart."

"Depart? Don't know him too well, but I'm certain he's taking a job, either that or he's on holiday."

"Well he's taken my job."

"Why don't you ask him?"

"Father Kreshen!" Yelled Sean the gypsy, running towards him.

"I didn't realize you were still here. I haven't seen you around for a while. Where have you been?"

"Around I guess. Besides, I could ask you the same."

"Well, Litus and myself are stuck in the mud currently. They are disturbingly quiet about all of this."

"Well I guess I'll pray for you, but in a way it's better that you're still here."

"Why's that?"

"You two are the most interesting men I've ever met. And besides being stuck here, having you two to speak with kills the time. And not only that, if you wait enough you might be able to book with our ranger, what was his name? Elliot?"

"Yes, that would be gracious of him, but we have already been booked and are trying to depart soon. We're just trying to find our departure information."

"I get that, I'd just assume that kind of information takes time, cause they're so cautious, or something like that. Just tossing rocks, really."

Kreshen kept suspicion close, and chose his question carefully, "well, when we do leave in a few days, you'll be short of company, I assume."

"If I could, can I join you guys. I'm just fascinated and want to record your journeys."

"Then why'd you travel out . . . "

"We gypsy folk can change plans on a dime, and I think I might just change mine."

"That seems brash, and I'm sorry I can't let you join us."

"Well that's a bit cruel," Kreshen was taken aback, "after all I helped you all."

"That's a large step in logic, my son. You may be confused, but we traded. You agreed to that trade, we both agreed. There is no debt."

"I'd assume a religious man such yourself would realize that debt goes deeper than that."

"Sorry son, but to me it doesn't in this case."

"Then I'll pray for your travels, best of luck, best of the certain and uncertain. Good day to you and Litus. Wherever he is," and he walked away into a crowd, and almost immediately he was gone from sight.

Kreshen – worried about Litus – rushed back to the room to ensure his safety, but to his hope, Litus was both unscathed and untouched. Kreshen sat in his chair wondering about that man, what had really caused that outroar. That hatred. And in the back of his mind he pondered that for the rest of the day.

Chapter Forty-One:

He was garbed in his finest cloth, in a sense he looked kingly; he wasn't the monarch, but he was the mock-ruler, and he purposefully decorated himself in these garbs to try and present a larger figure. An intimidating figure, for he never saw this lord Karaway, and assumed great things about his description from the priest and Bishop Lazith.

He purposely set his court in a previously dusty and almost completely unused small dance-room on the other side of the castle. But one of the reasons he chose it was a single hallway on the far east wing on the second floor with a wall of mirrors and a wall of glass overlooking the massive garden in the center of the hedge maze that sprawled to what appeared to be the horizon.

With a calm before the wind Eiger used his resources to create an image to mentally dwarf this lord long before he came to his door, but the time was still passing without his arrival. Though it was still the morning, so Eiger stood still.

More time passed. A half hour? Maybe an hour? He had a cup of champagne while waiting, and it grew flat in those fleeting moments. He only prodded at it.

There was a light creaking from the door as one of his guards let it open for – the assumed – Lord Karaway, and the lord strode with a seemingly uncaring swagger in his step. And he looked at Eiger with his purposeful confident blinders on, he didn't even notice the other men in his room, including Darien, and a high ranked member of the king's guards. But maybe Karaway only kept his eyes on Eiger cause he knew that the others wouldn't be threats.

Eiger changed his posture by increasing his elevation, and his eyes met Karaway's below him. Eiger made a short acute breath making sure to ask the first question, "Lord Karaway, I assume, you are finally here, I was expecting you to be damp from the snow before you ever step through that door. But I'm glad you received my letter, and returned a letter back very quickly."

"You assumed correct. I was hampered, dragged by my acquaintances, but now I'm here."

"You let your servants keep you late?"

"No, no. Not them. I don't have many servants as of now. But don't worry so much about my servants. What reason am I here?"

"You have affiliations with the church, do you think that is to clear your conscience?"

"Of course, I donate to the church often, and believe in repentance."

Eiger drew cold eyes on the lord, "you repent your sins, all of them."

"Yes."

"Yes? Is that it? Then all you do is repent your sins, wouldn't you eventually have repented all your sins? That is unless you keep producing sins you keep feeling the need to repent for."

Karaway sat up, getting out of his chair, and paced around before stopping and staring out an ornate window. "Far out there," he pointed outside, "that is my priority, my responsibility. I take good care of it. Of them. It happened quickly the devolution of the streets, people were bound to break the walls of others. I help them. I do."

"Alright, why would committing charity be putting civilians in harm?"

"Excuse me?" He puffed, removing his coat and tossing it in his previously sat chair, "that is slander. I've never done anything to put people in harm, that's vile. And I say that is slander."

"Put down your voice. I don't consider it slander, unless you could prove otherwise."

"What do you think I've done? In fact, why am I here?"

"Let me make this quickly clear, you are accused of running and profiting from robbery, and governing a crime-rink."

He looked at the duke with a vibrantly horrific face, he was completely aghast, "so you think I give to the church only to what? Guide my conscience?"

"If you could supplement a truth to remove this guilt, your guilt, then do it. But you can't, for I have the real truth of you, of your crimes."

"True, is that what you call truth? You haven't given me any reasons to believe there's a horrible criminal in this room, and too that it was me. What do you do? Are you the second in command to the queen? Because if so, saying you're dealing with the worst by putting those you don't like on stakes isn't a noble thing at all," he paused, grasping at a breath, "you aren't dealing with the lords running the crime, I am. I am the only one keeping the peace."

Eiger stopped him, and said, "do you think I'll put you on a stake, you're sorely mistaken. Hmm, you know," he said softly and confidently, "maybe I'm the one mistaken, and you're in the right. Since you're fighting an apparent uphill battle, what are the names of the men causing this organized crime? Surely if you're affected so much by this terror, you'd know of the men who caused you this struggle."

"What do you mean?"

"I felt I was crystal clear who is causing you this mischief. You stated that lords were hoarding the ex-soldiers. Which lords are causing you such grief?"

"I don't think I could tell, since I know not their names."

Darien made a slight movement that made Eiger wince at, and

he said, "that was a lie. Don't refute this, I know this. I know you just lied. You can't hide it now."

"Hide what, what knowledge of what am I supposed to know of? I don't know their names."

"You do, indeed."

Karaway noticed Darien's slight movement and uproared, "you've hired a truth-wizard to try and catch me!? But can your parlor tricks know the reality that I'm a holy man, and a charitable man. What you think is crime, is in fact governance. I am a noble man, who doesn't accuse others without knowledge. I am a righteous man, and a good man. The ones who bring chaos are the men of the unfaithful."

"Do not lie to me, do not say pretty words to try and inspire me, and do not try to weave this web, this image of holy supremacy over me as though you've taken a risk. Let's not prod here, you run a crime rink, you enforce your power over the common man. And I know of your men, your criminals who beat up old men over petty squalor. Do not lie to me, I will put your ass in an iron box and let the salt water rust it away."

"You slander me, I do not fester the crime, I try to break it. I don't have the manpower like other lords, nor the wealth, but I try to keep the peace. The men who act like a tyrant are those with small armies, made of the men separated from the army. I do not run some crime rink. I'm a good righteous man, a good queen's man too. I would never go so low as to threaten someone, like you," he got up, quickly draped his coat over his shoulders, and said to Eiger in a sarcastic grovel, "good day my grace, and may it be a good one," and he left the room.

Eiger barked at his men, "bring him back here, and keep him till I say so!" And immediately they left after him.

A few minutes later the doors were kicked open, and Karaway was thrown in the chair, while men stood by.

"You will not do that here, I can have you stripped of everything you own, by fire if I wanted. I will strip you of your titles and loved ones with the snap of my fingers," Eiger calmed his voice, but his eyes stayed piercing through Karaway's skull, "you will stay, until I tell you to leave. You will speak when I tell you to. You will blink when I instruct you to. Do you understand?"

"Yes," he said looking up at one of the tall men stationed right next to him.

"Do you know what is below the dark tower?" He pointed to the wall past the brick and air, the tower stood, and the image of the tower was in their mind, "do you know what makes the foundation?"

"You're going to have me executed!?"

"Down below, what makes the foundation of the tower is a prison. A prison far older than the bricks stacked high currently. There is where you'll be, but not executed. Far below, in a world without light. In the cold, and in the damp rat infested walls. And when you try to end it all, they'll find a way to resuscitate you, they always do. And if you starve they'll force feed you the bare minimum to breath. You'll be a prisoner until your heart cracks, and above the surface no one who you ever loved, or loved you will ever know your name, as your face is erased from their minds. That is what I give you, or I could let you go."

"Please," he cried, "I have a family, please just let me go."

"Then what are the names of your constituents?"

"There's three of us, myself, Lord Garet, and Lord Taryen. We each took control of blocks of the city. Please, will you let me free?"

"The land you control is now under my jurisdiction, and I'll make sure you remember. Your thugs are mine. You wont give a command unless I command you. And you will speak none of this to these other lords, and you if your men attack or mug anyone, or even try, or think. You'll never see the light of day again," he reclined back on his throne, and said to Lord Karaway, "now get out."

"Yes, your . . . grace," and he was pushed out and prodded till he saw the castle's tiled towers.

"So there's two more to deal with. And they have a sizable chunk of the defected army," he sat scratching his jaw, "now if the other two lords were this simple to coerce as this one, it'd be easy to do."

"It would still take a few weeks to find them, and convince them to come. I think in all respects we lucked out here."

"I do too. We don't know yet how much he had control over."

"Now with Karaway now a mouse in a cage, won't that leave the other two to fight over his domain?"

"His domain will still seem like his, before we take his men, make them soldiers. And heavily enforce those streets. And if I play my cards nicely, I should force whomever is the last of these lords to surrender, before too long."

"Then how do you determine you'll capture the other lords occupied land?"

"I believe what I've done here could warrant a discussion with old Pias."

"It could be a risky and dangerous idea."

"How so?"

"If those other 'lords' realize this plan, they might start throwing more coins towards Karaway's men. And they might even try to siege his lands, and then innocents would be in a grave situation. If he doesn't take the entirety of this, he might butt heads with you. I say it's better to leave the tower for the last, when we have the most men."

"Hmm," Eiger scratched his chin, "that is quite a predicament. If Pias doesn't accept my offer, he might go ahead with my current information and capture the lord's men for himself. But if I can convert men to soldiers quickly, and possibly get more redeemable lords at my table, then they won't be a threat, and that'll leave rebuilding the army in a difficult state."

"If this fails, it'll be a bloody mess."

"Yes indeed."

The streets reeked of filth, but even a seamen – such as himself – hated having to stand on the rocking floorboards of a naval vessel. But the ground of this island, of this city, was uncertain. Though the streets rank of shit, there were cheering and screaming over fire and crying, but what was heard over it all was that cheering.

It was a victory, and also his largest endeavor since becoming the grand admiral. It was a grand triumph, and now as he walked the ash caked streets, he relished in all the glory. Near the center of the city was a large garden, kept to remind its inhabitants of the nature they relinquished, but now what stood was a grand stage of gallows quickly built by the naval officers, and some of the thin stricken residents.

Tylock walked around surrounded by his troop of men with their hands on their swords, or fists clenched around their billhooks. His boots remained clean from all the dirt, ash, and other contaminants embedded in the ground. It was a small wonder no one stared daggers at him, or tried to stick a blade in him, for his propaganda was his shield. And the people bowed to the ground when they realized he was there.

Tylock himself was dressed head to toe in the finest of clothes that could be nabbed, a clean cut and sewn linen tunic, and his boots stained days prior. The cold blued and blackened steel of his buckles and ranking stars and the exposed hilt of his sword must have been cast and polished with hard diamond for weeks before he donned them. The edge of the sword itself must have been forged out over the span of a generation with how pristine it was assumed to be. Not a speck of dust stayed.

But the siege was over, and the gates to the city were open, and the border ports were seized by the navy, but the people still cheered. That's all they knew would break the hunger. Tylock had commanded lines of bread and soup to be set up in this same square. Surrounding the now yellow square were tall buildings of stone, almost cathedral like, including a cathedral that stood tall, maybe not as tall as the one in Porcelania, but not many structures were that tall on their own.

He walked into the cathedral where he was expected and was greeted by men in robes of three colors. They were the priests of the church, but each had donned a robe for each of their teachings. One man wore a robe of back, one a robe of gray, and another a robe of red. And the red robed priest was the finest garbed of the three. Tylock greeted each formally, saying very little, and presenting a seemingly lovely smile.

But he was escorted by the priest in red robes upstairs, and he came to an open balcony with other navy men waiting, and his guards stood out to guard him. Tylock watched from higher up at the people down. And almost immediately the masses noticed him above. He noticed their rags with splotches of white or beige in the cloth of mixed browns, reds, and some green, and blacks. But it mattered not what they wore, they were his people now.

Tylock said to one of the men next to him, "have them sent," and Tylock took out of his coat pocket a folded blue letter, and he spoke loudly and greatly, "for years, and years there has been a plague in this country and this city. But that ends today, and that ends here.

"I have come from the capitol on a mission to return this country to the days of gold and prosperity that was exempted from you all. The navy and I have rescued you all from the terror you live in. Look at the ash on the ground, and look at the filth packed in the cracks of the cobblestone, they did this to you. Your ports were swamped with piracy and crime, but not anymore. Your stomachs were empty, and children were injured, but not anymore. We shall bring justice to those who deserve it.

"In the history of this country, there have been times of hardship, and there's been times of corruption, but not anymore. There's been time of war, and there's been time of greatness, and we shall achieve those. And throughout our history, there have been those who oppressed us. Twenty years ago we were attacked by the kingdom to the east. Their ships met ours, and many men fell in those times, but today is different. The threat is different. A hundred years ago, there was an insurgence and worry of heirlooms which threatened our way of life, and that won't happen again. Today there will be a civil duty to uphold morality and humanity."

The rattling of chains stood in the new ambiance as a line of dozens of men were forced to walk. They used to be the noblemen and the high priest of the church: Bishop Barley. There were lords and city council officials, even the duke of Charian: Duke Ester was in the line. Their clothes, be it once fine linen and silk, were now torn and fecal smeared, and covered in dust and debris. It looked clawed at with dull knives, and pulled at by the hands of the desperate. But now they all were in this line, chained together with the rusty rattling end of the line.

"They once ruled this city with a tight grip, letting you all go hungry when in need, they steal what you have, and still tax you. Now look at them in their chains, this is the judgment they deserve, this is the judgment enacted on them by the gods.

"I have brought you peace and prosperity and food and clean clothes. The navy has rescued you from this tyranny. They were the problem in our society, they are the problem no longer. We will deal with the rats who chew our walls, how a rat deserves."

The men were pushed with a bound mace of sticks, and whipped with thin branches. They walked barefoot over the trash and the long dead grass. One by one each of the noble men, and city officials were stripped of their cold iron bindings and forced onto a chair. The loop of rope above is all they felt which wasn't cold but bare and filled with pins.

Bishop Barley looked at the people who he a month, or even a week or two prior was giving sermons and trying to keep some respect and humanity to the people he oversaw. Tears welled in his eyes as the people who he cared for only sought the kick of the chair under his feet.

"Back in the city of Porcelania I have bled for them, I remember the days where a fire being set was an inexcusable act of horror and treason. I was there to command and throw buckets of water on the fires that were spread from inside castle Renoi. And I bled that day, and you all bled together. Let this be your day, and let the day after that be your day too. And the day next, and the one after. Don't let the oppressors take your freedom, your families, your food. I have freed you, now take back your lives. Let me gift you your lives back."

There was a creaking from the wood boards below as their weight shifted uneasily. The crowds around began to cheer louder and louder, until all that could be heard was their shouting. Tylock continued to speak, but it all seemed to blend in. The Bishop cried as he watched the rest of the line glance over at him, and quickly advertise their eyes knowing their immediate fate.

The wood creaks were no longer loud. Nothing was, except when a series of men grabbed the backs of their chairs, and pulled hard. And then all the crowds went silent as they heard – just for a second – the crack of a dozen men.

"For what they've done they deserve worse than mercy. But we are the fortunate people, we aren't oppressors, we give mercy when needed. And a quick death is mercy, pain is what they seek to gain sympathy and is what they both do and don't deserve, and they won't receive it. We must make a hard decision and cleanse what we can.

The crowds roared with fury of fire crackers. The next dozen lords and politicians were unchained and put on the old wooden chairs.

"We will see a new light!"

Their chairs rocked with the ruckus of the sound they people made.

"We will bring a new peace!"

They tried to pray, but their hands were tied behind their backs.

"We seek what we must."

They looked at all the people, as the people began pulling the chairs from underneath their feet.

"And like the church, may we pray for peace and prosperity, and hope for good times."

They fell, all of them in succession of their predecessors, and the people roared.

"May you eat well, for we shall keep supplying till you grow healthy and strong. I will see to it, I will see to it all. Those who oppressed you are dead, the rats are dead. And you all are free from their curse. You're free. You may govern your homes for you are people of this country, you may elect and gain lands, for you are the people of this country, and you will rest safely knowing they are dead, and we are here."

And the people all around roared and chanted in unison, "long live the queen. Long live the queen. We are now free, and long live the queen."

"Long live the queen," he said, and Tylock repeated those words in his mind, *long live the   queen. For what I've bestowed upon them, they chant that tone.* He roughly folded his letter, pulled his coat around his torso, and stuffed the note roughly in his pocket. He bowed to the people, with a smile on his face, and muttered, *so long live the queen. Long live the queen. I'll find you Garnette, I'll find you Jane, cause the queen must live long it seems. You must live long and prosper.* He walked away from the balcony, thinking of golden hair.

Chapter Forty-Two:

Was it now a week when their ranger had disappeared from thin air, their money gone, their bills stacking up soon? Litus watched Kreshen become frustrated by the lack of knowledge being released, and by the organization – he thought he knew – was not turning a different light, nor revealing a new mask.

Just because Kreshen was worried didn't mean that Litus wasn't either. He just wasn't able to speak about his worries, but he knew that Kreshen was aware of both of their worries. So they remained where they were, and continued considering what to do.

It was midday at this time, they were about to give up their search for the day, when a knock was presented to them. Jane came in and sat next to Litus, and made herself at home, and asked, "why are you two so uncomfortable? What happened?"

Kreshen sighed, and said, "for days we've tried to find our Ranger Arbaton, and then we spent days asking the chancery anything we'd need to know before departing, and still nothing. We're tired of waiting, and tired of the silence."

"That sounds awful, I hope you find him soon."

"I do too, we gave him a sack of gold, and now he seems to have run away with it."

"Hmm," she thought, "I feel bad for you."

"My grace, I know of your visits and office with Morrosey, could you ask him of this transgression? We have been robbed at his expense, and now we are set back a much longer time than we wanted."

"If my word is anything, you might have to stay here, since winter is coming soon."

"I'm sorry, my grace, we can't."

"And why not?"

"This pilgrimage we're walking is important, and time is important to pace. Setback could mean we never seek our goal altogether."

"I understand, I do. I'm sorry this ranger did this to you two. But I'm here, if you need me, I'm here, and I think I'm going to be staying here for a while too, but at least there's comfort being around you two."

"I don't think Litus or I would hate it, in fact if you would like to come back later for tea we certainly wouldn't reject that notion."

"Thank you, I might have to take you up on that offer, but goodbye for now."

She left, and Litus noticed a certain grace in her step, one that wasn't there when they first met. It's almost comical to think she would be the queen's heir, but Litus certainly knew it more than she, though he did not know why for certain. Even though Jane had been uncomfortably and forcibly forced into this noble-like role, it seems to now stick to her, but hopefully not all the difficulties of the nobles, but hopefully not the politics.

There was this faint scent of clean fragrant soap, but he didn't know the scent. The smell lingered in the room with them as they waited for something related to a ranger to come.

After a few minutes of pondering, there came a knock at the door. It seemed odd that Jane would come back so early, unless she went directly to Morrosey to dispute this problem on their behalf. But no, it wasn't Jane, the knock was different. Kreshen came to the door, and the person who was on the other side, was not Jane, nor a queen, and neither a woman. It was a ranger returning from Tabier.

"My, my, are you back so early!? Come sit down, and let me boil a pot of tea. Elliot, what brings you here?"

"Pastor Kreshen, I promised when I returned I'd come to visit you at once. I was able to make the journey far faster than I expected, and I thank you. I assume you must have prayed the storm away."

"I pray indeed, it just seems to be a little late."

"When do you mean?"

"I was praying everyday while riding through the storm, and it seems to fall away with our travels."

"Yes, it did. Other than a few sprinklings of rain, the storm was essentially gone, for a week it rained hard, but it and its effects were surprisingly little. I just assume the ground took all the rain, and put it somewhere else."

"That's good, but I must ask you something important."

"Oh, what is it?"

"We need your help, will you take us through Mulder? Can you take this job?"

"Hmm," he said, flushed and fluxed, "I'm on holiday, but I can take your job after that."

"No, that's not what I meant. It may seem rude of me, but can you take our job today?"

"Like I said, I can't. Is there no ranger who could take your job? Have you checked the chancery?"

"We have, and we have had a job with another ranger, do you know of anyone named Arbaton?"

"Arbaton, not really. Wait, no I have, but ask if I can tell you the color of his hair, and I couldn't. If he had hair."

"Well we contracted a job with him, and he seems to have run away with our money. We've gone to the chancery, but they seem to not even know he exists, and soon we won't have enough to stay here, and it's important we get through Mulder."

"That's strange, quite strange, the guild never has this kind of problem. We have procedures to ensure this doesn't happen."

"But it has happened, and we don't know what to do next."

"Okay, I'll go ahead and take your job, but only if you can wait out one and a half more weeks, when my holiday is over," and shortly after Elliot left, and both Kreshen and Litus were struck.

They didn't have much money left anymore, and especially not enough for two more weeks. If they spent the rest of their money at basically the beginning of their pilgrimage, then what would they do to get supplies? Food? All they had was what Kreshen carried with him. Kreshen then said, "I'll be back."

He left for the chancery. And once there he asked for a list of any available rangers, but there were none whatsoever. The woman there was nice, but it didn't help. They were out of chances, and it appeared clear on Kreshen's face when he returned.

"What can we do now?" Kreshen asked himself, "all we can do is hope that Morrosey can extend our time here. No, Morrosey wouldn't do that, what are we going to do? He leads this guild with an iron fist, but won't raise a hand. What are we going to do?"

Litus realized all they could do was try to get Elliot to take their job. Somehow, they'd have to bargain quite a bit, but what had they to bargain? Not money, they had little, but Litus thought of something, and it could be something to buy a great many rangers, if need be.

The morning sky was cold with a crisp chill like a fresh apple. Outside the walls were a series of small campfires, with men roasting chickens and various vegetables on a spit. And that is where Litus and Kreshen found Elliot practicing the sword just shy from the heat. Litus watched for a split second as he began a duel, and within a blink it was over. Elliot went over to offer a hand, and was surprisingly greeted by the two of them.

"Pastor Kreshen, good to see you, have you found someone to take your offer?"

"Unfortunately my son, we haven't. That's part of the reason we're here now."

"I'm sorry, but I cannot take your job, not yet at least."

"We do know that, but we have something to offer."

"And what's that?"

"Do you know of the tale of the plain's knight?"

"The plain's knight, of course. It's something I learned when I was young, it's not some fairy tale?" And he chuckled.

"Indeed, if you can take our job, we'll give you the reward we reaped from one."

"That's incredible, but wait what do you mean you came across a plain's knight?"

"Well in our travels, before we entered the storm, we came across a silence, a fog wall and a bridge over a trench with a man of rusted armor standing there. Litus fought him, and won, and the knight fought with not a sword or spear or whatnot."

"What did he fight with?"

Litus drew into the void; plenty of men fell to the ground in fear as he pulled out the large enchanted scythe. Though it didn't appear special – although they were told it – Elliot gave a strange eye to it before he cared for the display, "a scythe!?" He mused.

Kreshen moved back, "an enchanted scythe in fact, and we're sure it was not done by any enchanter, but by the plains themselves."

"How do you conclude that?"

"The plain's knight used it against us."

"What did he do?"

Litus turned away from all the people, to the open ground where a lonely campfire sat. He swung the scythe once, and a visible ripple ravaged through the air towards the fire. And once it met, it shook the fire, causing it to wobble with the crashing of a wave, and after it was extinguished. The smoldering pit was a long distance away, and still it went out like a candle.

"That ripple in the air, is that similar to what you can do father Kreshen?"

"Quite so, and what I call it, is weaving. The plains enchanted it so, and the plain's knight was using weaving against Litus."

"Now one thing I know about enchanted items is that they break easily."

"As you use the enchantment it decays further and further, but the enchantment put into this scythe is great, I'm not sure you could use all the magic stored in it before you die of old age."

"Bah, I won't make it to then," he let out a sigh, "I'm sorry father I cannot accept this."

"And we were afraid you'd say that."

"Father," he broke in, "that's not what I meant. I can't accept this, because it is far greater than what I can provide."

"Please Elliot."

"Fine, but if I must, Litus I want to duel. I assume you defeated the plain's knight, and now that I know they were real, I'd like to fight one too, or better yet the one who won. So do you accept my duel?"

A duel for a job, fine. And Litus nodded. He put the scythe back into the void, and withdrew the two handed falchion for the first time in far longer than a month. He mesmerized the blade as it glinted in the faint light from a fire.

They stood three paces apart, letting only an arm's distance between the tip of their blades. They spun around, such like the turning of storm clouds. A vast whisper could be heard from the crowd who lingered to see the fight between the known and unknown. A man and a shadow.

And at once, like lightning their blades met. Was it over, not yet. Their blades contacted over and over again, with parries and blocks, and a swing and stab here and there.

Litus immediately noticed something different with Elliot, then he had with all others he had fought. *He's testing me, to know if I'm a predator, or prey.* Litus tried to break up the monotony of test, stab and parry. He threw a different strike. He crouched down and leaned up into a stab, knowing it would amount to little, but to see change in tactics that Elliot would do. Elliot grabbed his sword by the flat of the blade, and with a precise guard and push, he forced his blade close to Litus. Closer than comfort.

Litus shifted back, and got up to Elliots level. Again they twisted around a point, but now there was a new difference to it. There was a darkness of overlapping shadows. A complexity that seemed from the outside simple.

The crowds around them grew little by little, and a chant had begun as a murmur from a few individuals started them.

Elliot drew away, putting his pommel close to his waist, and it seemed like he was waiting. They shifted around the point still. This waiting game continued for one to make the next strike. For one to end, or to continue the standoff.

Elliot decided to break that stalemate, he lunged forward with a quick thrust, but as he came to Litus, he raised his sword into a block and put their blades together only for a brief moment. Litus drew back and came forward, and he too had his blade blocked. Litus quickly put his palm against the flat of his blade, and tried to twist his blade down towards Elliot's hands.

Elliot retracted his blade, and jumped back. "Hmm," he said, "the good clear day is so refreshing, It won't matter who's the winner is," he held his long sword outstretched by the pommel, and said, "it's quite neat."

It was quick, he ran forward swinging his blade forward, but fainting the strike and baiting for Litus' timed blocks to fall. But Litus took a few steps back, and held his blade out high. He caught a few taps from Elliot. Again he was being tested, and to larger extremes.

Litus twisted his blade around Elliots, and when he went into his second twirl he instead feigned and reached out for a simple stab. Elliot quickly backed off, while making a grunt while doing so.

"Let's stop dancing, and start fencing from now on," he said with a grin upon his face.

Elliot stepped forward elegantly and swiftly swung his sword from side to side. Litus in return met his steel with parries of his own. They matched blade for blade, with the tapping and reverberance shaking in his hands.

The storm swirled into a dark malice-like funnel, where it was all turned into a fiery tornado of explosive repulsion. Lightning was sucked into this vortex, and striking so often it quickly turned from a push to a pulsating reverberance of steel meeting steel.

There was a certain effect on all who watched when they saw the virtuosity clashing that caused their chanting to grow – though it were all to Elliot – it drummed up their duel furthermore.

Eventually they had begun coming closer, and swinging wider. There were shreds of some red tinged fiber being flung throughout the air and clinging to the weaves in clothes. It was all in a certain repetition, that either found hard to break off a strike, block, parry, and strategy. But strategy almost seemed impossible to think of. There was too much to focus on at once. Litus tried coming even closer to bind their blades for a brief second, but to his surprise, Elliot drew back. He maneuvered around quickly, causing Litus to have to turn to match him.

"What will come next?" He proclaimed, before feigning his attack, not once but twice going into a block.

Litus, expecting an attack, reached out to parry, but was met with Elliot's blade, slamming into one of his quillons. He raised his crossguard up, knocking it out, and went to attack, but was met with a block.

The clouds ravaged, the moisture that was present burst into flame. Sweat worked naught, and the lightning eventually disappeared, becoming a part of the ambiance.

Litus backed away, and lunged forward, his blade forward, heading down. Elliot with a surprisingly wide swing rose his blade from low to high to meet Litus' blade and he subsequently twisted it out of the way as well. Litus' hadn't known how, but his blade fell from his hand and to the ground.

Elliot stood blade raised high to Litus, before falling, and he proclaimed again, "it seems I have won," and the people around him roared.

Elliot picked up the blade for Litus, and once the clouds broke apart and dissipated, Litus could realize how injured they both were, especially Elliot. But he certainly didn't seem to care. Though his own cloak was only tattered around his sleeve ends. Now he realized that Elliot was thinking the entire time, and Litus accepted the loss.

So just like stated, Litus withdrew the scythe from the void and presented it to Elliot, and with childlike glee, Elliot began inspecting it himself. He came to them, and said, "meet me tomorrow, at this time, at this location. I won't be disappointed, and we'll leave only a few days after that."

Kreshen walked up to them, "and so we will."

Chapter Forty-Three:

Days had passed, and Jane was frustrated with her forced occupation here. There was always this feeling at the back of her mind, that the cult would catch up to her. Even though the ones clearly told were looking for her, were Tylock's navy. But still the mental image of the fire that ravaged, and the parasite that came from the queen's body, and this cult would do that to her too.

When she walked to his door, her guards followed behind and in front, and the guards at Morrosey's door looked slightly dismayed. *What were they up to? Did they finally find me, is this where I'll lose my humanity?* No matter how much she pleaded, Morrosey never listened. He was stuck in his ways, never changing from Eiger's letter.

When she walked in, there weren't any cultists with sharp daggers. Morrosey sat alone spinning his silver ring around his finger. He was clearly waiting for her, and he knew something grave, but Jane couldn't let him say anything first, so she barked, "you have to let me leave, please, they're coming."

"I know," he said.

"What!?" Jane said strangely and confused, "what do you mean?"

"They're here, and for what I know it's not the navy – which I'll get into momentarily – but I believe it's this cult you spoke of."

"Well I did tell you so."

"I do not work from superstition, I work from what is evident, and what is true is that some force, some cult has breached this keep and now you'll have to leave," he said, "and I know this to be a cult, because there isn't a commodore, or captain in the room with us presently."

"Alright then, well, where will I go? Eiger's keep couldn't be safe, and I for certain can't go to Porcelania."

"Indeed that's a good question, because where you'll go is across the forest."

Jane looked at him perplexed, "you're going to put me in danger to keep me out of it?"

"The guild is specialized at traversing the cursed forests. You'll be fine."

"How did you know they're here?"

"Eiger sent me two letters, one by pigeon, and the other hand mailed. And I had other paperwork written about you and for you specifically, and do you know what went missing without any eyes noticing, including mine?"

"The letter?"

"All of it. Everything is gone, and do you know what letter I've received this morning?"

"I don't," she said with goosebumps forming down her arm.

"A presumed letter from Navy High Command. And inside is a command of search and seizure for you and your wraith-like friend."

"No," she said with a layer of despair, "Is this not the navy command? What will you do with them?"

"The letter isn't formatted correctly for the navy, and I'll have a ranger send for their leave, but I need to deal with you first. You're the top priority."

"Then when will I leave, I want to tell my friends-"

"You will not be relating anything to these 'friends' of yours. None whatsoever. You're going to be leaving without a trace, and to the best of my ability, no one, not even most of my rangers will know you've left. I want it to be like you've never been here. And that's why you're not leaving right now, but later by dusk."

Jane walked fast around the halls, and she quickly got out of reach of her guards, and the hands of the rangers who were assigned to her. She pounded on his door, she said in a loud voice, "please Litus, are you there?"

Jaune came to her side, "be quiet, there are others who are watching."

"But, where are they? Did they leave?"

"I don't know, they may or may not have."

"Can you check please."

"Fine," he said reluctantly.

Jane returned to her room, and soon later so did Jaune, and he said, "I couldn't find them, my lady. I'm not sure if they left, but I couldn't find them, but please don't go looking."

Jane wanted to leave and search for them herself. She ever so did, but for some reason she stayed compliant. But most of all she felt despair. Again, it felt like she failed. Her friends just fell away from her fingers, from her grasp. *They were here only a few days ago, and now will I ever see them again? If only for a little while longer. And I tried to keep them from going. But, if only.*

It was darkened by now, plenty of campfires were kindled, their smoke rising high. The party of travelers consisted of herself, her four guards, and two rangers who professionally kept to themselves. Jane and the guards rode off on their great war horses from the duke, and the rangers rode on their own horses – who compared – were leaner. They had a few covered bundles of sticks as well as more than a week's rations of smoked meats and bread and butter.

The forest didn't seem too dark, but it changed only a minute from walking through. Their war horses almost immediately were spooked. Jane looked behind her expecting to see the castle camps directly behind them, but it was like an infinite mirror of forests.

One of the rangers moved to the back of the line, and the other led it. Jane watched their motions as the shadow of the forests created a dark vignette around her vision. Little specks of white dust fell from above. They fell coldly on the back of her hand, and delicately rested on the individual hairs on her head, and she said in both amusement, and contempt, "it's snowing."

The snow – even though it didn't appear to fall quickly – packed on the ground quickly, and almost unrecognizable at first. The light faded completely, and all the light they had were from boxed lanterns lit by the flickering flame of candles. This light flickered and little reflections of sparkles came back to them where they danced on the legs and body of their mares and themselves.

Over an hour happened almost instantly, and that realization hit like stone against steel. The darkness was everything that wasn't their candle light. And those little sparkled reflections felt like a shield, when the noises began.

It was like scuttling, at first. Just normal animals in the forest, but soon there was a loud thumping, a smashing sound of a creature far larger than seemingly possible. Jane was certainly a little jittery, but not so much as Pinky, or Sam. Through these three, she had been through a sliver of the southern Mulder forests.

The noises were in harmony with everything else, the trotting of their hooves, and the pace of their slowed breaths. The sound grew louder, and ever more louder. Until all that was heard was the sound of music.

She gripped the reins tightly, and put her hands to her ears to try and block the noise. It barely made any difference. The noise just penetrated her skull, and looked forward, and realized she was alone in the forest of snow.

The snow began to blow harshly, every little particle of ice blew like needles sewing their course through the air, and piercing her warmth. The trees that passed her were thin, tall, and scraggly. The limbs rose high in disturbing and unreal positions.

Her face was smacked by a passing branch which she couldn't see, it felt like a steel wire whip. It stung, and put a red mark on her cheek. she touched her face, and soon she realized that all the sound had vanquished. Not the blizzard made noise, and neither did that whipped branch make noise too. She panicked, "where are all you at? Where did you go? Where?" But her voice rang with no sound.

"Have you passed through the gates of slumber? My realm of which I give you access? Garnette Renoi."

"Shut up," she yelled out, "who are you? Why can't I hear anything? What did you do?"

"I've said before, and you know not still?" He chuckled in a low breathy song, "will you run from what you think is feet behind you?"

"What!" And Jane looked back, and she felt a heat, a power behind her, a fear.

She bolted the reins, having her mare rush forward away from the beast stalking her, in the wake of the panic she forgot it. All she could think was to run. The trees passed by like they were sprinting in the opposite direction, and the music began to blair loud once more, hellishly so. The ground became a tidal wave, the dirt and snow moving around with a great force. She tried so desperately for her mare to keep good footing, to maneuver around it all, but a large shove and tumble brought her crashing down, and it all went black.

She awoke, what seemed like a few seconds later in front of the rangers and guards, ready to grasp tightly to her sword or either their coats. But instead she found another ranger and pair of travelers.

"My grace?"

She immediately recognized his old tenor voice, "Father Kreshen? Litus?" And it was them, "Litus," she said while getting up.

He dismounted, and she ran to him, clutching him tightly, "thing's are following me! She said fearfully.

But all who followed were the rest of her party. Elliot had muttered under his breath, and related to the other party's lead ranger, who said, "some charming fever."

Both parties made camp. They put a little bit of both their supplies to make it, and build the fire while the snow slowed to a near halt. Though throughout the entire night she didn't leave Litus' side, she pestered him asking how they left, and trying not to reveal her secret while asking why they left.

She also kept a hand on her sword, and once sleep took them, she clutched the pommel. *Why did I falter, I didn't do anything? Why? I didn't even pull it out. But was it because it was a dream? Was it a dream?* She thought as she fell to a deep and dark sleep on the cold rooted ground.

Chapter Forty-Four:

He sat in a quite small chamber room, where at the large table in the middle bathed in the large orange light of a large assortment of clean burning candles. On the table was a large assortment of food, but that was to be expected from a gathering for the duke. If it weren't for what this gathering was for, it would seem very grand.

Eiger put down his silver knife, and he asked the head of the king's guard something quietly, "now where is this queen at?"

"Our royal friend takes her time similar to how a queen should."

"So, what does that mean?"

"Our queen does what a queen should."

"That's good it seems. We'll start when she enters," and it wasn't a very long wait.

She had a servant open the door for her, and the intern-queen walked in with immediate eyes from all of them. Particularly from Eiger and the king's guards. He remarked on her look. She was beautiful, incredibly so, and she looked eerily similar to the real Queen Garnette: Jane, but what stuck was a thin veil which masked her face.

She wore a well fluffed dress, clearly well starched and such. But what kept most their attention was her makeup, she wore nearly white paint, and around her lips and eyes painted like clamshells. She looked as though she was trained in her posture and design of elegance, but still she was good at it. She sat and it commenced.

"My grace," Eiger said, "I believe this is the first of our meetings?"

"Yes it is," she said in a quiet, but soft tone, "tea, pour me a cup," and the servant who came with her did so swiftly, "you, Duke Eiger, and the rest of the lord's you have sat here. If I am to guess, this isn't for what my kitchens will cook for supper, but for a discussion about what to do with this city?"

"That's correct my grace," he said, "I have gathered here a series of lords who were bound to your crown."

She looked around the room to see them all, and said, "why so little?"

"Most lords defected from the crown for nearly two months now. So the lords who sit at this table with you are the thrones' only allies."

"No, that's not true. My royal navy is perfectly intact."

"So it is," Eiger said, "but they're not here, and we need a way to keep the capitol in the right hands."

"Then use the tower?"

"We have been."

"Then what was the point of all of this?"

"The common man is weary, the lords both high and low, don't think that there is a monarchy anymore. They believe that this city has come to chaos and anarchy, and they try to allocate their own power, thus only adding to this apparent chaos."

"I haven't seen any of this? How do you presume?"

"Have you looked out there? Queen Mary essentially made it a mandate for those in the city to wear a mask, it showed loyalty to the crown. Now less, and less do."

"Fashion changes, regime changes, and those masks went with it. But fine, let's say what you say is true, and my city, my capital is uncontrolled, what do you say happens?"

"The nobles, the lords, and the people need to see the queen at least, in all glory and attire."

"No, that would not do. I am the queen, not a jest. We wait for the navy."

"And during that time the city will burn, and when winter comes will there be a well managed line to keep the people fed?"

"Why would that matter, just let them eat whatever."

"When the cold takes them, and their children go hungry they will seek those responsible," *and our heads will stand on spikes, and your gold hair matted with snow.*

The morning was wet, and cold. Even though there was snow on the ground, when they looked up, there was nothing but tree branches, and leaves and needles. And the ground in some patches was soft like moss, but the rest was lightly snowed on and hard like stone.

On horseback, Litus was able to tell Kreshen a wonder with magic – though it be with a series of hand signals, and some seemingly strange thought reading ability. In the discussion Elliot and Kreshen both talked about their weaving magics, and compared the differences. One froze the weaves of wind, and the other navigated the weaved pattern of the woods.

The next day was basically the same as the first, the cold, the uncertain little mounds in the ground filled with thick contorted roots and vegetation. Jane rode by his side rather than with her own troop. Which mostly made her guards upset, while the rangers partnered together to make a plan on where to go. With their guidance there wasn't anything that happened, almost nothing at all, besides the occasional rustle of leaves.

That morning had a colder sensation, and revelations too. He finally saw the perpetrator that the navy installed. She wasn't just

some common woman they found off the streets, she was too smart
for that. Unless they did, and the entire time of her absence was to
teach her politics. Or maybe she was some lord's daughter, maybe one
who aligned with the navy. Then he tried to remember her eyes, they
looked glassy, or like the foil on glass. They didn't look like the
Garnette's actual eyes. Her name fit far better, cause her eyes were red
like those jewels. The impostor's eyes didn't shine quite the same. It
was a cold bitter day, and became a cold bitter night.

The further they went the deeper the blankets were, and they
all froze inconsistently. Some patches were crisp, and others soft, like
a rotten apple. At least there weren't any things as they trailed,
especially no white bears, nor wraiths. Though she did still fear what
she saw the first day of their new travels.

"I don't know why, but even though we traveled, what? Only
two days, it feels like eternity."

"That's mostly because nothing's happened."

"I guess so, besides what I saw that first night."

"And what did you see, my grace?"

"Stop calling me that," she said instinctually, "no, I don't
remember much. But it felt like a dream. A horrible dream, actually.
Isn't that strange; I know it was awful, I feel it, but I can't remember."

"Do you not remember everything, or just most of it?"

"Yes, all I remember was a figure, with nothing, no detail, and
that's it," *was it Litus?*

They continued their travel, and it was still mostly boring, with
three rangers, nothing went awry. Though one of them went with
Pinky, who mostly begged for action to go hunting, and when they
returned, they in each hand had two conies. They cooked over the fire
with a meaty smell, it showed the stark contrast of the empty scent of

the forest. And they all ate close to the fire, not waiting for the meat to cool while they drank from their canteens.

The day dropped its curtains much quicker than the days prior, now the feeling of winter was dawning greater. Jane sat by the fire, while the rest of them were falling, and one of them stood guard off to the side. But as the fire kindled, and its flames danced; she watched closer, stuck in a trance. It twinkled and rose higher and higher, until it became monstrously high. "So you remembered me," was said in a cracked whisper, "you will be betrayed like you betrayed them," and the fire pointed abstractly to the ones sleeping.

"What are you . . . doing?" Jane said, backing up more and more.

"What is who?" Said Elliot, "are you talking to me?"

"No, well," she looked back at the fire, now a normal flame, "it was nothing."

"So you're the queen," and she shrugged, "I guess so."

"Hmm, I guess that answers a few things," he sat down, "then sleep well my grace. Sleep well."

The iron bars held what was left of his mind, and his body was drowning in the floods that came since the fall. And he was stuck there against the bars, and past it were half the city of crumbling bits and the hollowness.

His pale skin was washed of any humanity left. Any light which still lingered – if any – passed through his translucent skin. His shattered hand still gripped those iron bars. A blanket of smoke drifted over the water disguising all there was to be. He couldn't see what was there of the city anymore, it all became cloaked and imperceptible.

They drank from their chipped mugs, and roared, "we've beaten these thugs!"

"I pulled that old hag lord from his bed chambers and wrapped a rope around his neck."

"What did he ever do for us other than take our taxes and hoard it!"

"Fuck him!"

"Long live the queen!"

They all roared in unison as he quietly walked down the stairs at the side of the bar. He sat by himself loathing the ash he wrought, "I've lost him, and I don't know what to do with this all."

"Is he dead?" A man who sat next to him said.

"Might be."

"They could find him, the impossible was done, and this is far from impossible. No matter how awful."

"The navy!? No. I don't think I will. I couldn't care what they do anymore. They've taken so much already."

"So you do ask of the impossible. Why don't you drink till your head becomes reasonable."

The barmaid came to him and he said, "I don't care, just get me water."

"Water? Alright."

His glass was off colored, and smelt like sweat, "what's this?" He questioned.

"The water. I believe an animal died on the way."

"Is it in the aqueduct?"

"Is that what they're called? Then, yes I believe so."

He got out of his chair, but was interrupted, "wait, if you're gonna leave, could you check the aqueduct? I don't want to worry if a dog died up there."

The man who sat next to him said, "but if it's not an animal, I'll go tell the navy for you."

"Fine," he said while leaving, "I'll go check, but no navy business, yet."

He broke out of the door, and through the streets were covered in smog. He ascended the hill being filled with the black cloaked men with iron emblems on their chest. The sound of hammers were building up the windows that overlooked most of them now.

He kept to what he remembered, and crept through the city of what still remained. Up at the top in the aqueduct he walked the edges until he came to the drain where a man and his flesh were drowning in the water.

He dropped into the water – and with his heavy hands – he picked up the young pale lord. He pushed him over the walls and onto the ground. On the ground, he lightly slapped his face, hoping he'd breathe. And finally the lord spat and muttered in faded breath, but it was only sputtering noises.

"You're alive. My grace."

"I am. Your lord?"

"Yes, I'm sorry."

He sat there focusing on his breath for some time, "over all of this?"

"In title."

"How did they do it?"

"They hung him, the navy did."

"I'm the duke of half of this city home to one subject and a loop of rope. I'm now the duke of Charian?"

"Far more than half of the guards were loyal."

"Loyal? They were?"

"Till the very end."

"What do we do now?"

"I am bound to you, and I reason we need to leave this island."

"My home is gone?"

The guard nodded, "this siege is over, that navy has infiltrated the shores, and have set up their militia government. It's over."

"So I have to either hide in the sewers like a rat, or die? So I'll be a lord of rats."

"No, no! That won't be the case."

"The entire city is surrounded, what can I do?"

"I'll protect you, and see that you are saved from this all."

"Why?"

"Is it my duty?"

"What is duty to a low lord of no land, and no people, and no wealth, nor any standings to our queen and the gods."

"Do you kill dogs that whimper in the streets?"

"No."

"So stop whining. You've already decided to die. No, I can't let you die. Let it be for pity, and then-"

"No. I won't be pitied, and this is not my suicide."

"Good," he said slowly, "good"

He was dragged up the stairs of the inn, and was tended at his bedside by the maid of the strange establishment. Dust and ash filled the room from the fireplace and the incoming trepidation of stomping boots entering the doors. And the dust billowed on the windowsill blocking what little light could be let in, but then it was shut and replaced with the light of candles and the fireplace.

There was a gash inflicted down his leg which when wrapped by the cleanest linen afforded. As she was taking care to keep the blood from falling further down his leg and onto the bed, and the young lord pulsed between a feeling of ecstasy and the feeling of a knife driven through his mind. It was in these moments of the unthinkable that he longed to see past the dust on the windowsill. "My lord, there's only so little left, please endure it."

He muttered a single breath, "fine," and another breath of pain pierced the arch on the back of his skull.

He felt a numbing sensation the next day – close to night. They discussed behind the curtains and closed doors, "we're going to the twin city first."

"To Ser?"

"Where else can we go? I've found a longboat, we'll use that when midnight falls."

"The navy!? Are you forgetting about the navy? They will see us."

"Ships are breaking off of the circle every few hours. Soon there'll be enough holes in their ranks which we can leave unnoticed. And I know you're worried – and you should be – but I'm certain without a reasonable doubt, this will work."

"But we're not going to stay in Ser for long?"

"We could go in two directions, either find a vessel to elsewhere – most likely Hule, or we'll go on foot using the ranging guild to get to Hule."

"Why not Porcelania?"

"What!?" He said before letting out a laugh.

"I'm serious. The phrase 'in the lion's den' we seek the center of danger, for it is what is least expected of the lions, invertedly being the safest option."

"What are you talking about! No, we won't go that way. And we're not basing off of irrelevant sayings."

"What if Hule isn't safe either?"

"Then we'll have to figure that out when we get there."

It was past midnight. The sky was a blend of the clouds and smog, and most lights were dimmed for the night. He carefully made sure to keep his wrappings tight, before quietly exiting through the window. A pillow broke his fall, and was thrown into a dark dank alley.

He kept light on his feet, and a coat he'd nabbed helped to cover his figure and face. Tonight the streets were quiet. Not a peep or scream pierced the heavy to topple walls. He walked, seemingly wandered from any other perspective, but he did seek one.

Some naval men were walking down the streets lit by the orange light of their hand lanterns. He had tried to pass by, but when the officers barked, "you!" He looked at them almost dumbfounded.

"Me?" He said in a shrill voice.

"Yes you! What are you doing at this time of night, when everyone else is deep in sleep?"

"Sorry, sorry, officer. I just . . . had too much to drink, and need to get to my babe, and, and-"

"Stop your blabbering, I consider myself a kind man, and my men would too, so get home or you're going to have to come with us."

"Yes, yes. I'll be going."

He had taken a few steps forward, "what are those?" And the man said after, "stop, you!" A naval officer in the back said.

"Yes?" he said timidly, "I'm just trying to get back home."

"What are those bandages around yer legs?"

"Uh, uh."

"Come on," said the lead officer, "answer him!"

"Well, I was burned during . . . when we took down the . . . the evil duke."

"That was a great day, wasn't it. Saw the smoke rise. Sorry to hear about your injuries, you did a great service, my son. Now be off, and make no disturbance. People are sleeping."

"Alright, alright. I'll be off."

And they walked away.

He found the front gates of the manor in disheveled shape. The doors were broken down, but some rubble in the way blocked the door. And the windows shattered. In a matter of days it all fell into a terrible ruin worthy of and needed for demolition.

He had made a long detour – especially careful to stay away from faces no matter how dim or bright – heading through the dark abandoned tunnel but to two, and he climbed the ladder into the library inside the manor.

He pushed until the case fell, and saw the newly rested dust on the smashed and torn pages caked in the ground. As he walked through – trying to get past the shattered windows – he saw the halls he owned. It was gone. A broken mess, but a mess that will stay forevermore.

He walked to the room he once held, and saw what he owned ransacked, missing, and broken. A stain of blood was browned on the floor, and looked like a castle from where he stood.

The room where his father ruled from, was the most dire. It was a room shredded till it was imperceptible as a room for the living.

Half the manor was gone from flames lit some days ago and drowned by the rain which fell harshly. When he came to his father's bedroom, he could see straight through the burned down wall. He saw half the city through the wall. He walked to a night stand – or what was left of it – and picked up a blackened knife which was once chrome.

Although it felt like an eternity, it was merely minutes of the empty quiet halls of ghosts before he went back down the ladder. Once he met the ground at the bottom, it would be the last he'd see of the old manor. For some reason he expected him to be standing at the bottom waiting, but it was just the ambiance in that old tunnel. Ambiance and himself.

It was the next day which passed – and the night that followed – when they walked against the light that reflected into watchful eyes. People – even the lowly burglar – didn't walk where they had gone.

They had nothing, besides the clothes on their backs, and the long-ship hidden from the navy and the people.

"The city seems to hold a strange image in my eyes."

"It does for me too."

"It's a nightmare now. I don't want to ever see these shores and people again, for what they've done to me and my father. To my home. To my friends."

"I don't know what to say, my grace."

"I guess I'm not some duke, no longer. I hold no lordship other than blood. And what is blood, other than a document revealed for malice and which stains our streets and ceilings."

"Once you know the world from my age, you'll know that bloodshed is a given certainty. In the small, and large. And I see that no matter what we do there will be imminent bloodshed, whether it's our blood, or it's our hands."

They walked into the tunnel – once more – but now they passed the ladder for good. For an impossibly long walk through the dark tunnel. Eventually the floor fell down gradually, and they kept their feet planted as much as they could, until the end washed and blinded their eyes.

The longboat was on the shore sitting quietly as the waves calmly beat against the hull and sands. The tunnel was the only apparent sign of human trepidation and action, for the rock wall which stretched up against the beach was tall and void of touch.

The wind pushed air aloft with salt against their brows. They pushed the boat into the water, before jumping in themselves, and they used the oars to get them off of shore, and they rowed heavily to get past the waves.

Once they came to clearer waters they waded in the calmer waves and regained their strength. Not a ship in sight had come that night, with sails flown high and proud. "At least not now."

"But if a ship comes, what will we do?"

"Buck down, go flat, prone if possible. If the boat is flat enough against the water, we could possibly go unnoticed."

"What if a monster – a seafaring beast – brings this boat to the ocean floor?"

"It'll go for the navy's ship before it comes to us."

"And then what?"

"I can take it, just a simple brawl."

"But what if it's a massive beast, something larger than a naval vessel?"

"Then we will have died trying, at least."

"Can't a great mind think smarter than to give up?"

"I'm your guard, a warrior, I'm no scholar, albeit still educated. Sometimes the only thing you can do is give up, but as given by your scenario, it's impossible to deal with something far greater than I. But that shouldn't mean to give up at times, no matter how difficult, you should always try what you can."

"Alright."

" . . . You have nothing else witty to say, my lord?"

"I guess I don't."

"I'd grab a bottle of ale, if it weren't for the fact there is none on deck."

"There is no deck."

"This is about as good as I can do."

"Thank you."

"Now, it will hopefully take about the rest of the night for us to cross over."

"The entire night?"

"At a minimum, so if you want to get there, keep rowing."

"Alright, alright, but I'm not going to be gracious."

"Well you said to yourself you're no longer a duke."

"Just keep rowing."

The guard chuckled as they kept pushing forward as they imagined the milky bowl in the sky as clear as was told a thousand years ago.

He sat there, in that chair, and the sight of *him* was intoxicating. He felt the urgent rush in his blood, a seizing in his mind, but was blocked by something he wished was gone. An iron chain hung in a loop from the mantle in the ceiling. At first he shuddered at the sight of the cold iron links before seeing the rust fall away showing the bare metal. Underneath the chain was a single lonely chair.

"I'll do what I must."

The iron seared his palms with red marks and tore a hole through his hands. His blood dripped from his hands, pooling on the seat of the chair, and shattering the links in the loop.

He dropped the cracking iron, and it fell to the ground smearing an image on the pale floors. "I must do what I must," ran through his head.

He grabbed the dripping pile with what was left. Trying to stretch it out into a paper thin bar, but it collapsed. "I must do what I must," he said, trying to keep it together.

Somewhere it came to him, *A king of iron must make his throne. Don't you see son? You must make this chair into a symbol, the red iron the blood of those who've bored a hole in your grasp.*

"How? I'm perilous, nothing can be mended."

Take it by force, the throne must be made of iron, but taken by iron. For the iron-king.

He saw it before him, that spinning blade or crimson, both of them twinkling in the candlelight. Both casting reflections on his eyes.

The morning came swiftly as the waves rocked them and brought them to shore. As the lord left from the long boat, the salty water brought a stinging sensation throughout his legs. He fell into the water, getting his bandages soaked, and only held on by his grip on the side. The guard quickly came to his side, helping him up, and they were both able to quickly and brutally pull the ship to shore.

They looked back seeing only the very peaks of the city across the water as the sky began to glow. Soon a ship in the distance grew closer but its sail's were masked by the blur of orange. They looked back no longer.

Chapter Forty-Five:

The mundane nature of the forest became ever clear with each tree they passed and each time passing the right way was taken, "I thought this cursed forest was supposed to be, well, cursed."

The ranger leading the pack turned his head, "you know nothing of this forest."

"I lived next to it my entire life, I know."

"Then you should know the danger that exists here."

"Is the north even cursed, like the south?"

"You're saying that as though you didn't run into the abyss within the first hour of our departure, and experience a dream-like nightmare," he said, turning back, "your grace."

The day drew on like a slog, it was cold, and the low hanging branches from the snow piled trees made for a more than wanted ducking experience. A few hours passed, nothing quite grand or interesting happened, just small discourse from those around her, including that of her own guard.

Pinky asked Kreshen, "Father Kreshen, I've seen you do magic, I was wondering if you know what it's called. It's when you put magic in a thing."

"You mean enchanting?"

"Yes, yes, do you know it, could you teach me?"

"Although I know of the basics, and the history of enchanting, I can't exactly do it myself, I mean in teaching matters unfortunately."

"The history of it?"

"There was a period when enchanting was a pure art. It was considered different from conjuring, but now we don't see it that way."

"Why? Have we gotten better at it, or something?"

"In sorrow fact, it is the opposite, and it's because, a thousand years ago, during the war of change or sorrow, or also called the great war. The art of enchanting was almost lost. The great works were destroyed in combat. The relics we know of are often the small iron works which weren't subjected to war. This is also the war which killed the dragons, who were greatly important to the art. Nowadays it's rare to find an enchanter, and they'd only work with some types of wood. But did you know that steel could be enchanted too?"

"I actually did, Garnette has an enchanted sword. So enchanting metal is lost, but in those days where it was great, were there other things that were enchanted, like rocks or glass and crystals."

"Hmm, well firstly I can't enchant, but if I were to guess from what I do know, I'm not sure you could. That's either because they don't have the fiber you find with other natural materials and metals. It's either that, or for jewels it's a byproduct of the land. It's not really a natural material in an enchanting way. But we don't know if it was possible a thousand years ago, or possible in hundreds of years from now, because all who would know either aren't born yet, or they died in the war."

It was nearing the end of the morning, he had planned to discuss with Bishop Lazith about the other two lords who ravaged much of low Porcelania. Or at least try and get as much knowledge of them as he could.

He wore a coat of red, with red embroidery and pewter and silver buttons. It was a thick garb, while inside the castle it blazed to wear, but he knew that he'd rather wear it while out than burn while inside. He wore his heeled shoes with red soles underneath. And lastly he wore a few beautiful rings, most were silver, but the most beautiful one was encrusted with jewels like a flower, and made of gold.

Pulling up to the castle gates was an old reliable carriage pulled by young and strong mares. He stepped up and through the door, Darien followed up and sat across from the duke. "My lord," he said, "do you think that the Bishop would have anything on these other two lords?"

"If these other two, Lord Garet, and Lord Taryen are as 'faithful' as Karaway, then I'd assume at least one would have left a string for the Bishop to remember."

The carriage bounced on the hard rocks stuck in the crack of the road as they came closer to the cathedral. Until he could see the glowing stained glass high above the city streets. There was the sound of plinking from the incoming rain. The droplets could be seen crater to the ground, and they looked like beams of light emitted from the light behind the stained glass.

They rode every further on. There was this chill, unlike the coldness around them. It was a piercing dry cold which went through their skin and through their bones, but up ahead was a sight none of the rangers had expected. It was a large circle of red cobblestone, and grave markers. Some were in the rotary, and others lined it.

A few of them dismounted to see the graves. "Did either of you see this cemetery?"

"It's not a cemetery, there's no church, but no I didn't see this."

"No," said the last ranger, "this is a discrepancy in the pattern."

"Hmm," Elliot said, pacing back and forth, "something else is here. Something that swayed the will of the forest."

"We should leave, there's three of us, we can find a path to escape easily."

"And keep following us, like you said there's three of us, we can find whatever it is, and deal with it."

"I agree," Elliot said.

"Fine," said the last, reluctantly.

Jane watched Litus step down from his mare, and draw his sword out. He formed one of the fours to search. The rangers though just kept a hand on the pommel on their long sword. They walked around the graveyard. Passing by each stone, and every unreadable death board, they looked out into the infinite depths of the forest. Just waiting and looking for something. Was it an animal, hopefully so. But if it were something else, one came to mind, but she didn't want to think of it. She watched one of the rangers make a weird gesture. She was certainly confused, but she felt a strange aura in the air, one that made her put her hand on her handle and draw out the first few inches of her enchanted blade. She looked back at that ranger, and he was deeper in concentration, and now a foggy looking wobble appeared around him, completely visible. *Was that their weaving?* He turned around to see where the rest of the party were, before yelling loudly, "I feel something, I see something," he breathed hard, "be on guard!" Fleeting moments passed, and lastly he yelled that horrid string, "a wraith is close!"

Eiger strode through the front doors of the cathedral. There was the smell of rain and the falling dust like ashes from a bonfire. He saw a priest at the altar. Eiger walked up to the man, asking, "do you know where the Bishop is today?"

And the priest said back, "he's upstairs in his chamber, alone."

So he walked, with each step reverberating in the echo chamber where all the people stayed quiet. They prayed solemnly, but

Eiger couldn't be bothered to look at them, all he cared for was the discussion with this Bishop.

The chamber was cold, there were strips of light rain coming through the open door at the end of the chamber. He met Lazith sitting on a patio outside in this light rain. He drank from a porcelain cup, and as he turned to face him, he said, "ah, Duke Eiger, isn't it a pleasant day?"

"What makes today pleasant?"

"The rain does, come out here, and look up at the cathedral."

Reluctantly, he looked up at the rain plastered stone, "I don't see it."

"This cathedral is older than us, and hopefully we'll die long before it falls. But the rain is temporary, and the rain doesn't do much actual damage to the hard stone. But it's that small part of it which is dangerous. It could freeze and crack the stone. But it never has. I feel the same, there's this unchanging nature to me, to my position. But here I sit watching the rain try to bring down my life, my burden."

"Before I go, I need to know, if you know of two more lords."

"Two more lords," he scoffed, "do you plan to keep coming to me for information on anyone you don't think is good for your city?"

"I do."

"Hmm, " he said, "either way, it seems I don't have a say in this. The winter is coming soon, and it's raining currently, hmm."

"Either way? What do you mean by it?"

"You who live in the capitol's capitol haven't received a letter?"

The storm began to march headstrong and hard. Eiger began to walk back to his carriage, the doors to the cathedral were opened, and a man jumped from his aisle seat to the duke. He pushed the blade into his flesh enough times to drop the duke to the ground. Darien immediately used the sword which was kept clean.

It sounded like a thud, as a long fletched arrow came spiraling into Jane's chest. It was only then that any of the rangers, or guards, or Litus believed they saw the *wraith* at last. And it was only for that moment. Draped in red tarnished black robes, and withdrawing on horse past their field of view. Before they could all run to her, a horn for out in the forest was heard, a war horn. Loud and sharp. Jane fell to the ground clutching the arrow lodged in her chest. She dislodged the painful point and it was covered in both an oily dark liquid and bright painful blood.

He was on the ground watching the light fade, while the whole hall of the faithful was filled with vigor and yelling. He found himself in a coughing spree. It was ridiculous for a high lord, a noble, to be acting sickly in front of the common people, and even worse, inside a great place of worship.

The light, the light is fading. Close the door, the rain is coming in, the wind's are blowing cold air. But he never spoke about it, for he didn't feel the strength forever more.

Two men grabbed him from either side, pulling him up and into the carriage. Darien stood over his body, a knife in hand cutting away much of his dress – which now soaked and dripped on the cart floor. "Open your mouth, and bite on this my grace," Eiger barely did so biting on the leather wrap of a knife.

"Grab the shirt, and shred it into strips," and his assistant did so, "first we need to clog the wound."

They stuffed twisted linen strips into Eiger's wound. Blood dripped and the rocking of the fast moving cart made it hard to keep anything steady. "Come on, come on!" He said while winding the last bits of cloth around the wound.

Eiger felt nothing, no sharp pain, just a numbness. All the sound seemed to wash away into intelligible waves. Until one thought was transmitted to his mind that he could process, "is this it?"

They spoke – but he didn't listen, or he couldn't listen – he didn't know which at this point. And soon he could not remember what he had said at all. They moved his body around, and he jostled around like a piece of furniture being moved by a buggy. He was being pulled up, and wrapped with a white quickly turned red piece of cloth. He raised his hand and saw that his hand was the opposite of the cloth. The cloth was purely red, and his hand was yellow and pale devoid of red.

There was a creaking sound, and then he felt the trinklings upon his chest and face, it all felt numb. Little needles prodded his skin, pulling around flesh, and only now did it feel painful.

They rushed to her, guards looking out each side for more arrows, but what had stirred the rangers were that horn and what could come from it. They roamed around waiting for something to find its way there.

Kreshen observed the arrow tip, he wiped the oily liquid on his fingers, *poisoned*. He took a quick smell of it, "what is this?"

"Give me that father," barked Barrett, he too observed the poison, "I . . . I don't know, it's poison!? But I don't know what kind it is."

"We can deal with this wound at least," and so he went trying to undo her bindings and for a brief second he thought, "a wraith's poison? No, this is . . . northern poison, it's Blaekrot. It's Blaekrot!"

Jane pushed her head up, and spitting, "what's Blaekrot? What will happen?"

"It's a slow poison, it's grave to say, my grace."

"Is there anything you can do?"

"I don't know my grace, but firstly we have to patch this wound. My Grace, brace still," he said while weaving over her wound.

She tried to keep quiet but whatever Kreshen was doing was unbelievably painful, but she kept it to loud grunts and moans of agony. There was this waving pulsating sensation over her chest, and when she looked the air around her skin was too waving like steam. "What are you doing?" She said, but quietly, too quietly.

They tore some linen fabric, and went to work to wrap her body. They sat her upright, and she groaned in pain. *Is the arrow gone?* Jane looked over to the center of the graveyard, and the ground began to shake. One of the rangers ran up to her, and yelled, "get her back on, we're leaving!"

So they put her back on the mare, and sent her off, following and following the guards and rangers.

He turned quickly as a beast erupted from the unknown into the outskirts of the graveyard. A being of stone, and in the figure of a gargoyle. Its sharp talons clutched on the hedge stones which it shattered into small rocks and pebbles.

The gargoyle careened toward a figure closest: Litus. It jumped high with its wings of stone, and crashed down to the ground sending dirt and other debris around leaving small craters behind. Litus jumped out of the way, sword in hand. The gargoyle spun its long scaled tale around catching him off guard, and sending him into the ground, further away.

Elliot ran up to the beast, long sword in hand and meaning to see what the beast would do. He backed away from a swipe from those talons, and when he saw a chance, he went forward. Putting the point into the forearm of the stone beast, to find out it wasn't stone at all. The beast jumped onto Elliot, but Litus got up and stabbed at its tail. It jumped high away from the two and made a loud deep growl.

A series of growls repeated the message and soon they appeared. Two more ghastly and strange stone-like gargoyles entered the arena of death. Elliot yelled to the other ranger, "it's skin isn't stone, thrash and stab it till they die!"

They were each pitted against a gargoyle. The only defining look between the three, was one had two wounds already.

Litus backed away from the crushing drop of the beast. He readied his blade high pointed to the gargoyle's face. He dodged a wave and slash forward from the beast, but when he tried to ring around to its side, he was snagged by the cloak and fell. The gargoyle took this moment to try and kill its prey early, with a slash and a bite it tried to get Litus, but he wriggled his way out of the beast's clutches, and came up immediately sword in hand outstretched to the beast. When the thing tried to reach close to Litus he struck it with his blade. The gargoyle tried to jump on him, lunging forward clumsily, but Litus was able to jump away.

There was this dark shadowy vignette in her ribcage. She felt that arrows were releasing on either side of her waiting for an ambush. She wanted to halt her ride, but couldn't. *Can't I ride?* The figure in black was waiting for them, and a memory – now long ago – was that bear: the white bear. Was the white bear waiting for her, in ambush? A horse and a few men are so much weaker than that bear, it destroyed her home. No, it had to be something else. The cult, *yes,* she thought. They were what ambushed her, and soon the darkness took her mind, and she became a mindless zombie riding in this pack.

Litus cut at the arm of the gargoyle, a spew of red blood splattered the cold ground, and Litus dug the blade only deeper into the trench of flesh. The beast thrashed about in pain until Litus completely dislodged the hand from the gargoyle's arm. Instead of retreating away, it only became more angry, thrashing about, and jumping forward onto Litus. He kept his distance – only slightly. Striking what he could, leaving a small open wound all around the gargoyle. It spun its tail around smashing into Litus. He was thrown to the side, rolling in the rock and light snow. The gargoyle lunged onto him, grabbing at his chest, and throwing him about like throwing a stone. It was something which would have either severely injured or killed a normal man, but Litus took the scraped and shreds of his cloak and disregarded the damage. He held his sword in both hands, its long blade rushing forward and penetrating the skin of the gargoyle. The beast spun around only causing the steel to create a worse wound in its flesh.

He – quickly, and instinctively– grabbed onto the tail trying to stab the flesh or cut the flesh with the blade of his sword, a string of blood dripped as he cut away the flesh of the dying beast. He was flung off with a snap and whip of the tail.

The gargoyle turned to face Litus once more. It kicked up a screen of dirt before flying up to drop down on the figure, and so it tried, but Litus jumped a far ways back. He readied his blade seeing an opportunity, and ran forward again. As the gargoyle was careening to him, he too was doing the same. He swiped the steel around a wall of flesh, in an arc of precision, down went the gargoyle, headless, dead.

He got up from the ground as he fell from the succession of his conquest? He looked around, it was quiet, besides the fighting further away. He took a brief, short breath before marching on to the gargoyle closest to him. He ran quickly, sword kept forward, and like the gargoyles, he was racketeering towards it, cutting as he went.

The rangers were far more careful when fighting the gargoyles then he, but now that there were multiple on one beast, there wasn't much they could do. From both sides they stabbed and tore the flesh of the stone gargoyle, until all was left was the squealing of its death.

The third ranger was fighting the gargoyle by himself. Elliot yelled to the ranger, "wq\e're coming Lee," in hopes of drawing at least a tinge of the gargoyle's attention off of Lee and on them.

Lee – like Elliot – was keeping his distance, he was a current guard of royalty, and wouldn't budge to some gargoyle, but still he tried. He circled the gargoyle, keeping in the blind spot of its grasp and its tail's wrath. He took little strikes where he could, but it took one second that he took a wrong step. The tail wrapped around and swung into him, throwing him to the side far away. His sword had made a deep gash in the gargoyle's tail, taking out a sizable chunk of deep red flesh.

With his free arm he clutched his chest, a sharp pain and once the adrenaline dropped from his blood, so did he.

"Litus! Grab his body!" He said, clutching the scythe.

Litus ran around while Elliot went straight toward the beast. He at first dragged his body, Lee yelled at Litus. "Fuck, I think, fuck! I broke a rib, maybe a few. Get me back to my horse. I need to make sure our grace is safe," he did, dragging his body to his horse, but didn't help him mount, *there's already half a dozen with her, you'd make no difference so far back,* he wanted to say.

Elliot swiftly came into the gargoyle's reach. Every swipe the beast made, Elliot either dodged out of the way, or was able to snag a bit in his curved blade. He eventually cut away both arms of the beast before it began a desolate last attempt to kill the opponent.

It lunged at him, but the gargoyle, not realizing its arms were truly gone yet, crashed down in the dirt with tombstones and nameboards. He maneuvered around and with a quick wrap around and slash, he toppled the beast's head from body.

"My grace! Garnette, the poison will . . . " She could only make out so little in a stream of illiterate and muffled sounds.

Her vision in one eye was an oversaturated mess of paints and light, while the other had the fog. It grew deeper now. She looked up, and at that instant she was allowed to see the clouds far above and their deep swelling of mass, darkening ever more. And soon that colorful hellscape – which turned the blurred forest into an extreme, overstimulated experience – had the fog drape over that too, with the deep darkness she saw. She yelled out, scared, "I can't- I can't see anything!? Where is . . . what's happening?" But they couldn't hear her, and she could hear them.

Chapter Forty-Six:

The chimes played in a low reverberation. It was a blaring explosion of noise all in tune and all in time. She covered her ears, to mute the sound and still the sound pierced the flesh of her hands and was still perfectly audible.

She walked through the manor of cracks and soot. She didn't know where she was, but a divine force was guiding her through the maze-like structure to the infinite manor. It all came to the spiral stairwell which led higher and higher, and the more she ascended the louder the symphony became. Until blood the same temperature and hue of fire dripped between her fingers down on her nude figure.

An almost infinite time passed and she continued to walk up the stairs of uncertainty. *What is lying at the end of it all?* Then it was over, she reached the top, and what she found was a room with a figure at the end of it, sitting at a long table. He tapped his finger on the shifting wood grain. Two torches were to her sides. He remained cast in shadows.

"Who are you? Are you him?"

"Him," he cackled like the roar of fire, "I am it, I am inevitable. I am the future and the end."

"Then, where am I?"

"The imminent future for you, possibly."

"Is this the death-lands? The lands of the dead?"

"No, this is far from that puny realm. This is the realm quite high above the living, the realm for the infinite, and for the clouds, and the lightning, and the heat of stars," his arms waved up expressively, "have you ever seen the stars? Some, very few now call it the heavens."

"What do you mean stars?"

He gestured with his hand pulling her closer, and the world dissolved into a void of bright points. It was a radiance of color. He pulled her by one hand into his bosom, and then walked closer to the sun. its tendrils were a beautiful dance of flames, and as slow as they appeared it was beautiful. The celestial body burnt no soot, it was a pure passionate flame.

She looked up to him, expecting to see someone familiar, but it wasn't him. For he had a body, and a sharp face, and a head of long hair which spun and floated like it were suspended in deep water. And he spoke once more, but this time his voice was beyond noble, it was sweet like honey, and was graceful beyond monarchs, and he spoke, "that is a star. It's a large celestial body of fire. Come let's see it closer."

He took her smaller hand and they walked every closer to the sun. The closer they came, the more the heat embroiled them, not painfully, but comfortably. Each strand looked like the dots and splotches in a well crafted painting. It was made by the hand of perfect brush strokes. He whispered in her ear, "come let's dance," and she suddenly became entranced in it.

He took her hand and they turned around as dolls in a dream. His face was full of vigor as they spun around the stars oh so perfectly. They floated in the abyss like silk flowing through a pool of still water.

"This is the infinite I live in, and look over there," he pointed to the world, "they live under the cold hatred of that fog. They live, mull, die, and nothing else. They have no meaning, no hope in their life, but here you can float in the beauty of the stars."

"But," she stuttered, "I . . . "

"You don't have anyone down there, you only have poison, and imminent death, will you take my hand once again?"

"I still don't know who you are, I have . . . what do you want from me?"

"There's quite a lot I want from you, but I can give you something in return. It won't be a fair trade, for what you'll receive will make you a saint and a deity. You have done so much so quickly, and I think you deserve a reward in time. Only if you'll take my hand and dance once again."

"This is the realm of dreams, what you've spoken of before?"

"And what if I refuse?"

"There are many who wouldn't refuse, you'd be the first. I'll give you time to think, for in a week and a half, your time will come, or your life will begin."

Through the entire night and through the entire day they rode on through the forest with little slowing. It was a slog weaving around trees and searching for wraiths and an exhaustive ride which wore their back out, and made them groan.

Oh it was cold, bitterly so. She couldn't shift her toes in her boots. It was like digging a grave in winter. Their mares spit and wheezed in pain from the breakless trotting over uneven terrain. The rangers grew great headaches, and Kreshen's exhaustion painted on his face. They all rode still, for fear, to escape, and for most of them for her.

A week's time, for what? Till the poison kicked in, what was in my dream? Wait what did he say, a reward, for what? What would I get? If I could see, without this fog, I'd do a lot.

But after nearly an entire day of backbreaking trotting, the rangers decided to stop, seeing nothing in their gazes for hours and hours, they built up camp near the west border of Mulder.

She touched her wound mark which had this vibrating sensation. She didn't expect it to remain, but still, she asked, "Father Kreshen, are you there?"

"Yes, I'm here, what is it my child?"

"This um, feeling around my puncture still feels like it's shaking?"

"At the time we hadn't anything clean to patch that wound, or threads to tie it up. That sensation, the shaking is the wind, I've bound it to your wound to seal it shut. I'm sorry if that's causing you pain."

"When will my vision be restored?"

"There shouldn't be any reason furthermore to be worried about, my lady, we're close to the castle, and surely through all their hands, there's a set more skilled in treating poison than I."

She didn't have any dreams that night, or maybe she did, but it wouldn't matter since she remembered less and less of them now. But she was helped up by her mare, and rode with heavy guards to keep her from falling.

As she rode, there was a funny feeling. She felt as though her vision was getting better, and some of that pain – that caused cracks like glass in her as she shifted – began to mellow out. It was this euphoria, an escape from the pain. Maybe the poison wore out. So she touched her wound, and almost immediately that pain returned, and with it the fog which obscured her eyes was fully saturated again. For hours, this process, this repetition continued.

He took the arrow to preserve what that poison was, but he was still curious about it. He pulled it from the void, and just looked at it. It was a long arrow, but it was flimsy, it bowed without much pressure. If he held it from both ends and his mare stumbled over the terrain, it might very well snap. *But an arrow this flimsy from what I've heard of wraiths seems strange.*

He had put the arrow away, and as he rode he thought more about those wraiths. Everyone called him a wraith, they feared him greatly. Though that was all superstition. But Jane, and the guard they encountered only one, and a skilled man was slain, another dismembered, and it all happened in the flash of a lightning strike. But if everyone really knew how dangerous they were, would they fear him still? Or would they attack him, or his friends, his companions?

They rode the uncertainty through midday. Like expected, snow kicked off the hooves of his black mare, and their breath was visible. He kept both hands on his reins, while the others, even Jane – who currently couldn't see – kept her hand on the pommel of her sword.

There was this feeling as they came closer to the edge that the forest was thinning. Sam and Pinky who rode to his side were talking about it. Litus didn't notice how it started but he quickly understood what it was about.

Pinky said, "that's when they'll get us."

"We're expecting that, when they strike again, we'll have the advantage."

"What makes you think they don't know that already?"

"I guess I don't know, but we have better numbers."

"We know our numbers, but not theirs. There could be, I don't know, a dozen wraiths, and they'll . . . they'll-" he looked conflicted.

"Let's just keep our eyes sharp, and not fail our post."

They split up and rode on either side of Jane. They stayed as close as possible when the trees made them ride double file. And in those cases, even Litus looked out for wraiths, or just figures that looked like himself. If he went lost, would they hunt him the same way? Is the only reason he's not been killed already, is pure happenstance? *It can't be luck, I refuse it,* but he didn't know why he refused this answer. *There's always been someone who helped me, and they kept me from death. I will be certain about the future. I need to be.*

The day began its quick deterioration that came with the season. "This is when it'll happen," Pinky said.

"Don't be a fucking bastard, we're all scared, you're only making it worse," Barrett spoke to him.

He said back, "I'm sorry."

But as the forest became less and less, their fear only grew. It was like a person you trusted telling a story, and growing quiet and tense, and waiting for them to snap like a worn bowstring. They were wound taut. With each snap of twigs and crunching of small pebbles in the dirt, they became tighter. The rangers asked them to be quiet, they said it helped in this time of need. And they rode, and rode, and rode evermore. Until they saw the horizon far away with the sand dunes, miles and miles away.

They eased out and when they took their first steps on certain terrain, almost all of them, besides the rangers, and Kreshen looked back to see nothing further than a few feet into the forest.

Within a half mile of the border, was a large castle, built similarly, but only slightly differently than Esty. From the non decorative stone walls of crusted salt and coarse sand were the walls and fortification of castle Sebois, the sister keep of the Ranger's Guild.

Chapter Forty-Seven:

Eiger sat up pulling what available strength he had, and there was this awful burning sensation all over his chest. He brushed his fingers over the many scars which deformed himself. There was this large bump filled with fine twine, and the skin filled with the red puss from his own veins. He looked like the patched up and many resewn cloth doll of an aggressive child. There was this one stitch which was only slightly upturned; he hadn't known why, but he touched it. A rush of pain was punched up, and a bead of blood began to drip on his fingers.

"So, this is what has become of it. I survived, but marred."

A woman came to his side, she was a maid with an apron of pockets and filled with many little small glass and copper tools. She took a wad of linen – sourced from the old bed sheets from the keep. She dabbed up the blood, and said, "don't prod at it. We'd have to resew the stitches anew, so no meddling, my grace."

I was stabbed, hmm, six times. I let a man stick a knife in my chest six times. "What day is today?"

"You were asleep for two days, so that would be-"

"I give thanks to you. Do you know where Darien – the head of my guard – may be at?"

"The lean old fellow with the sword?" And Eiger nodded, "he comes around here every few hours. He has guards placed everywhere here. I guess it makes sense for a man of your stature."

Eiger pulled his blanket over and as he tried to get out, the maid went to him, "you should stay, it's not healthy."

"I have places to be, and things to do, so I'll be going."

"Not yet you impatient man."

"Excuse me, you will speak to me in that tone again."

Her face had scrunched up greatly, as she scoffed at him, "fine, your grace."

"Get out." He barked, while pain spiked through his chest.

She tightly gripped her blouse, and snuffed as she barged through the door. While the doors were open, Eiger watched Darien walk to his door, and had a look of surprise as the maid ran off angrily.

"She's only trying to help, my grace."

"She's rude, and I don't need to deal with that, while sailing to death's domain."

"My grace, I have something of importance to tell you."

"Go on."

"There's two parts, my grace. Firstly-" Darien was cut off, by the door opening up to reveal Lucerne in gloriously pristine uniform, marching in with a saberless scabbard.

"Duke Eiger, it's been a long while, hasn't it?"

"Yes, it has. Nearly two entire months," *where has he been, why did he abandon his post?*

"It's horrible what happened to you, here," he gave Eiger a dull metallic ring with a mosaic of a flower, "it's said flowers cure sickness. This one's made of silver, so it won't tarnish."

Eiger rubbed his thumb over the ring, it had a rough surface, "my partner, I want to know of any achievements you've had, surely?"

"Of buying soldiers, I've had offers, and made deals with great men, and I'm one step away from reforming a pirate crew to our cause."

"Darien, which end of Renoi are we in?"

"The west wing."

"Hmm, help me up, I want to walk to the east wing," and both Darien and Lucerne helped Eiger up on his feet, and he began to walk with light support, "why have you made deals with pirates?"

"I know naval strength, and pirates are, well they search for what makes them money. I gave a good price, and I'm letting that deal fester with them."

"In our deal, we agreed on acquiring the strength of the lost armies, and lords to rebuild the army. This was your deal, and now I feel as though you've pulled the rug under my weary feet."

"No, no, no. Pirates aren't like us naval men. They don't wear uniforms. And they have a great fighting spirit."

"And how are they any different from my men, or the men of the other great lords?"

"They're trained under harsh conditions, for one."

"And? I could say my men trained with the hurricanes coming from the east, and the constant rain and hard winters, and the curse of the forest Mulder make my men quite strong. I guess I don't see your point."

"I'm sorry for not explaining it better than I could, my lord. They are multi purposeful. And what I plan for them is to infiltrate the lord's land, and sway his people, which in turn will sway the lords. And over the period of a few months all the lord's men will have returned to being an army, and we'd be the top generals of this army."

"Hmm," mocked Eiger, he said in a low and calm tone, "at least you have this under control, and are using men of this kingdom."

"Yes, yes," he lied.

They were beginning to pass through the overlook of the courts; the now soot smothered, and lone filled court which held so many great and important men and women. "it's horrible Eiger, you haven't restored the halls."

"I believe I'm asking again, did you see the halls burn?"

"Why would that matter?"

"In a way it's beautiful how these halls, and an event which couldn't be known, would cause the entire kingdom to become engulfed in flame."

"I don't know about that."

"Hmm," Eiger subtly mocked again, "fine then. Now I wonder. Hmm. have you ever been in the east wing of the castle, especially from high up?" Before he let Lucerne speak, Eiger corrected, "or have you ever been in Renoi before this?"

"Not quite."

"Imagine a balcony, high above the maze of perfectly placed hedges, and in the far distance the ports are filled – incredibly so – with ships of merchants and the royal navy, and other ships of lords and fishermen."

"It sounds like a nice view."

"A nice view? No, it's something more. It's knowledge, and it's knowledge that I've had for nearly two months."

Lucerne stayed quiet, he appeared to feel a poorly hidden shame, and fear that Eiger would talk about something that Lucerne didn't want to hear. For a while in silence they walked throughout the castle; Lucerne learned to keep his tongue tied. Though it was clear, he didn't know exactly why, but he felt a reason to do so. *To be safe, maybe?*

Eiger walked to this large chamber room, it seemed to be a gallery, with a wardrobe of rare paints from all across the kingdom, and the world. There was this large portrait that was being worked on of the late queen. It was unfinished, most of the canvas was filled with red paint in the background, and her deep red eyes, like Jane's, were piercing and vibrant. He opened the glass doors to a large stone balcony.

"You were right, Eiger, this is quite a great view."

"The painter never finished that one it seems. Down below you can see so much of the hedge, and look further past, you can see the docks, can you see them?"

"Yes, he must have been painting that view quite often."

"I've found this room quite quickly. That's when I realized the painter was gone – doesn't matter now where he went – and I saw a slightly different view. Do you know what I saw?"

"No?"

"I saw a port, quite like that one, and do you know what was different?" This time he didn't let Lucerne answer, "empty. Absolutely empty. There were no ships for two entire months during the most desperate moment in this kingdom's recent history."

"Well, since the navy has been in control by Grand Admiral Tylock-"

"Then what? I won't even let you make your case, you were meant to defend our shores. To keep the capital safe, and you didn't."

"I thought we were on the same side, you and I."

"Lucerne, you have betrayed my trust completely. You beacon me to an unprotected city, while you buy pirates for an army."

"I don't understand, nothing happened, how could you be upset when no pirates attacked these lands, nor did any of our lands get invaded by foreigners. How I see it, I put my life at risk, and I've conquered much because of it. I'd rather be congratulated than persecuted. I think I've done a great thing for this city and the kingdom."

"You can see the entire port from here. The northernmost dock, to the southernmost. Where are these pirates? Wait there aren't any, because you have none. You risked all the sanctity of the city and kingdom, and for what?"

"Calm down. Let's talk this out like civilized men."

"We're talking right now, I have been able to diagnose and treat this city of the cancer which corrupts it. And I've put so much money and men towards doing so. I've established peace, and lords oh so many are requesting invitations and visits. You have nothing to show, and wasted your time and mine more importantly."

"What do you suggest then," he annoyingly pushed.

"Stick to being a commodore, and leave the army to me."

"No, you're just upset that this is a difficult job. I'll be leaving on this note, and will be waiting for-"

"Nothing," said a man behind the three, "commodore Lucerne of the twelfth, come with me."

"Who are you?"

"Can you not read rankings, are you a fool and a punk?"

"No, admiral, but what do you need from me."

"I'm going to shut this down right now," he clapped his hands, and three navy men rushed with wrought iron cuffs, while he held out his polished shining sword, "commodore, you are being charged with traitorous actions, disobeying commands of high officials, and conspiracy within her royal navy."

"Wait, wait, wait! What do you mean? You assume I've committed such heinous crimes. That is false, completely false. I serve the navy, and I'm a good officer."

"Do not try to back away from these crimes."

"Allegations!" He said, trying to push away the blade, "those are allegations."

"Don't make this difficult commodore."

"I'm not being difficult, I'm not going to be imprisoned for crimes which I haven't committed."

"Duke Eiger, what do you have to say?"

"Before you go on arresting anyone, how about you tell me who you even are? What reason do you have to be here?"

"Admiral Broarch, on navy command, your grace."

"How noble, and when you take him, where will he be sent?"

"That is the navy's concern, your grace."

"So it is. What did you ask of me again? I've seemed to have forgotten."

"Duke Eiger, what do you know of the crimes that Lucerne has committed, seeing as you two were in discussion right before."

"Well to tell, I was convinced to sail away from my land for fortune and prosperity, and when I arrived I was met with a defenseless capital."

"No!" He yelled, "that's not true."

"Take him away," he said, keeping him a blade apart.

"You can't do this," Lucerne yelled as the other men were coming to him.

Lucerne balled a fist and in a rapid succession he went to swing at Eiger, but his hand was caught by the officer, and before he knew it, Broarch – with the hard metal knuckle bar – smashed his fist into Lucerne's face. An immediate swell of blood ran down his nose and into his mouth.

Lucerne looked back with those streaks of blood running down his face, with eyes of fire. He was brimming with rage, and most of it was towards Eiger.

Broarch in one thrust scabbard his sword. "Your grace, I humbly apologize for this informal meeting. I've been meaning to meet Lucerne and you."

"Do you plan on breaking my face as well, and throw me in a cold cell?"

"Hmm," he chuckled, "no, I'm not here to do that. I hear you have ties with the church."

"I am a holy man, yes."

"That's not quite what I meant. I assume you have ties with the Bishop?"

"Yes, I do."

"And I know you're fond of the church which tried to take your life, but there are going to be changes, you should have known. If I can make another assumption, I'd say that the man who tried to take your life, was a religious zealot. A cultist if you may, one who was trying to make a display by killing a major figure to keep what they have in their grasp.`"

Eiger, had a feeling he knew who that assassin belonged to, but a cultist? No. But he took a minute to reflect, but was thinking, planning, "a cultist? That's folly. A cultist to what cult?"

"That is something I'm trying to find out."

"You as in yourself, or are you using the navy's power?"

"This is a project you could call it, of naval intelligence."

"Hmm, and how do you assume that the man – with fire in his eyes – was some fanatic?"

"I tell you with complete certainty, he was. You are a victim of this cult. Which helps me sift through the possible cultists here."

"There are cultists among all of us, is Renoi? You don't think they caused the fire which killed our queen? That was a strange night."

"Indeed, that's true. Much to be believed, even if it's hard to grasp."

"Admiral Broarch is it? Can I ask you an important question?"

"Go on?"

"Can I trust your word is true, and the plague which haunts this city is this cult you 're warning me of?"

"On the crown of the queen, and if the sword she carries is sharp, you can trust me."

"Thank the great lords, and thank the gods above and below us," he prayed the three points, "and if I may ask again, Admiral Broarch, how will the navy deal with this? I don't see that a cult could just be brought with what you have."

"You don't know?"

"Should I of known?"

"Before my arrival there were many dozens of letters sent by both horse, and pigeon. But nevertheless, I will relay this to you directly. In a quick description, the national church will now be split up by the gods. There is an oppression of the gods with insufficient and dated methods of faith."

"Outdated methods of faith? What? How so? What is wrong with the way we pray, and preach. I don't quite understand."

"I will describe in greater detail for you my grace. There are great terrors being put on the people. They feel as though their prayer to the gods individually is lacking, to put it lightly. And secondly, there is only one god left with a physical presence in our land. And for a thousand years no one rationalized how this affected us all, it's horrible. We mean to fix this discrepancy, because why would those who pray to the only god left in our realm of the living have to pray to the god of death, and a fallen god."

"And this is supposed to be effective? Somehow."

"With complete and utter certainty," he finished speaking low like a snake.

A port with two fleets. He looked out at the ships filling a void he'd taken advantage of, and when Broarch left – from that moment on – Eiger watched the ports and the hedges below. "Darien," he called, "is Bishop Lazith still here in the city."

"From what I know, he is."

"Good, have a footman bring him here. I want to know who attacked me, and whether he was partly responsible."

"I can have him in two hours."

"I don't want to see him today, bring him tomorrow."

"Alright."

"But don't let him know yet, have men make sure he doesn't flee. Just in case. Did you know about this?"

"What part, my grace?"

"Did you know about the church?"

"Yes, I did."

"Have they already started with their changes?"

"From what I know they've run into their first snag, and that being both Bishop Lazith, and the city herself."

"Did they already find out that half of this city is run by private lords?"

"I don't know, but it's more likely it's the common man causing the commotion."

"He's a better man than I first thought. The question is whether they'll force him to buckle, and what'll come of him."

Outside the clouds began to swell up, and a light trickle of rain began to pour down.

"So what Broarch told me was a lie, but I want to know why they're changing the church in such an extreme way? Hmm, and this cult he spoke of. Was it Jane who first told us?"

"I do believe so."

"And parts of what he talked about, the cult in particular, were true?" And Darien nodded, "if I were to make a guess, they would be servants under the chaos god. Splitting the church would cement their power to this land. Wait no, they've already had power in this land, it would only be more noticeable. Did you hear anything in the cathedral? What the admiral was planning to do with it, when he got his hands on it?"

"I found a letter they sent with instructions on what they plan to do, my grace."

Under the darkness of early morning, Darien hid in the shadow seeking Bishop Lazith. The hall in the darkly early morning was quiet, far more quiet than it was before, and it was quieter than the outside streets and alleys. A mouse's heart could be heard beating from across the hall, but Darien made little to no sound whatsoever. His hand remained completely attached to the handle of his sword, and his cloak was wrapped around his body so much so that his figure was hard to see without squinting.

He knocked at the door, it was only a short time until that figure, moped, and revealed himself. He had a little hand lantern which he put to his face as he said, "what do you want with me? Is the duke alive? If so, what does he ask of me?"

"Today, in a few hours, you'll be summoned to Eiger's hearings. You'll promptly go to castle Renoi, and meet him there. He'll want as much as he'll ask of you. We both know what he'll want to know, so you'll tell him everything."

"Wait, um, alright. He'll send someone in a few hours," he rubbed his palm, "so why are you here? If that's the case."

"Because I want to know what you're going to say, before you go to Renoi."

"Fine, well then, um, what do you want to know?"

"Let's start off on Lord Garet, have you met him. I want short answers here."

"Yes."

"Was that recently, within the last week?"

"Also yes."

"Do you know if he were talking about any of his men when you've seen him?"

"I guess, I don't know if they were his men, but he was talking to alot of men, and I've seen the same men time and time again."

"How often does he come here?"

"He's quite religious, always asking for a private service after a normal service."

"When's the next time he'll come?"

"Usually in two days from today."

"Have these private services been in his own home?"

"Only once, his manor isn't as massive as I assume Duke Eiger's is, but it's a short distance from here."

"Now let's cover the other man in this problem, Lord Taryen, have you met him? How often, and did he speak to any men while here?"

"I also have met him, and um, he doesn't come here often, but I've never seen him talk with someone else."

"Alright then, when's the last time you saw him?"

"Actually he was here not that long ago. I believe I saw him last week talking with Lord Garet."

"Hmm, then do you have an idea of when he'll be seen again?"

"I wouldn't have an idea, he's not a very religious man, or at least he doesn't pray here often. Is there anything else you, you need from me?"

"I do not, I'll be gone, and you won't say anything of this."

"Are you not supposed to be here?"

"Just because you don't see me wont mean I'm not there, so here," he gave the Bishop coins of gold, "and shut the fuck up."

The day was still new, and the light of the sky was still less than silent. Darien walked through the sloping slums, and kept away from the sight of only men his age, and apparently near blind. At the very end in an overgrown garden was a manor guarded with rows of old black steel pikes. And the gate entrance was locked, and so were all, and so were all his side entrances. But not only that, but his lord's crest was patrolling the grounds. Some outside, and many inside.

He jumped the fence easily, falling on soft grass. It helped mask the sound. He quickly, but assuredly entered through an unoccupied window, and inside he went to the lord's door. It was unguarded, and went inside. He stood right by Karaway's sleeping body, watching, before he checked his room. Nothing of importance. He left quietly.

He traversed the halls, there were these small paintings that were strewn here and there. He saw further down the hall a man walking away from him, clearly not knowing Darien was there. So he followed this man. There were doors here and there to back away from if necessary. The man was wearing a cape which covered the emblem on his tunic. He watched the cape shift around as it shifted in the air. The guard passed by an open window, curtains blew with a soft light air. The guard turned to close, and Darien had a good look at him. He recognized both his crest and face.

Darien fell back, and went into an empty room, away from sight. For quite some time he did the same checking all around the manor under the sight of none. The day had begun to lighten, and he knew he had to leave before a head saw him. So he retreated the way he entered. And out the window he jumped the fence over again, and walked away like he wasn't there.

As the light began to sweep into the city, Darien kept notice of the light before that time came. He intended to get to Renoi before too long. The life of the city began to show, as women opened windows of their home, and smoke from chimneys released a large puff of new smoke from putting in a few new logs on the coals. With this were people going around knocking on windows and less people trying to sweep the glass from the streets. Once he came to the higher posher end of the city, he passed by a few watchmen, and soon there were less navy men, and closer to Renoi were Eiger's men.

Darien entered the keep, the morning was high, and the duke awoke in a bed attended by a maid.

Chapter Forty-Eight:

"Your grace," Darien said to Eiger while standing in the duke's chamber, "the navy are starting to patrol, like they were the watchmen. Although I don't know how many numbers they send."

"How many total ships do they have, because as I know there's two fleets here. That could be anywhere from a near thousand to a few thousand men. Then we'd need to know how many men could hold the ship, and how many the admiral would be away while in the city. And this blasted note," Eiger said, throwing the paper on the desk, "they're splitting the church into three, but why?"

"We're trying to get a few men into their ranks to see what they're doing."

"And when can we expect that?"

"Most likely within the week. "

"With both the tower, and the navy, do they search the slums?"

"Yes, they do, but from what I know, not many ever actually are there. Mostly all their patrollers go around it."

Eiger thought for a second, "do I have enough men to spread around the city?"

"Currently, not many, you have about half of the men the tower has, if that, and possibly a third or a fourth of the navy."

"I'll have letters sent to certain lords from across this county, and city. Any men they send will be better than not."

"But currently what do you want done?"

"How many of Karaway's men do we have in retainer?"

"From the men we know of, we have the vast majority, maybe eighty or ninety percent."

"I think it's time to start the reformation process."

"But most of them are just thugs, and thieves."

"But they have hands, and already know where the point of a spear goes."

"We still don't know who the man who stabbed you is, and who he is tied to."

"I believe it was the other crime lord's men, is there a contradiction to my inference?"

"No, my grace, but I think we shouldn't deny the possibilities of others, like Lazith, Pias, or someone else, or even this cult."

"Well I have limited resources, and need to consolidate as much as I can towards whom I think is most likely possible."

"The men shouldn't all be consolidated around the slums. It would draw attention, until eventually either the tower or the navy finds out about the crime lords."

"There's not much I can do about it. Do you have an opinion on this?"

"The men in Karaway's land, wear your crest. Don't let any watchmen think that the men are yours. A crest doesn't make an alliance, or honor. So make most of them go crestless."

"That wouldn't work. They might see a series of nameless men as a gathering of suspicious men."

"Then they'll be dressed in Karaway's crest."

"If the navy happens to stumble onto Karaway's land and sees a monstrous number of men, they might be suspicious," he poured a glass of tea, "while you're still here, I want to keep you my eyes and ears?"

"But, my grace, if they wear your crest, they'll be even more suspicious."

"If they hold no crest, the navy, or Pias might have those men imprisoned for carrying their gear. So no, they'll wear my crest, and

I'll tell them I've made great acquaintances with Karaway, and that'll be that. Has anything new come from the pesky lords?"

"Nothing substantial enough that hasn't been said from Bishop Lazith in your meeting."

"I want them to watch even closer. I want to know when these lords eat, and sleep. I need them even closer, much closer."

"Currently I don't believe that is possible."

"How so?" He said before drinking his tea.

"The only way to get closer would be to infiltrate their premises, and if our men were caught there would be plenty of consequences for them."

"What about the women? Have we tried putting maids in their manors?"

"We haven't, but if they know that they're being spied upon, they might keep an eye out for any behavior."

"Then how difficult would it be to get in contact with his maids?"

"If we could somehow get in contact with their maids, then it would only be a matter of time, but in this case as of today It's not possible. It would simply be easier to take their manor by force, or try to write a letter to them like you did with Karaway."

"Either way, I want men closer to these lords, to track everything," he took another sip, "I send men to find information I want, and so does the navy, and so does Pias in that dreaded tower. How about them, those pesky lords, have they been seen sending spies after me?"

"Most likely so, but I don't think they'd be nearly as effective as us, they mostly lack resources."

"I would agree, but close to a week ago now a knife was

stuffed in my chest a dozen times. So I'm clearly not as effective as I think I am."

"Well you're not dead, so the navy will have to wait to give no-one time to dig a grave, or to not send letters to those who should be receiving."

It was a mist filled morning, he was walking through the city's slums like he was told to. He kept a knife in his coat, and pulled his boot straps up, to keep mud from entering and giving him some rot of some kind.

He passed by this one shop, it had stained glass windows, and he assumed it to be a pewter shop. That's what he saw while looking inside. Along with a thief who broke the lock and was sacking a series of silver plates, and knives for scraping butter.

The further he went the more he saw. The blocks under Lord Garet had seen little light of day. This was his second rotation on these streets. For a few hours as the morning took it's time to start, and a series of fearless old men with knives on their hips walked their daily draw. An old woman looked at him, and she gestured.

"Hey you, young man," she yelled to him, "you, come here for a moment."

He took this bait, walking up to the old woman, she said to him, "I've seen you walk up and down these streets with such a face that looks like you're always looking for something. Do you need help? Are you lost?"

"I suppose I am," he kept his hands disclosed in his coat, "this town is confusing."

She rubbed her arms, "chilly isn't it. Come in, I'll make you some hot water."

"No, that's alright."

"I insist, come in, it's much warmer inside."

He looked around, there was this man with dark eyes watching him, before darting his head away. "Alright I'll come in."

The house was quant, and at first it wasn't apparently warmer, but eventually it felt only slightly so. She put a kettle made of copper on the fire, the rays reflecting across the room. "It's dangerous out there, ya know."

"Oh I've seen some. If it's so dangerous, why do you live here?"

"Cause it's my home, and I'll be damned if those crooks push me out of my own home."

"I know some people who need that spirit."

"If you don't adapt, you die. And for a lady at my age, I'd say that's quite grand."

"I'd say the same for my mother. Those are good words."

She grabbed the pot of water – now sufficiently hot – and poured two mugs for herself and him. The steam which drifted from the surface of the water danced in the dusty air. She asked, "where are you heading to, young man?"

"I'm heading far north, but it'll be a long time till I get there, so I guess I'm wandering till I get there."

"Well I've never left this kingdom, but that's stupid."

"It's gonna be winter soon, so I'd rather wait till it passes."

"Just go, if you keep waiting, you'll never make it. No use being a virgin in a dangerous city like this."

"Is it just criminals, why is the crime so bad?"

"Could you check the door?"

"Alright," he sat back down afterwards, "draft too cold?"

"Son," she said, "it's gangs, and they like to spy on us, and if we say something they try to do something. Horrible things."

"It's that bad? I've seen some crimes here and there since staying here, but nothing that bad."

"No, no, you don't understand, it's not just gangs, it's a gang of gangs."

"You know I think I still don't understand."

"Do you want a knife in my gut boy? There's horror in this city. You must have seen it?"

"Who's causing it, I'll go kick his ass."

"Lord Garet wouldn't like that, he'll send someone after me."

"Really who, has he sent men after others?"

"Why are you asking all these questions? Get out, strange man, get out."

He finished his mug of water, and placed it neatly and quietly on a table, and he said, "good day."

He rubbed his hands together and breathed into them, a chill of mist escaped his fingers.

Chapter Forty-Nine:

She was bedridden for that day, and she was in such a state where she couldn't even wash herself. Around her wound, right below her chest, was the smell and look of death. It was a slow acting rot, but rot nonetheless. Whenever clothes brushed against the wound, it stung like a dozen bees. Kreshen helped where he could, but this poison was advanced. He looked grave constantly while trying to treat the venom, but whenever Jane pointed it out, he put on a false mask to keep her from being distraught. It reminded her of Porcelania, and all those clay masks, somehow.

"Father Kreshen, can you help with the pain?" She knew he wouldn't be able to since he hadn't yet, and as expected, he said, "I'm sorry, your grace. This is the best I can do. But not long from now the surgeons will help you, they'll heal you."

"You're in safe hands, my lady," said Jaune, "just cooperate, and you'll be as graceful as you were meant to be."

"I'd rather be in a fighting position, where's my sword?"

A minute passed, Barrett brought that sword. It's long handle, and long leaf blade, it was still polished like a mirror. With her little strength she rubbed the edge, "don't cut yourself," Kreshen said, but she didn't.

"If I were to, would that pain be something that distracted me from this one? How could I know that this pain would ever go away? Every day feels like a week or a month; an absolute eternity of this prolonged pain, and I don't believe it'll ever go away."

"And what would you do? Keep cutting yourself? You would only make your pain greater. Your hell would be twice as worse. Make it easier on yourself and us, and think about your actions rationally before you do them," Jaune said.

"I never said I would hurt myself."

"This is a hard time for all of us. We have just made a point of relative balance. Let's keep it that way, please."

"A place of balance? I'm stuck in a bed slowly rotting to death, and Litus isn't even here, I'm surrounded by people I barely know."

"The rangers and keepers here were suspicious and scared of him, so he's stuck in a cell."

"A cell!?"

"I don't think it'll be for long, but they wanted to make sure he wasn't some shadow spawn, or reaper, or wraithkin," he said with a shudder.

"It's only going to go further and further down."

"My grace, don't say that, life always has its funny things, but the disturbances around you will eventually be met with equal luck, and as for what we can do now – I know you're not fond of it – but pray for your safety."

She scoffed, and as her diaphragm sheared from movement, she had a jolt of pain strike her back. Kreshen prayed and brushed her wound with an open palm. With a jolt of electric sweat, he eased the pain slightly. When he released his hand, there was a red mark on his palms. Jane breathed heavily, sweat fell down her face, "I can't think rationally, when all I know is pain."

"It'll hopefully be over soon," Kreshen said, keeping his strong mask looming.

"Aren't I the queen? Can't I order them to come to me sooner? Or to release Litus for fucks sake?"

"They're going as fast as they can. They need to make sure what they do won't kill you instead," Barrett ushered, "it may be difficult, but have patience."

"What happens if I die before they meet me, or they kill me? What will you all do then?" She looked to Kreshen first.

"My lady," Kreshen said slowly, "you shouldn't think about that."

She turned to Jaune and Barrett, "what about you all, what would you do?"

"We'd bury your body, and return to Lakeholm. There's not much we could do. But you won't die. We won't let it happen."

The sound of a door opened, and quickly, vigorously men rushed in ordering with a roar to her guards and the priest to back away. Jane whimpered out, "Litus," *This is it?*

They stripped her body, removing what clothing hid her skin. It felt humiliating, although she couldn't do anything about it. Her senses in that moment became sharp, and she could hear the cackling of a fireplace, and part of its warmth, the only warmth. There was a humming and praying in what seemed like a tongue that she couldn't know or say. Close by she tensed with the smell of rot, protruded and reaped a disheartening which followed with pain, an impossible plague.

With what strength she had she bobbed her head up to see a gathering of men, she didn't know with tools of what appeared to be glass, and some of a bright metal. One of the men grabbed her head, and he yelled in a grossly and booming voice, "bite down on this, it's leather, with the pain, you don't want to bite your tongue off," and she did so.

She lowered her head onto a soft pillow, and soon their tool went forth, and henceforth all that feeling dissipated. Except for pain. All she could think, and sense, and feel was that pain. A pain so indescribable, it would be like describing unknown words, or whatever could be beyond the sky. And for a moment, she fell through the bed. Falling slowly, limbless, deep below the ground, through dirt, and the gaping halls of some castle.

And soon she drifted into an ocean, and could remember distant thoughts, a recent thought shot into her head, of vibrancy. There far below the ground, a red sun, deep of hue, and sweltering heat. Its rays swung around and at the ends were these whips of black flame. She drifted closer and closer, and in an instant a pike of black flame penetrated her body, and again and again. She wheeled and cried, with no sound to escape. The pain was vibrating, and electrifying, and orgasmic. It was a shaking pain, and an ecstasy above all else. The pike kept prodding into her flesh on and on again, leaving no mark except for the one in her chest.

Her head was raised up, and she was now chewing on a small cut piece of bark. She spitted it out as quickly as she realized it was there, and said – in what was supposed to be a cruel way – "what happened!?" But it came out as a gentle plea of exhaustion.

Those series of men and women, all rangers and maids, were around her bed, while Kreshen gave a prayer to her, which she didn't cut off. One of these rangers, an old man, with stable hands looked to her, and she put her head up, and there was a pool of black blood streaming out of her wound, and she realized they were keeping calm. She felt she couldn't move, one of the maids pulled out a freshly cut piece of bark, and whispered to Jane, "open your mouth, and don't spit this out now."

The cell was cold. Although it was filled with grains of sand from previous cellmates, the cell had a lightless chill. There in front of him was a single stream of pale light, it twas a harrow sight in the crack of the wall. He tried to reach for the light, but couldn't. Not even the dust could touch him.

There were footsteps coming; a deep thud each one. And at the cell door, were two men who looked like rangers, and said they were too. They held out two keys, one for the door, and the other for the shackles. "She asked for you. You know who. If you were a wraith, you'd be the poorest one of all. So come out, you're supposedly safe," and As they walked out of the cell, Litus let the pale light fall over him, and the light was cold and thin.

They walked him through the halls, from the dungeon, to the ground above. The inside of the walls of Sebois – although different from Esty – was eerily similar. *If they took me, what about Elliot?* It felt comical, because shortly after thinking it, Elliot was found. He had ran up to Litus and the rangers escorting him, yelling, "what are you doing with my Client?"

"Orders," he said.

"He's not some prisoner, and he's not some wraith. You hide intentions, like a child hides guilt."

"On the queen's orders," he said with a blunt hammer.

Elliot repeated those words quietly to himself. He said under his voice, "he's not a toy," and he followed them.

Elliot didn't let them shake him off, but once they got the chamber where Jane was held he was forced to stay outside the door.

Kreshen didn't even notice Litus at first, but Jane looked but couldn't say anything; her lips quivered but fell with exhaustion. Eventually Kreshen had pulled away from burning himself out, and he looked at Litus.

Litus had kept the arrow, never able to give it to anyone who truly knew the poison, so at this moment he drew the arrow from the void, and presented it to Kreshen, and he said "you didn't believe that the poison was Blaekrot. But here, this was the arrow which pierced her," Kreshen sputtered.

The ranger took the arrow carefully. Subtly and easily bending the shaft, "surprise it didn't shatter," he pulled the tip close to candle light, spreading the black liquid with his fingers; the viscosity as it pulled back over the trench, "it's the rot," he muttered and sighed distastefully.

He turned to the maids and other rangers operating on Jane and he took them away for a short moment, and amongst themselves they discussed what to proceed with after. After a minute they returned to where they were, cleaning up what they've done, and stitching up the wound on Jane's chest.

They rubbed the wound free of blood, and poured over to cleanse skin pale hot sand. What was left on her skin was a fine layer of dust. Which was soon lightly swept off.

She raised her head – with assistance of a maid next to her – and was nearly upright, noticing the vague semblance of reality. Her sight wavered around, while the small candle light pulsated in her eyes, and by the time her headache and senses returned, she noticed a man who was speaking to her had just finished. And everyone had a strange queer look. Even Litus, whom she could only see his bright eyes.

"Could I get some water?"

"Do you understand what that'll mean, my grace?"

"What? What do you mean? What did you say?"

"Have you ever heard of blaekrot? It's often called just the rot?"

"Well yes, Father Kreshen said that the poison on the arrow was it, why?"

"Well we know it for sure to be it, and we don't have anything to deal with that."

She looked around at them all again, "so am I . . . going to die?"

A maid came in with a set of clothes from her truck, and a vase of water with a stone mug.

Jane was dressed in a thin and fine silk and linen dress which was not the gown which she'd come accustomed to. But she wore it finely and sickly. The sounds of the fabric being pushed over her was all which was audible in that room.

"My grace, we won't let that happen."

"What is going to happen to me then?"

"We've realized that what pastor Kreshen has done was the best treatment for you, so he's agreed to follow you to the city east of here."

"What? Why? I can barely move, everything hurts-" she took in a deep breath, "and you're going to have me travel, where?"

"The city of Prame, home of the surgeons guild. If anyone can cure this, they can and they will."

"Then have them send men, surgeons here? I'm being treated by Kreshen like you said."

"We won't have time to send a letter to them, by man or pigeon, and then have surgeons sent here. Time is not on your side. You could fall from this any day, and each concurrent day that poison will only grow closer and closer to that outcome. We can't let that happen."

She grew solemn, watching their faces once more, before being handed a mug of water. Kreshen reached out for it first. "It will taste bitter my grace, but you should drink some tea, instead," and she didn't argue against it anymore.

He took the mug and placed a few flakes of dried leaves into the mug. Soon he made the water heat and the leaves dissipated until steam made the tea steep. He gave it back to her, holding her head in his hand, deeply exhausted. She took a sip of the tea, and like he said, it was incredibly bitter. Her face scrunched, and she backed away from the mug for a moment. She then put her strength into it, downing the rest of the drowsy tea, and gave it back to the maid. The bitterness stung as she drifted away, but at least it wasn't as sour as the wound which momentarily left her mind.

Chapter Fifty:

The sands drifted through the winds and across the infinite lands. The sediment layers split apart. The particles clung and swaft around him. He watched a figure ahead with sand compacted to his form drift, and when he fell there was nothing left. The dust flew away from this figure and the lands continued as they were.

He kept the stride, as his walk drifted on and on. Till eventually he fell as well. His body shattered into a billion pieces of dust, and he swept through the dunes and upward towards the sky. Far in the distance which he was heading was a mountain. It was a wide being, with multiple peaks of red and orange layers.

The dust continued to drift higher and higher through the clouds, until he met the other side. He reached and pulled himself out of the clouds and the stars high above all surrounded like refractions of a fish bowl. Up here the clouds were dunes, but instead of dust, it were swaths of a mist with little fragments of water beginning to form into a crystal.

He walked on newly formed crystal ice paths just obscured by the cloud mists. The dunes passed one by one, as below he could sense the mountain peak. He walked, and walked for a near infinite amount of time, his body decaying, and each particle slowly falling away and down to the ground below where it sought. He walked and walked further, until he was down to the last grain.

He jumped, and as the last of his body fell through the clouds, and the weave of forming ice crystals. The wind threw him every which way; his freefall was not in his hands. So he drifted, on and on. Till the ground was there in a short time.

He fell in a cup held by a man with the face of a malkin, and a body of a malkin, so he was assumed to be one. And was carried on, in that cup jostling around, as a grain of sand. The malkin walked up the mountain's stones, and he and others climbed so often they were worn into stairs. One side was a wall of rough orange and beige rock, and the other was a sheer cliff below, and only growing steeper and more sheer the further they walked up. At the top of the mountain which he hadn't seen yet was an immense palace carved from the stone and weathered by the sand storms causing an entire castle to disappear at a far distance. As they jostled to the entrance which held a doorway larger and grander than most palaces, or used to be, like the sides of the castle the door was sputtered with sand and dust. Though they walked through the door on the side, made of a light wood.

Inside was a hall of pillars and marble stone so intricately cut that it seemed to have been made by a race that died long ago in a grander more sophisticated time. Though it was an assumption. Along the walls were stacks and rows and shelves of scrolls and books, and papers. Some were kept together, others slightly eaten by book worms, and others were fragile to near disintegration possibilities.

The pillars were evenly distributed, and untouched by weathering, untouched by skin. But the whole floor was made of either marble or another stone which wasn't known. Light spilled through a stained glass window far above, in the very back of the church, above a statue of a mysterious figure. The light of many hues and colors danced as they bounced and reflected and twirled around the reflective floors.

The little pitter patter of malkin as he walked muttered in the air creating a little symphony in the ambiance which made this holy light waltz grandeur and grandeur.

The statute was but a tall veiled man, but a little strand of silver gilded hair seeped out. He stood in the center of an ocean of silent waters. It was held in a bowl, not far away from the land. The malkin knelt down, filling his mug with the waters, and mixed it around. He then let the mug fall and drift in the water.

"Do you know the odds of catching sand in an open mug?" He said in a tone of two.

"Yes."

"That is a grand idea: fortune."

"It infuriates me."

"Oh I know, I know a great deal."

"Tell me."

"Everyone's eyes are on what is physical, not of light, or warmth, but precious silver and gold, and either a hand on a pike or heads on one."

"And this is not how things should be?"

"No, not at all? Why is fortune won by the winners?"

"By what medium? You ask about the medium of war?"

"War is won by strategy, luck, and resources. It's rarely fair, except those who step back, and see with eyes of clear clean glass. And nothing's fair, except an equal bet. I thought I knew you, or knew of you."

"I think you know more of me than I know myself," he chuckled.

"But you've seen dreams?"

"Of what kind do you wish?"

"Your dreams such as this one, of a key and gate."

"Have I told you this?"

"The key and gate at the end of a hall of dark stone, you've seen."

"How are you related to me?"

"Very apt, quite a clever one. You'll sense my presence in time, hopefully."

"Besides gates – which I seek – what about betrayal?"

"Funny that."

"How is that?"

"How do you know you won't betray yourself?"

"In saying that, have you, or will you betray us?"
"How about a gate?"

"Do you know where it is?"

"The gate with which this key fits?" The malkin tossed the key into the water, it landed in the cup.

"Yes," he said softly.

"But you should not go past that gate."

"And why's that?"

"You'll alienate most of all the land you tread, and the seas you sail."

"But I have to know, there is something there, my memories possibly."

"And what knowledge would you receive there that's not here?"

"Don't you know, just as well as I?"

"But you'll learn plenty. For that gate will destroy us."

"If that's the toll," he said, "show me the gate."

The malkin nodded. He walked past the statue, and the end of the hall was completely made of that stained glass image of something tangible and irrational. The light of the infinite shown down on the holy and the forgetful. How it erupted, and broke by each lead stitch. The glass warped into a bridge with a street lamp made of the sun, but past it all was darkness.

"We will eventually track into a gravely pain of our making."

They crossed, while the sharp edges cut their feet leaving a trail of blood behind. He could only see through the veil. He looked at his pale hands, how they were blurry and stone-like.

It was a shortened period to what it felt like, an instantaneous flash of time. They had walked past the entrance without realizing where it was. He spoke up gracefully, "where is this? Is this the future?"

"No, this is destined."

They walked still, little glass marbles still littered the ground. Soon shifting from their insanity of color, and subtly shifted into a glowing black presence. They dominated the cold. He looked back, a set of doors made of the shards closed and its light diffused through from behind reaching with faint hands to where he was going. Walking further and further still, he sensed something, so he asked, "so is that the gate?"

There was nothing, and now he knew that. It was a short walk away, he held the key, and the gate was just. Would nothing stop him from going through? So he trudged through. A pool of mirror-like water rose to his ankles. Penetrating the pores in his smooth porous skin. The chill reached and cracked like the end of a bull whip. They latched onto him, biting into his skin, piercing and corrupting when they sowed.

He tried to push through, but even with this new form it was decaying the same. But there it was, shortly ahead. He had to push, just a little bit more, *what is behind that elusive gate? Past will solve all my problems.* His skin thinned and soon with a snap, he was hobbled and stepped on the stump he was left with. He stepped further, and dust fell away like the blood did too.

He jumped at those cold iron bars. A chain rattled as he tried to get up. A hefty lock swung from side to side with the struggle. He tried to draw from the void, *but what is the void?* Everything around him looked like the void. *The pillars of that church? Cathedral? The castle? Whatever it be, those pillars, it could have been the true void, before I've lost my mind, and memories. But how could it be, it wasn't accessible.* He couldn't keep or grab the key, wherever it was.

He banged on the chains, and clutched the lock with a firm grip. Chalk painted the outside of the lock. He pulled and pulled, but it wouldn't budge still. He turned it toward him, and with his blurred vision he saw no opening. No key could fit, there wasn't an opening for it.

The smoke of a single candle far past the bars drifted on towards him. The glass box which held the candle too drifted closer and closer as the cold chips and shredded dust off his leg. A certain stream of this smoke twisted and twirled around a single point just above that glass box. He kept pulling at the lock, trying to break it. He kept pushing his hand into himself, trying to reach for the key, only to find in the darkness ahead it was held by a figure of the smoke. A grumble and laugh protruded forth in a haunting echo chamber. "This is what you're looking for?" He jingled the key.

"Please help," he said, "I'm dying, please open this gate! I need to get through!"

The gate opened and he was thrust forward by a force, and landed by the feet of this shadowy figure which almost resembled something familiar. "Here, you dropped this relic," he said while tossing the key.

He held out his hands to catch it, but instead it dissolved into the soot of smoke. "This isn't the key?"

"That wasn't the gate either. You already told yourself that this was a dream. Wasn't that so?"

"If this is a dream, show me the gate."

"This is a dream, but you won't control it."

"Can you tell me where the gate is?"

"You are not something worthy yet."

He looked up and the figure had horns that – like the smoke that billowed – swirled into a bar that protruded straight up. But his face was a dark cloud, and within the emptiness were two trailing flames of purple. His eyes shifted along the same as the flame of that encased and protected candle. He looked so similar to Litus. "Are you Litus?"

"That is not a valid name for me nor you."

"Then who are you? That malkin was him, and so am I, who are you?"

"When you find the real gate, you'll know everything. Absolutely everything. It is then you will know who we are."

"What will happen after?"

But the figure didn't speak. "Turn back from which you've come, then come back the righteous way. It is only then that," he figure disappeared.

He limped back on his stump towards that kaleidoscopic insanity. When he touched the water, the process began anew. The freezing ate at his skin, tearing chunks off, sheering sand from the surface of dunes. The pain of following a path with which he wrought not to follow, but forced to, only cascaded the intense pain which he endured.

Chunks and chunks fell more and more. There was now a stump per leg, and it only climbed up his torso. And all he looked at was the rainbow light behind that blurry veil. He crawled, gripping the ground with his hands. His silver hair falling into the lake of ice. The light which came from the door cascading out and combining into a false purity of white light. He fell down trying to watch his reflection in the pool, but the ripples and veil shrouded all he could know and make sense of. The doors opened into a true light, and his reflection was even further lost. He crawled further and further, refusing to give up – even when he was legless and a loss of an arm – and he kept pushing forward.

The door was only a few feet away, but soon as he disintegrated, it fell further and further back out of reach. He made one last ditch effort throwing himself forward towards, and it all faded into nothing.

She awoke with a lingering numbness on the surface of her scar and went to instinctively rub it, but pulled away before the pain had a chance to pierce her so early since awakening. Litus sat by her side, she didn't know for how long, but it wouldn't matter. "Litus," she asked, "could you help me sit up?"

He came to her, pushing her up. "Have you ever known someone so low?" And he didn't know how to respond, "I guess that's a no. I thought and was told so many countless times that this luck of mine would turn, and I would be the luckiest girl alive, but no. I'm stuck in this perpetually tumble down an ever steeper hill," she looked at him for something, "it has been so long, but I guess I still forget your condition.

"No," she said, "I'm sorry. I've thought often about how you've saved my life so often, and I've never been able to repay that debt. Now I don't think I'll ever be able to do that anymore."

He got up from his chair, patting her arm as a maid was entering the room, and Kreshen followed her in. Litus left the room, only looking back once.

Pinky brought Garnettes mare out from the stables, along with the other guards and rangers. He fastened a saddle and a mount for her bags. He was instructed by the rangers on how to fasten these rope looped harnesses which looked like they were for looping boots into.

All the other rangers were saddling up horses, a couple were coming from the woods with bundles of sticks all ranging in size. They packed chests full of cooking supplies and food, and all her grace's clothes, and ointments, and plenty of the leaf Kreshen brewed. They brought a couple of mules to carry water and other heavy supplies like arrows.

Shortly after – while the morning went on like the dew of fog – Queen Garnette was escorted out by guards and was more placed then helped mounted. She clutched her chest the entire time.

The gates opened and the hills were sprawled of thin grass along with the thin collections of sand.

Through the hills they marched, and agony was exhausting. They rode up hills and down into deep ravines, the sand crept further in. Soon enough in the dry desert they had to come to a stop when Garnette's bandages had begun to grow full of a yellow and green puss, and needed changing. They unpacked clean linen, and dealt with the wound with a splash of clear alcohol and hot sand then wrapped the wound anew.

They had traveled on, with the sandy chunks of grass being kicked up every which way, and they only had to stop for Garnette's pain. Pinky often was one of the people requested to help from the other rangers and Kreshen. He hadn't known exactly why, but he liked the acknowledgement from them, and felt he needed to help as much as he could from what he caused.

The night dawned forth, they made their campfire boiling water to clean the wound better. Her grace apologized mostly to Litus, the strange half wraith, or that's what Pinky thought of him. Kreshen, Jaune, and a few of the rangers did thank him, and her grace gave thanks later as well which he accepted, but felt embarrassed. There was very little he could do to deal with the death he was responsible for. So as he looked at the sky, there he thought he felt a man talking with the voice of Garland, but there was no one like that around.

Litus and Jane both looked up at watching the sky pass, but what they saw were different things. She saw the infinite passing of dark clouds only growing darker, and Litus saw near the opposite. He saw an infinite passing, and stopping, existence, and non existence all within the clouds which shackled the sky.

Chapter Fifty-One:

When they awoke, with cold sand on their clothes and cloaks. Their mares once dark now lightened with itchy dust. They tended to Jane's wound. It was obvious that pain, the stinging. It's constant blaring. Over and over, unending, and undying. A reminder of information she didn't ask for.

They packed what little things they unpacked, and kicked sand over the crumbling ash and used coals. Refusing the campfire to produce thin rising streams of smoke. They mounted and began their walk over the sandy dunes. Particles of dust brushed over the dunes like smoke off a burning log.

Litus rode his dark mare behind Jane, and her guards were on either side of him. He was forced to listen to their talk being stuck between it. He eventually grew quite tired of their talks but it never ended.

"What does the guild do better than us?"

"Well they consistently practice. Meanwhile, if you practiced the sword more, you might be a competent swordsman."

"No I mean, why is Blaekrot so difficult to deal with? I've been meaning to ask, but why?"

"You're asking someone who knows the same amount as you."

Elliot overheard this babble, and moved up to meet their place. "Do you know anything about poison you two?" He asked, "what do you imagine poisoning is like? Or how fast it would occur?"

"I would assume poison would kill someone in at most a day," Pinky said.

"Rangers, not all, but most know the cures to poisons that work that quickly, as well as poison that is found in Mulder, but

Blaekrot is a long crawl, and it doesn't even come from this continent."

"Oh, but is that it?"

"Well I suppose it's not just that, but that it's rare as well. Even in the lost kingdom of the Tens where it originates."

"Is that why all the rangers back at the castle were so quick to denounce it?" Asked Pinky.

"Well yes, but that makes me wonder, why was it here?"

"It was from a wraith as well," Barrett said.

"They do travel very long distances, but I guess it was a strange coincidence."

"No it was no coincidence. I'll tell you that."

"Now you're sounding like Garland," he chuckled softly.

"Yeah I guess you're right. Isn't that odd?"

"A companion of you two?"

"Yes, and a good friend too. He died to a wraith on our travels, to a wraith."

"Hmm," Elliot though, "as much as we like to think we know about wraiths, we never truly know what makes them tick."

"Well I know they strike fast with their sabers."

"They do indeed, but the sword is never specific."

"I get that, but I don't know, maybe I'm seeking something, or wanting to believe I know why one killed him so."

"That was nearly two months ago now, what are the chances that same wraith attacked us in Mulder."

"If it were, the next time that bastard dares to approach, I'll stick this blade so far through his chest, the quillons will reach the other side."

The day passed, anew began, and the sands they crept were deathly cold under the early morning's sky. On large dunes and on the horizon they could see it. A sprawling city, home to one of the greatest guilds in the kingdom, looked smaller than a worm, but that was still a few days away.

Jane felt this strange heat build as they traveled great distances. She grabbed at her chest, trying not to touch her bandage, but just her clothes, "poison," she muttered garishly, "my chest is burning up like a leaf on hot coals."

"It could very well be a symptom; you should drink more water," Kreshen said.

"I feel it getting warmer now that you mention it," a ranger said.

"It's a symptom of the rot, it's not getting warmer out here," Kreshen said.

She had wished that the heat was due to the sand, or the air, or that there were something to blame, but it was pain that radiated. It hadn't been replaced, but added to the pain in which she hated. She rubbed her chest, trying to numb some of that pain, to contain it where it was. To try to.

The sky shifted over into a deep slate of darkness. But they continued to travel some distance, they could see that the city grew larger with each hour, and each climb of a great height. They made camp at the tall top of a dune, although they kept their fire low. The night kept marching forward. And it never stopped. Time never stopped.

They all awoke within minutes of each other, and began their travels for the day. They didn't unpack much, and escaped quickly. Just like the three days prior they walked and walked. The sand was quite loose, their footings were much less manageable than before, but that didn't stop them. All they did and could do was push and continue to push further.

The dunes dust blew and the sky was dark during the mid day. Even with Jane's pain, they looked on to the incoming city gracefully. It felt weird though. It had only been a few hours, and the city ahead was significantly larger than it appeared before. But still at first with the tiring drudge up and down the steep and increasingly speckled sand.

It would be another hour passing and a deep climb of a surprising stiff dune in which they saw a sight quite different. The city of Prame was further ahead, but it wasn't the sight that grew much quicker than they expected. Between them and the city were an arrangement of tents, of which Litus, Jane, her guards, and Kreshen didn't realize what they were until the ranger leading them uttered, "bandits."

Elliot checked to see if his nice recurve bow was by his side, the lead ranger called him out, "you're not going to go attack them are you?"

"If they are bandits, we'd have the advantage of surprise."

"And what if they two had bows, or a man with a preloaded bolt quick to fire. What then? We're not going to put in any more danger than is necessary."

"So we're going to go around, for how long?" Jane entered.

"My grace, we're taking the safest route."

"We could also create a diversion, lead them elsewhere while the queen goes straight through."

"And what are the chances of that failing, I'd say high, we're going around."

"We have an advantage: surprise."

"This is over, we're going around, cause if we just found out they were bandits, they might think we were wealthy merchants. They'd think that, and then who really has the advantage of surprise. We go around."

So there they went, they turned in a great direction to retreat some ways back, and to trek another path to the side of the troubling tents. Now they felt the sand in their boots, and could hear the subtle heaving from their horses.

They lost precious time, and stopped much less than they did days prior to make some back. They all felt the same thing. Every once in a while they looked to Jane to see if she was either still alive, or wasn't in pain. Some of them had a face that wasn't distinguishable. *Nothing will cure this, not the poison, and not the rules of the world, does it?*

The night sky began to dawn once more, and they still weren't at the city yet. For hours and hours they circled around the street bandits trying and hoping not to be seen. With their special caution, fueled with determination, hope, and skill they appeared to not have attracted a single eye from the tent men. They hoped to not see the glare of a looking glass. Or at worst hear the tramping of hooves.

The sky became a bright red. The hooves were marred on the repetitive march that ran further and further on. Although by then the ground was no longer such a loose sand and was more of a harder clay or denser mineral surface. They didn't care what surface was under the hooves of their mares; they cared for one thing: the persistence for survival.

The blood in their ears and the beating of their heart was all they could hear. If a war horn was blown, they couldn't hear. And even as the sun dawned and the moon invaded, they marched on and on. And then they could see behind them directly those same dreary men, but it was so dark the torches and its short light was all that could be seen in mass for each pirate rider.

"Look over there. It's the city. I say we push on, and within the night or morning we'll make it there."

Elliot nodded, "what's a bit more pushing then."

It was quiet as they rode on. None of them wanted to speak. For most they were just exhausted, but for some they felt this pushing on their frames. Like being stuck in a box of spiders or ants. But they didn't quite know just why they were quiet, but they were.

Sometimes when Litus turned his head, he saw the flickering of light of the tents, and other times he thought he saw no light emanate from the city gates. And in a flash there was absolutely no light at all.

It was cold, all they felt was this cold and the brushing of wind and sand across their skin, and the sound of turbulence in their ear. It was quiet still. And they moved slower, evermore. Till all they could hear again was the slow beating in their chest.

It came like a howl in the dark, as a small arrow whizzed by, landing by their feet. They didn't have to speak to know no matter how hard they tried in their detour, they were spotted.

Elliot and others pulled out their short riding bows and returned the fire which came to them. In the dark they couldn't see what attacks were coming, they knew for absolute certain they were coming, but not how many.

The trotting of horses pushed forward, and men on horseback came darting at them. They reared up, trying to ride to their blind spots. There were two, no three, or more of them, they thought who encircled them.

Litus pulled from the void the long two handed falchion. He held it out in one hand as he entered the out wall of their company. Elliot pulled out first, with the scythe in both hands, and trust in his horse. In a gap between two of the riders he came out encircling them, but in reverse. The first on his left which roared to him was swiftly thrown off his horse, and a slash came across his chest although it was not a deadly one.

Litus then took his opportunity and pulled through another gap in the raiders line and he too had an advantage of surprise, landing a splitting blow across the bandits neck. A spew of roses came from his gaping neck. He joined Elliot's rear and formed the raiders' anti-circle.

And as the raiders came closer and closer, their blades swinging so much closer to their arms or legs or necks, a few hit. Jane was stuck in the center of all of this, she watched the rangers from Sebois start to get hit, but they wouldn't quit. They tried to find an opening in any way they could, but the circle grew smaller. One of the rangers had been taken, and fell down to the darkness. A different pulsing of trotting was coming. How many more were coming with their wrought steel, and their sharpened spears.

Litus had come into contact with these incomers. He was thrown out of the circle from an attempt to destabilize their incoming attack. He too caught them by surprise. A single strike threw one off and was brought down with his mare.

Elliot swung once, missing the raider, but the next swung true and low to high, throwing the raider dead, and spewing his blood out in falling seeds through the air. Now with only one raider left, they were forced to retreat, and ran back, but this is when Elliot realized it wasn't the last raider, and more were immediately there.

Barrett ran around, breaking from their prison, and followed Elliot. They both then followed Litus and attacked the new group, who were in greater numbers.

Pinky was so stuck where he was, he feared pulling his sword in case he accidentally struck one of his own. But now with new found space he pulled his sword out, and was conflicted from going with Barrett or protecting Garnette. He yelled out, "what do I do?"

In a rough tone, Jaune quickly yelled back, "protect your queen!"

Pinky tried to encircle her, to protect her from all sides, but mostly he was disturbed by the fighting, and scared to be attacked directly. But he knew that he would disgrace not just the queen, but Jaune, the duke, and Garland of his crimes if he failed to protect her, or failed to fight. So he continued where he was, and tried to be ready to fight and see his enemies first from the right end of the blade.

Litus and Elliot tried to attack the great force, but found they weren't anything small. There were nearly a dozen of these fighters. Elliot and Litus tried to attack a rider or two, but before they could strike they found the number to be a great risk. They had to pull away, and Litus observed their racketeering, as they plowed through to the thick of the company.

Barrett escaped their incoming attack with a cut to his leg and a slice of his horse's rear, but neither were lethal, or would stop him.

He ran to the end of the volley, and with a large wide swing, he had a head roll down into the void of the ground.

Litus ran back, knowing Jane was defenseless. *She can't even swing a blade now. They'll get her, and what then? I'll have done nothing.* His horse pushed on, her dark skin blending into the background. His cloak dragged in the wind, and he kept his shining sword to his side ready to swing where necessary.

Pinky, Sam, Jaune and the other rangers left around them all formed a circle to guard Garnette. She was stuck, but when the whole mass started swinging their razors, that line started to break. Pinky was able to block what he could, and he was successful in blocking plenty of those blades, but some reached in, and pulled parts of his garb with a small trickle of blood, and they marred his legs, and the back of his horse.

Elliot and Barrett each were taking the legs and other limbs of the raiders, and Elliot had dismounted one or two more. His reach was great, and his strikes were straight and true, but the raiders weren't always keen on accepting his strikes. The keen eyed ones noticed his strike and were able to go only slightly scathed. Two or three of these riders stuck around, and they tried to encircle Elliot and Barrett not realizing one's brutality, and the other's reach.

A lance had come through the middle, stabbing one of the rangers – that Jane knew very little of – though the shoulder. He fell off, and the horse went down too. Another horse stumbled and was trampled on one of the raiders. It came down like a wave, and it happened all too fast. Jane tried to back up fast, trying to be far

enough away from raiders to either escape, fight, or *where's Litus?*
She reared far too hard, and was pushed off and fell into the dark, and
her horse in shock tripped over, and kicked trying to escape hands.
Jane was put into an adrenaline rush. She forgot her pain, and rushed
to grab the scabbard from the fallen mare. In one hand she held the
scabbard, and the other the sword. On the ground she raised it high,
ready to strike where she could. Waiting for an attack to befall her.

Litus pulled up going far around them and saw Jane standing
there helpless except for her sword. He raced to get her. A single
bandit was seen running the same way on the opposite side of the
mass. He ran, and ran, and he swung his blade true, as the bandit raced
too to take the lone woman standing, waiting to die. And they both
swung their blades. One caught metal; the other caught flesh.

Litus had taken the head off the horse of the bandit coming to.
Jane fell back guarding herself from the slash, and once the bandit
fell, she jumped bringing her blade down into his neck drawing blood
in the moonlight. Litus pulled up to Jane, holding his hand down to
her, and when she took it he pulled her up.

He looked to the mass, and then to the city enshrouded in
darkness, and made his decision. He heeled his mare and rode off.
"What are you doing? We need to help them, they'll die if we don't."
The first person who'd die would be you.

He looked back once more, and saw the flame light glint on
metal coming closer. He tried to ride faster, and push harder than
before, but there was only so much he could do. And he looked back
once more, he could tell there was only one bandit riding, and closing
in, but if there were others trailing him, he'd only hope not, but
prepared to drop heads again.

"What are you doing? Stop this, we have to turn back!" She
said again, *Don't you know we'll die?* "I'm your queen, turn back
now," She yelled out lastly.

He didn't turn back, not now, and not ever.

When he checked to see if the bandit was getting closer, he nearly missed a blade to the throat. He leaned to the side, nearly causing his mare, and Jane to fall. He swung his sword out, only to hit the bandits ghost.

The bandit had run to his other side without Litus noticing. A swing came without Litus' seeing. A clash of metal from Jane's sword sprang Litus' attention, with one good swing he took the bandit off his horse, and they ran off further for a while.

For near an hour they rode that exhausting trail; the city in the distance seemed to gleam in possible light. Torches were visible from where they were. Jane held Litus tightly with one hand while holding in her other the scabbard sword of her birthright.

By their distance they were merely a half hour to an hour away. Jane had fallen asleep, still clutching what she had. She felt cold. Her breathing was slow, and cryptic. Litus tried to push further and faster still, but he'd more likely get kicked off his horse.

The city was expansive, and the path they walked soon became a real road, made of real packed dirt and stone. The city was also greatly tall, and its center was this massive castle many centuries old. Although it is all shown by what light was given from the torches and lanterns planted around its walls.

By the time they were in less than a half hour's travel from the city's walls it was only beginning to show any form of light from the sky above.

Litus watched the city draw closer and close still. A single light was present from above the wall. It flashed momentarily, but was quickly snuffed out. Litus wondered if it were some city guard, so in case he pulled his cloak tight, and put into the void, both his and

Jane's swords. He kept his in hand just in case, but now it would have been a liability instead.

He squinted as he saw exactly two tiny lights flickering in the distance. *The city guard. They shouldn't have a reason to attack, hopefully.* For a few minutes he rode forth and waited for them to come. "Halt! Stranger," they yelled out, "halt now!"

He did so, and both carried lantern poles with the flickering light of candles illuminating their faces. "Why are you here!" He yelled, "answer me now!"

He tried pointing at Jane and hoped it told them what to know. "Those bandits got you, didn't they?"

He nodded fervently.

"What weapons do you carry?"

He shook his head, and with hand motions made a cross. "Traveled the dune's without a weapon? You're either a liar or an idiot. Where's your weapons? Dismount now."

He did so reluctantly, and the one yelling jumped down checking Litus' body. Litus feared what would happen, the guard patted him down for a long uncomfortable time. He reached through his cloak, "perfect," he said, "you're safe to enter," he shifted to look at Jane, "she doesn't look too good, she should see the surgeons guild. You see that castle, the tallest building? It's there."

That was it? Litus remounted his mare, trying to keep Jane from falling. The guards had started riding towards the gates first, and Litus followed it after riding quickly through the narrowing and widening streets of the city.

Chapter Fifty-Two:

In a chamber on the east most wing of the castle, Eiger sat waiting. Outside the window he saw only hedges and sometimes a gardener, or a guard passing by. The time passed on and on as he waited. He tapped his ring-dressed fingers on the hardwood table. He took in a deep breath, and said to Darien behind him, "the disrespect of that man, to make a duke wait for his dinner."

"He'll come, I've gotten word of it."

"I have little time to waste," and he waved his hand.

Soon being brought into the dining room was a short man with a quill pen. Eiger asked, "is the door monitored?"

"Yes, my lord."

"Good, good. Let's start. I want two copies of this letter, but have the names be different for the addressees."

"My lord, he's here."

"We'll continue this later," he waved, the writer nodded and left out of the door on the other side of the room.

Eiger commanded the doors to open, and in came Admiral Broarch dressed in his finest black naval garb. He kept a hand on his royal naval sword. Eiger got out of his chair, "it's no good making a good lord wait, admiral," he said with a smile.

"I was busy, as any *good* admiral is," as he smirked back.

"Well sit, sit, Admiral Broarch, we'll dine in a few short minutes, as they plate the table, but sit, sit, beside me."

"Alright your grace," he said, "times are new, but food is goodness for good sake."

"Indeed it is. The church, it's been a week or two since the beginning of your religious restructuring?"

"What about it? Are you still questioning something about this all?"

"Call me conservative, but I still don't quite see eye to eye with you."

"I suppose that's fair. I guess I might try to reaffirm your concerns."

"I guess, let me lay off one. With your quick religious adjustments, I'm finding it quite hard to find who sent that man who tried to kill me."

"How does that involve the church?"

"It's where it happened, and I'm weary of it all."

A servant came to Eiger's ear and whispered something to him, "alright," he said, "bring it in."

In came a grand series of all the servants who began plating the table on ornate chrome plates full of hot roasted chickens and lamb-racks. They spent a few minutes preparing this all. Two of the servants carried a mirror plate for both the duke and the admiral. And by request of the two diners their plates were made. With goblets poured with wine as red as blood.

They tried to talk over the little twinkles of the utensils on their plates. "Whenever I return to Lakeholm, I think I might pirate all the chefs here."

"Hmm," the admiral said, "not if I have any say in that. Might I request them for my fleet?" He chuckled.

"No, I can't allow that. Now where were we? Yes, you can't begin all of this religious business till we find the man who tried to murder me."

"You know how much crime is in this city?"

"Of course I do."

"And you went to the cathedral alone?"

"I'm not so blithe to do such a careless act, but the man who stabbed me did so, so quickly no one could blink during the time it transpired."

"Folly," he said, "I think that's nonsense, how would you men let a murderer get away then?"

"They didn't," Eiger thought for a moment, "they dealt with him at that moment. It's the circumstances which make it strange. And I've been thinking about what you said when I awoke, about this cult here."

"So you've come to the conclusion of who tried to kill you. Is there anything else you wish to speak about?"

"No, I'd like to stay where we were. This doesn't make sense, yet."

"What more is there?"

"There are boroughs of this city where crime rules above us, but the cathedral, and the lords and great officials of this city are clean, or try to stay clean. But I was still stabbed by a man under the roof of the gods," Eiger raised his voice, coughing from the pain of his wound.

"My grace, please don't raise your voice so."

"I won't let my near death be brushed over like dust," He said grimacingly.

"I understand your frustrations, but I have a duty to uphold."

"Duty, over justice or honor?"

"I think you misunderstand it all," Eiger tapped his fingers on the table, but the admiral continued on, "I am not bound by you noble folk's idea of justice or honor. I am purely a man of duty, no more, and no less. The reformation of the churches will continue."

"Fine, I accept your bound by duty, but as this noble folk you speak of, I am bound by honor and the practice of the church. And if you won't help, please by the gods' grace give me time to find out by myself."

"Alright then, I'll delay the reformations by a week, my grace, will that be suitable?"

"It will," Eiger said peevishly.

"Now, I don't want to seem so invasive, but just as you had to ask of me, I ask something of you."

"So be it, I see we have been distant and grown quite spiteful to each other. I'll answer what you ask of me, in hopes of rectifying all of this turmoil."

"Alright then. I guess let's reverse some of what we said. The crime. My men too have seen those boroughs you spoke of. And I completely agree. So many great pieces of the pie have rotten in the pan. What will you do then? You wouldn't eat a slice that's touched another? You bake a new pie. It may be a crude analogy, but it works. This city needs a fresh start is what I'm trying to get at."

"And that is what Tylock and yourself are doing, by yourselves? What about the queen?"

"The faithful are the hearts, we make it beat a new stream, and the brains and veins will flow and think greater and stronger. And we have word of her grace, I'm surprised you haven't heard much from her."

"Then overall, what do you ask of me?"

"You have your own men roam the streets acting like watchmen. I don't have to ask why. The tower has been in a quick and crumbling decline, and that's so very obvious as they can't even protect the streets they've been for centuries."

"So what do you plan then?"

"That'll be up to high command and the queen too. There's important things that must be done to reestablish tower control, and keep it out of some lords thinking to corrupt the weak men for their own use."

"The tower is supposed to be in the queen's control already, is it not?"

"It most certainly is supposed to be, but you know as well as I that since the fall of Queen Mary, low men have tried to flock to power which should be hers."

"And you say that there's men who could try and take control, do you refer to this same cult?"

"Quite possibly."

"It sounds like they've nested their roots into every crevice and opening in the city."

"Absolutely. That's why I plan on meeting Lord Pias at the top, and work my way down removing everything that harms us all."

"As if that'll work."

"Hmm, do you have something against this?"

"Yes, I do, but first have you ever met lord Pias?"
"No, I haven't."

"Well let me tell you, as much as the people will dislike your changes to their faith, he has the power to stop you. How many men do you have?"

"I can't say that."

"What you have, he has twice that."

"That's if he'd attack – which he won't – my fleet is smaller, yes, but the size of the navy is grander by far. And other than that, who'd want to be the man who starts a measly battle over this all?"

"Don't underestimate the chance at taking away toys from a man who believes he earned them."

"If you were in my place, what would you do?"

"I'd wait and see more, and know more about this city you try to break."

"I'm not breaking it, I'm fixing it."

"No, what you are doing is digging your grave in winter. Food will be shortened first off, but you'll also put the tower with the people, by pushing them. I suggest you try and defend the borders instead, and wait."

"I see what you're saying, and the strategy you've acknowledged, but I need to catch up with these zealots who know the city better than you, and get the tower on the side of mine. And what you talked about the people, I think is false. The lords have taken so many hands, that these men are loyal to the lords, they're not a unified force. And once we have the tower tamed, the lords will come back, and the city will heal, and be ready for a new face."

"For now you have to play a thin game with Pias. He knows just as much as you, and more. And don't think he isn't strategizing how he'll deal with you. He's dangerous when you try to bully him."

"So he is," Broarch put his utensils down, "I have to go, may I have a leave of absence, my grace?"

"Yes you can leave," and so he did.

Eiger awoke early in the morning. He'd thought for a long while about this all. "I'd have control of the castle," he murmured to himself, "that will only be though, if he's not already bought.

"Who would be in his pocket? The king's guard maybe, but since Lazith spoke true in our discussion, that rules them out. Denoth has never told me lies, he's to be further learned. And that leaves the tower, and maybe this cult?

"What I've heard so much, but seen nothing of.

"For decades we've lived under the nose of a monarch, who wasn't ours. How did none of us ever know?

He fell back into a chair, and poured himself water. Sipping silently, he thought out loud, "they've had to have worked with these cultists before. Wait, at the ball, they were above, in the balcony. They wore robes of red, but without a weapon. How was it so obvious? How didn't I know?

"Hmm, what I tell him, wouldn't be of concern with those cultists. It's only a concern of the navy and possibly lord Pias.

"But if he were a pawn of the tower? Hmm. No, probably not.

"Tylock is separating the churches in three to deal with the zealots. If the purpose is to reduce their power, that doesn't make sense. Giving your enemy a platform to stand on. Tylock the fool, the seasick fool."

He got up, and rang a bell. A maid came in asking what service she could provide, and he said, "get me some clothes," she nodded and did so.

When she returned, she asked, "do you have any other service of mine, my grace?"

"Get me Denoth, the head of the king's guard."

Eiger got dressed, with help of a separate maid, and soon Darien came to his door. And shortly after Denoth came too. Denoth was in boiled leather, and was stunningly clad in his red plated armor above it. Casually resting on his silver falchion, he said, "my lord, you've called for me, and here I am."

"Yes, I most certainly did," Eiger snapped his fingers, and some of the servants went to close the blinds, lock the doors, and light candles, "this is better, put down your sword."

He stood where he was, and kept his hand on the pommel, "you've been suspicious of our own queen for over two months now. It's obvious in your soul you don't think she should wear that crown above her veil."

"This is slander, it's not true."

"That was a lie," Darien spoke.

"I know you are loyal, but that loyalty can only stretch so far when this queen of yours is someone you aren't so sure you should be protecting."

"I trusted you, Duke Eiger. I've done so much, and this is the graciousness I receive? This is slander, and I won't take it."

"Why, it's true? This queen you protect isn't the queen. You saw it with your own eyes. And that meeting some time ago, when she first revealed herself in two months, both of us saw her. Albeit behind a clever disguise of a veil and powdered makeup, but that wasn't the woman you saw fighting Mary all that time ago on the day of the royal ball? I would know, her ship crashed onto my shores, some days later. And my truth wizard Darien was able to figure out her truth."

"So the woman who sits on the throne, is not our queen? So she really is a puppet of the navy?"

"Precisely. I don't know who that woman is, if she is noble born, or not. All we know, only us in this room, some of my men in Lakeholm, and her grace herself know of the true monarch."

"How do I know you speak the truth"

"He is," said Darien.

"That's not an excuse."

"Do I have a reason to lie to you at this time?"

"Every man has a reason to lie, but not every man has a reason to tell the truth."

"In a few days I'll receive a new letter of the whereabouts of our real Queen Garnette, although she goes by Jane. It'll contain the state she's in, where she is, and where they're going. Last I heard they were heading to Sebois. If you want to make sure that I tell the truth, send a rider there."

"You sent her across Mulder? Why not send her to Fer and Ser instead, if you want our queen in absolute danger?"

"I have trust in the Rangers Guild, and I sent her with half a dozen riders, and by now she should have a dozen men protecting her at all times. I'll send a bird with a note for a rider if you intend on doing so. If you do intend on sending a rider, I'd do it sooner rather than later. Apparently this siege on our own cities has just ended."

"May I sit?" Denoth asked.

"Go ahead," and Darien pulled a seat for him.

"I have a duty to protect only my monarch. But if you are correct, then what? The navy will send men to take the castle, and either abolish the king's guard, or replace it. Most likely it's the ladder."

"What I'll say, which you don't need to heed, but would be wise. Keep acting like whoever she is, is your queen. But I'll also need your help and the help of the rest of the king's guard to ascend Jane."

"How would you go about doing so? That would most likely lead to war, would it not?"

"Yes, a civil war, most likely. Second in our modern recorded history. There is a very thin line in which we do not cause, or war is sprung. I don't intend to bring chances like those on us."

"Then you ask me to do nothing then?"

"No, we need to build up our power and secretly switch the queen's place, which causes the navy to fall."

"The navy already has a lead greater than we'd take in a long while. You'd have to pray something great happens which can give us that lead."

"I'm not in such a sorrowful state yet, my friend. What we need is men. We need lords – doesn't matter if they're noble, or low born – we need the lords to ally with us, behind me, so that if conflict arises, we can ascend the queen in an army of new strength."

"Let me ask you something now. Would you rather fight a threat you know of or one you don't."

"One I know of."

"I'd rather as well."

"Remind me, when was that last letter?"

"A few days ago, although in a few days another will come."

"When the new letter arrives, I wish to see it, and then I'll act. Besides that, I must be off. Good tidings to you, my grace. Good tidings and good day."

When he left the room, Darien asked, "you can trust him?"

"Who else can I? He's too honorable to be a threat to our fight, which is the right one."

"I'll have the servants come in here, and deal with the dust."

He looked out the window, watching the morning light rise in, and the fall of glittering flakes of snow. And then the winter's chill became apparent again.

Chapter Fifty-Three:

The peace was new, but the winner wasn't yet known. They'd lost less than liked, and the two greatest of those who were the binds of their journeys. Kreshen and Elliot for Litus, and the queen's guards and other rangers for Garnette, were missing.

"I've got a cut up my arm, do we have any bandages that weren't lost?" Asked Jaune.

"Jaune," Pinky said, "you have more cuts on your back, you need great help. Father Kreshen, can you help us?"

"I'll do my best, but we should try and get to the city before these wounds eat you up," he reached through a horse pack, and came back to Jaune the leader, "bite on these reins, I'll pour this alcohol on your wounds, it will hurt greatly, and then I'll wrap up those wounds. And like I said, it will hurt."

He did so, and Jaune tensed his muscles as the clear and cold liquid pinched his open wounds. For some time he went around trying to patch up the wounded men in the company, and all the while they worried about Litus and the queen.

They walked drudgery, and over the hours they found that the sky had begun to awaken, and the infinite expanse of both the clouds and the city's walls were concerning. Although there was a light in the middle of the dark, that castle. In the center of the city was their holy balance of power.

The gates were opening when they arrived. A few guards had come out to inspect them. "Your weapons? Reveal them," and they did so frantically, the citywatch had barked at them, "why in such a rush," and then they noticed, "the raiders attacked you? Where? How far back?"

"A few miles back," Jaune said, and another ranger finished, "we killed many of them, but I couldn't tell it was pitch black."

"Get to the surgeons guild as quickly as possible. See that castle, just go straight ahead. And for your weapons keep it revealed at all times."

"Wait," Jaune asked, "were there two people who came here some time ago? A man and a woman?"

"Many people come in the night. A man and a woman, a few last night, so possibly."

They rode out quickly. The cobblestone sounded the beating of drummers. Pinky looked to the side gripping the reins harshly, and saw the tanned skin people watching them in distrust. Among them he saw Garland. And then he was gone.

The buildings all around that made the city were built of bricks, but the style was significantly different. They were thin, narrow, and covered in a layer of sand and pink salt.

Elliot had made it out of the conflict without much injuries. Although his tunic had suffered and same with his mare. He kept a hand on the pommel of his curved blade as they rode suspicious of the unreasonable.

After some little time spread over a year they were at the open gates of the Surgeons Guild of Prame. Although the castle was old, it appeared from afar to be the only one in the city. They had such power in stature.

They dismounted and walked through to be quickly greeted by a man and a woman with tanner skin than theirs, but both dressed in servant-like garbs. "We saw you all coming by, you all need help. We can get you all rooms quickly."

"Was there a man and a woman who came here in the night, or recently?"

"How recently?"

"Maybe within the last few hours."

"And what did they look like?"

Jaune thought about his words cautiously, "the woman had pale hair, and the man wore a black cloak. Does that help? Did they come here?"

"No, I don't think that we have. Why, should we have?"

"Yes, yes you should have. It's important! To me!"

"I'm sorry, you should have one of your unharmed men go seek the citywatch. They might help you."

"And where are they?"

Jaune and the others who were badly injured were forced to stay behind and put into rooms, while all who were left departed to find if the citywatch knew anything. "I think I see it," said Barrett, "a tiny little guard post."

"You should have stayed behind."

"I've suffered worse, and besides they reeked of something sickly."

"What would you expect?"

"I wouldn't know, but I don't like it."

"Again you're sounding like that companion of yours," Elliot said.

"I guess he'd have known what is happening here more than any of us combined. He was a true guardsman, a protector till the end, and a friend too."

"If they didn't go to the guild, where would they have went?" Asked Kreshen.

"Maybe they got napped by thieves when they entered at the pitch of black," Barrett said.

"No, it's more likely Litus would have killed them," Elliot said, Kreshen nodding, "but he could have been assumed to be a wraith who held a noble woman hostage."

They entered the hold, it was short and dim, lit by a few too little candlesticks. They walked to the office space for public concerns and there they met a man with eyelids dropping so low, they appeared to be closed. Father Kreshen prayed quickly and asked the man, "have you seen a man or woman recently, one blond the other cloaked?"

"That's a vague description yer lads gives. You want some missing people as of recent?"

"Yes!"

"We have none, even within those . . . restrictions," he slowed his tone, "if you wait a little longer, there may be what you seek."

"Do you have anyone who fits that description in your holding cells?"

"Again, I say no. You might want to search where they were lastly, or where they're going to. I can't help yer any further than that."

They left, and all of them we either pissed, or – like Barrett, – fuming. "We should split, I'll head north of the guild, Father you head south. And Elliot you being the best of us, check back at the guild, I feel something off with their lot," they all nodded and began their ride out.

Their ride for the first few minutes was in a singularity. When they came to the breaking point, they all nodded to each other as though they were walking into a death trap. *This could be their last time alive, or mine, or all of ours. My grace I've failed you. Garland, you too.* He made sure the scabbard on the side of his hip was fashionably attached, and then he rode quick and hard. He constantly trotted up and down the streets, through every alleyway, and asked locals of the vague description they were already attuned to give. He would ride these short distances so quickly and look so often he got cramps in his neck. But in it all, he could still see that castle in the distance, whenever he was riding back.

Kreshen nodded, and rode out south, and there he looked in the places that he didn't see on his initial ride up to the guild. He prayed whenever the alleyway he rode down was empty, and asked locals whether they'd seen someone, but it all went to naught. *It's as though they disappeared. What if they've never made it to the city to begin with? No. Litus wouldn't fail that easily and quickly.*

Elliot rode back to the keep, he too could smell the scent that Barrett had picked up earlier. It was a peculiar smell, he'd never in all his time in this city, or elsewhere in his travels sensed something so sterile. He wandered around the outer walls of the guild searching for something that could give some clue as to where they went. *How could a dozen thousand people miss a wraith, a noble woman, on horseback, even at night. Where did their horse go?* Elliot searched for what felt like an excruciating long time until he saw their stables. Under the shadow of the roof he searched through their mares. And there in perfect darkness, was Litus' dark mare.

Chapter Fifty-Four:

He was no longer waiting, they were. Two who received their letters, and two who were willing to come with their own guard, and they were the one's waiting. Eiger took his time, and calculated his strides walking through the hall of mirrors. Oh that room, it invigorated him. It was a perfect farce. Now it was an even greater one. He had ordered the servants to rearrange the room in such a way to give his recipients sitting at the table a perceived power.

He walked through the door held open to him. In the room were a few men clad in boiled leather behind both of the men sitting, and then there were his men standing behind Darien, and Denoth with a few of his king's guards behind him.

He sat with his back to the door, as another farce. "Well let us begin this," as he was handed a map of the city and sprawled it over the table.

"No food? No roast chicken," snickered Garet.

"At least a glass of wine?" Said Taryen.

"Ah, it seems you two know me so well," he snapped his fingers, and a chest was put onto the table, followed by crystal cups, and a bottle of champagne, "it's not wine, but it is something greater than rude language to your grace."

"We kid, your lord, nothing but a jest of what we've heard of you."

The glasses were poured, and passed to each of the men. One for himself, another to Taryen, and the last to Garet. Eiger was sharing a glass with criminals, and he made sure not to seem disgusted. "It's a bit more bitter than I'd like," shared Eiger, and the others nodded subsequently.

The case was put away, and they all stalked their goblets ornate in flowers with thorns. The aroma of the sparkling wine was like said bitter, but had this sickly sweet aftertones. It was quite unique, unlike the grapes pressed in Porcelania, nor Hule, something further north it seemed. It was anything from crisp though.

The map was brushed off of any dust that lingered. Eiger took a pen of a deep red ink and he drew onto the map a detailed border of two. "These are the lands which you two have taken for your own good natures."

"No, no," said Garet, studying the lines, "how do you know that in detail?"

"How wouldn't I? Your men linger, and where they linger most, is where I know you have control over which the great dark tower has none of."

"Hmm, the tower isn't so incompetent as I assumed," said Taryen.

"Yes, yes the tower sure isn't as incompetent as you believe," he scoffed and then laughed, "they're worse."

A man to their side with a pointing rod handed it to Eiger, and he pointed to each of their territories, "like said these are your territories, in which you've stolen and are ruling in place of the just."

"What just?" Taryen said, "I don't believe there is a queen that is ruling, the tower is all there is, and you."

"Yeah what just is this you refer to?" Piled on the other.

"You are having punk goons beat up old men over little, and are robbing the common folk. You are a menace to this city."

"What makes you believe that, I rule and tax this land such as any lord, and if the tower weren't incompetent, I'd have to reason to have men enforce my ruling."

"Now your grace, it seems like you are doing the same. Only you're worse, you've come from a land that isn't yours, you've taken the most prestigious castle in this half of the world, and now you expect the actual good men of this city, of this land to bow down to you?"

"You misjudged me completely. I'm not some intruder, and you also are not without a queen. I am the one that is working in her place."

"What?" Said the man.

"I am the minister of rule as of recent. I'm to restart the ruling of this city. You two are walls that I must either build around or break down."

"I don't believe you, not one bit," said Taryen, and nodded the other, "why does no other lord know of this chicanery?"

"It isn't for knowing yet."

"Huh," Garet grumbled.

"Are you going to question me, or will we discuss the lands which you two hold," before he could let them answer, he said, "now this land is yours, and this neighbor is yours."

"Now that I think about it, where is Karaway?"

"Your right," he gave the brush to one of his soldiers and he drew his border, "I guess it's an unfortunate end to his rule, and a sad thing for you two to know now."

"What did you do to him? Where is Karaway? You killed him, you had him killed!"

"Karaway, unlike you two, is a reasonable man, and he is alive and breathing just well with his family in his arms close and sitting warm by their fireplace."

They sat in silence as Eiger took a drink, and then ushered them to do the same, "now if anyone is a troubling sight to us and the peace of the crown it's the defective and tyranny of the watchmen tower."

Both of the mob lords looked at each other, and Taryen said, "what are you planning against the tower?"

"Upfront with the blasphemy it seems," Eiger chuckled, "I'm not against the tower as you think."

"You are a confusing mess of a duke."

"Plead my forgiveness if I have brought on this aura," he said wiping his brow.

"Can we snuff a candle or two?"

They snuffed out some of the candles on the walls, and in the soft darkness hid plenty of their men. The pinkish hue from the candles on the round table is all the light they had.

"Let me say something crude?" And they nodded, "the tower is an incompetent mess that oppressed all they touch. And I'd say their regime before the fall of Queen Mary was far more oppressive than anything you simple lords could even compare. Although they were just, there was a sense of order, albeit a complex one. When was the last hangings?"

"Two months ago, Duke Eiger?"

"With the immediate chaos brought on the massacre of the royal ball, everything fell apart, as you two know."

"Why do you bring up what is old, what do you want?"

"A long peace and prosperity, and winter to already fade into a long long spring and summer."

"I want to keep the land in which I govern," said Taryen.

"Yeah I want insurance for what I rule over. I spend so much money to make sure my, what did you call it, governance is in order. Men and money. I want to make sure that the money is safe."

"Well now that you talk of money, let me make it clear that the money you sow is stolen from the crown and those who were put into control of the boroughs."

"Well if you would tax us, the only thing that would allow us to keep control of our territory to a satisfactory level, and temper."

"So you would expand?"

"The only thing we won't expand to is each other's domain," the other mob lord agreed.

"And the church?"

"They are sacred, you know that."

"And the tower, when they fall, and the queen appoints a new man to govern."

"If they get in the way, they'll be in the way."

"So you wish to bring in fighting?"

"No, I don't wish that."

"Then your rules will be to nothing."

"Are you threatening us?"

"Surly lords such as yourselves would know I would never say such blatant grim remarks? No, what I want is your loyalty to me and the crown. You will be in charge of taxing the people you govern over, in your boroughs, and you will lend men to me, and in return gain a share of control. And you will follow the order of laws truthfully."

"A share? You want my men? You want me to just give up my men!?" He did not ask but laughed loudly along with the other mob lord, "that's the, the," and he laughed some more.

Their laughter had shaken the table. Ripples waved in their glasses, and the candles flickered too. The mob lords were wiping sweat from off their brow. "He wants men for little, Duke Eiger, your lord-ship. You kid me, you are a true brooding comic, of which I've heard of."

Eiger reached through his pocket for the vials he was sure he had. He pulled out both of them, and drank the contents of one quickly and visibly. He put down the empty glass vial on the table, along with the other full one. "For you to accept the crown's taxes you need to expand the land you govern, so."

"What's with that vial," said Garet, fanning his neck.

"The poison's antidote, and here is a second one. The only other second one."

"You, you poisoned the wine, by the gods you poisoned us. What is wrong with you!"

"Yes, the champagne we all drank was poisoned, and before your jump up and try to kill yourself faster be reasonable. And answer this one question. It will all be done with, and this whole fighting and bickering will be below us. Nearly two weeks ago, a man was sent to assassinate me. Which one of you sent him?"

"We haven't done anything wrong, just give us the vial!"

"And leave me to die?"

"Now, now, before you get antsy, there is only this one vial left on this continent. So which one of you tried to kill me?"

"It was him!" Yelled Taryen.

"It wasn't me!" Garet yelled back.

"A lie," Darien said, as the king's guard and the duke's men went killing lord Garet's men.

"Here," Eiger said, tossing the vial over to the fumbling lord Taryen.

He frantically opened the glass and drank the contents. Garet reached for his sword. It was clear that his vision had deteriorated. His heart beated quickly, but he didn't fall yet. He ran blade first to the duke, and his sword was caught and pushed down by another. And lord Garet fell to the ground grabbing his bleeding neck, and died.

"Horrible, wish the poison got him sooner."

"You poisoned us!"

"You've made a great acquisition, all you have to do is accept my preposition, your men are mine, your rule is yours, and I want to see a cart of taxes at the castle gates in a week."

"Yes, yes, my lord . . . my grace. Please let me live, I have a family."

"A good day to you too."

Eiger got up. He was a little woozy from the effects of that poison, but he affirmed his stance and walked out of the now darkened room. Taryen watched him leave, as he and his men remained in the blood and the light of too few candles, and their pinkish orange hue.

Chapter Fifty-Five:

The void, where is the void? My cold dark hall of pillars of a strange stone, I don't yet know what. It was cold, a secretion on his neck bit like the teeth of a bat. He kept walking and didn't have control of where he was heading. The pulsing in the air was a feat of incoming heat and sand long lost to time and was an immediate peril soon waiting. But he kept walking forward.

The threat was a being he had seen and felt, but couldn't ever be let to know. It's presence in his body was new, it was a catalyst for terror and hatred. It's face was currently in his memory a being of shadow, but so was everything else locked up here. *What is this disease?*

Dust had fallen off the tall pillars in clumps. There was this stinging pain like hair being pulled from his scalp. No matter how far he walked, this pain persisted. It wouldn't matter if he was locked to a bed, as a sickly woman was pulling skin with pliers. These clumps as they gathered on the ground had the eerie sensation of snow that clung like oil to his skin. He wiped off this oil for what seemed like forever, it just spread further. Stabbings were shot down his spine.

Who are you! Get out! He thought, but was given silence, so he thought again, *Who are you! Get out!* And again there was no response, so he tried once more only asking – in thought – *who are you? Why are you here?* "Quite persistent," she said in a sultry tone, "a locked box within a locked box."

You didn't answer it. "I don't need to, once it's over, we'll be quite similar. A toolbox within a toolbox."

Get out! Reveal yourself! "If you can find me in this labyrinth, then you can try feeble wraithkind. I pity you very much. I pity you so much in fact, I'll give you one gift to help your endeavors," she said as she partially revealed herself.

Her face was pale and half covered in a pure veil. Her eyes were red like a ruby or garnet. They looked cut like his, or a mimic of his eyes, but red. Was she dressed in a robe, or was there nothing? He couldn't tell from the lack of light that could emanate before she left.

He was left in the crumbling castle. He kept walking and hoping to find the heart, and to find the disease that infiltrated the void. *Could it destroy all of this? Will it end? I will never let it sow my mind into a deep pit of deathly dirt.* He kept walking and walking through the infinite expanse.

Under a single spotlight he could see it, the floating great sword which wielded what felt so long ago in the realm of the living. There was this false wind that blew as he encroached toward the handle. "What is that?" She asked from nowhere he could immediately tell.

He began running towards the sword, with one hand outstretched he tried to grab it, but as he came so close. His sight had begun to fade away. "Not so fast," she said in a sultry tone, "this might be quite useful."

"Here," she said, "is your new reward. I found it not so long ago."

It all faded into dark for one quick swipe before re-revealing reality in a forest with a thick blanket of snow. It was a dense forest, with barely room to breath. There was this path that he could remember of all things. It led to this thick rotten tree, with deep roots and carvings that weren't very legible anymore, if ever. A corpse now all skeletal was strewn on the bed only barely peering out of the snow.

I've seen this before. He said walking the path. More skeletal corpses lay about. Further ahead, he came into a full graveyard with its surrounding gates broken. There were new bodies which he couldn't remember lounging against the walls. They stood in stillness, serenity.

He marched through the snow, not caring if the coldness felt like needles upon his skin. *Demorte.* The town's buildings – even though they were newly built of brick – were near demolition. New recipients held the roofs, and occupied its rooms.

He walked onward, there was this force in the center of the town. It radiated a heat which also appeared in the ground below. The inverse outline of the snow made the image of a sun, a bright burning star with tendrils which lashed out trying to grab onto as much land and beings as possible. *The followers of Gruel.* He crossed the worn bridge now made of rotting wood, as everything was rotting. The building that immediately followed no longer stood, no guard stood. No guard, who was the residence of the town which he remembered. No it was those followers everywhere, looting and ripping the life out of the town.

In the center of the town, was the worshipful, the hateful, and a great big bonfire. A roaring fire, so high its smoke touched the heavens. And that smoke swirled around a collected pool of the smoke from the months they've taken, and that pool began to pour down to the ground. As little droplets of translucent black oily water dribbled down.

As they fell, they caused the bonfire to spread further and further out. It engulfed the zealots' legs, but they still prayed. They still prayed in their woolen sacks of robes, and let the fire engulf all there was to see. Before the fire could take all of the ground. He raced to enter the door of the house, the old malkin he used to know.

He swam up to the top of the ocean's surface. Climbing through the ethereal clean water. He could see the sky without a surface. Just stars and a black ocean just as large as the one he swam through. The time will come, when ships fall into the sea, and more. He plunged deep into the water as that was the only thing he could do.

He found himself clinging to the wretched remains of a shipwreck, *but which one? In my memory of the past there are two shipwrecks. Which is this one?* Oh the storm clouds turned into a spiral of pure malaise. It was the melancholy of finding the death spot of a loved one long passed. He kept his grip onto the floating lumbar. It rocked back and forth over the waves. He kept his grip tight as the lumbar constantly tried to tumble back and forth over the rough waters.

A lightning bolt struck eerily close. Its plasmic shell fell off into the cold and floated on the surface like oil. He drifted closer and closer to the film. It was either a flight or sting. He didn't want to fly, and to fall into the water. It started as a stinging sensation, the more he drifted into the mass of film, and the film clung to the lumbar and himself, it stung more and more. It became a burning sensation. A horrible burning, and writhing sensation. His muscles shook and twisted without his control until his fingers which were the last appendages which gripped the plank failed.

As he fell motionless down through the depths of the ocean he saw the sails fly above. And the snuffed candles drift out of the capsized cabin, and the maps of the known world were torn and turned into mush. Documents lost to time. Over there he could see – before the light took him – a map half a century old when the kingdom of the Tens was whole. And over there, some massive kingdom surrounded by the Haute Mountains, and these maps, these documents decayed by the touch of light, and were long gone forever.

The pressure built and darkness rose as he fell further down. The film was flung up the further he fell, the tingling sparks subsiding, as he regained some control of his arms. He tried to swim up, but he only was pushed further down, and he struggled more and more. As he looked down into the infinite darkness, *The void,* he thought, *The void!* He began to swim down, and he fell further and further into the darkness. Until that was all there was.

He fell down onto the ash covered ground. The pillars were thinned, the sediment of the older layers were made of a gray smooth rock. There was this scent of rainfall after a fire.

He walked through the hall. Passing by each pillar, searching. Searching for that sword. In the distance he saw it gleam for a split second, before her voice boomed through the hall, *Not yet you. Go back, go back somewhere lost.*

She appeared and pushed him through a fabric, a veil of earth, and he fell through to the other side.

Inside a stone temple, long draped in foliage and deep rooted vegetation five hundred years old. He picked an old piece of leather, with letters pushed into the flesh. It was once a book. But nothing was left except the front cover, now long tarnished.

A horn blew from far away, and almost immediately thousands of years of dust fell from the roof, and the beams which held it up for so long with many heavy creatures thumpings. He coughed and whispered something unintelligible. Another set of stomping had erupted from that, and with a large crack it fell through dropping large stones to the ground.

The gargoyle roared with a tight pitch, holding its stone pike upwards. The door emanated an alluring light that he had to try and get to somehow. The gargoyle quickly backed away close to the doorway to have room to thrust the stone spike forward. He was able to dodge the first, and against the second. The beast roared and waved the pike around the room trying to clip him. But he was able to back away far enough to miss them all. To him the gargoyle moved slowly, and traversed the space with a crawl. And once he realized that, he passed through. *A beast of stone doesn't move.* He passed through the doorway of light, and he could see something other than some pure light, it was a true light, a half light, but once he passed it, he realized it wasn't any light of truth, but only a fragment of a fragment.

It was a pool of fire, in the middle was a flag waving but it was burnt harshly. *What flag is that? Which kingdom, country?* A strong gust of wind picked it up, and threw the flame into a whirlpool. It rose high into a tornado, and in a moment time froze and the tornado was flung across, and the fire was gone flying away like a bird migrating.

The island which he stood on was empty, but much farther ahead in the horizon he saw shadows of migrating human figures.

The fires erupted once more. The stone burned, the foliage of grass and dirt turned to soot. The stained and glass ether turned to goop, or shattered under the heat. He could see from outside, the lines of navy officers carrying buckets and troughs of seawater to the keep, and the great nobles and leaders in the navy and army dead and half charred. The army officers were in large troops running around the castle trying to find any servants to punish, or dead lords to carry out. And then the infighting began within them. Lords were coughing blood pulling out their coins of gold to try and pay someone to save his life over others. There was Tylock, with little scars compared to the rest of them, barking orders, and having his sailors save the right people. Here he saw it from was that quiet cell at the top of tower black. And half the monarch's great palace was lit brighter than the sun. *I did that all, the blood and fire.*

Before he knew it the hot sands and small mountains were under his feet. *Over there,* he pointed to the peaks in the far distance. *The archive, the cathedral, and the void. I need to return to the void, bring me back.*

He ran, and furthermore still, not knowing what was ahead, or that he could stop. The time skewed through forever, and the skies above flashed all the tempers of the times of days, like lightning.

In the distance he could see a figure walk through the dust. On either side were the echo mountains. Each scrap of cloth – although muted – reflected back at him, and in the far far distance at the figure ahead. And in an even great distance ahead of that, were another figure who fell into the sand. And the following figure – closer to him – fell only minutes later.

I will not fall next. I will not, I have to get there, to the void, and I won't fall, I can't. So he walked, and walked, and ran, and ran, and when the sand burned his feet, and the skin charred and began peeling away; he still walked further.

The sky fell down in the presence of water. It was a being veiled in thin mists, with long hair made of ice and frost. "Where are you going, my close friend?"

To the void, I need to find the void, "oh the void, the void. Why can't you find the void?"

You already know why, "I thought asking might make it better."

What are you? "You also know that."

I won't flail about while you kill me. I won't fail. "You're already here aren't you?"

He walked forward, on and on, the scorching deserts had passed, and the rocky fields were now under his feet. He walked further and further up the rock carved stairs. And at the top, carved into the peak of the orange and red sediment mountain was a cathedral, with massive swinging doors sputtered with the weathering of all the sands. But he knew to take the door on the right.

The screams and chanting cacophony of sound all echoes and blared through the round. They were segregated off from all the crowd looking down from atop their walls, and their carved seats. Under shadows he sat waiting. It was dark, but there was no void.

I need to get there, "and how will you do that, just do it," she laughed in cold chimes.

That gate, I can't pass it without something. I just need to wait for my turn, "and so will I."

A brutish man of no discernible features stood next to him, and with a fading gesture threw down sword, and a helmet, "my, my, my knight will fight, and make me much rewards it seems. It is only just, my just knight. Here, a set of armor for my just knight, or whatever you should think you are, and I."

The prophecy of the Malkin again and again. So to find freedom I must be their knight of justice? "Who else would you be fighting?"

The armor fits. "Everything will fit a being such as yourself."

A candle was lit which removed more light from the chamber. Another after that, and another after that. It was a room of twinkling light, as they waited for the gate to open for him. He could see the other side through a small porthole in the walls. He clutched the pointed sword in his hands, it was nicer than expected, but here everything is nicer than expected, or so it now seemed. He rubbed the scale off the blade, it was not a great cutting blade, but a piercing one. *This will be a step closer to the end of this all.*

He waited behind, and soon the gate raised. He beat off sand from his silver boots, and on the other side coming from a gate shrouded in darkness, was he. Shimmering in his steel, with all the light making an iris-like shimmer around his figure. He beat the sand off of his light embraced boots with the tip of his estoc.

It's there, even as the light blinds me, it's there, the void. I must go. Both gates closed behind them. The people of no discernible features, and from some angles were just blurs, shouted and careened more and more, stomping from their seats. He looked around at all of them, and saw nothing he could recognize with the memories he made recently.

They ran to each other, with their estocs just outside of reach. "Strike me if you can, cause I'm the image that's deep within. How can't you kill her, if you can't reach me?"

You are you, and I am me. "Or so it seems? Now stop wasting time, and face me, coward."

He thrusted his sword, the other dodged. It came to a parry and deflect, their motions were almost perfect for each other. "No, no, you're nowhere close to keeping this. Bah," he said, "in only fifteen seconds, or the blink of an eye have I been able to realize I've been talking to a child, it seems. You aren't not even close to earning that thing," he said, pulling the iron key from his pocket, "you were given this prematurely, I have taken it from you, but I'll give it back, when you've earned it. Now let's see if that's now?" And he snapped his fingers.

His figure disappeared. Out from the sides were two greater figures. It was two women, far taller than he by a head. They were blinded and deafened. They felt the vibrations from the roots in the ground.

"They should prove to be, else, that key will not be yours yet," he bowed and the mist of his skin turned into clouds that were observing from the heavens.

They marched up to him, they wielded the same weapon as he, but they shined greater. He tried to walk around the arena in the sand, with that dust billowing in their drapes. The sand spun in a string of vortexes as their blades of glass pushed towards him. He tried to dodge both at once, but found he needed to drop.

They backed off, as he tried to jump away. He got up brandishing his sword. *Where's that key!?* They lunged at him, point forward. He made a sweeping slash, knocking their blades away from him. He pounced back. *Where's the key!? Where is it!?*

On the other side of the rotary was the open gate of darkness. *He threw the key near the center hadn't he? The sky is watching every scene in which I am moving forward, isn't he?* He looked to where he thought the key was, and to where the open gates were.

The women were on either flank. One came first, sword bearing forward to him. He feigned his block into a deflect, and he ran to the center, but was intercepted by another blade. It slid deeply into his shoulder, right between the armor and pauldron. She sank the blade deeper, the other refused to follow.

He stepped back, pulling the blade out of his shoulder. It scraped against the metal of the pauldron, and the blade was no longer glass.

He paused for a long slow time, they didn't move, they knew the outcome. He walked forward, sword falling, and with each step he kicked sand which blew forward.

There was an imprint in the sand where the key was, he went to grab it, but dust quickly smothered everything.

He walked to the gate, and from the bright light of the arena, all there was, was the absence. And on the other side, was the coast. He saw ships break in the long distance with men boarding and slaughtering others and flying an orange square flag.

He watched from the tower far above, stricken by the winds of a hurricane. "You failed, as I expected," roared with the winds.

A flag from behind him collapsed. He looked down to see which it was, but all he could see was a flash of purple. He climbed down a side ladder. Beads struck his back. The closer he got to sea level, the louder and louder the sounds became. Lightning struck the masts of ships, not caring for which side. Different weapons clashed, and so did the waves of the sinking ships, and the bodies smacking bodies. His feet fell before him, from a rotten rung in the ladder.

Through a grate, and into a crypt he fell down. It was all quiet. Wet and quiet. He sat up, *is this the void?* He asked himself. He gripped his shoulder, it still stung in pain. The liquid which emanated from the wound was warm, and sickly. It smelled of his finger which was covered in his blood, it smelled like a fresh corpse.

Anxiety rummaged in his stomach. Thoughts and images peered through his skull, *outside these walls are.*

He marched on, carrying something in his hand he didn't know what of. The water below rose. The walls of the tunnel were hard like stone. No matter how hard he thought the walls couldn't fall, he had to keep walking forward. He was reminded of the desert, how its cold fluidity tried to grab anyone unworthy, and pull them down with the rest of the losers. But he didn't want to be a deadly loser, he wanted to persist no matter what. So he kept walking as though he hadn't been walking and walking and walking.

It was to his waist at this point. No matter how much slashing he tried, the water kept rising. The cold embrace, meeting the corpse which was soon upon him, and the tunnel was an infinite husk of a corpse who was trying to do something he couldn't speak about.

The ground shifted in an uproar of hatred as it took the top of his torso. *Not the wound!* He cried, but once the water rose and the feel that the poison brought, felt like an arrow of death. *Jane.* he collapsed to the ground, his entire being submerged. His head started to shut down, as the effect took hold, and the blood in his body turned colder and colder.

From under the surface he could hear a wire being echoed in a warbly tone. It grew louder and louder as it came closer. He had to duck even lower once it dozed above, it was a wire of waxed strings. *This won't be it, this can't be it. Not this far, not this close.* With one arm he grabbed the top of the rope, he walked its length. He needed not to breathe here, he walked closer and closer to the end. And there was a true darkness, a trapdoor below. He jumped down, and landed in the hall of pillars and the void stank of hatred and fire.

He held it behind his back, obscured to sight as he walked back into the hall from behind a diminishing pillar. He stood behind her, as she tried to take the hanging great sword. A gleam of sickly green light emanates from her attempts. "Oh how my attempts go to so much shame, when they are ruined by the rat lord of this establishment. You can't walk up to me, I have you strung like a doll. You bow down to me. Look at you, you've struggled so much, give rest. Let me do what I'm best at, and it'll be over, once you give me all your strength," but he stood there walking closer, "I only need so little time left. I've sent you twice into the maze. Little mouse."

She floated towards him in a newly found and more graceful way, which emanated her beauty. She would have entranced any man who could see her. Her figure glowed brightly from behind the bright green flames which lingered. She waved her arms forward, and floatless leaped onto him, "I shall send you far deeper, where this won't be found so so easily."

She twisted her hand around his shoulder, "ah, the feat of my doing is so powerful, can't you feel it?" She said as her fingers stuck in the wound, "ah, look at it, I did this, praise it!"

Get off me! He tried to get off the estoc to wield, "use up your energy, when I send you far away, and you'll only give me more time. Thank you for this time."

Underneath her she created an opening, which his legs began phasing through. "Oh my beautiful beautiful host, I wish to see you go, to see you squirm as your energy drains away."

He fell deeper, with his injured arm, he grabbed onto her leg, her cold skin in some seconds felt like glazed porcelain, and others felt like a seashell. As he fell deeper into the portal, he maintained his grip on her leg, "ooh," she said, "I'll hate to see you go. How you try so often and fail so pleasantly. Look, you're trying to take hold of my leg so as not to fall," she bent down grabbing his arm, "you want to be rescued so badly here," she gave him a glimpse at the pillars once more before sticking her finger back into his wound, "habits never die I suppose," she said dropping him and holding her pretty face.

The portal was a door, and he refused to go. He held onto the doorway with his bad arm, *It does seem habits die hard,* he thought looking past her at the sword. He breathed heavily, with a little bit of his strength he pulled himself up and out with the sword. She had already come back to the floating great sword, and she looked at him with pure anger, "you didn't fall? Why do you disappoint so often, this joke is too bloated."

He held the estoc forward, *I lost the key, but I remember something else.* His eyes were closed, as he remembered that moment. She came forward, with a needle in her hand made of any inky black substance. "Honey don't you get it?"

That moment is the moment I seek, "put it down, and go into the memory."

He put lowered his guard for split second as the pain jolted, and she dashed to him, "you should of-"

"Death," he said, and it was over.

He awoke in an old dirty pond, stuck to the wall with rusty chains, in a cell cold and stuffy, with the absence of light. He tried to break free with as much force as possible, and after grunting in a muted voice, he broke the old chains.

She lay motionless in the water. The door to the prison cell was opened, by a dead fool.

Chapter Fifty-Six:

"I have something to say," growled one of the men inside. "Shut up all you, I have something to say," and all the men inside put down their ales, and listened, "our lord, hasn't returned from his meeting with the queen and hand. And neither are our brothers, and that is because they've been killed."

Gasps rang, and the panes of thick glass vibrated on the touch of it. "They would dare!"

"Yes, they dared, and now they think we will bend to them. We should bend over for them, and do you know what I say?"

"Nay!" They roared.

"Yes, we say nay. We say nay to that!"

"Nay!" They roared. "Nay!"

Waves beat on the sides, splashing salt into the air. "Gah," he said, "what we do for the right cause."

For an hour, wind slapped around their eastern flag, but now it started to cool down, and the wind pushed them forward. "Oh we sow the heaven to the land below, and soon the land will rise past the clouds. Ever seen the stars?"

"I don't think I ave, but you funny folk ave?"

"If you pray enough you see the stars as they truly are."

"We all pray."

"Not as great as I though, but I extend my hand to you."

It was dark there. Cold, dark, wet, and inhospitable. "The key," he said in his soft but gruff voice.

He tried searching for the key in the void, but nothing. There were magic objects, weapons, and tools, and such, but no key. "So it is gone," he said to himself, and Litus realized, "I'm speaking?"

He looked back at the corpse, her poison, the wound. He felt a soft bruise on his shoulder, but no incision. There was a grumbling from behind him, he held his sword to her, "get up."

She fell on her back, grasping the wound he'd given her. "You didn't. You. how?" She spoke.

Litus looked around the cell. "Where am I?"

She spat up as she laughed, "not in a dream anymore."

"Get up," he croaked and whispered ethereally, and walked up to her, "get up."

She breathed heavily, and refused, "you are my puppet, what have you done!?" He grabbed her arm, pulling her up firmly, "if you let me live, I'll let you escape."

"I'm not escaping yet," he looked at her wound, "you might live, if you pray to your god."

She coughed up a chuckle, "alright. So it will be."

Outside the cell was a long hall of reflective lightless pool. There were cells all around the pool. "Down the hall, there will eventually be a door," she breathed in the musty air, "if it's open, you'll have an easier escape."

"And if it's closed?"

"I'm not entitled to give you that. That secret would die with me."

"You are willing to help me escape, that's not very faithful of you."

"This isn't court, wraith," she groaned.

As they walked throughout the pool a sound emanated from far ahead. It was a large splashing sound. Litus looked at the cells. A flood of light pierced through and reflected the entire pool so bright that the torched flames looked white. He broke down a rusty cell door, and pushed himself and her in. falling to the ground smothering her mouth with part of his cloak just in case. He put himself in the deepest corner of the cell. She didn't squirm, as though she expected him to gag her.

Three of them passed by the cells, wielding a torch, and a brass pitchfork. And the last held a wand up his sleeve. Their robes blended in with the light they carried. Then they passed by. Streaks of their abstinence lingered. Litus went to leave. "No, no!" She said, "you'll get caught easily, so let them pass."

"And let them find an empty cell?"

He pushed them both to the other corner waiting for them to pass back. "Two cells away from here is a hidden gate."

He got up to check their position, she coughed up, "what are you doing?"

"Waiting for the right moment."

They were just feet away from that empty cell, "which cell?" he groaned in a breathy whisper.

She pointed with her black stained hands. He dragged her while breaking through that cell door. *They're too easy to break.* "Open it."

"Over there," she whispered, and he brought her over, "it's open, come let's go."

"And why should I trust you?"

"Why stop, you've come this far. I have nothing to live for."

"No, no."

She tried to yell out, but all that came out was a deep inhale and spurt of an inky black substance.

There was a crash of metal audible, and unintelligible speech. He snuck back into the dark cell. They ran from that empty cell, to where she was. They waved their torches and held the pitchfork, like a pike, as they stormed through the cell. He drew out his falchion and walked up behind them as one of them muttered. "What!"

He put the blade through the back of the closet. The prongs of the pitchfork struck near him nearly missing the dead.

The torch bearer in stupidity tried waving Litus off with the flame, but with one clear strike, took off the man's hand, and down with the man, and the light.

It was clear they wanted to speak, but uttered nothing. They pushed him back with their reach, Litus parred every few attacks. He drew into the void, and held his hand behind his back. The barbs of the pitchfork pushed forward and grabbed the blade of the curved sword and parts of the cloak. Threads were ripped out along with the sword, and with one last thrust the pitchfork barbed cell bars. Litus was below the man piercing his gut with the point of his estoc. The man fell, and Litus gathered his things.

He returned to her cell, and only his outline was visible. He came to her, and grabbed her arm. "Your deception won't last, cultist!"

"Do it," she muttered.

"No."

He dragged her outside the bars, and checked their bodies. Taking their keys, and taking their weapons, including what he assumed was a wand of enchanted light. They walked to the end of the hall where a large door of iron stood. He listened through the other side, and there was nothing audible. Passing through onto the other side there was a hall of doors. Dozens and dozens of doors which he assumed were dungeons such as this, and he asked, "these are all the same?"

"Yes," she said in a sultry voice under the light of calm lanterns.

The hall was lit by these small candles in glass cages, and their light was few, but was plenty in comparison. "There's no window's anywhere. How far below ground are we?"

"Why would you assume we were underground?"

"Where would this all be then?"

"That's greater than I could say."

"Then where do I need to go?"

"You don't seek freedom, so how could I possibly know?"

"You searched my dreams; how wouldn't you know yet?"

"It was poison, no funny tricks. All of it is your imagination."

He pushed on her wound, she moaned in pain, and Litus ushered, "then this pain is forfeit?"

"Stop! Stop! I was controlling the poison, but I . . . I didn't. I was controlling the poison until you got me."

"Where is she?"
"Most likely in a cell."

"One of these ones?"

"Was."

He dropped her forcefully to the cold darkness. "Which one?"

"I . . . I couldn't know. I only knew yours."

He opened the first door and inside was a hall of cells same as the ones he was stored in. Except it was bone dry. He held the light of a fire wand, and ran down and back throughout the hall. In the neighboring hall, he did the same. He ran down the hall, and back. Nothing. The hall neighboring that, he ran down, and back, and nothing. "They're all empty?"

She didn't answer.

"How many are here?"

"How many? What? Humans, Malkin, *Zealots,* or halls?"

"How many halls are here?"

"I've never checked."

"Fine then. They're all empty, as it seems. Why?"

She coughed up a sickly tone, "how you seem so sad, why don't you come here, and I'll say."

In a soft voice, he said, "where are they all?"

"Keep checking."

He went back through the halls, one and then another, and another. Each as empty as the previous. At the end of the hall of doors he heard an anthem. It was faint, only sounding like a whisper from a deceiver. *Jane,* he thought and began running back. And once he saw her, he said, "there's no others of you."

She stood up, "and there's sounds from over there," Litus said.

"We call it a symphony."

"I need to see it, where do I need to go to see it?"

"At the end of this hall, there's a door much like these ones, and it's past that."

He grabbed and pulled her up. They came to the end of the hall, and Litus asked, "which door."

"That one," she pointed to the one on the right.

He opened the door, and the moment he looked through, there were the sounds of footsteps. There were only a few of them, but more than none, but their stepping was audibly leaving, and he said, "so it's where they're going."

"You don't know that."

He pulled her along, as he followed them up a stairway, and at the top he overlooked a church and orchestra of fire, and people far, far below. There were the orthodox garbs of the people of Gruel. Or the people who worshiped Gruel.

In the center stage a thousand feet away was a massive cartwheel, with iron shackles, and a person. An inhumanely tall man stood next to it, waving a silvery dagger which waved like the fire they adored. In his other hand was a large bowled chalice whose sparkles reached the wall behind Litus, from a deep red to an almost pink flower.

The symphony of screams and the shock horror of mutilation and carnal desire to continue was exuberant among all the people who wore their robes of a deep crimson red, and a mask of gold or porcelain. In perfect harmony, they all shouted, "to our god, our only god, he blesses us tonight, and further nights."

The tall man beckoned these cries as he waved that dagger around, until in a crack of light, it pierced the man, posted at the wheel, and his skin boiled in mere seconds. And the only sounds that came from him, was a scream, and a sound akin to a kettle whistle.

He rushed back to the keep, and during his run, the guards that stood post in the castle had asked for identification. Darien took down his hood and pierced the guards skull with a stare, before continuing on.

"It's Darien, I'm coming in," and he burst through the duke's chamber door.

"What are you doing? Do not not just barge into my quarters wherever you seek!"

"His men, lord Garet's men, are planning a revolt. They're planning to riot. And to riot tonight."

"What!? How do you know!? Explain."

"I just received truthful knowledge that his men, his servants, goons, personal guard, however they call themselves. They know what's happened to their lord."

"Do we know where they are planning to riot?"

"We don't, my lord."

"Then have his region's border secured. Inform Taryen of this situation, and make sure that none of this is known to the tower."

"There is no way of this falling on deaf ears. He'll know."

"Then let's deal with this situation quickly. I don't want a knife in the side from Pias too."

"My lord, you shouldn't have done this."

"Done what, my hand Darien?"

"Poisoned him, my lord. You shouldn't have poisoned him."

"He admitted to an attempt on my life. It does not, what you think. You will do what I ask of you. I know my moral bounds, and this will pass as judgment under our lord, Selziar."

"Then, shall the rioters be arrested or executed."

"I'll put it to individual judgment. Never dealt with a riot, I'll see what is most efficient, and what's the best course of action."

"Alright, my lord," Darien bowed, and left clutching the pommel of his thin sword in his palm.

He marched in uniform to the traitors cell near the bottom of his own vessel. Followed by a scholar, and an armed officer. One of whom, he wouldn't admit, was a truth wizard. The light of the midnight sky emanated from the secretive waves of the ocean. Silent whispers of captives were skittering like mice, except for Lucerne who appeared to sit serenely. "Is that you Broarch?"

"Why are you sitting like that?"

"I'm not imprisoned due to sitting, am I?"

"Has this sitting given you a new perspective?"

"Sitting? No."

The waves slapped on the side of the hull, with the sound of flows around them. Despite the turmoil of this man's actions it soothed him. Broarch was calm as the dead, "I think of you quite poorly. I need to repeat the tyranny you've put onto us. You abandoned your post. Left thousands and thousands of innocent women with babes at their tit to the hands of those who try to take them for treachery and turmoil."

"You say that as though you have something great about yourself."

"Pray for the gods, the two of them. Any practical man would do so in your place. You have nowhere to hide, and you're further behind all the others here."

"At what?"

"Being a mouse. Although," he chuckled, "you're quite a rodent," the other men laughed, and soon followed Lucerne.

And he said with a polite smile, "I can see the writing on the wall, and it seems I am in quite a pickle."

The admiral quickly turned sour, as the waves grew a teensy tiny bit grandful and less, "get up," he ushered, "that porthole, look through it. Do you see it?"

"No, I don't."

"Hmm," he chuckled. "Neither do I."

"What's over there?"

"A continent, and a series of islands, of a political nature that isn't ours."

"No, no, there's something out there."

"That was true," said the scholar.

"What do you see?"

"Ships."

"You're enamored with what I've done with your ships and crews. They're doing night patrols."

"I know how the look of light bounces off my sails, and nails of my ship, especially at night."

"Truth."

"Then that's a matter for me, and not you. And do you know what's also a matter of mine, you."

"I know that, but-"

"Silence. I'll ask again, of all reasons, why did you think that you'd find the city as how you left it? How is it that you couldn't understand what would happen to you?"

"Blue flags fly in the midnight air which we will soon . . . soon see."

It was a fiery showmanship for all the little terrors of the world, for the few to see and preach in this echo chamber. He ran back down and grabbed her arm, and she moaned in pain. In his breathy tone, he lurched, "death hasn't taken you yet."

"I don't pray for death, I pray for the flame to twinkle further and further on."

He took the red robe and wore it instead. That clean bleached mask of an animal he wore as well. The twisted antlers wrapped around the hood and clipped the disguise tightly. In one hand he held a wand and the other something else.

He walked back holding arm to arm with this vile woman. The entire time he thought only of Jane. He asked, "how do we get there?" And he let her direct.

The halls were as grand as they were red, like the skin of a shined apple. The quant tea lights that filled the dungeons, now became beacons. Bright flames were lit in gilded sconces, and they produced no visible soot.

Cultists passed by them, and each time, either twisting their head, or giving a seemingly curtsy nod. He tried to pass them by unnoticed, "do it back, don't be a fool."

"Why."

"Then don't.

"Whomever you're seeking will be turned into ink."

"Ink?"

"For the reclamation over the lands that are ours."

"I'll nod," *So she knows about Jane, but how much?*

"You see that corridor? We need to head there."

"Alright," he said as they walked down.

There were paintings which lined the walls. Litus didn't recognize the figures presented, but he could see that they were extravagantly garbed, nobly so. In a corner he could see, a woman tall and pale, with the same red eyes which he'd known for half a year?

"That's the dead queen."

"Yes, and you killed her."

Her deception run's deeper than I believed. "You must be a high ranked member of this all."

"Very perceptive."

"Your wound seems to be healing?"

"N- No?" She stuttered.

Litus with one hard thump, punched two fingers into her sternum. A blackish-red ooze secreted and dribbled onto the floor.

"Ah," she tried to take in the air, "but, I'm trying to help you?"

"You're going to die. I can promise you that, and it'll either be from this wound, your own brethren, or something else."

Her eyes were black behind that mask. Her heart still croaked, in a slow beating drum. She bled onto the ruler's hall; each and every one was like the last. "Where do we go next?"

She coughed before saying, "at the very end."

He kept her arm while they walked, and she dragged a foot.

The end of this painters hall, held an enshadowed doorway. Litus peered around, making sure that there was no-one to encroach. He jumped out, and walked down the dimly lit halls. He kept to the dimness, that is where it was safest. It was quiet, the sound of the roaring was eerily distant. He let her guide, but he was ready to retaliate if the time came.

Even now, when the sound was completely silent, he still felt needles prick at his skin, but what confused him was that he didn't feel them while holding this cultist woman. He felt a sharp prickly thread the further they walked forward. "What's there," he pointed forward.

"A doom for most."

"Why are we going to it?"

"We have to go deeper down, to meet the doom maker. I thought for a moment that my doom hasn't come, but he's down there, most likely. And yours most definitely."

The door at the end of the hall had blurred panes, which exacerbated glowing ashes, and rustling sounds all reflecting off the gold and red porcelain walls.

It is soon now. The thought came to him with a piercing. *Is it past that door? Or is it further from it?* He had to know he jostled her and he ran to it. Footsteps entered behind them, and followed with a yell in a different tongue. *Past the door. Past the door.* She said, "wait, there's someone coming."

He knew and didn't answer, "behind us, and in front."

"In front?" And from the windows he saw a figure without features.

There were two of them, in the dimness. The light turned gray. It all came down to a masquerade. Once one of the cultists passed through that door, he walked solemnly. He held her close to him, to disguise their pain. "Just pass slowly, and bow when instructed."

He nodded. The man behind them ran up quickly to meet the cultist that just passed those doors. Litus remained calm, as they did so. He bore the stinging with grace. The man nodded, and Litus stopped and nodded back. It came like thunder. A bar smashed into his back. He dropped his hands, and she fell to the side. Litus could hear the sound of chains thrashing towards him. He got smashed on the side again, needles were pulsating as clear as an empty sky.

Before he could get struck again, he kicked at the man's legs, pushing himself and causing that man to stagger little, but a significant sum. He held that wand firmly. He rolled over that bruised side, and came to his feet. The men tried rushing, but Litus in one thrust of his arm, cast the fire of the wand forward. And in a split second a beam of pure unbridled light exploded out of the tip of that wand. The light flickered, not like a candle, but like the roar and terror of lightning strikes. The beams split and cracked every few feet they traveled in that fraction of a fraction of time they traveled, and each split found an end and reconnected. They flowed down the hall, and through their bodies. They jostled for mere moments, before falling, with a kindle burning in their chest.

The wand burned a hole in his sleeve, and the hall seemed so much darker. He turned his head, when he heard the rustle from the side. She was sitting, trying to avoid sparks which lingered in the air like flies.

"You knew this all."

"Yes."

"You failed."

The yelling was massive. It started with possibly a dozen men, and it only expanded further on. He dropped down, and entered the stables out back. He grabbed the first mare he could, and with a boot and a grunt of the horse, he rode out. It grew to at least a hundred men strong, all shouting protest. He could see men growing as he looked back.

He came to the outside boundary, and from the horse he alerted the men of the ensuing riot. "Stay on guard! I'll send word of what to do next. So stay put, and if they come, keep them surrounded. It's not gonna be pretty. Be ready men," and Darien left to the keep.

He passed by the first few guards, and at the entrance dropped down from his horse. A footman pushed a halberd in Darien's face, "who are you! Identify yourself!"

Darien pulled up his hood while spitting, "you should be charged with treason," he said fully revealing his face.

Once they saw his face, they let him go, and promptly nodded and apologized, "stand guard,"

He marched to the chamber. The door clattered, and swifty slammed shut. "My lord, there is a riot forming in Garet's former land. Possibly hundreds of men, almost all armed. You have to do something."

"Hmm, is this information true?"

"Yes."

"Does lord Taryen know? If not, send a man to alert him, and send a man to alert Karaway. Have the border secured."

"Is that it, my lord?"

"Make certain none of this is known by Pias, or at least not the scale of this all."

Darien nodded, and left the guard.

Grabbing a billhook from the armory he watched the empty ground past the noble lords guarded homes. There was a long echoing clattering like an army of blacksmiths or lumberjacks doing their work. Or maybe, it was drumming. The sound of drumming. He watched for some time, and the sky dimmed a little more.

There were many of them. He included. There was fire, and it stormed through their veins. He was dressed in a covering over his face made from scrap cloth. A hammer with a hand forged spike on one side smashed into the door knob, and it was thrown out of the door frame.

An old woman screamed as she ran off to another room. He ran through any cabinet. Searching through drawers and drawers of nothing but papers and little else. He ran to where she went and found her quivering on the ground holding a knife. When he approached she tried to swat at him, but he returned the favor with one clean blow. In the semi darkness there was a stain that occurred across the ground and on the walls. He rummaged through many pockets, finding a single ring made of a thin brass band and a gem made of age-worn wood.

An old man screamed from behind, he swung a hammer at the intruder, and again with the hand ax in his other hand. The intruder poorly rebounded that hammer spike towards the old man but found no resistance except for a metal hammer in his back, and on his head.

Within only mere minutes, glass littered the streets like rain, like snow. They ran picking up the weapons they could, including breaking the ends off of bottles adding only more glass to the floor.

It was a tower tall and deep. And a stairway spiraled around the inner walls going high and low a long long way. He looked down without falling off, and it truly looked infinite, both ways. And Litus looked around this immensity, and still birds hung from high, and were empty at this time. More and more captured and stored all around to gaze and to laugh at by the cultist in this base. It disgusted him, the torment, the wrath of a silent conqueror.

He continued to drag her down and down further with him. As she cried for the fates to take her already. She prayed to the god, he was set to destroy. The stairs were kept cleaner and were polished from use and labor greater than even the castle Renoi.

Pins and needles prickled in some seconds, and none in others, but the intensity and speed between these grew shorter and shorter till it all felt like a stinging sensation. There was an entrance at the bottom of the stairwell. At the very end of the dark tunnel was red. He took the blade he thrusted through, wiping the red away, and hiding it.

It was funny, there was a crow, and so laughed the man stationed up top, clutching his coat tightly waiting for the next man to come and take his cold place. In his pocket was a wrapped sleeve of a hard flat bread, he broke off chunks feeding some to that crow, and the bird thanked him with a caw that flew away. He watched that bird gracefully fly off through the horizon. Until it was gone in the night sky, and then he watched further on. He saw a glimmer of light, only for a moment. Looking closer, he waited, another shimmer of light bounced, and another. With steady eyes he saw with the clear air between them, the illuminated face staring right at him. He reeled back, knowing what he saw, and rang the bell high above. "Pirates! Pirates!" He yelled across the horizon. "Far port side! Far port side!"

"My grace, I need to alert you, Lord Pias, has heard of this commotion, and is sending men including himself to deal with it."

"You can't keep a mouth shut," he told himself, "is this the consequence?" He reflected for a moment before asking, "do you know how many men he plans to send?"

"I do not, my grace."

"Then a lord will do lordly things. I have four dozen men here, I want three dozen to be alerted, and ride out with me."

"I will alert the duke," he bowed and left.

Eiger wasn't sure if his plates would fit, it'd been many many years since the war, and he was only a child then. Set to inherit his seat. When he came down to the armory with smiths pounding on their anvils carefully with their massive and tiny hammers, and their face when their lord came was a gobsmack. They all put down their works – as carefully as possible – and bowed to their grace. Pulling their hands through their short beards, pulling out any stray embers. "What can we do, my grace?"

"Armor and steel my friends, I need to know if I still fit."

"Right away, my grace."

This is war armor, not that frilly tourney armor with gold embedded and steel horns strafing the sides in a mimic of dragons to reapers, and to the duke's surprise it still fit him like a glove. The armor hadn't a patina, but the dust covered it like frost on a window. And Eiger had a long sword with a broad blade fashioned to his hip, and he went to the stables, where all the soldiers would wait with him.

A man in bright red armor already seated on his mare, yelled out, "your grace, Duke Eiger!"

And the duke presented himself, "Denoth, I am leaving to deal with this discrepancy, have the queen well protected."

"That won't be the case, my grace."

"Oh, and why's that?"

"You can send your men to death, but I can't allow yourself."

"As I enter, as you say 'death' ride with me and protect me if you must."

"Our grace needs to be protected as well. As you know. I cannot leave my post, for a lesser man."

"Then trade one of my men for yours, a trusted man for another. And then I'll ride, with your protection or not."

And so Eiger mounted and traded his knight George Smith, for one of the king's guard: Sir John II. They marched for thirty minutes past the cathedral.

The sound of the many was a great boom. It was no wonder the tower would know, Eiger felt it like a heavy slap over his ears, like a knife in the chest. The quality of the buildings steadily degraded as they passed by. Eiger noticed the sound grew greater the closer they came. That and the armor brought back memories he quite forgot.

To his left he could hear a concert of hooves clop the ground. When he looked, Pias looked back. He rode his mare to Eiger, and they both stopped before they entered the road which led to a great fire storm.

Pias wore a set of gilded armor of scrolls and such, with a white leather bound scabbard on his hip. Eiger looked at the armor glint from the lantern light he held. He looked up at eye level, and he said, "what commotion brings the watchmen here? Is this the whole of the Tower?"

"The same one that brought you and the men of Renoi. Including one of the king's guards. Do you know what the deal with this riot is?"

"I should be the one asking, your men are supposed to keep the peace, you should know of the tensions which brought this upon us."

"My Grace, Duke Eiger, I only ask to get more information on how to handle this chaos. If you wish to be cooperative, then just follow me."

"You wouldn't lead my men, when you know not of the threat."

"By the law enacted by the crown, the watchtower, and myself would be in charge of dealing with this, so stop bickering with me, and follow my orders."

"No, no, no," said Eiger, "there is procedure, and a riot at this scale, couldn't be performed by the tower, this is a matter of the army."

"And this is the army?"

"Yes, and I'm in command."

The bickering had continued for an eternal five minutes. In history more had died in less, but they couldn't decide who would command whom. Everything grew more and more, diction and contradiction, noise noise noise. It grew from an opera to the sound of an ocean of fire. Both of their footmen had a look of anguish as they looked around the block they stood in.

Eventually it all changed from their standstill to being dead silent as they watched the incoming men holding their torches and makeshift pikes, and swords they stole. A great immensity of them all. Hundreds of men, all of them, standing waiting.

"Stand in line," yelled Pias. "Stand in line!"

All the footmen in his regiment shifted to take up the road with their flat shields raised forward. The rioters stopped their running and the look of over a dozen men shifted as they were surrounded. There were the men who had faces of anger, and men whose faces were covered.

One of the men shouted with a sword raised high. "Don't give in to fear! They are the few! They are the fearful!"

And near two dozen men ran down the road with whatever they wielded. Their shields were trusted in their arms, but mostly they kept still.

Eiger had his horsed men find entrances on either side to snuff the opposing forces. Their flank fell through small alleys on either of the buildings in partial ruin. In a little sparse of time they had, soon coming out were thin streams of cavalry. What they saw as they entered the mobs from the side, was that the line stretched far further down the road than believed.

There were many hundreds of people behind the frontline. They tried to pierce through the people. To separate the frontline from the rest, but it was far too vast an ocean to break the waves. They hoped to be the ship, but they had sunk in their sail, with no plain sailing.

They tried to break through to the front, or retreat through the alleys they came from. Not all of the men went in to begin with, but there were some who didn't escape.

There were thousands amongst them. Hundreds stood right behind the stage with an infinitely long line of believers in their balconies, and more high above in their boxed seats. They chanted and prayed, as the tall man on the stage drove his wavy blade through the prisoner with grayish and copper skin. The scream of agony was the melody to this choir, it resonated and died in his chest with the skin peeling away from the wound with blood boiling into a sludge which dribbled into a porcelain jar, help filled by all the rest of the prisoners. They all roared from this, chanting in a strange tone, *More,* and they prayed. As the blood dripped into the pot, it released a char steam that quickly thinned.

He stepped out from the dark hall, into the back of the crowd. Litus made his way through, pushing past many, who wouldn't care, or couldn't pay attention to him.

The man was taken from his crucifixion and was pruned. His body was placed upon a steel bed altar. A flame was quenched below, being fed but a drop of the black sludge blood. It erupted into a flame not of red, but in a great bluish paint. His body began reacting to this flame. His body drifted up with the flame. His limbs drifted down, as his chest was the peak closest to the ceiling of the great great keep. From his chest the fire pierced through, puncturing a hole in a piece of stretched leather. The ash from his body shimmered in the hue of many hues. Ash floated weightlessly up to the sound of shearing parchment. The hole expanded outward till his body had evaporated, and all that was left was his disintegrating limbs. And then all was ash, and floated up, and the blue fire was snuffed. The particulates continued to fly upward, until they were invisible.

He pushed through further and further, till he was half way away from the stage, and the tall man who waved, conjured about in a holy fashion. It seemed that wisps of air were woven around the tip of that blade. He put the blade down on a table to his side, and he spoke in a loud commanding boom, "we pray to this great man who relinquished his strength for the sake of the many, rather than the few. We pray to the dark times which have befallen and the light we bring while protecting others in the shadow. We pray to the new peace we shall hold tightly to our chest. And we pray to our god, Gruel Keroth," they all became silent and brought their head down to pray the one point: tapping the tip of their fingers to their forehead, and heart.

Litus continued to walk through the crowd pushing more and more away to get closer to that stage. And the closer he came, the higher it was from the ground. They brought out another prisoner, this one with splotched gray skin. The ritual began anew.

Are they sacrificing everyone from the cells? The hanging cells, the dungeons? What do they know about me? Do they know this prophecy? Did they sacrifice Jane? He still pushed thorough, and the crowds closer to the stage were only more densely packed. *Is she dead?*

The procedure went the same as before. His skin boiled, his blood taken, and that blue fire pierced and turned his body into flash paper over a candle flame. And then they prayed at one point. Litus had gotten stuck, his progression was little from here on. They brought out another and the series of motions began again. It felt like Litus was within just a touch of that stage, and the man said, "and here we begin and finish a new age, a new life, a new kingdom, so pray to her, and pray to our god, Gruel Keroth."

Out they walked in chains of brass Jane in the nude. Her hair washed, and illness cured. There wasn't a scar on her body. The man held her and placed her on an altar. The man raised his blade high and held his arms out outstretched to the sky. High above them the ash which hung reformed as a single swirling mass. "Come our grace, a daughter of god, chosen ruler, and shall be commanded by the lord."

Litus forcefully pushed through, letting his arm escape his sleeve. He put his hand on the stage. The ones that surrounded him, let out a gasp, if they even paid attention to see. He kicked someone trying to stop him, but with one motion he jumped onto the theater of war.

With one clean motion, her body began to levitate with no strings, only fire was below her, and ash above.

He stormed out of the cell room. His men followed by each man by his side, and when they saw those ships in the distance, they almost couldn't keep their eyes away. There were flags being flown, and he had an idea of what they were, or who they belonged to, but he wasn't so sure who they belonged to. "Men at arms! Men at arms, on my command!" He yelled.

The ships sailed closer, and their flags were now clear as day. The blue naval flag that wasn't theirs. It slapped against the mast, as the ships curved towards shore. Their horns blew heavy tones. Three ships were ready to meet theirs, and the men were falling out of their bunks to keep other ships ready to sail.

The wind blew south west, they now had six vessels. Four of these vessels were row powered galleys. They hoisted their sails high and mighty, and they pointed the great ten ton hammer offset diagonally from the invaders. The rowers – one hundred and thirty five in unison – were first slowly rowing to keep their tired arms from snapping awake.

It was no longer night, as the fires were held in containers over the calm. Archers clutched their heavy arrows between their fingers. The storm league were sharpening their short arming swords, and preparing the corvus. The rowers sat by heat waiting for their duty to truly begin.

Broarch watched from the quarterdeck. The tall commanding ships held a long view of the waters, and port holes on their sides for archers and pikes, but mostly for pyromancers. It twas a shame they held only fools with wands rather than the trained men of long ago. Crates were cracked open, with two of each dusty old wands, for each of the storm league men. They were tracked and marked. And they manned their positions.

The two large vessels fell broadside away from the coast, and the ships sat apart by a quarter mile at most. They were behind the swifter ships.

It started with a crash. Lanterns were thrown off their holsters, throwing hot wax against the treated wood. Splinters from the deck came crashing through, and rained down upon the men ready to storm the navy sailors of the land of insanity.

Broarch barked commands, but when he saw the speed at which these ships had sailed he was astonished, *Even with the wind in their favor, how did they?* A stray skimmer passed by their flank, it almost went unnoticed, but it was caught in just enough time to take action. Broarch grabbed a projectioning horn, and passed it to an officer's arms, "you tell them to fire when on my command."

He waited by the side, having his men act and sail as though they never noticed this skimmer. It was dark, and Broarch kept to the dark, and waited till they drew close enough. In a blink of a grappling hook wrapped around the lip of the ship, Broarch yelled. "Fire!"

And from the broad side a massive wave of brilliant red flame engulfed the skimmer sending a dozen or two men to the bottom of the sea bed, or charred to ash.

They were forced to ram the side of the ship, having failed dropping the corvus down on time. A half dozen arrows went flying at the rowers in the galleys, but didn't stop the men maneuvering the corvus. They lifted and dropped it down on the taller ship, and quickly running up the ramp the blades came piercing through the invaders. The sounds of pinging metal went like the flapping of hummingbirds. "Fire!" They heard, and a few of the men on the other side of the ship had flicked their hands and a stream of fire and bright lightning sprinted forward through men and enemy alike. The air singed and all the water perspiration exploded when in contact with that lightning. And right after, another helping of those arrows were released, and even more men stormed the ship board, and they returned their own arrows, and brought on their fire.

The flags of blue and purple spun around in a harmony like the dancers in a ballet. The Rientonem navy men were angling their corvus to drop down onto the ship of the invader. While they were trying to break their defenders with the multi-ton ram hammer to the side. And it all came with splinters and shattered planks. Men fell down from their post, and were crushed with the crumbling ships. The Rientonem sailors grabbed their swords, and the storm league readied their wands. The first wave sent fourteen men and lost five to a stream of arrows. And another four to the fire.

Soon within the minute, rain had begun to fall, and with it thunder and lightning much brighter and louder than the conjurer's magic. A single beam of electricity fell down with a smite onto the masthead of the man of war ship: the Periot. The mast crashed into the ground, and left behind liquid fire on what was left.

Broarch took full control, with his amplifier he spouted commands, and had his large vessel break through the middle. Behind the ships already there, and ready to meet the incoming ships with a viscous boarding, after a barrage of arrows and fire and thousands of pounds of steel weights.

They rushed as fast as they could. Picking the stream of heavy wind while rain poured and lightning struck like a dropped bolt on the hard ground, Broarch yelled to his men, "be on both sides, and on my command your fire and release."

"They're pushing through the park," he riled, and a moment later he sputtered again, "they've pushed through the park, sir!"

"How many? When will they?"

"Hundreds and soon, sir Darien."

He clutched the handle ready to draw. "I need a third to ride with me," and he yelled over them all, "Company B, you ride with me! Company A and C, hold against them, keep your lances and pikes raised forward, ready to strike when close enough," he drew his sword, slender it be and waved it in the air, he projected ever greater, "ride with me! Company B, cavalry division!"

Darien kicked the back of his horse, and he with nearly three dozen riders raced to meet the escapee rioters at the green. Down the city streets women were holding their children's ears while men were pulling them in and locking the door behind.

A drunk old man was leaving a pub and when he saw the duke's men, he raced to put his mask on, and fell backwards through the pub doors. They didn't break for others as well, knowing the consequences of lost time.

They had raced through two blocks one posher and one poorer, and at the end was a small keep – insignificant compared to Renoi – and the Watchmen's tower. The parkway was past there. A man who stood at one of the battlements watched with wide eyes as a storm of cavalry went storming by, and he noted.

Darien could see in the far distance behind a line of brush a storm of men with their pitchforks and torches. He split the company to take their flank. And once he came to the peak of a hill, he saw their numbers. It was meek. There were significantly less of them. *This was a distraction at least.* He commanded with his fist to slow their descent on the peasants.

There were even women and children within the group, and priests as well. *Are they using them as some shield?* He dropped his hand, signaling to his men his thoughts. They surrounded them from one side, the rioters stopped in their place. They held their makeshift pikes out, and waved their torches trying to wade off the Darien's men.

While in a safe distance away he shouted at them all to lay down their arms. He shouted for long, but they neither laid down their arms, nor continued on.

From behind a few dozen or so rides came from the fort they passed. And adorned leading the men was a man stationed on top in his black armor on a white horse: Lord Temberton. He rode up behind them all. To the rioters it must have been a crying shame for themselves. They would soon be accosted with spikes where they would be resting against their jowls and be flayed off loose skin. But it was not so, when the lord came shouting and came to Darien he parked the butt of his long spear on the once soft ground. "You! Captain for the duke of the flash fields: Pagmonila. What is here that you bring an army against."

"I work in the name of the duke, the queen, and for the people. These are those who seek chaos, which should be kept low. Those who expand further and further on, encroaching lands which aren't theirs. They break homes, steal, and burn."

"You stopped."

"There are priests and women and children among them."

"You plan to starve them here?"

"We are breaking their pace."

The father stepped back in disgust. "You encroach on this like a fly on flesh. I cannot allow maggots to grow from your violence intruder." The blade extended into a long shimmering flame that drew from his hand to the floor and scratched into the porous material, "you defiled our god with your presence heretic! I shall absolve you of sin, and I thank thee," and he prayed.

Litus watched Jane be lifted out of reach. He kept the blade forward to the pope. "You raise your blade to me, a demon wraith in our church. Then let me pray to you as you pray to me," and the priest bowed.

He raised the flame high and spun it like a whip. It caught the end of that cold estoc and the sound was a crack. Bits of flame rose and fell like the sapling and fruit of a tree soon to ripen and die of old age.

The priest's movements were slow, but his blade struck before it appeared. Every movement struck before it should have, but there was no foul play. That poison in his system was gone, it was the pope who was supernatural, but differently so than himself. Litus didn't know if the priest was even human, nor did he know just what he was, but all he did know was the swiftness of the priest's beating blows.

It was like a long memory faded but rekindled anew, and the horror it showed was a blasphemous display of hubris on who's ends? The flame had pierced his femur at the speed of a blink, blasting an embering hole through his cloak. Litus touched the painful gash that was left with one hand, but in his other he kept the point on the priest.

"And so it begins anew," he prayed, "from the soot of sinners gets pressed into a gem greater than this cathedral and the jewel of the city and us. This is history and art and all the beauty of the world. It is life, and grandeur, and peasantry too," he extended his arms out holding the flaming sword in an even greater extension as all that ash which touched the ceiling came dropping like black snow onto Jane's body.

An image pierced his mind, and in a swift motion Litus drew from the void a flame of his own, and a gift to all the zealots. Soon the ash flew up again with the new heat and ash produced from the tinder of potent hearts.

He swung his sword over his head looking down at Litus, and shouted calmly behind that antler mask. "Blasphemy," and the blade extended ever further until it cracked its whip tip just feet away.

Litus parried the tip away, flinging it away from him, as he lunged forward. He plunged the sword deep into a cone of metal. His blade was brought up by the hand and knocked away. And Litus backed away from the heat.

Jane hung with that ash which helplessly sat on her skin, and bled into her golden blonde hair. A streak of black dye dripped down her scalp and onto the ground between them.

Litus kept the blade extended as they turned around the droplets. He clutched his thigh with an open hand. The pain was non existent till he touched the wound, and it left immediately once he took it off.

"The cancerous root, we weed out those who don't swallow the poison of shame. Who doesn't swallow the pity of others. The great king shall rise again, in a time that is new. But first we weed out the roots from the community for they don't bring ill blithe terror, humility and humanity to our sleeping feet."

The red ash from the hundreds of hearts reflected a passionate light onto half of their faces and made the other in dark. The father brought the flat of his blade to the bridge of his nose, and prayed once more and then disallowed the touch of the sinner's blade to encroach his being.

It all occurred too fast. In the center of it all, beyond the control of his riders, or Pias' the people were smothered with the hammer blow. Many tried to scatter, and others were the fuel, and the breath in their lungs weren't theirs anymore.

The flames were a grand display, a horrible display, and a display of uncertainty. Eiger yelled. "Out! Retreat!" But he wasn't sure if anyone could hear.

Pias kept his ground, as he watched people fall into flame, and others escape through the cracks in the city which he didn't see. It was like a cobweb of fury. It stretched and stuck to everything, and before he could blink it stretched across the street. From side to side.

The rioters' fury was like the fire. They erupted into anger and threw anything they could find on the ground at Pias' men. They thrust their pikes and met shields shattering and splintering on the ground. He barked. "Hold your ground!"

Eiger had recovered a sizable sum of the men he sent in, and there they formed a rank behind Pias. He could see with his eyes the full scale of the ash which flew high getting clung to brick and the sky above. The light of the fire was bright. Their lanterns were dim like the reflections off of the ocean bed. All the light in the world was a single holy red flame.

There was no bloodshed when everything was this giant red. There was no pain either. Spears went through shoulders. And bottles of flaming alcohol were thrown and burst on the ground in a small orange tidal wave. And all was the same. There was peace in knowing that what was, was this. It was a pure animal instinct, but above all it was fire.

It was like an anvil. A hard cold stone against the heated malleable billet chosen to take any shape that cuts. All cuts were reforged and welded whole again. Little sparks were flung and it mattered not, for they seemed insignificant altogether.

Litus backed away, turning his sword against the flame. He looked up and swung high to deflect the attacking steel. He pushed forward the bar being met by another. For a little while it was this game of slash and counter. It was more of a testing of abilities. Litus took this time to look around his surroundings, and see the footings of the clear stage. It was a dish floating in a pool of blood. Soon it felt like their movements rocked that dish, and the blood would climb the porous material. The edges of the dish radiated hateful energy which tore the strongest of materials into tiny delicate parts.

There was that table. He could possibly be able to grasp and take Jane from the position she's trapped in. *Then where?* There was no discernible exit, but maybe it was behind the pope. He shot out a bolt of lightning from his offhand, and in an instant the pope dodged the bolt. His hands shook holding that flame. He held the blade against his hand, giving it a small cut. Once the blade of flame, now less slick with blood, made his hands shake less. He swung that red drops of blood hissed as they flew off the blade. Litus saw his hands had a bone protrude, and glisten against the light.

Litus needed the edge, and the old estoc wasn't so sharp. He backed as far as he could, to draw the falchion, and in that time the pope made the distance. Their swords bound. Litus tried to push the blade over the flame, but with one kick he was thrown to the ground. The tip of the flamberge was against Litus. The cult leader stood above him, and he said in his dark tone, "you destroy so much, but I know what you are, or what you seek. Ser wraithkind of poor thoughts," he pushed the tip closer. "Look at them," and Litus did so, watched a pile of burning corpses and people try to leave, and others watching them praying, with faces masked and unmasked and eyes he seen a million times, "I thank thee, and I pray that thee brings peace after the day begin anew. Angel of fire."

Litus reached for and pulled from the void the estoc again, since the falchion left his hands. He swung up, picking up his feet. The father backed away and paced around Litus, "that fire, imagine it, see it in the dark."

Litus tried not to touch those thoughts. He jumped forward and was met with the front of a wall of steel, and blocked and tried to continue forward, but he dodged it, jumping to the side. He threw the blade towards the priest, and in those few seconds there was a parry, counter strike, and strike. They were back to this game once more of prodding and backing. Litus both knew it and that the father knew too.

The fire began to crawl high. Pushing that ash even higher, until it all melded into the soot which sat before. The fire was liquid falling upstream, clinging to the walls and piercing it like a boar spear pierces flesh. Soon the rock began to light with the light greater than the sun. Every scratch, visible and poignant.

Litus feigned the strike, and pushed his blade close to the head, only scratching the mask. The father in a rage slapped away the blade, and went to grab Litus with his skeletal hand. He thrusted the flame blade into the dish, cracking it for the blade. He lit a fire from the tip of his finger. "By the light of the gods," and he touched the hilt of the flamberge.

From the crack, a wall of fire, encircled Litus and Jane floated above in the center. It was like the fire wall from many months ago now. Before he could do anything, he was stuck in the fortification. He braced for something, a strike, maybe for the ceiling to come crashing down, killing them all.

A large drop of a blacking bloody dew fell on the ground next to Litus. It shined like a freshly cut jewel. From above many more of these drops fell in clumps. They dropped from the ceiling covered in soot. Most of the drops never hit the ground. Their landings were the beds of white ash.

The reverend preacher met Litus by sword, and received a slash in return. Litus was feigned and received a cut to the arm. But still, he kept his guard up with two hands.

The dew stopped right above Jane's body. It all started to pool together in one material. The black soot and the white ash refused to combine, but rather stayed apart on the dew. They formed these bright clean stripes around the material. And the material wasn't some smooth ball – it was more like a figure – soon with the shape of a head, and a body, and bat-like wings with sharpening spikes at each limb end.

Litus looked up, for a moment. In that split second he believed he saw that parasite. *It is what it looked like*. After that second, the father swung his sword low, to escape being cut Litus tried to jump back, but stumbled and fell. The father again stood over Litus, blade to him. "Oh merciful god, I pray this wraith to be," Litus couldn't hear it, over the tinder chanting.

The creature creaked and motioned like a rusty door hinge until it stood outstretched, throbbed, and slowly, slowly opened its eyes.

Litus tried to reach for the estoc, the father put a foot on it, to keep it out of the wraith's hands, and he continued his preaching. The fathers' free hand emanated this flame and glow, that rose high, fueling the parasite, and directing it. With his bad arm, Litus grabbed the blade, and pulling it up from his chest. The father looked back in ecstatic lust and awe as he reached for the blade to bring forth through Litus' chest. Litus reached and threw a bolt of lightning high above, wrapping around the wet parasite. It fell to the ground onto the flaming pile. Before the cult leader could speak, he received the cold estoc in his chest and immediately gutted out as Litus now stood before him, bathed in the red.

And the fire kept rising, the smell was apparent. It was infinitely greater than anything else in the city, and it smelled like meat, crisp meat, and the simmering fat would be pleasant, if it weren't for the dust which littered the street clinging to the grout in bricks, and the legs of pike-men.

Eiger put a cloth over his face, but it barely helped. He was in awe at the collapse of a building made from the kindling beams. All the bricks fell like a playing card house. It was a gamble, and they all lost. Himself, and all who die within the heat.

"My Grace, what do we do? The fire is spreading," said a soldier, by his side.

The cards were reshuffled, and Eiger came to his senses, "where's the navy? And the fire marshal?"

"We don't know where the navy is, but the firemen are tackling the flame from the other side, but some of the rioters are invoking fights with them."

"Where is the fire greater?"

"Currently here, my grace."

"Alright then, I'll ride to retrieve the navy, inform Pias of my departure, and tell him to maintain any loose rioters, on the queen's name," *for how long it was, it was strange the navy didn't have a single sailor,* he though as he rode quickly with all his men following, and then he saw it, the ships and the fire over waves.

Everywhere through the clean lens now covered and smeared clouds of cruel particles. It billowed high and created a bed of chaos a thousand feet high and a thousand feet wide, and it stretched all above the cursed forest, and being the first direct contact of massive cities in the first time in over a thousand years. Thunder enveloped and cracked through the grain of cooked fiber, and cooked flesh. And the ash carried little bits of fire which wouldn't snuff and compacted into a red cloud. And it only shows itself more and more with the flashing of blue lightning over all the land. It spun into an ever combining hue of terror over terror, and crack and thunder for a long while, but soon it would rain blood and ash for all below in the sea of chaos.

Glossary:

Gods:

God Selziar, Lord of the Realm of the Living

God Keroth/Gruel, Lord of the Realm of the Living

God Mortith, Lord of the Realm of the Dead

Unknown:

The Traveler/Litus

Unknown

Human:

Andrew, Armorer of Diende

Ranger Arbaton, Ranger

King Ariston Renoi, King of Rientonem

Bishop Barley, Bishop of the City of Fer and Ser

Barrett, Guard of Duke Eiger / Queen's Guard

Commodore Barwyn, Commodore of the Royal Navy

Batwit, Shipper of Maud

Admiral Broarch, Admiral of the Royal Navy

Knight/Father Darien, Head guard to Duke Eiger of the Pagmonila Fields

Knight Denoth, Head of the King's Guard of Rientonem

Duke Eiger, Duke of the Pagmonila Fields

Ranger Elliot, Ranger

Commodore Erik, Commodore of the Royal Navy

Duke Ester, Duke of half of the city of Fer/ Duke of Charian

Lord Garet, Lord of Porcelania

Garland, Guard of Duke Eiger / Queen's Guard

Queen/Princess Garnette Renoi, Queen/Princess of Rientonem

Knight George Smith, Guard of Duke Eiger of the Pagmonila Fields

Jane

Jaune, Guard of Duke Eiger / Queen's Guard

Knight John II, King's Guard of Rientonem

Lord Karaway, Lord of Porcelania

Pastor/Father Kreshen, Father/Pastor of Trinity Church of Tabier

Bishop Lazith, Bishop of Porcelania
Ranger Lee, Ranger

Commodore Lucerne, Commodore of the Royal Navy

Queen Mary Renoi, Queen of Rientonem

Ranger Morrosey, Head of the Ranger's Guild

Duke Pelile, Duke of the Flumen

Admiral Perot, Admiral of the Royal Navy

Lord Pias, Lord of the Watchtower of Porcelania
Pinky/Peter, Guard of Duke Eiger / Queen's Guard
Roswell, Maid to Tylock

Sam, Guard of Duke Eiger / Queen's Guard

Sean/Seran, Gypsy of Pachu

Lord Simon, Lord of Porcelania

Admiral Taylor, Admiral of the Royal Navy

Lord Taryen, Lord of Porcelania

Ranger Telemond, Ranger

Lord Temberton, Lord of Porcelania

Lady Thinithe, Lady of Porcelania

Grand Admiral Tylock, Grand Admiral of the Royal Navy

Malkin:

Carrion

Taresh/Terry

Tiamon, Priest of Tabier

Tolk, Elder of Diende

Rouvel

www.ingramcontent.com/pod-product-compliance
Lightning Source LLC
Chambersburg PA
CBHW062058290726
48975CB00001B/32